Peter Watt has spent time as a soldier, articled clerk, prawn trawler deckhand, builder's labourer, pipe layer, real estate salesman, private investigator, police sergeant, surveyor's chainman and advisor to the Royal Papua New Guinea Constabulary. He speaks, reads and writes Vietnamese and Pidgin. He now lives at Maclean on the Clarence River in northern New South Wales. He has volunteered with the Volunteer Rescue Association, Queensland Ambulance Service and currently with the Rural Fire Service. Fishing and the vast open spaces of outback Queensland are his main interests in life.

Peter Watt can be contacted at www.peterwatt.com.

Author Photo: Shawn Peene

Also by Peter Watt

The Duffy/Macintosh Series
Cry of the Curlew
Shadow of the Osprey
Flight of the Eagle
To Chase the Storm
To Touch the Clouds
To Ride the Wind
Beyond the Horizon
War Clouds Gather
And Fire Falls
Beneath a Rising Sun
While the Moon Burns
From the Stars Above

The Papua Series
Papua
Eden
The Pacific

The Silent Frontier
The Stone Dragon
The Frozen Circle

The Colonial Series
The Queen's Colonial
The Queen's Tiger
The Queen's Captain
The Colonial's Son

Excerpts from emails sent to Peter Watt

'I have just finished reading your latest book *The Queen's Colonial*. It is without doubt the best book I have read in 2018. I found it absolutely riveting and could not put it down. I can't wait for the next book!'

'Just finished *The Queen's Colonial* and as usual it was superb. It never ceases to amaze me how you research the details in history and weave them into a fictional story which is so believable. I will be waiting anxiously for the next one.'

'Just finished *The Queen's Colonial*. Excellent detail . . . you haven't lost your touch! Another enthralling family saga.'

'I have just finished *The Queen's Colonial*. Truly excellent. I have now read all nineteen of your books. I thought the Duffy/McIntosh series was great, the Papua trilogy was fabulous (I have read those three twice) but I feel that the new book is possibly your best book yet. I am looking forward to the next instalment. Keep up the great writing.'

'Damn you, Peter Watt . . .!! Just finished *The Queen's Colonial* and can't wait to get the next one. Love your work.'

'A real page-turner. Your source for the Crimean War was inspired.'

'Just finished this wonderful book. You never cease to entertain me with your fantastic writing. Please keep writing. As always I'm waiting with bated breath for your next book . . .'

'Just finished *The Queen's Colonial*. Thoroughly enjoyed the book. The military history aspect is interesting to me and the storyline intriguing. What a family!'

'Thank you for taking the time to write the way you do. When I am reading one of your books I am in the scene with your characters.'

'I have just completed the Papua series. Your writing has been a constant companion and escape . . . It has been an absolute pleasure to immerse myself with the characters in a thoroughly entertaining blend of fiction and well-researched fact.'

'Another most enjoyable read. Having generally read factual military history most of my life it was pleasurable to read a fictitious work wherein I could not only enjoy the woven stories, but see and feel the characters. Well done!'

'Thank you so much for the years of storytelling, especially the Duffy/McIntosh saga . . . Your books will always take pride of place on our bookshelf to remind me of the many hours of enjoyment spent reading them. I think I will have to start over and re-read! Thank you again and please keep on writing.'

The Queen's TIGER

PETER WATT

PAN
Pan Macmillan Australia

Pan Macmillan acknowledges the Traditional Custodians of country throughout Australia and their connections to lands, waters and communities. We pay our respect to Elders past and present and extend that respect to all Aboriginal and Torres Strait Islander peoples today. We honour more than sixty thousand years of storytelling, art and culture.

First published 2019 in Macmillan by Pan Macmillan Australia Pty Ltd
This Pan edition published 2022 by Pan Macmillan Australia Pty Ltd
1 Market Street, Sydney, New South Wales, Australia, 2000

Map on page viii taken from *The Cambridge Modern History Atlas* by Sir A. William Ward, G.W. Prothero. Sir S. M. Leathes & E.A. Benians, 1912, copyright Cambridge University Press, reproduced with permission.

A catalogue record for this book is available from the National Library of Australia

Typeset in Bembo by Post Pre-press Group
Printed by IVE

The paper in this book is FSC® certified. FSC® promotes environmentally responsible, socially beneficial and economically viable management of the world's forests.

For my wonderful wife, Naomi.

Map 123

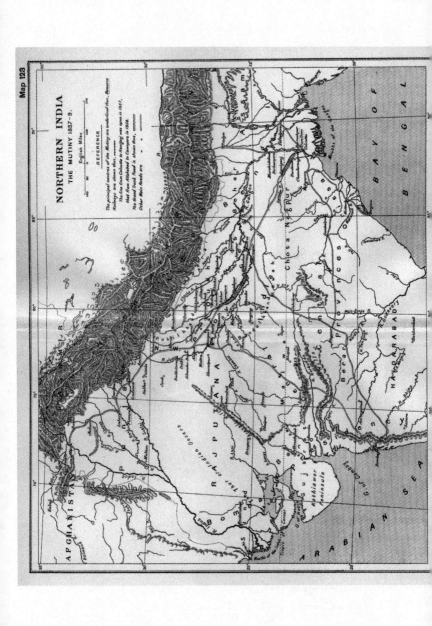

NORTHERN INDIA
THE MUTINY 1857–9.

English Miles

REFERENCE

The principal centres of the Mutiny are underlined thus, Benares

Railways are shown thus,

The lines from Calcutta to Hooghly was open in 1857,

that from Allahabad to Cawnpore in 1858,

The Grand Trunk Road is shown thus,

Other Main Roads are

PROLOGUE

The Bengali Dry Season

India, 1857

Mrs Alice Campbell, née Forbes, the bride of Dr Peter Campbell, Canadian citizen and former surgeon to the British army in the Crimean War, marvelled at the exotic lands she and her husband had passed through on their journey to visit Peter's brother. They had arrived by ship in the Bay of Bengal and travelled up the River Ganges delta to Murshidabad in the Bengal Presidency of north-eastern India. Here Major Scott Campbell had a posting with British East India Company and, according to Peter, had become more British than Canadian.

The British here certainly knew how to hold a ball, thought Alice, looking around her. She and Peter had only arrived in Bengal this morning and already they had found themselves invited to a magnificent ball held for the expatriates of the region – senior civil servants and officers of the East India Company. Great fans moved the hot evening air around the candle-lit ballroom, which was alive with the colourful uniforms of the officers and the glittering jewellery of their ladies. Scattered around the room were Indian servants wearing smart uniforms, and on a dais a regimental band played dance music.

Peter wore a dinner suit and Alice an off-the-shoulder silk gown, although little in the way of jewellery. Major Scott Campbell was taller and more broad-shouldered than his surgeon brother and cut a dashing figure in his cavalry dress uniform. He strode towards them holding out two crystal coupes of champagne.

'Here, Mrs Campbell. Old chap,' he said, passing the champagne first to his sister-in-law and then to his brother. 'Welcome to India.'

Alice and Peter had met with him that morning when he had escorted them to quarters in his villa. The newlywed couple had been welcomed by a staff of Indian servants, both male and female, dressed in traditional clothing.

'So, my little brother saw action in the Crimea,' Scott said, taking a flute from a passing Indian servant circulating amongst the guests. 'You will have to tell me all about your experiences. Damned long time since we fought a war with a European nation. Not since Napoleon.'

'Not much to tell,' Peter said, sipping the chilled champagne. 'Just the usual – men dying in agony and calling out for their mothers as they did so.' It was obvious that Peter did not wish to remember the horrors he had encountered on his operating table, usually an improvised kitchen tabletop.

'I can see that you were able to marry the most beautiful woman in England,' Scott said with a glint in his eye and a broad smile that made Alice feel as if his compliment was almost a challenge to his younger brother. Peter was nearing thirty and clean-shaven with short hair, whilst his brother, a couple of years older, had a thick black beard and moustache. Scott was single, but Alice guessed he could have any single – or married – woman in the room if he chose.

'Thank you for the compliment, Major Campbell,' Alice replied.

'You must call me Scott – after all, we are family,' he said, clinking his glass against hers.

'Sir,' a young officer interrupted, 'I must apologise but the colonel wishes you to read this despatch from Berhampore barracks.'

Scott took the sheet of paper and read it with a frown. He passed the communiqué back to the young officer.

'You look concerned,' Peter said.

'It is nothing to be too worried about,' Scott replied. 'Just notice that our sepoys at the barracks have refused to attend musketry practice at the range there.'

'Why would they do that?' Alice asked.

'It is the new Enfield rifles,' Scott replied. 'The sepoys have to bite off the end of the paper cartridge case to load the powder into the barrel. There are wild rumours circulating that the paper is greased with pig fat, which is not acceptable to our Moslem soldiers, and Hindu soldiers have been told that the cartridges are covered in beef fat, and *that* is not acceptable to *them*. We suspect that the rumours are being circulated by nefarious types who would like to see a rebellion against us in order to seize power for themselves.'

'Well, it is their country,' Alice said, and both men looked at her as if she had suddenly used a profanity in the company of the Queen.

'I am afraid that the Indians are like squabbling children,' Scott said. 'They are not a united people. The Moslems and Hindus will kill each other at the drop of a hat, and the Sikhs are no better. They need us to keep them from slaughtering each other. At least my men are loyal to Her Majesty the Queen and not to some foolish idea of independence.'

'You might require the services of the British navy and army here,' Peter said cautiously.

'The East India Company has conquered and controlled this great subcontinent without any assistance from England,' Scott said. 'The matter at Berhampore will be rectified in due course and things will get back to normal. By the way,' he continued, changing the subject, 'some of us from the regiment are planning a tiger hunt in a few days and I would like to invite you and Alice as my guests. We shoot from elephants.'

'I would very much like to join the hunt,' Alice said. 'I think it would be thrilling to ride on the back of an elephant.'

'Good show,' Scott said without asking his brother's opinion.

The band struck up a waltz and Peter swept Alice onto the floor to join the swirl of sweating faces.

But beyond the extravagance of colonial India and the ballroom, a simmering volcano of nationalism was about to erupt and swamp the Indian subcontinent in a fire from hell.

Part One

Persia and India, 1857

ONE

I t was a typical day in the life of a soldier in Queen Victoria's army.

The rain pelted down as Ian Steele, known to all as Captain Samuel Forbes, led his company of riflemen through the mud and sand of the desolate lands of the ancient terrain of Persia.

Ian bore a remarkable resemblance to the man whose identity he had assumed. In his early thirties, he was in fact more strongly built than the real Samuel Forbes – a legacy of his days as a blacksmith in the colony of New South Wales. The secret pact between English aristocrat, Forbes, and colonial blacksmith, Steele, had been forged for mutually beneficial reasons and had to be maintained for at least another seven years.

Leading the force Ian was part of, which comprised five thousand British troops and artillery guns, was the competent English lieutenant-general, James Outram.

The march had commenced in the filthy, disease-ridden Persian coastal town of Bushehr, captured the previous year by British forces. Their mission had been to attack the Persian army entrenched in its position forty-six miles from the ancient town of Bushehr, but the enemy had fled before the British artillery, rifled muskets and bayonets, leaving its military camp intact.

It had been one of Captain Steele's valued men, Corporal Owen Williams, who had discovered the small but valuable hoard of gold hidden under a carpet in a Persian commander's tent. Without any of his fellow soldiers observing, he had pocketed the coins which would later be divided equally between himself, his commanding officer and his best friend, Sergeant Conan Curry.

After a couple of days, everything else of worth from the captured Persian camp was packed for removal back to Bushehr, then enemy ammunition was destroyed in a massive explosion.

The night was dark and bleak as the British force marched. Sergeant Conan Curry strode easily beside Captain Samuel Forbes. A special bond had been forged between officer and non-commissioned soldiers on the bloody battlefields of Crimea only months earlier, but there was more to this relationship than that. Sergeant Curry knew the real identity of his commanding officer and it was a secret Curry had sworn he'd keep till the grave. Strangely, Conan Curry had once been Ian's best friend. They had grown up together in the shadow of the Blue Mountains outside Sydney, but their paths had separated when Conan had chosen an indolent life of easy money with a few of the bad apples of their village. They had come together again a world away, in England.

Ian had been able to have Conan attached to his company as acting sergeant major, whilst the third member of their trio, Corporal Owen Williams, remained with a platoon commanded by the brother of a close friend, Captain Miles Sinclair, who had been killed in the Crimean campaign. The young platoon commander, Lieutenant Henry Sinclair, was barely seventeen years of age and this was his first taste of war. Ian had asked Owen to keep an eye on the young officer and quietly guide him in his role.

'A bit bloody disappointing the Persians did not put up a reasonable fight,' Conan growled.

'They call themselves Iranians,' Ian said. 'Iran is the ancient name for this part of the Persian empire.'

Conan accepted this correction without question as he knew how knowledgeable Ian was about history. However, he was less interested in the name of their enemy than in the reason for their flight. The new Enfield rifled musket he carried was changing the nature of battle. The Enfield had great range and accuracy, whilst the old muskets their enemy carried required close-range volley fire to be effective. No doubt knowing they were outgunned had factored into the Persians' – Iranians' – decision to flee rather than fight.

'I don't suppose you know why we are in this godforsaken Musulman country,' Conan said as the rain drenched him to the bone.

'The old story, Sergeant,' Ian sighed. 'We are here to keep the Muscovites from extending their influence into India. For years the Tsar has been encouraging the Persians against us. Now we are taking a stand.'

Ian was about to give a short history to his acting sergeant major when shots interrupted him. The shots were coming out of the darkness at the rear of their column. The order to form a square was given and Ian ensured that his company fell in with the rest of the regiment. He was aware that two-thirds of his men were raw recruits out of the London barracks and hoped his veteran non-commissioned officers would steady them in the confusion of this unexpected event.

Ian took up a position in the front ranks of his soldiers. He knew the primary role of the British officer was to lead his men by personal example. Ian was armed with a rifle like his men, but also carried two loaded heavy-calibre revolvers in his waistband. He had found them far more effective than the sword at his waist, which denoted his rank as an officer of Queen Victoria.

Ian was crouched on one knee when he became aware that a man on a horse had just galloped past their front.

'That's the general!' Conan exclaimed. 'The silly bugger will get himself killed out there.'

Ian agreed and wondered why General Outram would do such a foolish thing as to detach himself from the defensive square in the dark.

'Mr Upton, you are to take command,' Ian yelled to a nearby officer.

He leapt to his feet and Conan followed him without question. They moved quickly in the direction the general had taken and eventually, somewhere ahead of them – Ian calculated it to be about a hundred yards away – they heard a horse whinny in pain.

Both men raised their rifles, surging forward to a small clearing amongst the desert scrub to see the vague shape of a horse down, its rider trapped beneath.

'I think it is the general,' Conan whispered. Both men could barely make out the downed horse with their night vision at its most acute.

'Over there!' Ian hissed. 'Figures moving around. They have to be Persians.'

Conan raised his rifle, not bothering to make an attempt to sight but firing blindly in the direction of the moving men. Ian removed his pistols and delivered a withering volley that seemed to scatter whoever was trying to encircle the downed horse and rider. The Persian soldiers quickly disappeared, probably unaware of the importance of the man they had attempted to kill or capture.

'Who is out there?' General Outram called as he brought his downed horse to its feet and remounted.

'Captain Forbes and Sergeant Curry, sir,' Ian called back. 'Are you injured?'

'Just my pride,' replied the English general, bringing his mount under control. 'I thank you, Captain Forbes and Sergeant Curry.' With that, he spurred his horse back to the British lines, leaving Ian and Conan to follow.

Ian resumed command of his men. They waited out the night and when the sun rose on another day of miserable, sleeting rain, they saw the Shah's Persian army formed into infantry squares to engage the Anglo-Indian force.

Ian glanced up and down the front rank of his men and could see little fear in the faces of his new recruits, both young and old, as they gripped their Enfield rifled muskets. Ian sensed that they had confidence in their training and their modern weapons. He had issued orders to his platoon commanders to ensure that the powder for the rifles was not damp and the soldiers had recharged with fresh powder. The Persians were wary and remaining a safe distance from the deadly accurate long-range fire of the British rifles.

'It's going to be the job of the cavalry to break the Persian square,' Conan said to Ian who was kneeling, using his rifle as a support.

'Very impressive, Sergeant Curry,' Ian grinned. 'We will make a soldier of you yet.'

Conan smiled. 'But not an officer.'

Even as they looked on they could hear the jangle of cavalry bridles, and Ian's men raised a hoorah from the ranks when they observed the Bombay Light Cavalry form their squadrons to charge the Persian square. The cavalrymen broke into a canter, then a full gallop, charging the Persians to Ian's company's front. It was a thrilling sight emphasised by the thundering hooves of the warhorses. The Indian unit smashed into the Persian ranks, wielding heavy sabres, slashing and stabbing with the fury of men possessed. Dust rose in swirling clouds, partially obscuring the desperate clash, but within minutes the Indian horse soldiers rode out of the melee with uniforms covered in the blood of the Persians. It was all over in mere minutes. Seven hundred of the enemy lay dead, and Outram's force was able to capture a hundred prisoners and two of the enemy's guns. Ian could hear the disappointed grumbles of his own company, as they'd had little to do with the victory at what would later be called the Battle of Khushab. Still, he knew it would not be the last bloody engagement in this campaign.

'The colonel wishes to see you, sir,' said a junior staff officer from regimental headquarters.

Ian followed the young officer back to the rear where he saw the man he most despised in the world, Colonel Clive Jenkins. His commanding officer had originally served as a lieutenant in Ian's company before being rapidly promoted thanks to his highly placed social contacts and family fortune. Ian had witnessed Jenkins' craven cowardice in the face of fire during the Crimean War and knew he was incompetent to lead soldiers. Jenkins hated Ian for this knowledge and had placed him in almost suicidal situations in Crimea.

Jenkins stood now with two of his senior officers, and when Ian arrived he reluctantly saluted.

'You wish to see me . . . sir,' Ian said. Despite their mutual hatred, Ian had had no choice but to swear his loyalty to the man he knew was a coward. Jenkins was of a similar age to Ian, but that was where the similarities ended. Jenkins was slim and had the patrician looks of an English gentleman; in contrast Ian was broad-shouldered and had a face that was not handsome but was nevertheless ruggedly appealing.

One of the officers present was a major and the other a captain. Both served on Jenkins' personal staff.

'I was informed that you left your post last night without permission,' Jenkins said in an accusing tone. 'You have a history of running your own show without respect for the established role of an officer and gentleman.'

'Sir, I had an urgent choice to make and did not have time to request your permission to temporarily hand over my command,' Ian said.

'Nothing can excuse your lack of obedience to your superiors, Captain Forbes. I will be –'

Jenkins did not get any further before a major from Lieutenant-General Outram's staff interrupted him. 'I am sorry to intrude, Colonel Jenkins, but I was informed Captain Forbes was at your headquarters. He is wanted by Sir James immediately.'

'Of course,' Jenkins replied, annoyed and confused as to why the legendary senior officer would want to speak with one of his company commanders. 'He is dismissed to accompany you.'

Ian did not bother saluting but turned on his heel and followed the major to a tent where James Outram sat at a small field desk scribbling notes. He was alone and looked up when his staff officer approached.

The major saluted. 'I have Captain Forbes, sir,' he said.

Ian stood to attention before an impressive man in his mid-fifties. Outram had a strong face, neatly cropped black beard and a receding hairline.

'You may relax, Captain Forbes,' the British general said with a smile. 'I summoned you here to express my personal thanks for your assistance last night. I suspect that if you and your sergeant had not found me, my head might have been stuck on the end of a spear for all to see when the sun rose. I did a stupid thing in riding out alone. I wished to ascertain the extent of the enemy opposing us, but I should have left that task to my staff. Your rescue cannot be mentioned in dispatches, although you deserve a mention. I pray that what happened will remain between you and I – and Sergeant Curry.'

'Yes, sir, I fully understand, and I can assure you that Sergeant Curry will be discreet,' Ian answered.

'I have been informed of your remarkable record of service in the Crimea,' Outram continued. 'And I am aware that there is some animosity between you and Colonel Jenkins.'

'Sir, despite my private opinions, he is my commanding officer and has my total loyalty.'

The general pushed himself from his desk and stood. 'An excellent answer, Captain Forbes.' He extended his hand to a startled Ian. 'If in the future I can be of assistance to you, do not hesitate to make contact with me. This is my way of thanking you for your service last night.' Ian accepted the handshake and felt the strength in the senior officer's grip.

'Oh, by the way, I have been informed that Colonel Jenkins had you summoned to remonstrate with you about your temporary absence from your post last night. Major Starke will inform your commanding officer that you were acting on secret instructions from my staff. I am sure Colonel Jenkins is wise enough not to question my authority.'

'Thank you, sir,' Ian replied, letting go of the general's hand.

'You may return to your men, Captain Forbes, and I hope that one day you may join my staff. I need competent officers around me.'

Ian saluted and marched away, knowing that this was a man he would follow through the gates of hell if asked.

Ian did not bother to report to his commanding officer, who he guessed was now being told in no uncertain terms that Ian had been acting on Outram's orders. Jenkins, for all his high-placed connections in England, would not dare question James Outram, a darling of the British government.

Ian was met at his tent by Conan, whose worried expression asked the question.

'Sir James asked me to thank you for our service to him last night but would rather it remain between the three of us,' Ian said.

Conan nodded. 'I was told by the boys that Colonel Jenkins wanted to see you. Whenever the bastard asks for you it only means trouble.'

'Ah, yes.' Ian smiled. 'Thankfully, a major from the general's staff rescued me from an accusation that I had deserted my post. I don't think Colonel Jenkins will raise the matter again.'

'That bastard Jenkins is out to get you killed,' Conan spat.

'It's not easy to kill us colonials,' Ian said with a grin, glowing in the knowledge that his and Conan's actions hours earlier had garnered the appreciation of the British force commander. He hoped that it would not be easy for Jenkins to cause him any further mischief in this campaign.

TWO

A man in his early thirties stood with his hands clasped behind his back by the great window of a three-storeyed house. He was gazing down on a vacant area of swamp and bushy scrubland lightly covered in snow. It was said that the vast vacant plot in the middle of the sprawling American city of New York, originally established by Dutch colonial pioneers, would be developed into a great park.

Samuel Forbes was deep in thought when another man entered the room.

'Samuel,' the man said, noticing the disturbed expression on his friend's face. 'Are you unwell?'

'No, James, but I have just received upsetting news from my dear friend Jonathan in London,' Samuel replied. 'It appears that Ian is in Persia fighting yet another campaign for the Queen.'

James placed his hands on Samuel's shoulders. 'Ian survived the worst of the Crimea and has proven to be a great soldier. You should not worry yourself about his welfare.'

Samuel detached himself from his friend, walking to the small polished teak table to retrieve the letter sitting next to a copy of *Uncle Tom's Cabin; or, Life Among the Lowly* by Harriet Beecher Stowe. The letter was from Jonathan, a former schoolmate of Samuel's. They had been in boarding school together and it was with Jonathan that Samuel had discovered a mutual attraction forbidden by the laws of England and the English Church. Jonathan had been able to remain close to Samuel's family – especially his sister, Alice – and regularly reported on events from the other side of the Atlantic.

'I do, though,' Samuel sighed. 'When we made our pact to exchange identities I did not give much thought to the fact that Ian would be constantly fighting in the British Empire's wars. He still has another seven years left of the ten-year period I was supposed to serve in my grandfather's regiment to be eligible for my inheritance. I feel that I was being absolutely selfish placing his life in jeopardy.'

'You know that Ian was more than willing to serve the Empire as a soldier of the Queen. It was as much his burning desire as it was your ambition to seek revenge against Sir Archibald, your supposed father. Captain Steele is where he always dreamed of being.'

'There is not a night that passes I do not have nightmares of Ian's body lying on some godforsaken battlefield,' Samuel said. 'I feel the need to return to England and speak with him. He may wish to renege on our agreement.'

Samuel, however, was not telling the entire truth. He did wish to return to England, but Ian was not foremost in his thoughts. Privately, he agreed with James that the man was more than likely content where he was. But how could Samuel tell his partner in life that he still dreamed of the precious moments he had spent with Jonathan in his youth, and of the deadly consumption that now racked his former lover's body? That he wished to see Jonathan – perhaps for the last time – and explore his feelings for his old friend?

'I doubt it,' James scoffed. 'From the little I learned of Mr Steele when we were in New South Wales, he was born to battle. His father fought at Waterloo and Ian expressed his overwhelming desire to follow the colours. If you return to London you might be recognised as the real Samuel Forbes, and that would incriminate Captain Steele as well. You have to consider that. You are by nature reckless and impulsive and I love you for that, but I fear your nature may one day get you into trouble you cannot escape.'

'I feel guilty that I am enjoying this privileged life while Ian takes all the risks in my name,' said Samuel.

'Are you sure you do not wish to return to London to see Jonathan?' James asked, his question tinged with a note of accusation.

'No, no,' Samuel quickly dismissed the idea. 'I will love you to the day I die, dear James. I have grown to love this country as you do. But I am not Ian Steele.'

James fell silent for a few moments. 'I will make a booking for us both to journey to London, then,' he said reluctantly. 'But you must promise me that you will not under any circumstances put yourself in a compromising situation with your family.' From what Samuel had told him about his brother, Charles, and his father, Sir Archibald, nothing good could come of encountering them.

'I promise,' Samuel said, embracing James with affection. 'Besides, my darling sister has married and is currently in India, so there is no reason for me to wish to contact my family. Although while we are in England I would like to visit the memorial to my late brother.'

James knew that Lieutenant Herbert Forbes had been killed fighting against the Russian army in the siege of Sevastopol, and understood why Samuel would wish to pay his respects. All that truly bothered James was that Samuel might renew his relationship with his old friend and lover, Jonathan. He reassured himself that it was his wealth that currently allowed Samuel's extravagant lifestyle and that his lover would not jeopardise this arrangement – at least until he was able to claim his inheritance from the vast Forbes fortune.

★

The London home of the Forbes family, situated in the most desirable suburb of the great city, still had an air of mourning about it. Servants moved quietly around their master. Sir Archibald had taken the death of his youngest son badly. He spent hours staring blankly at a black-framed sepia photograph hung on the wall of the library. It showed a handsome young man still in his teens wearing the dress uniform of an infantry officer, his hand on the hilt of his sword.

Charles Forbes secretly sneered at his father's grief. Sir Archibald was growing soft and sentimental. For himself, Charles was overjoyed that the family fortune need not be shared by his youngest brother. All the more for him. If only his sister, Alice, would also disappear – perhaps she would die of some exotic disease in India – that would leave only Samuel, and he would meet a painful end on the battlefield if Charles' plans with Clive Jenkins came to fruition. Then he would be the sole inheritor of the Forbes estates.

'A terrible tragedy,' Charles said to his father as they both gazed at the photograph.

'It should have been Samuel,' his father replied bitterly. 'Not Herbert.'

'Give the army time,' Charles replied. 'Officers on the Empire's frontiers usually have a short life span.'

★

Alice Campbell was never bored with the exotic culture she encountered daily in the Bengali city of Murshidabad. From the palace grounds of the rich and aristocratic Indians, peacocks screeched as they spread their colourful fan-like tails amongst an army of gardeners tending to the lavish gardens. The markets were filled with the aroma of a rich variety of unfamiliar food, spices and fruits. The mango quickly became her favourite delicacy. Each afternoon she would return to her brother-in-law's sumptuous villa with its beautifully manicured lawns and colourful shrubs and flowers, all surrounded by a high stone wall. Inside the villa high ceilings and marbled floors were a cool relief from the Indian sun. It was so different from the homes Alice knew in England. She felt herself being drawn into this exotic life in India.

However, there were plenty of reminders of the London life she had left behind. She and Peter would often attend tea parties at the homes of the British employees of the East India Company, where Alice found herself growing irritated at the patronising attitude towards the local Indian population. Not that she always disagreed with the British views, especially when she heard stories of wives sometimes being burned alive on their husbands' funeral pyres – a tradition being stamped out by British justice.

It was during the third week of their visit that Peter was

called upon by his brother to provide medical assistance to a British officer who had accidentally shot himself in the leg.

Peter packed his surgical bag and was escorted from the town by a section of four lancers from Scott's squadron. He was warned that it would be a week before he returned.

Alice was alone and bored when Scott visited on the second day of Peter's absence, reminding her of the tiger hunt that had finally been organised by a local Indian prince. Alice hesitated to go without Peter but Scott was persuasive, so very early the following day she was escorted by a tall Bengali trooper to a place outside of the town where ten elephants stood with baskets on their backs and handlers sitting forward on their necks. The sun was just above the horizon and Alice could see Indians milling around the elephants standing patiently in the dust. Scott was speaking with a richly dressed and rather handsome Indian with a jewelled turban and he broke into a broad smile when he saw her. Her brother-in-law was wearing his field uniform and carried a double-barrelled shotgun in one hand. He excused himself from the Indian and strolled over to her.

'Ah, Alice, your opportunity to get a taste of the real India,' he said. 'We will be going into the jungle in pursuit of the vile creature that attacks and eats humans. We are guests of the local ruler of these parts, and you and I will share a howdah. I am sure you will have a tale to tell my brother when he returns. Shall we mount our beast?'

A ladder was brought for Alice who wore a long flowing white dress and a broad straw hat with a scarf tied under her chin. Alice climbed the ladder and sat down in the basket. Scott settled down beside her, producing a second weapon, a wicked-looking double-barrelled pistol that resembled a shortened version of his four-bore percussion elephant gun. Its barrels were also loaded with great lead slugs. 'The pistol is just in case we need very close protection,' Scott said. 'Do you know how to fire it?'

'I suppose that I simply point it and pull the triggers,' Alice replied casually, causing a broad grin to break across Scott's face.

'That's my girl,' he said, and turned his attention to the mahout, speaking to him in Bengali. The man, wearing little more than a loincloth and holding a short rod with a metal spike, replied. Under the prodding of the Indian elephant controller the great beast lurched forward, as did the line of other elephants with their passengers, who comprised local royalty and a couple of Scott's fellow officers.

The convoy of elephants left the town behind and soon entered a thick green jungle of giant trees and shrubs. Alice felt as if she was back on the ship that had steamed to India weeks earlier as the elephant seemed to pitch and roll in its heavy gait. They were following a well-worn track to avoid the heavy foliage of the forest. Birds shrieked and monkeys howled in the treetops as the elephants plodded on. There was an alien strangeness to this land that was so different from the cold, wet country of her birth.

Alice leaned back against the edge of the basket and took in the aromatic and earthy scents of the jungle, both pungent and sweet. Despite the heat and the sweat now running in small rivulets down the inside of her dress, she started to doze. Suddenly a great cry rose from the men of the convoy. Alice immediately came fully awake and looked around to see what had caused the commotion.

'There!' Scott shouted, raising the heavy-calibre weapon to his shoulder. Alice saw the flash of yellow and black in the shadows of the jungle. A tiger!

The blast of the elephant gun almost deafened her, leaving her ears ringing. Scott fired the second barrel and other guns opened fire at the tiger that had disappeared into the heavy undergrowth.

Scott was quickly reloading. 'I think I got him,' he said as he poured black powder down the twin barrels and dropped the heavy leaf balls after it. The percussion caps followed and he leapt from the howdah to the ground below, leaving Alice alone as the elephant shifted nervously. It was obvious that Scott was going to hunt the tiger on foot but it had all happened so fast that Alice had had no time to react or protest. She saw Scott disappear into the jungle, followed by others from the hunting party, leaving her and the mahout alone.

For a while all she could hear were the shouts of men stalking the wounded animal, but gradually she became aware that the elephant she was sitting on was shuffling to one side of the track. The mahout was shouting and using his stick in an attempt to bring the great beast under control. Alice gripped the edge of the howdah with all her strength, and suddenly the elephant trumpeted its fear. Disbelievingly, Alice saw that the wounded tiger had doubled back and, in its rage, it leapt onto the hindquarters of her elephant. Alice swivelled to see the tiger clawing its way up the great pachyderm towards her, and she realised that the elephant was now preparing to launch into full flight to shake the beast off.

Alice could see the head of the tiger only a few feet away. She was both absolutely terrified and mesmerised by its beauty as it snarled in wounded anger. Alice was vaguely aware through her terror that she could smell its pungent breath. In the distance she could hear the concerned shouting of men crashing back through the heavy undergrowth, and realised to her horror that the mahout had deserted his animal in his own desperate fear.

The tiger fixed her with its smoky eyes and Alice knew that she was close to death. The muscles in the tiger's shoulders bunched as it prepared to make the last leap onto the back of the elephant, which now burst into full flight, smashing its way through small trees and heavy foliage.

Whether it was instinct or luck, Alice felt the butt of the pistol in her hand and she brought it up, almost touching the nose of the tiger. She pulled both triggers, and the tiger disappeared behind a cloud of gun smoke. The recoil of the pistol almost flung Alice from the basket. There was no time to pray, so she closed her eyes, awaiting the inevitable gory death the claws and teeth of the great cat would bring to her. There was not even time to think of Peter as she fell back in the basket, hitting her head.

Then all she remembered was a babble of voices in English and Bengali. The terrified elephant was standing still, trembling, as she lay on her back in the howdah.

'My dear Alice, have you been hurt?' Scott's worried voice drifted down to her as she opened her eyes to see his face above hers.

'No, I don't think so,' she replied, shaking her head to ensure she had not been dreaming the nightmare of seconds or minutes before. 'The tiger?' she asked.

'You bagged it,' Scott replied. 'We have never known a woman do that. What a story you will be able to tell my brother.'

Alice pulled herself into a sitting position in the howdah. Scott helped her climb down a ladder and she could see the bloody claw marks on the hindquarters of the elephant's thick hide. She could also see a few feet away the body of the tiger she had killed. Men were gathered around it, and when she stood unsteadily beside the elephant, a cheer rose up from all those present, from the loinclothed elephant handlers to the richly dressed Indian aristocrats. Alice could see admiration for her feat in their expressions. The turbaned and bejewelled figure Alice had noticed talking with Scott earlier that day stepped forward with a smile. She could see that he was in his mid-twenties and had a handsome, dark face. He sported a neatly clipped short beard and his brown eyes were full of sparkle.

'I think we should call you the daughter of Kali,' he said, taking Alice's hand and kissing it. She was surprised to hear him speak in fluent English, although she did not know who Kali was.

'Thank you,' she politely replied, her heart still beating hard in her breast. 'But I shot the tiger because I was terrified.'

'No matter why you did it, you faced the fearsome beast and triumphed.'

'Khan,' Scott said, addressing the aristocratic Indian, 'may I introduce you to my brother's bride, Mrs Alice Campbell.'

Alice thought that she detected a note of annoyance in Scott's introduction but dismissed her suspicion as she gazed into the face of the handsome young man.

'I must present you with a gift to celebrate your great victory today over the demon tiger,' the Khan said, taking a huge blue sapphire pendant on a gold chain from around his neck and pressing it into Alice's hand. Alice gasped at the beautiful piece of jewellery and began to protest the generosity, but the young Indian prince shook his head.

'I was educated in England and I know that it is your custom to present soldiers with medals for bravery. This is my medal of bravery for you.'

Alice was at a loss for words. When she gazed into the dead eyes of the tiger at her feet, she felt conflicted about what she had done. She had seen the beauty in those eyes before she killed the magnificent creature, but at the same time she realised that had she not killed the tiger, it would have killed her.

'I must return to my servants,' the Khan said with a polite nod of his head and he turned away, leaving Scott and Alice alone.

'Who is Kali?' Alice asked, and Scott frowned.

'These damned savages have so many gods, but Kali is of particular importance to them. She is their goddess of death, time and doomsday. But she is also associated with the mother earth figure and, dare I say it, sexuality and violence. The Khan is one of those jumped-up rulers we have to pander to in these parts. It seems that we will be ending our hunt and returning to the city. You have the honour of bagging the only tiger today.'

Alice held the precious pendant in her hand, her thoughts still reeling from the deadly encounter and the mystifying events that had followed. It was a day she knew she would always remember.

That night she returned to her brother-in-law's villa and went to her room to sleep. As she passed into the dark world of dreams she remembered a verse from a poem she had once read when she was young. William Blake's poem echoed in her dreams.

Tiger, tiger, burning bright
In the forests of the night,
What immortal hand or eye
Could frame thy beautiful symmetry?

Even as Alice tossed in her sleep, at the Barrackpore barracks, only miles from the scene of the hunt, a mutiny had just occurred and two British officers had been wounded. Already the opening events of the Indian mutiny were beginning to ripple out, and those ripples would become a tidal wave of death and destruction.

THREE

Captain Ian Steele spread the coins on a wooden table in his seconded quarters in Bushehr where he and his regiment awaited the order to move out against the Persian army. Corporal Owen Williams had divided the prize he'd discovered hidden in the tent of a Persian commander into three equal parts and handed Ian his share in a small leather bag. Under the flickering candlelight Ian could see that it was a tidy sum to add to the considerable fortune in jewels his company had taken from a Russian baggage train as the Muscovites fled from the battlefields of the Crimea. The fortune he'd always dreamed of as a soldier of the Queen was coming true.

Ian scooped the coins back into the leather pouch and secreted the pouch within his bundle of uniform kit. He leaned back in the rickety chair to stare at the mudbrick wall of his tiny room. His quarters were in what had once been the residence of a Persian businessman who had fled the city when the British army came.

'Sir,' a familiar voice called from the other side of the wooden door to Ian's room. 'The commanding officer wishes to speak with you.'

'Thank you, Mr Sinclair,' Ian replied. 'Inform the colonel I am coming immediately.'

Ian threw on his jacket and straightened his uniform. No doubt he was in trouble again. He walked through the evening shadows to the HQ building where he was met by the regiment's second-in-command, Major Dawkins.

'The colonel will see you now, Captain Forbes,' the major said in a tone that did not bode well.

Ian stepped inside the room being used as the office of the regiment. It contained little other than a map on the wall, a table and three chairs. Jenkins sat behind the table, which was strewn with papers. Ian saluted but Jenkins did not return the salute.

Jenkins rose and walked to the wall map, his hands clasped behind his back. 'General Outram has ordered that the regiment remain in this godforsaken place while he continues his advance against the Persian army upriver,' he said in an irritated voice. 'However, he has requested that I allow your company of rifles to join his expedition with Brigadier Havelock's brigade.'

Ian was thrilled at the opportunity for his men to join the mission to confront the enemy. Living in Bushehr was miserable, with the desert winds blowing dust so fine that it was able to penetrate into every crevice of the township. The regiment had been stood down but Ian still took every opportunity to take his company beyond the town's walls to conduct light manoeuvres and target practice. A few of the new recruits grumbled at the duties but the old hands explained it had always been the habit of the officer nick-named 'the Colonial' for his long time in the British colony of New South Wales. There he appeared to have taken on some of the colonial's philosophy of equality amongst men, regardless of class. The old hands also knew of the company commander's courage, wise leadership and daring, and admired him for that. They were similarly aware of their colonel's poor record during the Crimean War, but they kept that to themselves as good soldiers should.

'Sir, I will lead my company with the knowledge that I must uphold the regiment's sterling reputation,' Ian replied tactfully. From the dark expression on Jenkins' face, he suspected that his commanding officer was angrier about this potential opportunity for Ian to bolster his already glorious reputation than he was about being left out of the coming battle – about which Jenkins, in his cowardice, was probably quite relieved.

'I cannot understand why General Outram would specifically request your services when we both know that you are not a true representative of the gentlemen officers I have in my command, Captain Forbes. I was sorely tempted to inform the general of your poor performance as a company commander.'

'Sir, it does not fall to humble soldiers to question a general's orders,' Ian said, and received a glare from the man he knew was using his self-purchased commission to further his prospects of a political career in England. It had been ever thus since the days of the Roman armies, Ian thought.

'You are dismissed, Captain Forbes. You are to join with General Outram's expedition within forty-eight hours.'

Ian came to attention and saluted Jenkins who, once again, did not return the salute. But Ian felt that nothing else mattered except to join the continuing war in this ancient biblical land.

His first stop was the quarters of his four junior officers to inform them of their new mission. They in turn summoned their sergeants and with them came acting company sergeant major, Sergeant Conan Curry.

'It's on,' Ian said, and a broad smile spread across Conan's face.

'Sir, is the regiment going with General Outram?' Conan asked.

'No, just our company,' Ian replied. 'The regiment remains at Bushehr.'

Conan grinned again. 'It pays to save the odd general from time to time.'

'Paddy, it certainly does,' Ian replied, using Conan's company nickname. 'I want you to assemble the company on our parade ground within the hour and I will announce the good news.'

'Sah!' Conan replied with a smart salute. 'The men will be happy to hear they will be earning the Queen's shilling.'

Conan hurried away, bawling to the men in their quarters to fall out with arms, whilst Ian glowed with a feeling of deep satisfaction. It was rumoured that the small war was near an end, and he wanted to see the last battle before they returned to their barracks in London. This was the life he had chosen. But as Ian packed his kit for the expedition, the same old fear nagged at him: would he prove to be the leader his men expected?

★

Dr Peter Campbell stared at the beautiful sapphire pendant his wife held in her hands.

'You must return it,' he said with a frown.

'It was a gift from the Khan in recognition of my killing the tiger,' Alice protested. 'It is not the monetary value of the gift that I care about but what it symbolises.'

Peter had barely returned to the gates of Murshidabad before he had been regaled by stories of how Alice had single-handedly shot a large tiger. Even now the tiger's magnificent pelt was being prepared by the Indian prince's staff to be presented to her.

The couple stood in the garden of Scott's villa. Beside them a fountain trickled water into a pond covered with colourful lilies.

'I trusted Scott to keep you safe whilst I was away,' Peter said bitterly, 'and what did he do? He took you into the jungle to hunt tigers and you were almost killed.'

'It was not Scott's fault,' Alice countered. 'I was missing you, and it was boring being left alone here. What occurred on the hunt is the most exciting thing that has ever happened in my life! For a moment when the tiger attacked I felt both desperate fear and absolute exhilaration. I think that I now know how you must have felt during those battles in the Crimea.'

'I never experienced exhilaration,' Peter said. 'Just fear – and helplessness when I could not save all the soldiers who came across my operating table. There is something unnatural in what you are saying.'

Alice strode away to slump on a divan. 'I have only ever known the mundane life of an Englishwoman and suddenly I find myself in a world of strange sights, sounds and smells. It is exciting and even wondrous to me. I am truly happy we came because when we return to London I will once again have to assume the stuffy and boring life of an English matron.'

Peter stood staring at his wife and felt a surge of love for her. She looked so vulnerable and yet had proved her steely courage under the direst of circumstances. He walked over to her, knelt down and took her hands in his own.

'I will tell our children when they are playing on your tiger-skin rug how their mother shot a ferocious man-eater in the wild jungles of India.' Peter kissed his wife's hands. In spite of his misgivings about the tiger hunt he was starting to realise that this woman was a diamond with many facets.

'Ah, how romantic,' Scott said, entering the garden in his uniform of red coat, tight white trousers and knee-length boots. A sword dangled from the belt around his waist.

Peter rose to greet his brother. 'You put my wife's life in danger,' he growled. 'I ought to give you a thrashing.'

Scott came to a stop paces away, a tight smile on his face. 'If I remember correctly, when we were younger I gave you the thrashing of your life. I would take you up on the offer, except I have been recalled to duty and do not have the time. Two of my colleagues at the Barrackpore barracks have been wounded by the sepoys there. This mess about the cartridges is getting out of hand, and it appears we will have to disband the native infantry unit until they execute the ringleaders of the mutiny.'

'Will you be in danger if you go?' Alice asked, rising from the divan.

Scott turned to her. 'My dear Alice, it is touching that a beautiful woman would be concerned for my welfare, but I can assure you that this is not the first time I have had to face down rebellious natives.'

Peter's anger was spent when he considered Alice's concern for his brother's safety. There had always been a fierce competition between the two brothers, but there was also a deep love. He would not wish his brother to be harmed in any way.

'Go safely,' Peter said gruffly and Scott grinned.

'I go knowing that Alice is safe in your care, little brother,' Scott said, and turned to walk away into the house. Peter suspected something facetious in his brother's departing remark and glanced at Alice, whose face reflected nothing but genuine concern for her brother-in-law.

'Do you find my brother attractive?' Peter blurted, startling Alice.

'Goodness, Peter, he is your brother,' she replied. 'It is you I find attractive, and he is almost your opposite. You are a good man, a healer of the sick and poor. I think your brother is what might be described as a cad. It is you who I love.'

'I am sorry, that was a stupid question,' Peter mumbled, and Alice placed her hand gently on his cheek.

'Do I sense a little jealousy?' she asked. 'If I do, then I can tell you that your thoughts are misguided. I am the proud and loving wife of Dr Peter Campbell.'

Even so, Peter could not shake off his distrust of his brother. He tried to banish from his mind the dark thought of an affair between the two people he most loved in the world.

*

Ian gazed at the riverbanks covered in thick groves of dates, beyond which was a desolate land of arid desert. The warship conveying them upriver flew colourful signal flags and the blue-coated Indian sailors worked quietly and efficiently. On the deck of the steamer stood Ian's company of around eighty men watching the shore drift by.

Now and then herds of cattle were seen on the shoreline, along with native herdsmen. The river was only about three hundred yards wide and Ian wondered nervously why the Persians had not chosen to set up ambushes on this narrow strip of water. A fusillade of fire could sweep the deck clean of his infantrymen.

Orders were issued before nightfall and Ian understood what he must do when they encountered the Persian river defences upstream. He tried to repress the bloody memories of hand-to-hand fighting in the Crimea, praying that the Enfield rifled muskets would do the job of defeating the enemy from a distance as they stormed ashore.

It was just on nightfall that the expedition observed the Persians throwing up earthen berms to provide cover for two artillery field guns. But an accompanying British ship commenced firing its guns at the Persian artillery, and the explosions indicated the devastating effect of the ship's fire. When the smoke cleared, the men could see the shattered bodies of the Persian gunners and others fleeing to safety.

Night fell without any further disturbance and a party of engineer officers used the dark to make a reconnaissance of the Persian defences. They were accompanied by a raft towed into the channel on the far side of a low, swampy island. On the rafts were two eight-inch mortars and two five-inch mortars.

Ian spent the early evening smoking his pipe and sharing his small stock of brandy with his junior officers. Sergeant Curry moved amongst the soldiers, sharing a quick nip of rum, joking and generally reassuring the men that the following day it would be Persians – and not Englishmen – who would die. The eve of a battle was a time for reflection on the meaning of what could be a short life with a violent end.

When his officers made their way back to their respective men, Ian lay down on the deck to stare at the star-filled night sky. The difference in the constellations of the northern hemisphere was something he was growing used to, but he missed the reassuring set of stars so well known in New South Wales as the Southern Cross. He dozed off with his rifled musket by his side and his two pistols. Through the darkness came the whispers of soldiers unable to sleep, and the sound of a mouth organ playing a mournful tune. Ian slipped into a deep sleep, although it was racked by nightmares of exploding Russian artillery shells and the screams of the dying.

Ian was jerked awake by the sound of an exploding mortar bomb as the first rays of the sun touched his face. He leapt to his feet, scooping up his pistols and rifle. When he looked to the shore he could see the smoke rising from the enemy fortifications. The battle had begun.

FOUR

'Fix bayonets!'

Ian roared out the order above the din of the exploding mortar bombs and the sound of the long deadly bayonet blades clicking as they were twisted into place at the end of the Enfields. Very soon they would be storming ashore, shouting defiance at the entrenched enemy, and Ian knew it was inevitable that many of his men would fall to the enemy's musket balls before they could get close enough to wreak havoc in hand-to-hand fighting.

For the moment the flotilla of British paddle-steamer warships continued to pound the formidable entrenched positions of the Persians. The Persian artillery batteries responded with a hail of solid cannonballs that ripped into the British warships.

As he stood on the deck of the troopship, his sword at his hip, his two revolvers tucked in leather holsters and his bayonet-tipped Enfield gripped in his hand, Ian noted vaguely that it was a clear and temperate day with a gentle breeze. It was too nice a day to die. When he looked up and down the river he could see the colourful flags flying from the masts of the warships and thought that it could have easily been a regatta day – except for the explosions threatening both Persian and English soldiers. The river was glittering under a rising sun and the smoke from the naval guns drifted gently in the air.

On the riverbank Ian saw colourfully dressed Persian horsemen riding between the groves of date palms. He heard the heavy thumps of trunks hitting the earth as the naval shells smashed into the trees. Ian's men were crouching on the deck with grim faces. No doubt each man was pondering the fate that awaited him when they finally went ashore to engage the Persian infantry hidden behind their carefully prepared earthen parapets. What was reassuring to Ian was that the naval bombardment was slowly reducing the defences. For three hours the cannonade continued. In that time Ian relaxed, drew on his pipe and puffed smoke that curled away in a lazy cloud. He was joined by Sergeant Conan Curry, who also took out his battered pipe and lit it.

'It reminds me a bit of the Redan,' Conan said.

'But this time we have the navy providing artillery support,' Ian replied. 'All we have to do is wait for the navy boys to do their job smashing holes in their defences. Make sure the men have a good supply of water in their canteens and drink as much as they can now before we disembark. It is going to be thirsty work.'

'Will do, sir,' Conan answered. 'I notice that the Persian guns are going a bit quiet.'

Ian could see that the fire from the shore had slackened off and that their ship was altering course to disembark them a few hundred yards north of the Persian artillery guns. The point of landing was relatively clear of date trees, although swampy and intersected by creeks that clearly filled at high tide. Scattered musket shots covered the landing point and Ian watched as the fierce Scottish Highlander infantry – accompanied by grenadiers – poured ashore.

'Riflemen! Time to go ashore!' Ian yelled to his men.

He felt the mud grip his boots as he clambered from the troopship, followed by Conan and the rest of the company. Very little musket fire met them as the enemy skirmishers fell back at the advance of the British troops while the company slogged its way through the mud, relatively safe from enemy fire for the moment.

The order came down from General Outram's HQ that the company was to form a defensive ring to protect the British artillery being offloaded to provide support to the infantry. By mid-afternoon this was completed and the rising tide was filling the muddy creeks of the landing place. It was time to move. Ian was pleased to be with his company in the advance on the main Persian camp beyond a date grove on the riverbank.

En route, the company was fired on, but the musketry fire proved ineffective. From time to time Ian ordered his men to engage an enemy target, and the result was a string of dead Persians off to their flank, having foolishly exposed themselves to the lethally accurate Enfield fire.

The order was passed down to Ian that the infantry were to halt at the edge of the date grove. General Outram rode past Ian's company and Ian saluted him. The general returned the salute, calling out, 'Damned fine work by your men, Captain Forbes,' before continuing his reconnoitre of the enemy camp now clearly visible to the advancing British and Indian troops. The general sent forward troopers of the Scinde Horse to get a closer look. His military secretary who had gone with the Indian unit reported back that there were two camps on either side of a village and the Persians had drawn up their army into a formidable force to resist the advance. Even as he reported, the men with Outram's expedition could still hear the navy guns firing in the distance at a few remaining Persian guns.

A rider came to Ian, who was smoking his pipe and leaning on his rifle.

'Captain Forbes, General Outram would request that your company be used as skirmishers in our advance on the enemy encampments.'

The young lieutenant delivering the message was breathless with fear and excitement and Ian suspected that this was his first action.

'Inform General Outram that my men will be in place within ten minutes.'

The young officer saluted, wheeled his horse around and galloped away.

Ian called in his officers and senior NCOs to instruct them on their role in the advance. It was a quick briefing and the orders then delivered to each and every soldier. Under command of the junior officers the riflemen deployed to the front of the line arranged for the attack. Each rifleman moved forward, selecting any cover he could find, always ready to pick off an enemy target.

Ian had placed himself just behind his line of skirmishers with Conan at his side. They could clearly see the Persian troops opposite them prepared for battle near the town of Mohammerah. British artillery had been sent to their flank to provide cover fire, and the assault forces was composed of a combination of British and Indian infantry.

General Outram had chosen to initially attack the encampment to the left rear of the village where his opposite, the Shah-zadeh, had the bulk of his artillery and cavalry. It was obvious that the British general knew he must knock out the Persian's most potent weapons before taking on their infantry in the second encampment about five hundred yards to the right, where groves of date trees provided some cover for the Persians.

Ian gazed at the distant target and felt a knot in his stomach. They were to advance across an open plain. This would be the time they were most vulnerable and it was possible many of his skirmishers might die.

Bugles and drums signalled the advance, and Ian stepped forward, his rifle across his chest as his own company moved well forward of the red squares of the vastly outnumbered advancing British troops.

'Tell Molly that I died well this day,' Conan mumbled as he and Ian trudged forward, acutely aware that they would probably be the first to die when the enemy commenced firing. Ian was very aware of the love that existed between the colonial Irishman and the pretty Welsh girl. Molly was the sister of Owen Williams; a bright, educated young woman who had invested her brother's money – as well as Conan's – into a very successful confectionary shop in London.

'You bloody well tell her yourself,' Ian replied, staring at the mass of waiting enemy still holding their fire. Range was all-important to the much shorter-range enemy muskets, and Ian was pleased to hear the occasional crack of one of his riflemen opportunistically firing at a target.

Before the advancing British formations, the Shah's army seemed to dissolve. They could see the Persians fleeing the front lines, throwing away their arms in their haste to make their retreat faster.

'Bloody hell!' Conan swore, hardly believing his eyes. 'The bastards are running away when they had the best opportunity to defeat us in our advance!'

A strange thought went through Ian's mind that it was, indeed, too nice a day to die.

'Conan, spread the word to the skirmishers to keep a lookout for landmines,' he said, aware that the Persians often buried casks of gunpowder with protruding metal tubes that when stood on fired a charge into the powder. He had witnessed the devastating effect of such hidden weapons in the Crimea.

Suddenly there was a massive explosion from within the Persian camp and the shock wave almost blew Ian off his feet. A thick column of smoke rose into the blue skies and he guessed that the fleeing Persians had detonated their reserves of ammunition. The British squares continued the advance until they were inside the rows of tents. The desert earth was strewn with muskets, small-arms ammunition, bedding, carpets, saddlery, band instruments and even half-eaten meals. Amongst the debris of war were a few unexploded British artillery shells. Very few Persian wounded remained and it appeared that most of the wounded had been carried away or had sought refuge in the nearby village.

General Outram would not rest until he had finally cornered the Persian army and brought them to the point of surrender. He ordered his units to continue the pursuit, leaving the Persian camp behind. Outram despatched his Scinde cavalry to track the path of retreat but they returned to report that the enemy were fleeing so fast that only cavalry reinforcements had any hope of catching them.

The order was given to camp for the night, which proved to be bitterly cold in the open. Neither soldier nor officer had tents, and after looking to the welfare of his junior officers and their men, Ian huddled by a small fire that Conan had been able to make. A tin pot boiled water for a much-anticipated cup of hot tea. They were joined by Corporal Owen Williams, who was offered a spare mug.

'We never had the chance to go through the Persian's camp for any loot,' Owen complained.

'No doubt the local villagers have done the job already,' Conan added, sipping his black tea and adding a good dose of sugar to sweeten it.

'You are both alive, that has to be a consolation,' Ian said, poking at the small fire as if attempting to extract more heat from it. 'This war is not over and we might run into a rear-guard defence by the Persians. They still outnumber us.'

'What I wouldn't give right now to be back in that pub near the barracks with an ale and a big meal of Yorkshire pudding by the log fire,' Conan sighed.

'You forgot to mention Molly on your lap,' Ian grinned, knowing that his friend had promised the pretty Welsh woman that he would marry her when his term of enlistment was up.

Conan glanced at Owen, a hint of self-consciousness visible on his face in the flickering shadows of the campfire. 'That, too,' he said quietly.

'You had better do the right thing by my sister, boyo,' Owen said good-naturedly.

Rank and class did not exist around this small campfire under the Persian night sky. These were three friends bound by blood and war.

'What do you think General Outram and Brigadier Havelock plan to do next?' Conan asked.

'If I were them, I would continue to pursue the Persians upriver until they sue for peace,' Ian replied. 'We have a formidable flotilla of warships, and from what I have gleaned the enemy has a well-fortified position on the river at Akwaz.'

Conan nodded, trusting Ian's knowledge of military tactics and strategy.

In the darkness a jackal yipped its call and the three men settled into the comfort of their companionship and small campfire.

*

When the sun rose over the desert the order was given to return to the town of Mohammerah and occupy the abandoned Persian camp. By day Ian's company took shelter under the shade of the date palms, but they moved camp to the desert at night to avoid the malarial waterways. They moved between diurnal swarms of annoying flies and nocturnal clouds of biting sandflies. Ian had to release many of his company to guard private property in the town, which at least garnered respect from the local inhabitants who had expected their homes to be looted and burned to the ground. Nonetheless, the British army had acquired great stores of grain, a good amount of ammunition and some cannons left behind by the retreating Persian army. However the stench of unburied Persian soldiers mixed with the other pungent smells around the town, so it was not a pleasant place to be.

Mohammerah was located at the junction of the Karoon and Euphrates rivers and was a filthy mud-bricked settlement with a large bazaar. Its only redeeming feature was the governor's house with its well-maintained gardens. The town was surrounded by a patchwork of swamp and cultivated farmland. Beyond the village was an endless horizon of flat desert. The river was the lifeblood of the people, who lived as they had for thousands of years. Throughout the day the British and Indian troops heard the routine call to prayer from the tall minarets of the mosques.

Ian had a chance to tour the town and was impressed by the variety of fruit trees in the governor's garden. He saw apple, mulberry, plantain and pomegranate trees side by side and noticed a small boy selling the fruit by the road. Ian guessed the boy had used the confusion of the fighting to raid the orchards, and admired his enterprise. Ian purchased a basket of mixed fruits for distribution amongst his troops and determined to send back a party of his men with money to purchase more so that each man would have at least one piece of fruit.

Ian had been tasked with carrying out a review of the Persian defences, accompanied by a villager who had a good grasp of English. The old man had once worked in the lucrative local trading houses when goods from India had poured into the town. Conan also went with Ian, as well as a platoon under the command of Lieutenant Sinclair. They crossed to the right bank to examine the earthen ramparts the Persians had erected and came across three dead horses still harnessed to a capsized gun carriage. The bodies were bloated and decomposing, covered in clouds of evil-looking flies. Beside the carnage lay four human bodies with massive injuries, and it was apparent that an English naval shell had found its mark, taking out the gun crew. Ian recognised the rank of captain on one of the corpses and knelt down to search his stretched uniform, maggots falling onto the sandy desert as he did so. He slipped a letter out of one of the pockets and passed it to his interpreter.

'What does it say?' Ian asked as his men stood upwind of the foul stench of death.

The interpreter scanned the letter. 'The man writes that

he might die in the great battle to come, and wishes that his brother in Tehran look after his wife and children if that happens.' He passed the letter back to Ian, pointing out a forwarding address.

'Sergeant, see that this letter is passed on to brigade HQ for posting,' Ian ordered.

Conan frowned. 'Yes, sah. It will be done.'

The party spent the rest of the day moving amongst the shattered bodies of their enemy. Arms, legs, decapitated heads and entrails lay scattered around them as they continued the review of the defences on the riverbanks. It was not a day Ian wanted to repeat, and that night he prayed that the advance would continue and put some distance between them and this obscene place of death. He had made the same prayer when he was in the Crimea.

Over the next couple of days, the expeditionary force of British and Indian troops went about the business of landing more stores, including tents. The work kept the men of Ian's company busy whilst General Outram planned his next move. As Ian had predicted, the fortified town of Akwaz, on the river upstream, was his objective.

Ian's company was to board the steam warships allocated the task of taking the town by force of arms. This time it appeared the enemy was going to make a determined stand and Ian knew that his company's bayonets would be stained red in the battle to come. He also knew that many would likely be killed and wounded, and the faces of his soldiers boarding the Indian navy ships showed that they knew it too.

Ian had little interest in the politics of campaigning. All he knew of their reason for being in Persia was that an emir in the Afghan province of Herat had rebelled against the occupying Persians and, with the support of the Kabul emirate, had appealed to the British in India for support. He knew, too, that the reasons for war were complex and varied. What really mattered to Ian was that God was on their side – and the Enfield rifled musket.

FIVE

There had been an air of unspoken tension between Alice and her husband since his return. It annoyed Alice as she knew she had nothing to feel guilty about. She had remained loyal to Peter, although she had to admit that Scott flirted with her whenever he had the opportunity.

The endless round of tea parties, visits to the homes of influential families of the East India Company and afternoons spent under the shady trees of the villa garden were becoming boring. It was as if she was still in England, albeit with an unfamiliar world beyond the gates.

One way to break the boredom was to visit the local markets where the colourful mix of people and cultures never failed to fascinate Alice. Whenever she took a trip to the markets Scott had insisted that one of his troopers accompany her to keep away the riffraff that loitered to pick pockets or even rob the wealthy – Indian mostly,

English rarely through fear of the severe reprisals that might follow.

Alice had planned such a trip today and was waiting impatiently at the spacious residence for her escort, who had failed to arrive at the designated time. Peter was away treating some of the poorer residents of the Bengali town, so apart from the servants going about their daily chores, the house was deserted. Alice impulsively decided to go to the markets on her own. After all, she had looked into the eyes of a tiger and defeated the great and magnificent beast.

Parasol aloft, Alice made her way out of her relatively safe neighbourhood dominated by European homes. After several wrong turns she eventually found herself in the marketplace crowded with vendors selling everything from local produce to imported silks. A man sat cross-legged playing a musical instrument Alice did not recognise whilst a deadly cobra appeared to sway to the rhythm of the music. Alice stopped for a moment to watch in fascination at the seeming bravado of the turbaned man in the loincloth and dropped a couple of coins at his feet, carefully keeping her distance from the hooded snake. She approached a stall festooned with colourful silks and began looking through them. Gradually she became aware that the mood of the people around her seemed unusually sullen. A man bumped into her roughly and growled something in a language she did not understand. Others in the marketplace cast angry looks at her. Something had changed since her last visit and she experienced a twinge of unease.

'This might not be a good time for an Englishwoman to be alone in the markets,' a familiar voice said behind her, and Alice turned to see the Khan. He was not dressed in his finery but wore a loose-fitting long shirt over a skirt-like cloth wrapped around his waist. He was accompanied by a bodyguard of four bearded men wearing turbans and armed with curved swords. The silk vendor bowed his head, obviously recognising the importance of the man speaking with the Englishwoman.

'Prince, it is good to make your acquaintance again,' Alice said, relieved to have his immediate protection. 'It appears that the people here resent my presence.'

'It is understandable when one knows of the hanging of a mutineer leader, Pandey, at the Barrackpore barracks,' Khan said. 'His stand against the Queen's Empire made him a hero to the common people, and now he is a martyr to them. You are in the wrong place at the wrong time, and I would strongly suggest that you allow me to escort you safely from the markets. My palace is only a short distance from here, and I am sure you would like to see how the other half live.' There was something facetious in his last words, and they were accompanied by the hint of a smile.

Alice had to admit to herself that she was fascinated by the Indian prince, who was handsome, charming, very intelligent and had a wry sense of humour.

The crowd made a pathway for the prince and his bodyguards as they escorted the Englishwoman away, closing behind them with shouts of anger. It seemed the prince had arrived just in the nick of time. Soon Alice was free of the stifling mob and on a wide avenue lined with shade trees. They walked for a distance until the pungent smell of the markets was behind them. Eventually they came to a whitewashed wall surrounding a magnificent building rising three storeys above the street.

A great wooden gate ornately adorned with Arabic script swung open and the party of six entered a beautiful garden with manicured lawns and flowing stone fountains. Servants in loincloths tended the garden and well-dressed male and female servants greeted them at the top of the broad stone stairs leading into the palace.

'So this is how the other half live,' Alice said with a grin, feeling secure and comfortable in the company of the young man who wielded such power.

'Perhaps you might enjoy a cool sherbet before you are escorted back to your husband,' the Khan said politely. 'I am sure that my wife would love to meet with the daughter of Kali.'

Alice was fascinated with this introduction to the palace of one of the ruling elites of the Bengal region. From what she had learned from Scott, these princes owed their positions to their alliance with the East India Company.

'I would be honoured to meet your wife,' Alice said as the prince escorted her to a room with marble floors and sumptuous divans. Two servants hovered nearby and the Khan issued instructions. They disappeared and moments later a beautiful dark-eyed young woman wearing a long silken dress embroidered with pearls entered the room with a young boy Alice guessed to be around five years old. He was dressed in the rich traditional clothing of an adult, with a turban, like a miniature version of the Khan on the tiger hunt.

'This is my wife, Sari, and my firstborn son, Ali,' the Khan said. 'Neither speaks English but I will be sending my son to England to be educated next year.' The boy standing by his mother stared intently at Alice, and the prince noticed.

'My son has never seen a beautiful Englishwoman with hair the colour of gold,' he smiled. 'I think he would like to touch your hair.'

'If he wishes,' Alice replied, and the Khan summoned his son forward. Very gently the boy reached up to touch the hair piled on Alice's head. He looked into her eyes and smiled shyly, before running back to his mother, who smiled with the same shyness. The Khan spoke some more words and Alice could see a sudden look of interest in Sari's dark eyes.

'I told her how you single-handedly killed the tiger,' he said. 'My wife is impressed. You may be the daughter of Kali to my Hindu subjects, but I suspect that you are our Queen's tiger to your own people. But now I should extend our hospitality.'

As if on cue the two servants returned with silver trays upon which were crystal glasses filled with sherbet and ice. They were set down on a low polished teak table and soft cushions were brought for the Khan and Alice. Alice realised that the prince's wife and son had disappeared from the room. She suspected it was not quite proper for her to be alone with the Indian prince, but to say so would only cause offence; besides, she was intrigued. She took a cushion opposite the Khan and accepted the glass he passed her. The thick, cold drink was delicious.

'Why do the people resent us?' Alice asked without the polite niceties of genteel conversation.

The prince raised his eyebrows at her bluntness. 'I am sure that Major Campbell has told you about the issue of the cartridge cases,' he said, sipping his own drink. 'But there is the underlying issue of being free from the yoke of the British or, in our case in Bengal, the East India Company.'

'But my brother-in-law has informed me that you hold your position because of the East India Company's administration of this region of India.'

'Before you English came, my father and his father before him ruled an area ten times larger than I do now,' the Khan said, and Alice noticed that he was frowning. 'The Company cunningly took our lands for their own purposes and promised that they would protect my rule. But now they have disobedience in the ranks of the army and I fear this will become a full-scale rebellion by the people of India bent on throwing out all Europeans.'

'If that eventuates, how would it affect your family?' Alice asked.

For a moment the Indian prince did not answer. 'I would have to see which way the winds of war blew,' he said in a quiet voice. 'My priority is the survival of my family and my regime. But I do know that it is very much in the Company's interests to ensure my safety.'

His answer sent a chill up Alice's spine, and for the first time she had a sense that she and Peter ought to cut short their stay in India, despite Scott's reassurances that the mutinous acts of the East India troops were being squashed. How could such a tiny number of Company soldiers and administrators guarantee control over a land of such huge geographic size and vast multitudes of people?

'I have arranged to have my carriage take you back to Major Campbell's residence,' the Khan said, as if displeased with the conversation Alice had initiated. 'It has been a pleasure having you under my roof for this very brief time. My servants have almost finished preparing the pelt of the tiger. I will have it sent around when it is ready.' He rose, extending his hand to assist Alice from her cushion. She accepted and felt his firm grip linger even when she was on her feet.

'You are a beautiful woman in any culture,' he said softly. 'Dr Campbell is a fortunate man to have you in his bed.'

'And you are similarly fortunate to have such a beautiful wife and son,' Alice stammered, embarrassed by his choice of words. She slipped her hand from his and bade him farewell.

Alice was escorted to the carriage and delivered to her residence. She was met by Peter, who was standing in the gateway as she alighted from the coach. She could immediately see the dark expression on his face.

'I was informed that you left for the markets without a bodyguard,' he said by way of a greeting. 'If I am not mistaken, that is the local prince's coach.'

'I chose to go to the markets alone as the trooper Scott assigned me did not keep his appointment. I have been before without mishap but, I must confess, the crowd in the markets was not very hospitable and I was fortunate the Khan happened to be in the area and could provide me with a safe escort home. He has proved to be a good and honourable man.'

Peter frowned and without a word turned and strode back to the bungalow. Alice hurried after him.

'Peter, what is wrong?' she asked, and Peter suddenly stopped.

'Do you know how this looks to the people who live here?' he said with a pained expression on his face. 'Every time I go out on my medical rounds you seem to find entertainment in the company of my brother – and now that has extended to the local royalty. Do you know that the Khan has four wives?'

'I did not know that,' Alice answered. 'I only met one of his wives, and her son.'

'That is the low morality of these people,' Peter said. 'Bloody harems and forced marriages. Is that the type of person you would rather socialise with than your husband?'

'That is not true, and nor is it fair,' Alice exploded. 'I love you, and I have no romantic interest in any other man. Surely you know that.'

'All I know is that you get presents from a bloody native

prince and my own brother takes to you as if you were more than his sister-in-law. All my childhood Scott was the favoured son and would make a point of taking anything that I valued. Now I think he wants you.'

Alice was disturbed by Peter's revelation of his insecurity. It had never occurred to her that this gentle and courageous man who lived to make other people's lives better could doubt her love for him.

'I think we should consider returning to England,' Alice said.

'Would that change anything?' Peter retorted. 'Or would you find comfort in the arms of another man there?'

Shocked, Alice stumbled in tears to their room, leaving Peter standing alone.

He cursed himself and shook his head. What was wrong with him? He walked slowly to the garden, grabbing a bottle of unopened Scotch whisky on the way. He did not need a glass. He would drink from the bottle.

Peter sat down on a stone bench. It was mid-afternoon and the hot sunlight blazed down, filtered through the leaves of the shady trees. If only Samuel were here to talk with, Peter thought, and not off somewhere in the biblical lands of Mesopotamia fighting another war for the Queen. Alice's brother was Peter's closest friend. The soldier and the surgeon had shared so much on the battlefields of the Crimea only months before. No doubt Samuel would tell him that he was acting as an insanely jealous man and that he should put more trust in Alice.

Peter opened the bottle and took a long swig. Meanwhile Alice lay on the big bed, sobbing tears of frustration for her husband's lack of trust. She only wished that her brother Samuel could be here to talk sense into the man.

★

Captain Ian Steele watched as his men boarded one of the three steamers conveying troops up the river to engage the Persian army. He was pleased to see the look of confidence in their faces as they passed, and many gave him a nod of respect.

Ian had attended the briefings at brigade HQ and knew that what lay ahead would take lives, but he reminded himself that this was the lot of professional soldiers. He was reassured to learn that the naval commander of their small fleet was a man with a considerable reputation in similar campaigns in Burma and China.

A company of Highland infantry had boarded the steamer lying alongside their own, and a cheerful banter was exchanged between the English and Scottish troops. Ian could see that morale was high amongst his men.

At ten o'clock in the morning the steamers pulled out of Mohammerah. The steamship the *Comet* led the flotilla, towing the slower *Assyria*, whilst the *Planet* brought up the rear. Each steamer also towed a gunboat armed with two twenty-four-pounder howitzers, artillery guns capable of firing at a high angle to drop explosive shells behind fortified constructions. Ian passed the order for the men of his company to prepare the tea that the British army marched on.

'At least we don't have to march to the next battle,' Conan said beside Ian. 'And this is not as bad as the bloody troopship that brought us to Persia. At least it is hard to get seasick on the river.'

'Very true, Sergeant Curry,' Ian said. 'I'd consider transferring to the navy if all wars were fought on rivers. No marching through sleet and cold, or living in the open in drifts of snow, wondering if rations will be delivered to fill my empty stomach.'

'But it is the seasickness,' Conan said, knowing that his company commander had suffered badly on the sea voyage to Persia.

'Yes, the bloody seasickness,' Ian replied with a twisted grin. 'How about you fetch us a mug of tea as sweet as you can make it, Sergeant?'

Conan nodded and went in search of tea. Ian gazed across the water at the right bank of the waterway fringed with palm and date trees intermingled with shepherd boys grazing their herds of goats. How far he had come from the riverbanks of his favourite swimming hole in the shadow of the Blue Mountains that hemmed in Sydney Town. The real Ian Steele was long dead now, and he was Samuel Forbes.

SIX

Great flocks of duck and teal scattered before the bow wakes of the war steamers pushing up the river. On the banks dwarf poplar and thick willow trees flanked the flotilla, beyond which the desert dominated, with the occasional tufts of coarse, dry grass. No longer were there orchards of date palms or any other signs of human habitation.

This was what the real Garden of Eden must have looked like, Ian thought as he stood gazing out at the riverbanks.

It was just after sunset when the flotilla anchored below the ruined Arab fort of Kootul-el-abd. Ian landed with a party of officers and found the fireplaces of the enemy's bivouac within fifty yards of the river. They also found the wheel marks of artillery guns and Ian knew they were closing on the retreating army as the impressions were relatively fresh.

The following morning the flotilla set off again, and by mid-afternoon the ruined mosque of Imaum was spotted.

Again, a party of officers landed and found evidence that the combined Anglo-Indian expeditionary force was yet closer to their objective. They found freshly dug graves and a ruined mud house that appeared to have been the temporary shelter for the Shah-zadeh himself. One thing Ian commented on to his fellow officers was the absence of the usual scraps of food around the enemy campsite. They agreed that the Persian force must be low on provisions. It was hoped that they might reach the vanguard of the retreating enemy before it could reach the prepared fortifications. However, the next day the flotilla ran into a series of narrow bends in the river where the water was channelled into a strong current that slowed them down.

On the third night the Anglo-Indian steamers came opposite the Arab village of Ismaini where information was gleaned that the Persians had passed by the previous day with seven regiments and two thousand cavalry. It was still a formidable force. A straggler from the enemy army had been captured. He was almost dead from hunger and informed his captors that a couple of the Persian commanders had died from their wounds and had been buried back at Imaum-Subbeh. More graves were discovered, and even the footprint of a desert lion.

Eventually the Arab encampment of Omeira was reached and the unwelcome news imparted that the previous day the Persians had arrived at their fortified base at the town of Akwaz, fourteen miles north of their current position.

The fleet was secured for the night against a surprise attack and a reconnaissance organised for the following day. Ian knew his men would see action tomorrow against a large dug-in enemy force. He gathered his company on the deck of their steamer and addressed them as to the forthcoming fight. He spoke calmly and reminded the red-coated soldiers that they were the finest light infantry in the British army and would make the regiment proud. His quiet and calming talk brought about a cheer from the men. Ian dismissed them and was joined by Conan.

'So, this is finally it,' Conan said, plugging his pipe and gazing at the star-filled sky rocking gently above.

'Let us hope that the Persians repeat their efforts of the last time we met them,' Ian said, also looking at the night sky, wondering if the people of the Bible had done the same thing in the times described in the Old Testament. 'I have noticed that Molly has been writing to you,' he commented.

'She is a grand lady,' Conan sighed. 'I don't know what she sees in me.'

'Neither do I,' Ian grinned. 'But she *is* a grand lady.'

'What about you, sir?' Conan asked. 'Is there someone waiting for you when we return to London?'

'I don't think there is anyone waiting for me,' Ian replied, but an image of the beautiful young Ella Solomon, waving goodbye to his ship steaming from the London port, flashed before him. He tried to dismiss the memory of her sad smile. There was no future for a soldier of the Queen and the daughter of Ikey Solomon, one of London's most ruthless men. After all, her Jewish religion put them in different worlds. Although Ian had been baptised a Catholic, he had never really been a religious man. His mother had been a Presbyterian who had despaired of her only child ever practising any Christian faith.

As well as Ella, there was Ian's first true love, Jane Wilberforce, who had mysteriously disappeared when she was pregnant with his child. Ian had not given up his search for her, even though it seemed very likely she was dead, probably at the hands of Charles Forbes. Jane's identical twin, Rebecca, certainly thought so. Rebecca had been adopted as a baby and raised by the rich and powerful Lord Montegue and his wife. The sisters had been reunited in secret only months before Jane's disappearance.

The bell on the steamer tolled the time, as was the naval tradition.

'Funny how you think about those you love just before a battle,' Conan reflected as he puffed on his pipe. 'I suppose it is somewhat selfish to do what we do. If we fall, we leave the living to continue without us.'

'From what I have heard of Molly's business she will not be destitute,' Ian consoled. 'But we aren't going to fall in battle tomorrow. It will be the other bugger.' He sighed. 'Right, it's probably time to get some sleep.'

Both men tapped their pipes on the boat's railing, watching the sparks of dying tobacco fall into the dark waters of the river.

Neither slept well that night on the deck under the Persian stars. Ian could hear the worried, whispered conversations of his company around him, and he understood their fears. Eventually, sleep came, but with it the endless nightmares of the Crimea as men were blown into scraps of bloody meat by the Russian artillery and bodies shattered by the hail of musket balls.

*

It was early dawn and the British flotilla steamed to within three thousand yards of the Persian defences, partly screened by a low range of sandhills. Three enemy artillery guns were seen positioned near a small mosque. Persian cavalry galloped along the bank, observing the flotilla.

Some Arabs hailed the war steamers from the bank and they were taken aboard. It was well known that the Arabs had no love for their Persian occupiers. They informed the

British high command that the force opposing them only consisted of around five hundred infantry and thirty cavalry, tasked with the protection of Persian army stores. It came as a pleasant surprise to the British force but also a caution that the enemy's main strength was somewhere ahead of the advance. It was decided that the town on the opposite bank should be taken as soon as possible as this would ensure the landing force was out of range of the deadly Persian artillery. As such, one of the gunboats was tasked to engage the enemy guns.

Again, Ian gave the order to fix bayonets, and his company was landed midmorning. The order came down that his best men were to be deployed as skirmishers, leading the files of Scottish Highlanders into the town. The order to the troops was to destroy any enemy supplies they encountered. In the distance Ian could hear the explosions of the artillery duel between gunboat and on-shore Persian artillery.

Ian, with the bulk of his company, followed his skirmishers, ever alert to any possible resistance from enemy snipers. They did not see any civilians on the streets and alleyways, which were bordered by miserable stone and mud hovels, and Ian guessed they had wisely remained indoors. But it appeared after some time that the town was undefended.

'Sir! Sir!' A young officer from Brigadier Havelock's brigade staff hurried towards Ian, his face flushed with excitement. 'Compliments of the brigadier. He wishes all his officers to know that the Persian commander has surrendered.'

'Why in bloody hell would they cede to us when they have the advantage of numbers and arms?' Ian frowned. 'Is it some kind of trick?'

'From what I have heard, the sheik has bad memories

of our bombardment back at Mohammerah, and is under the impression that our expeditionary force is merely the vanguard of a much larger force,' the young officer replied with a smile. 'It appears that his army has chosen to retreat another hundred miles to Shuster. The brigadier has also issued an order that none of the private homes in the town are to be looted.'

Ian passed on the order to his company and retired to the riverbank as the Scots continued guarding the town and searching for supplies. He and his men watched the vast Persian army marching away. They had no provisions and had chosen starvation over confronting the numerically smaller Anglo-Indian force.

The Persian cavalrymen numbered around two thousand and wore the distinctive black lamb-skin cap. They wore long blue robes, lighter coloured trousers and a white belt. Each cavalryman carried a sabre, with a matchlock musket slung across his back. They appeared to Ian to be a formidable enemy and he shook his head in disbelief at their retreat.

Suddenly a musket shot broke the silence and Ian saw that one of the cavalrymen had concealed himself as his unit retreated. The shot was wild and fired towards the town before he leapt on his mount and galloped away to join his squadron.

'At least one of the buggers made a stand,' Conan chuckled. 'I think the boys are pleased that they did not bloody their bayonets.'

'So am I,' Ian said. 'The best kind of war is one where no one gets killed – except for the foe. But you can bet we will get back on the boats and steam after them. Sooner or later it will have to come down to a bloody confrontation.'

However, orders were issued to regain law and order in the town as the Arab occupants fought each other for the

Persian stores that had not been destroyed by the British troops. Conan grumbled that they were not acting as fighting troops but as policemen.

Ian and his company of men camped outside the town, awaiting further orders. From here they could see the snow-topped Bakhtiari Mountains a hundred miles away rising above the arid desert lands.

A day later Ian and his company boarded the warships and steamed back downstream to Mohammerah, where a fully functioning city of army tents awaited them a mile from the town on the vast plain. The returning men were also provided with the welcome news that a peace treaty had been signed in Paris, bringing to an end the small but decisive war with the Persian empire. Ian's company was to re-join the regiment and return to England.

A translated copy of the *Tehran Gazette* provided some amusement to the soldiers before they departed. The version published for the local population proclaimed that the British army had suffered terrible casualties in their encounters with the Persian forces along the river; in fact the British had been soundly defeated.

Conan found a copy of the newspaper, tore it up and wandered off in search of privacy to put the paper to good use.

★

In the sumptuous villa of Major Scott Campbell, the tension grew between Alice and Peter. Very few words passed between them but their schism continued in relative privacy as Scott was often away dealing with the ongoing unrest amongst the sepoy troops.

Peter spent the days tending to the local people. He had set up a clinic to treat the many exotic diseases and injuries presented by the people who waited for him in long lines.

His reputation as a healer spread, and he received the gratitude of the poverty-stricken populace.

One evening in April Scott returned home to inform Alice and Peter that he was being posted west to a Bengali regiment at a place called Meerut near the city of Delhi.

'I think you should both travel with my squadron,' Scott said, pouring himself a large whisky from a crystal decanter. 'After all, you have seen so little of the country.'

Alice frowned. She would prefer to depart India and return to England. She could sense the hostile glares of the people on the streets whenever she travelled to and from Scott's residence to the houses of other Europeans. She felt that she was living on the slopes of a dormant volcano rumbling its warning of an imminent eruption.

'Alice and I intend to return to the coast and take a steamer back to England,' Peter said, and Alice glanced at her husband, pleased to hear him express her wishes.

'I have an ulterior motive, old chap,' Scott said. 'We could do with a battle-experienced surgeon to accompany us to Meerut. I feel there may be some unrest amongst the natives and I know that you will be safer with me rather than risking a journey to the coast by yourselves. It will only be until we settle this matter with our sepoys, then things will get back to normal and it will be safe to travel again.'

'Is it that bad?' Alice asked quietly.

Scott turned to her. 'I do not wish to alarm you, but we need time to get the situation under control. In the past a few rabble-rousers have attempted to stir up trouble and the East India Company has quelled it.'

Peter turned to his wife. 'What do you think?' he asked gently, and Alice felt a surge of love for the man who had in recent weeks avoided her.

'I will let you decide, Peter,' she replied.

For a long moment Peter pondered his decision. 'I accept the opportunity Scott has offered us to see more of India. It is not worth the risk of returning to the coast until the Company has ended the unrest.'

Scott swallowed the last of the whisky and held out his hand to Peter. 'Good show, old chap. I promise our journey will reveal to you both the real India, the one so many in England only read about. It will be an adventure, and you will always be safe around my men and I.'

Alice gave a wan smile, and Peter reached for the decanter of whisky to pour himself a stiff drink.

'I have to return to the barracks but will inform the commander and have extra provisions made for you both. I must apologise that we will not be able to take a carriage but we will provide good horses for your journey. We leave within forty-eight hours.'

When Scott had departed, Alice went to Peter. 'You were gracious enough to ask my opinion on whether to leave now or later,' she said. 'You must know that I am your wife and love you more than any other man in the world. No matter your decision I would have happily agreed.'

Peter did not reply but took a long sip of the fiery liquid as Alice walked to their bedroom, which she had not shared with her husband for some time.

He watched her leave and pondered her words and actions. He placed the stopper back in the decanter, leaving his almost full glass, and followed her. It was time to swallow his self-righteous pride and ask forgiveness for his unfounded jealousy.

SEVEN

Back in Bushehr Ian delivered his report of the river campaign to regimental HQ where it was read by his commanding officer, Colonel Jenkins.

Ian stood at attention while Jenkins finished reading the report.

'So, you brought no glory to the regiment,' Jenkins scowled.

'We gained a lot of experience for the regiment,' Ian replied. 'Of more importance is that we did not lose any men to enemy action.'

'We have been ordered to return to England,' Jenkins said. 'According to regimental records you are due a month's leave, and tomorrow you are to report to General Outram's HQ before we depart. God knows why when you have done nothing of any significance with Havelock's brigade.'

Ian guessed that the general was simply going to thank him for his command of the rifle company on the river expedition. When he looked into the face of his commanding officer he saw the bitterness of being left out. After all, unlike the earlier clashes of the Anglo-Indian forces who first arrived in this war and saw bloody action, this expedition had proved relatively safe, and Ian knew from past experience that this would have suited Jenkins well. A chance for glory without the danger.

'You may go, Captain Forbes,' Jenkins growled, and Ian stepped back, saluted and left the regimental commander stewing in his anger and resentment.

The next day Ian reported to General Outram's HQ, one of the better buildings in Bushehr.

'Captain Forbes, please be at ease and take a seat,' the general said kindly. 'I wanted you to know that your service with my expeditionary force and the way you led your company were exemplary. I must admit that I am bitterly disappointed the Persians did not stand and fight. I would have liked to have shown them the truth worth of British arms.'

'By simply being on the battlefield we succeeded in winning the war, sir. And that, I believe, is the prime reason for our existence,' Ian said.

The general smiled. 'You sound more like a damned politician than a soldier, Captain Forbes. But I have another reason for summoning you here. This correspondence has been sent to me from London concerning one of your men, a Sergeant Curry.' Ian took the sheet of paper with the royal coat of arms embossed on it and read the few words written there. Ian's eyes widened and he let out a small gasp.

'Do you concur with the elements of the letter, Captain Forbes?' the general asked.

'I most certainly do, sir,' Ian replied, passing back the sheet of paper.

'Then as Sergeant Curry is currently still under my command, it is done, and I think I do not have to tell you that the contents of the letter remain a secret between us until the appropriate time.'

A faint smile passed across Ian's face. 'Sir, I completely agree, and thank you.'

'Sergeant Curry should be thanking you, Captain Forbes, as it was you who submitted the original report.'

'Sergeant Curry is a fine soldier and deserves what he has won,' Ian said.

'Before you return to your regiment I want you to know that my offer of a place on my staff will always stand. I am returning to India after this rather unsatisfactory campaign and expect to see some real soldiering there.'

'Thank you, sir,' Ian said respectfully. 'I am honoured that you would want me on your staff.'

'You are free to leave now,' General Outram said, and Ian stepped back, snapped the best salute he could muster, and marched out of the office with the words of the report swirling in his head. He knew that what was to occur in England would change Conan Curry's life forever.

*

It had taken just over two weeks to journey across the Atlantic Ocean by steamship from New York in the United States of America to Liverpool on the west coast of England. The real Samuel Forbes and his friend, James Thorpe, had travelled in style as befitted their wealth – or rather, James' wealth. After disembarkation they travelled by coach and steam train to London, where Samuel travelled under the assumed guise of Ian Steele, English traveller and man of means.

At the end of their long trip a coach brought them to a respectable gentlemen's club on London's Pall Mall.

'I feel that you have made a bad choice in returning to London,' James said fretfully as a porter unloaded their luggage. 'What if you are recognised?'

'Do not worry, my dear James, it has been so long since I was last in England that I cannot think of anyone who would recognise the callow youth who left these shores so long ago. I doubt anyone would ever remember me from my time in England.'

'According to your friend Jonathan, Captain Forbes is campaigning in Persia,' James said as they followed the porter into the expensive club. James had telegraphed ahead from New York to make reservations, and when they entered he was impressed by the elegance of the interior. 'But from what is printed in *The Times* it appears he will be returning soon as a treaty has been signed over the issue of Persian territorial claims in Afghanistan. I still think it is extremely risky for you two to meet in person.'

'I doubt that we look very much alike now, dear boy,' Samuel said. 'The risk is minimal.'

James was not reassured and had an uneasy feeling as they were ushered to separate rooms, elegantly laid out for visiting men of substance. They met later in the dining room where they were surrounded by many of London's most notable and wealthy merchants vying for a way into the ranks of the English aristocracy. James was further impressed by the decor and the dining room. They were shown to a table laid out with a white linen cloth and fine cutlery.

James perused the menu carefully. 'The meals here seem to reflect a certain amount of good taste,' he said, looking around. He shifted uncomfortably in his seat, glancing over Samuel's shoulder. 'I don't know if you are aware but a gentleman at the other end of the room seems to be watching us with more than the usual amount of interest. As a matter of fact, he is leaving his table to approach us.'

Samuel blanched. Who could ever recognise him after all this time? He'd been so sure he would go unnoticed.

'Mr Forbes, it has been a long time since we both served in New Zealand with the regiment,' said the tall man in his early forties, extending his hand.

Samuel recognised the man immediately. Captain Brooke was one of the commanders he had served under when his regiment had been garrisoned in New South Wales, before its deployment to New Zealand to face the fierce Maori warriors.

'I must have a rather unusually similar appearance to this Mr Forbes you mention,' Samuel said, standing and accepting the handshake. 'But, alas, I fear you have the wrong man. My name is Mr Ian Steele, of New York, sir.'

The tall man frowned. 'I must say that you bear an uncanny resemblance to an officer I once served with,' he said. 'I would dare to say you could pass as his twin. You even sound like him. I apologise for my interruption and will recommend the lamb cutlets if you are new to the club. The lamb comes from Wales.'

The man returned to his table shaking his head, and as Samuel sat down he realised that his hands were trembling.

'That was damned close,' James hissed, leaning across the table. 'I warned you that returning to London was a grave mistake.'

'I am sure that I was able to convince Captain Brooke I am not the man he thought I was,' Samuel replied, but James was not convinced. Already he could see another man joining Captain Brooke at his table and Brooke speaking and looking across at them. It was obvious what the subject of their talk was. Samuel had suddenly lost his appetite but knew he could not leave the dining room without first eating as that might raise further suspicion.

The lamb cutlets arrived and they were as good as Captain Brooke had promised. Both Samuel and James ate in relative silence and when the waiter arrived at their table they waved off any further courses. The journey had started on a sour note and Samuel was beginning to think that maybe he should have taken James' advice and stayed in New York.

★

A military band on the wharf met the troopship as it sailed in from Persia. Rain sleeted down from the grey spring skies of London. The regiment disembarked and the only people waiting to greet the returning soldiers were a few women and children – families of the soldiers. Unlike the farewell for the Crimea, the action in Persia had not attracted the attention of the English public who were used to troopships returning from the minor wars that glued the Empire together.

Amongst the people waiting on the wharf was Molly Williams, the love of Conan's life. She was waving with a small handkerchief and looked as if she was almost bursting out of her skin.

'You have a duty to your Welsh lass, Sergeant Curry,' Ian grinned.

'Yes, sah!' Conan replied, a smile so wide it seemed his whiskered face might split. He saluted smartly and hurried down the gangplank. He held out his arms and the slight, pretty young woman ran into them, embracing Conan tightly.

Ian felt good that the man who had come to be as close as a brother to him had found so much happiness. He knew it was stupid but he gazed around the crowd of civilians milling on the wharf for one particular face. Although he had not encouraged Ella's attraction to him, he admitted to himself that he would have given anything to see her upon his return. But the beautiful young Jewish woman was nowhere to be seen.

The regiment would soon fall into ranks and march with the band to their barracks, where many would be granted overdue leave. The pubs near the barracks would do well in the next few hours, and Ian arranged to have his kit taken to his club where he intended to have the most expensive meal on offer, followed by a couple of bottles of their best wine.

'Are we ready to fall in, sir?' Lieutenant Sinclair asked.

'Yes, Mr Sinclair, inform Sergeant Curry he is to parade the company and join the regiment.'

'Very well, sir,' the young officer replied, saluting and marching towards the gangplank.

Ian sighed. The young officer was so much like his brother, he thought. But Captain Miles Sinclair lay buried on the Crimean Peninsula – as did so many other fine British soldiers and officers.

*

Once he had been granted leave from the regiment and spent a luxurious night at his club, Ian made his way to Soho, to visit Ikey Solomon. He was met warmly by the big, bearded man with a handshake that almost crushed his hand.

Ian had hired the services of the shady but very wealthy Jewish entrepreneur to investigate the mysterious disappearance of his lover, Jane Wilberforce. Ikey had not been successful, but during their dealings Ian had met his beloved daughter, Ella, who had become smitten with him. Sadly their love was both dangerous and forbidden. Ian was a Catholic and she was of the Jewish faith. Such a match was frowned upon by both religions.

However, Ian had not been able to dismiss Ella from his mind and had decided he needed to see her again, despite all the obstacles facing them.

'So, my friend, you have returned from Persia,' Ikey said. 'I think your victory over the unbelievers requires a toast.'

Ikey produced a bottle of gin and poured two tumblers. One he handed to Ian.

'To the glory of the Queen's Empire,' he said, handing a tumbler to Ian. 'May the sun never set upon her.'

Ian responded, taking a swig then setting down his glass on Ikey's desk and taking a seat.

'What can I do for you?' Ikey asked, wiping his beard with the back of his big hand.

'I was hoping that you might have had some news on the whereabouts of the lady I sought before leaving for Persia,' Ian said.

A dark cloud spread across Ikey's face. 'I am afraid, my friend, that there has been nothing, and I can assure you that if Miss Wilberforce was in London I would know by now. My thoughts are that she may be dead.'

Ian took another sip of the clear, fiery liquid. 'I am afraid you might be right,' Ian said quietly. 'Now I need to know why – and who is responsible.'

'That is a matter for the police,' Ikey said.

'I doubt they would be interested in investigating the disappearance of a country girl from a Kentish village,' Ian replied. 'But I would put my trust in your people to keep an ear out for any rumours on the streets. I am prepared to pay.'

'There is no reason to pay me any more,' Ikey said. 'You were more than generous the first time. If I hear anything I will inform you immediately. You were very kind to my princess and I know that she speaks fondly of you.'

Ian felt a twinge of guilt as he knew Ella's feelings were more than fondness, and he remembered her passionate kisses when they had stolen time together.

'How is Ella?' Ian asked, trying to sound nonchalant, and noticed a touch of anger in Ikey's expression.

'The foolish girl has gone to America to study medicine. She has aspirations to become a surgeon – which is impossible, of course. Medicine is a man's profession. Unfortunately, she fell under the spell of Dr Elizabeth Blackwell. This Blackwell woman was able to receive her medical practitioner's certification after attending the Geneva Medical College in New York, and Ella has gone to America to attempt to enrol in that same college. I have foolishly provided financial support to her endeavour, but suspect she will return when they reject her admission.'

Ian remembered how Ella had said she wished to be a doctor, but even Dr Peter Campbell, more liberal-minded than most, had scoffed at her dreams to become a surgeon. Ian was disappointed to learn that Ella was on the other side of the Atlantic Ocean. But for now, while he had leave from the regiment, he had a mission. He would return to the Forbes manor in Kent and begin his own investigation into Jane's disappearance.

EIGHT

Samuel stood before the entrance door to the elegant tenement house in a salubrious part of London. He was trembling and he felt racked with guilt. He had told James he was going shopping for a new hat. When James had said that he would join him, Samuel had replied that he would prefer to go alone, leaving James hurt and disappointed.

The front door opened and a severe-looking middle-aged woman fronted Samuel.

'I am here to visit Master Jonathan,' Samuel said, passing her his calling card. 'I am sure he will accept me.'

Without a word the woman closed the door and Samuel continued to wait nervously. Within a couple of minutes the woman returned, ushering Samuel inside. She led him through a hallway adorned with paintings to a bedroom where an emaciated man lay back against heaped pillows.

Samuel was shocked when he looked upon his first love.

Jonathan lay pale, gaunt and sweating in the bed. Samuel smiled weakly at the face he had not seen since it belonged to a healthy young officer of the London barracks many years earlier.

'Ah, dear boy,' Jonathan said faintly and fell into a coughing spasm, spitting up blood into a handkerchief. 'You should not have come all the way across the ocean to see me in my present state.'

Samuel recognised the dreaded signs of consumption and knew that Jonathan was in the final stages of the insidious disease. 'When you wrote about your condition you did not say how bad it was,' Samuel said, moving across the room to the big double bed and standing over Jonathan. 'I would have come earlier if I had known.'

Jonathan reached out a hand and Samuel gently took it in his own. 'I am glad that I have the opportunity to see you one last time. I find comfort remembering when you and I were boys and discovered our love beneath the branches of the willow trees on your family estate. It was so beautiful by that stream watching the waters flow gently past,' Jonathan sighed.

'I often remember those times,' Samuel said softly, forcing back the tears.

'You have written of your friendship with an American,' Jonathan said. 'I do not blame you, dear boy. I know that your service for the Queen in the far-off colonies forced us apart. Possibly I could have followed you, but I selfishly chose to study at Cambridge. I confess that I too found a new lover. So do not grieve for what was lost between you and I. Time moves on and life must keep pace with it.'

'Is there someone in your life now?' Samuel asked.

'There was, but he is now with the Church and a rising force. He chose religion over me,' Jonathan said, a slight note of bitterness in his tone. 'But you are here in my last days on this earth,' he said, squeezing Samuel's hand. 'It is good to see you, though we both know that your being in London is putting your venture with Captain Steele in dire jeopardy.'

'I had to see you again,' Samuel said, tears now trickling down his cheeks. 'Nothing on earth was going to stop me.'

'You should return to New York immediately,' Jonathan gasped, a coughing spasm once again racking his frail body. When it was over he removed his hand from Samuel's and stared at the ceiling of his bedroom. Jonathan smiled. 'If only time and circumstances had been our friends . . . but you have always been an impulsive soul.' His voice tapered away.

The stern woman came back into the room. 'I think Master Jonathan should rest now,' she said, assessing her patient's condition. 'I am sure that you understand, Mr Steele.'

Samuel glanced down at the illness-ravaged face of his first love and realised that the nurse was correct. Jonathan was on the verge of drifting off after the emotional exertion their meeting had caused them both.

Jonathan's family was as wealthy as Samuel's, but his parents had distanced themselves from him when it had been revealed that his attraction was to those of his own sex. They had exiled him to this London property with a generous allowance, and even when he contracted consumption they did not visit him for the shame he had brought upon their family name. Instead they had appointed a full-time nurse as a way of compensating for the alienation.

Samuel leaned over his dear friend and former lover to brush aside the long, lank hair falling over Jonathan's eyes. He bent down and kissed Jonathan on the forehead and turned to walk away. Samuel could not bring himself to say goodbye; the word had a terrible finality to it.

He stumbled out onto the street and hailed a hansom cab.

As the horses clattered through the streets of London Samuel reflected on the emotions that had coursed through him upon seeing Jonathan after such a long time. He felt guilt that his passion of the past had not come rushing back to him, but at the same time he knew there were still remnants of his first love deep within his being.

Once back at the club, James immediately sensed that Samuel was extremely upset but wisely did not ask why.

Samuel turned to James with tears streaking his face. 'I love you, James. I always will.'

James felt the conviction in Samuel's words and was satisfied with that. Maybe now, he thought, they could get out of London and return to New York.

★

Ian took a carriage to the Forbes manor in Kent, and when he arrived he strode up to the grand entrance of the impressive stone building. He was met by the head servant, a man who had been informed that Master Samuel Forbes was barred from the house.

'I'm sorry, sir,' the man said, standing in the doorway, 'but I must ask Sir Archibald for permission for you to enter.'

'Do that,' Ian said and the man disappeared, closing the door behind him. After a while he returned and said that Sir Archibald would see him. Ian followed the servant inside and was met by the man who was supposed to be his father, although both men knew that he was not. The real Samuel Forbes had been fathered by Sir Archibald's brother, George, now living in the British colony of New South Wales as a successful farmer raising sheep for the lucrative wool trade.

'What are you doing here?' Sir Archibald asked in an angry voice. He was attired in a dressing gown and slippers. Ian thought that he had aged since the last time he had spoken with him. His hair was grey and thinning and he had lost weight. 'You know that I issued an order for you to be barred from my home.'

'I thought you might welcome home the man who is bringing glory to the Forbes name,' Ian said sarcastically. He knew this meant little to the English aristocrat; Sir Archibald was more interested in the profits the colonial wars brought to the Forbes fortune, supplying provisions to the army and navy.

'You still have not answered my question, Samuel,' Sir Archibald reiterated.

'I have leave from the regiment and thought that I might receive temporary accommodation in our house. After all, after ten years of service with my grandfather's regiment I will be entitled to a share. I promise I will not overstay my welcome.'

'I expect Charles to arrive tomorrow, and your presence here will not be welcomed by him.'

'I am sure that we can stay out of each other's way,' Ian said smoothly.

For a moment Sir Archibald appeared to consider the request.

'You may stay, but only in the guest cottage,' he relented. 'I will have the stableboy assist you with any luggage.' Sir Archibald issued an order for this to be done, then turned and walked away.

The stableboy arrived at the front entrance. 'Is there anything I can carry for you, Captain Forbes?' he asked, clearly in awe of the man whose reputation preceded him. He was a gangling youth in his late teens and awkward around this heroic figure.

'Just help me get my luggage inside the guest cottage,' Ian said. 'You must be Harold,' he added, and the boy puffed up with pleasure that Captain Forbes would remember his name.

'Yes, sir,' he replied. 'Most people just call me Harry.'

'Well, Harry, it is good to see that you are still in employment here.'

Ian was guided to the cottage, which was built of stone and comfortable enough. Harry placed the luggage inside the room and began to help unpack. His eyes widened when he saw two revolvers inside one of the captain's bags.

'Did you use those against the Persians, sir?' he asked.

'We did not get much of a chance to do any real fighting,' Ian replied, placing the pistols on a table for future cleaning. 'But they came in handy in the Crimea.'

Harry would have given anything to handle the big six-shot cap and ball pistols but he dared not ask.

'Have you ever held a pistol?' Ian asked, noticing the fascination on the boy's face.

'No, sir,' he answered.

Ian passed an unloaded pistol to him and Harry almost fell over in surprise. He took it gingerly in his hand.

'It's heavy,' he said, then blurted, 'I want to join up and go away to fight the Queen's enemies.'

Ian smiled, taking back the pistol. 'Soldiering is not an easy life, and there is always the chance you could be killed – or maimed,' he said gently. 'Life on the manor is much safer, and you don't have to sleep in the rain or march under the desert sun. I would think twice about joining the army if I were you.'

'Yes, sir,' the boy replied, disappointed that Ian had not encouraged his aspirations to become a soldier. 'But you get to go places I have heard are strange and exotic.'

'That you do,' Ian said. 'But for now you have the estate's horses to tend to, and if you did ever enlist you might find the cavalry to your liking. They have fine uniforms and don't have to trudge the paths we do in the infantry.'

Harry departed to go to his duties, his head suddenly full of ideas of enlisting. Maybe he would consider the cavalry, but his real ambition was to be a member of Captain Forbes' company.

Ian organised for a horse to be saddled, and in the clear crisp spring air he rode to the village and secured his mount outside the pub. His arrival drew curious glances from a few of the locals hunched over tankards of ale and smoking pipes. Ian walked to the bar where a surly innkeeper wiped the suds of spilt ale from the counter.

Ian withdrew five gold coins from his jacket and placed them on the bar. The publican's eyes widened at the sight of the small fortune.

'Tell all your customers and anyone else in the village that whoever brings me information on the whereabouts of a former resident, Miss Jane Wilberforce, will have claim to this money.'

'The witch,' Ian heard one of the customers mutter.

Ian scooped up the coins and left, leaving a loud murmur of voices behind him. He had hardly stepped onto the street when he noticed young Harry standing by a small cart and horse. Ian recalled that Harry had mentioned he was to go into the village to pick up supplies. The boy was surrounded by three lumpish-looking lads and Ian could see that they were menacing him.

Ian strode over. 'Lads, you are preventing Harry from going about his duties for me,' he said, and the three older boys turned to face him.

'Who are you, mister?' the eldest asked with a sneer.

'Captain Samuel Forbes,' Ian replied. 'And killing is my profession.'

The latter statement was delivered with an icy edge that caused uncertainty to cross the faces of the three youths. They shuffled away with their hands in their pockets, unsure if the tough-looking but well-dressed gentleman was bluffing.

'What was that about?' Ian asked Harry when the three young thugs had disappeared.

'Ron Berwick says I have been too nice to his girlfriend, Emilia,' Harry said. 'He and his pals were going to teach me a lesson, but you stopped them. Thank you, sir.'

'I have no doubt that you could have taught Ron a lesson had he been alone. Have you been too nice to this Miss Emilia?'

'I like Emilia a lot, but I am poor, and she will step out with someone who has money, not me,' Harry sighed. 'If I had money, she might think about going for a walk with me to the river on Sunday when Sir Archibald allows us to attend church.'

'It sounds like Miss Emilia is another good reason for not joining the army,' Ian said. 'I don't think those three ruffians will bother you again today.'

He walked back to his horse, mounted it and rode out of the village past the ancient tree-topped hill where the small circle of Druid stones was located. It had become almost a shrine for Ian to the memory of Jane.

When he returned to the cottage a meal and bottle of wine was brought to him by one of the servants, and Ian was thankful for both. He had laid the bait and hoped the idea of owning the gold coins might prompt a response. Someone had to know something about Jane's disappearance.

★

News of the reward spread through the village faster than a bushfire in the colony of New South Wales.

Harry was loading the cart when the shopkeeper told him about Captain Forbes' announcement at the tavern. So that was why the captain had returned to the Forbes manor, Harry thought. He had heard gossip from the other servants that Charles Forbes had been known to visit the local witch, and from time to time Harry had glimpsed the beautiful young woman when he visited the village. He had trouble imagining Jane Wilberforce as a witch because all the stories he knew about witches described ugly old crones with warts on their faces. He was not sure why Captain Forbes would be interested in the woman's whereabouts, but he wished he had some information to give in exchange for the reward. If he had that much money, surely Miss Emilia, the daughter of the shopkeeper, would take him seriously and step out walking with him. He could buy a new suit of clothes and a beaver-skin hat.

As Harry journeyed home to the manor with the supplies that evening, a thought came to him. A while ago, and he thought it might have been around the time Jane Wilberforce disappeared, he had woken in the night when he'd heard Master Charles returning late on his horse. Harry had stumbled from his bed, but Master Charles had already gone up to the big house. Harry was still waiting in the stables some time later, wondering whether he was needed, when Master Charles hurried back in and saw him.

'I heard you return a while ago, Master Forbes, and thought that you might need my help putting away your horse,' Harry said nervously. He had always been somewhat afraid of Master Charles.

But the master had dismissed him curtly, and Harry had swiftly departed.

He hadn't been able to sleep, though, worried that the master's horse would need brushing down and feeding and watering, so Harry had crept back to the stables. There, as he tended to the horse, he'd found something under the hay.

Harry had recoiled when he smelled the blood. Nonetheless he picked up the item and saw that it was a frock coat soaked with blood. He recognised it at once as belonging to Master Charles. Had the master had an accident? he wondered, although the man had not appeared to be injured. Harry had suddenly grown frightened. He'd wrapped the jacket in a hessian cloth bag and hidden it behind a loose plank in a space between the walls where, he presumed, it still was.

Harry had dismissed the distressing memory – until now.

He knew that it was the downstairs kitchen staff who had all the gossip about the family. Bridie, the seventeen-year-old kitchen hand, always seemed to know the latest snippet of news.

Harry delivered the provisions to the kitchen, where Bridie was cutting carrots.

Harry did not know that Bridie had a crush on Master Charles, and that the skinny young girl with the lank hair daydreamed of being his wife. It was an impossible dream, but the young woman didn't care.

Oblivious to this, Harry sat down at the table where Bridie was working and decided to confide in the girl.

'Did you hear about the reward Captain Forbes has offered for any information about the disappearance of the witch who used to live in the village?' he asked.

'Everyone knows about the reward,' Bridie sniffed. 'A traveller told us this afternoon.'

'What do you think happened to her?' Harry asked.

'She was a witch, so it is possible she used her magic to disappear and is with the fairy people,' Bridie said, reaching for sticks of celery.

'Do you think that Master Charles might have done her some harm?' Harry asked cautiously.

Bridie paused, her hand hovering over the celery. 'Master Charles is a good man, he would do no one harm,' she answered defensively.

'What if I said I have something that might prove otherwise?' Harry said, and Bridie paled.

'You are a fibber, Harry, what could you possibly have that would show Master Charles harmed the woman?' she asked.

'I have a coat he was wearing one night and it is covered in blood. Maybe I should take it to Captain Forbes and see what he thinks.'

'Where is this coat then?' Bridie asked, trying to sound nonchalant.

'I hid it between some loose planks in the stables,' Harry said, pinching a piece of carrot and getting a slap on the hand from Bridie for his trouble.

Bridie seemed to contemplate this. 'Well, I don't think it is our business to meddle in our betters' affairs,' she said eventually. 'I think you should forget about the coat.'

Rather disappointed by this reaction, Harry left the kitchen to return to the stables, where he began to brush down the horses in his care. As he began rubbing down one of the stallions he decided that, despite what Bridie thought, he would take the frock coat to the guest cottage and give it to Captain Forbes. Maybe the coat was important and he would receive the reward, and with it Miss Emilia's respect. He was unaware that Bridie had already passed on his news to Master Charles, who reacted by telling the smitten young girl that she was to tell no one else under threat of dire punishment. Frightened by this reaction, the girl agreed.

The horse he was brushing snorted and shifted slightly. Harry realised he was no longer alone in the stables. Under the dim light of the lantern he turned to see who had entered and saw a shadowy figure approaching. Harry peered into the gloom and saw that it was Master Charles, a pitchfork in his hand. Before Harry could cry out, he felt searing pain in his chest.

He tried to scream but instead slumped to the ground, gasping out his last breath.

Charles withdrew the pitchfork prongs from Harry's chest and knelt to look into the eyes staring blankly at the roof of the wooden building. If what a breathless and excited Bridie had told him minutes ago was true, Charles was safer with this young miscreant out of the way.

Charles quickly went from one stall to the next, ripping away the old loose planks. Finally his terrible secret was revealed. He did not touch the mouldy item of clothing still stiff with the blood of Jane Wilberforce, but instead found a drum of kerosene which he tipped over, letting the liquid run along the stable floor. He went around and opened all the doors to the stalls, where the prized Forbes horses were stabled. Next he took a lantern, flinging it at the trail of kerosene, which burst into flame, enveloping the stableboy's body and licking at the dry hay all around. The fire ran up the old wooden walls, engulfing the stables in an inferno. The terrified horses bolted past Charles to safety.

Satisfied the fire as well alight, Charles retreated, leaving the evidence and potential witness to be consumed by the roaring flames.

He was already back in the manor when the alarm was raised. Charles raced outside in the dark with the servants, pleased to see that the building was beyond hope of saving. He shuddered when he saw Ian standing alone, watching the fire. It was too bad, Charles thought, that the man he most despised in this world had not also been in the burning building.

NINE

'He was a brave young lad,' Charles reflected as he, Sir Archibald and Ian stood at first light gazing at the smouldering ruins of the stables. Servants milled around sniffling back tears and, in a couple of cases, sobbing. Bridie stood to one side, pale-faced and silent. 'He must have released the horses when he realised that he had accidentally started the fire,' Charles continued.

Ian said nothing but began to poke amongst the ruins.

He found the barely recognisable charred corpse of Harry lying on his back, hands curled inwards like a boxer's. Ian was used to death, so he leaned over to examine the remains of the naïve and gentle lad. What struck him were the two almost bayonet-like wounds to his chest. They could hardly be seen by the untrained eye but they were clear to Ian from his experience of seeing charred bodies on the battlefields of the Crimea. Nearby he saw the head of a pitchfork used to toss hay, and he noticed that the spacing of the wounds was approximately the same as the distance between two of the prongs of the pitchfork.

'We will arrange a decent Christian burial for the boy,' Sir Archibald said. 'He deserves at least that much for saving the horses.'

Ian stepped back from the corpse and walked across to Charles.

'Where were you when the fire started?' he asked in an icy voice.

Charles looked startled, stepping back a pace. 'I am not sure what you are suggesting but I resent your insinuation. As a matter of fact I was in the house, and in any case, why on earth would I want to cause any injury to young Harold? What has happened here is a terrible accident.'

Ian knew he could not prove Charles had been involved in Harry's death, even if he could persuade the police to investigate, which was unlikely given the Forbes' influence. He stared hard into Charles' face, which still bore the faint scars of the time Ian had attacked him before steaming to the Crimea. Charles blanched, and Ian took some satisfaction in that, then shook his head and walked away.

Later that morning he took a coach back to London. His regiment had informed him by letter that a dinner was to be held for officers and his attendance was required. Under military protocol, the request could not be ignored.

He signed into his club and was handed an envelope by one of the staff.

He read the contents and almost fainted when he saw the signature at the bottom – Mr Ian Steele!

★

Ian followed the directions to London's Hyde Park. Despite being early spring, the weather had a chilly bite and he wore a heavy overcoat. He walked towards a park bench and immediately recognised Samuel sitting with the American, James Thorpe.

'Ian,' Samuel said, standing to shake hands. 'It is good to see that you are safe and well.'

'Samuel, what the devil are you doing in London?' Ian greeted him with a frown.

'My sentiments precisely, Captain Steele,' James said. 'But it is good to make your acquaintance again.'

'I have been haunted by our pact,' Samuel said. 'I fear that you may not survive the ten-year contract we made.'

'It is not the Queen's enemies I fear, but your father and brother,' Ian answered with a hint of a smile. 'At least on the battlefield my enemies are generally in front of me, not trying to stick a knife into my back. They really hate you. Are you not afraid that someone in London will recognise you?'

'Too late for that,' James said pointedly. 'Samuel has already been recognised and we have had to change our accommodation as a result.'

'Damn!' Ian swore. 'Your presence here could make life difficult for me – and for you, of course.'

'I am sorry,' Samuel apologised. 'But I had other reasons for returning, not least to visit Herbert's memorial.'

'He was a fine young man,' Ian said sadly. 'I was with him when he was killed at the Redan.'

Samuel lowered his head, and Ian could see tears in his eyes. 'He died bravely,' he added awkwardly. 'He was as close to me as a brother. I understand your need to travel to Kent, but I feel it is too dangerous.'

'We shall go in disguise,' Samuel said. 'I will dress as a woman.'

Ian shook his head, suppressing his alarm. 'Something could go wrong and then both you and I will be exposed.'

'I promise that James and I will return to New York as soon as I have visited my brother's memorial,' Samuel said.

Ian sighed. 'It is not wise for us to meet again. However I wish to reassure you about our pact. Despite the horrors of war, I am doing very well and wish to continue as Captain Samuel Forbes.'

'Thank you, Ian,' Samuel said with absolute gratitude in his voice and face. 'You have put to rest the guilt I have felt since we last met.'

James rose from the bench and extended his hand. 'I, too, thank you . . . Captain Forbes,' he said. 'May you remain safe and well.'

The two men walked away, leaving Ian worried. Although London was a populous and busy city, at least one person had recognised Samuel. How could the man be so foolish as to stay?

★

Charles Forbes was a member of many gentlemen's clubs, but his favourite was the oldest established club in London, situated on St James Street in Westminster. At the White Club for aristocratic gentlemen the stakes at the card tables were high, and Charles had had to draw on the Forbes fortune in order to indulge in his favourite vice.

His wife, Louise, was almost permanently away, living in Italy, in a Tuscan chateau.

While she remained out of England, Charles was able to indulge in his second-favourite vice as well, which was seducing young ladies. Now he was considering adding murder to his list of favourite pastimes. The power he experienced from taking a life and getting away with it was thrilling. He felt like God with this new authority over life and death.

Charles was feeling lucky and the club offered him the opportunity to prove it.

He sat down at a table opposite a man he vaguely knew, a Captain Brooke. Charles remembered his name from the time Samuel had served with him in New South Wales. The cards were dealt, brandy served and cigars produced for the game.

'I think I ran into your brother at my club,' Captain Brooke said, puffing on his cigar as he dealt the cards.

'You probably did,' Charles said, taking the cards in his hand and fanning them out. 'His regiment has returned from the Persian campaign.'

'The odd thing was that the fellow denied he was Samuel Forbes. He said his name was Ian Steele,' Brooke said, taking a sip from his brandy.

'Very odd,' Charles commented, gazing down at his hand of cards.

'I served with Samuel for three years and I am sure that the man I met was he.'

'When did you meet this Mr Steele?' Charles asked. When the army officer gave the date of the incident, he replied, 'Ah. That could not have been Samuel as he was at our manor in Kent at that time.'

'Are you sure?' Brooke countered, and for a moment Charles stared at his cards without seeing them.

His mind started whirring. When Samuel had first returned from the colonies, Charles had doubted his authenticity. The boy who he had once bullied mercilessly had transformed into a tough and confident man. Charles had been persuaded by his father that he was Samuel returned to them, but there was something that did not ring true about this new, powerful version of his brother.

'How did this man look?' Charles asked.

'He looked just as I remember your brother,' Brooke said. 'Still the callow youth who stood with us against the Maori in New Zealand. He has not changed.'

Charles played badly that evening, his mind going over and over what he had learned. Was the meeting simply a case of mistaken identity? Yet Brooke was so adamant he was right. Surely he would know, as he and Samuel had served at least three years together. But if Brooke was right, why would Samuel claim to be someone else? So many questions without answers. Charles decided that it was vital he find this Mr Steele and ascertain for himself whether he was in fact his brother, Samuel Forbes. After all, the Samuel Charles remembered was a shy and introverted young man. The man who had returned in his place was the opposite. Surely a man's character could not change so dramatically?

★

Dr Peter Campbell stood alongside his brother at the edge of the Meerut barracks' parade ground. The sun beat down on the ranks of Indian cavalrymen standing to attention as the eighty-five prisoners were brought out to parade before their comrades.

'They are lucky devils,' Scott said. 'The original sentence for refusing to use the cartridges, a crime of mutiny, was ten years' imprisonment, but General Hewett has commuted the sentence to five years.'

Blacksmiths stepped forward with their tools of trade and native soldiers watched with sullen faces as ankle irons were hammered into place. The prisoners cried out for help from the men on parade, as well as cursing the British Empire.

'The men on parade don't look happy about British justice,' Peter said. 'They appear to be on the verge of attempting to rescue their fellow troopers.'

'They will not,' Scott replied. 'We have the artillery gunners standing by, as well as the Dragoon Guards. It would be suicide for them to try.'

The process continued for an hour, and all the time Peter noted uneasily the barely restrained hatred in the faces of the sepoys forced to hear the sentences read out and enacted. Eventually the prisoners were marched to the barracks' cells by a guard of sepoy troops and the men were dismissed from the parade ground.

Peter and his brother returned to Scott's temporary accommodation. He had been billeted in a small but comfortable and well-kept bungalow in a neat, well-maintained compound. It had been designed to cater to the tastes and needs of the British families accompanying their East India Company men in military service and civil administration.

They were met by Alice, who gave Peter a peck on the cheek.

'I have asked the house girl to prepare drinks,' she said.

Scott and Peter followed Alice out to a veranda over-looking a stand of tall tropical trees filled with raucous birds. Soon the sun would set and Alice had requested a native meal of spiced lentils and other local delicacies for them to dine on in the evening breeze.

'So, what do you think about this part of India?' Scott asked, taking off his sword and hanging it on the back of a chair. 'Are you pleased that you chose to travel with us to Meerut?'

'It was certainly an adventure to travel here,' Alice said, remembering the weeks-long journey on horseback through small villages, along winding roads that took them through primeval forests filled with wildlife. They had often camped under the stars and occasionally experienced heavy downfalls of rain, but it had been a thrilling experience for Alice.

The servant girl, wearing a long flowing colourful dress and headscarf, brought a tray of alcoholic drinks to them. Gin and tonic was the preferred choice, and she poured the gin with a dash of bitter tonic water.

Scott raised his tumbler. 'Chin, chin,' he said, taking a sip.

'You are not worried about your troops causing trouble after what happened today?' Peter asked.

'Not at all,' Scott replied. 'The purpose of the display was to ensure the rest of the rabble knew what was in store for them should they disobey orders. It will all settle down now and we can get on with the job of administering the territory.'

'Do you have concerns, Peter?' Alice asked, noticing her husband's expression.

'I watched the faces of the men on the parade. I saw hatred there, and fury at their powerlessness.'

'Your concerns are unfounded,' his brother scoffed. 'This is India and the natives know their place.'

Peter was not reassured. It was eerily quiet when he and Alice retired that evening and he lay on his back under the mosquito net, staring into the dark. He had a bad feeling and wished that he had chosen to leave India before the journey to Meerut. But it had been an opportunity to share something exotic with Alice before they returned to the grey shores of England.

Alice also found it hard to sleep and thought about the news she still held secret. Maybe she could share it with her husband when his disquiet about today's events was lessened. She resolved that she would tell him after church the following day, when the sun was setting and they were alone on the veranda. Hopefully then they could share what she imagined would be a peaceful and precious moment together.

Part Two

Mutiny!

TEN

Major Scott Campbell settled back on the veranda in a comfortable cane chair to read *Dombey and Son*, a novel by his favourite author, Charles Dickens. He had cheerfully seen off his brother and Alice as they left in a covered light-sprung one-horse coach to drive to the chapel for a service on this pleasant Sunday evening.

Scott was not a religious man and the choice between God and Charles Dickens was an easy one. He reached for the gin and tonic at his elbow and flipped open the pages of the book. All had gone well today. The sepoys had learned their lesson and things were calm at the regimental barracks.

The sound of voices drifting on the gentle evening breeze was faint, but Scott set down the book, listening with a frown on his face. He swore that he could hear the word *maro* being repeated. He knew that was an Indian word for *kill*.

Then it grew louder, *Maro! Maro!*

Scott leapt to his feet just as one of his Indian troopers rushed in shouting, '*Hulla goolla!*' Riot! The young soldier was in uniform and flushed with fear and excitement.

Scott was aware of key phrases in the local language and asked his soldier what was happening. The soldier breathlessly explained that the native regiments had gone on a rampage, with weapons seized from the regimental armoury. At first Scott tried to convince himself this was simply a small-scale mutiny by a few disenchanted sepoys protesting the treatment of their comrades. The young trooper was surely carried away by excitement and had exaggerated the situation.

Scott quickly dressed in his field uniform, strapping on his sword and holstering a loaded revolver. He mounted his horse, leaving orders to the trooper to remain in the bungalow in the event Peter and Alice returned. He galloped from the gates of the compound towards the regimental barracks, where Scott could see a cloud of dust being raised by a mob swarming towards him. A few of the men running ahead of the mob reached Scott on his horse, and an infantry sepoy slashed at him with a sword, cutting Scott's right shoulder lanyard. Scott had no time to draw his own sabre as the horse lunged forward, knocking down the sepoy infantryman.

Scott wheeled his steed around, sword in hand, ready to engage the soldier on the ground, but the sepoy was not prepared to engage a mounted cavalryman and wisely fled over a low wall to safety.

Scott pulled his horse around again to see a small column of his cavalry troopers galloping towards him from the regimental lines. For a moment he felt a sense of relief and ordered them to halt. They did, but immediately encircled Scott, and he knew that they were not friendly but hostile. Their sabres were drawn and they attacked immediately. Scott was hope-lessly outnumbered but he parried the many slashing blades aimed at taking his life. He was an expert with the cavalry sword, and it was only his many hours of practice that kept him alive. From the corner of his eye he could see one of his mounted junior officers galloping towards the melee, cutting down one of the Indian cavalrymen threatening Scott. The sudden intervention of a second British officer was enough for the small enemy detachment to scatter and gallop towards the compound bungalows a few hundred yards away.

'God, sir!' the young officer gasped. 'The rascals are heading towards our unarmed loved ones attending church.'

'I can see that, Mr Craigie,' Scott said, observing that the detachment that had attacked him had already disappeared into the compound. His first thought was to gallop after them and save his brother and Alice, but he knew he was probably too late. All he could hope for was that they had found some kind of safety, but for now he, as a senior officer, had to address the main problem of the mutineers. It was an agonising decision to make – rescue those he loved or attack the main problem in the regimental lines.

'Follow me, Mr Craigie, we must reach the lines!'

Scott and the young British officer galloped into the lines and entered a confused melee of Indian troops and British officers milling around the great parade ground. Scott's hopes fell when he saw many of his men already mounted, brandishing swords, firing off pistols and carbines in the air. Others were saddling their mounts whilst horses careened wildly around the parade ground. It was a scene of absolute chaos. Scott could see his fellow British officers attempting to bring the mutinous soldiers to their senses, sometimes pleading with them, other times threatening them, but nothing was working to quell the mutiny.

Scott was pleased to notice that the mutineers at the barracks were not attempting to attack the small number of European officers but yelling at them to be off and that the days of the British Raj were over. It was then that Scott sensed this was no longer a mutiny but the beginning of a full-scale rebellion by the people against Queen Victoria's Empire in India.

The young officer accompanying Scott was a fluent speaker of the local language and had been able to persuade around forty of the would-be mutineers to avoid joining their comrades.

The sun was beginning to set and the dust was like a ghostly haze.

'Sir! Sir!' The frantic words came from another one of Scott's young officers galloping towards him. 'The mutineers are attacking the gaol and releasing the prisoners.'

As the loyal Indian troops and the British officers galloped towards the gaol, they passed crowds of Indian civilians along the road cheering them on.

'They think we are mutineers,' Lieutenant Craigie yelled to Scott. 'It does not bode well.'

Scott could see the clouds of smoke boiling up from burning houses near the prison and suddenly he felt something hit him in the chest, flinging him from his horse. He hit the ground, stunned for a moment. When he regained his focus and sat up he saw Lieutenant Craigie reaching down to him.

'They have cut the telegraph lines,' he said. 'You had the misfortune of being caught up in one.'

Scott scrambled back into the saddle of his horse and to his horror saw a driverless hooded carriage slowly making its way along the road. A mutineer cavalryman was riding alongside, plunging his sabre into the carriage. The two junior officers wheeled about to attack the mutineer and he was killed by Lieutenant Craigie with a slashing blow to his neck. Scott rode up and when he looked inside he could see the blood-soaked body of a European woman slumped across the seat.

Nearby another mob of around twenty mutinous cavalrymen saw their comrade killed, and in their rage commenced screaming, '*Maro! Maro!*' but dared not attack the determined body of troopers accompanying Scott and his officers.

Scott and his party of loyal sepoys reached the gaol but the prisoners had already been freed. A few scattered ineffectual shots were aimed in their direction.

'What do we do now, sir?' Lieutenant Craigie asked.

'There is nothing we can do here,' Scott answered wearily. The sun was just disappearing beyond the horizon. 'I think we should ride back to our bungalows and ascertain the situation there.'

The British officer nodded agreement and Scott led his troop back to the European residences. As he rode he tried not to think about the bloody state of the dead woman he had seen in the carriage. Would he find Peter and Alice in a similar state? When they wheeled about, the full horror confronted Scott. Flames rose above the rows of bungalows and it did not seem that any had been spared. He broke into a hard gallop and his men followed.

★

Scott's residence was fully aflame, but Lieutenant Craigie's large, double-storeyed bungalow, surrounded by a mud wall, had been untouched by the mutineers.

'Sir, I will see if my wife is safe,' Craigie said, leaping from his mount. Scott continued staring at his burning house but could see no sign of his brother and sister-in-law. If they had been fortunate enough to return at the first outbreak of the violence, then their fate had been sealed when the house was ransacked and set alight.

'Sir! Your brother and his wife are safe in my house,' Lieutenant Craigie called to him, and Scott felt a surge of elation. They were safe! He dismounted and rushed into the house where he saw Peter holding Alice in his arms. Peter broke the embrace, taking strides towards him.

'You are safe,' Peter said, grasping his brother by the shoulders. 'God help me, I thought you might be dead.'

'How the devil did you dodge the murderous mob?' Scott asked.

'We were in our carriage driving through the village when a soldier burst from a side alley. He was being pursued by a mob of villagers. He was shouting for help so Alice and I pulled him in and drove as fast as we could back to your bungalow. The mob were on foot and we soon outdistanced them. But when we got back we could see that they had already got to the compound and had pillaged the houses and set them afire – except for Lieutenant Craigie's residence. We climbed over the wall and found Mrs Craigie, who immediately provided us with shelter. I was told by the brave woman that her husband had weapons in the house, and I secured them. Our arms consist of three shotguns, with an ample supply of powder and shot. We were prepared to make a stand here.'

'You do the Campbell clan proud,' Scott beamed through his fatigue. 'Is Alice in any way harmed?'

'No, but she is in shock – as is the soldier we brought back, and Mrs Craigie. I think seeing her husband safe is helping her state of mind. What is happening?'

'I think the mutiny is more like a rebellion,' Scott said,

exhausted. 'In that case, we are on our own until word gets to our general HQ that we need reinforcements. God knows when that will happen, so we have to take all measures to protect our women and children. I have a troop of loyal men outside but I cannot vouch they will remain loyal as this rebellion gathers force.'

'I think I have an idea, sir,' Lieutenant Craigie butted into the conversation between brothers. 'I have a fair understanding of the local Indians. I will go outside and talk to the men.'

'I have faith in your knowledge of these people, Mr Craigie. Do what you can.'

The young officer stepped outside and those in the residence could hear his voice ring out fluently in the local language.

'I wish I knew what he was saying,' Alice said, joining Scott and Peter.

Craigie ceased talking and returned. 'I need to escort your wife, Dr Campbell, and my wife outside to meet our men,' he said.

'Why?' Peter protested. 'They are safe in here.'

'Dr Campbell, without those men's loyalty I dare say we will all be dead by first light. Please trust me.'

'Mr Craigie knows what he is doing, Peter,' Scott said, laying his hand on Peter's arm.

'I am not afraid to go outside,' Alice said. 'It cannot be as frightening as facing a tiger eye to eye.'

Alice accompanied Lieutenant Craigie and his wife to the Indian cavalrymen lined up in disciplined ranks on the horses as if they were still back on parade.

Peter and Scott watched with some trepidation as the young British officer made another address to the troops, who suddenly flung themselves from their horses. Peter raised the shotgun ready to fire at the unexpected movement. But the men were prostrating themselves on the ground, sobbing and reaching out to grab the feet of the two ladies, laying their foreheads on them.

'They are promising to protect the ladies with their very lives,' Craigie shouted back to Scott and Peter. 'I know they will remain loyal to us.'

Both women re-entered the house, a little overwhelmed by the touching display of sworn promises to die for them. Meanwhile, Scott ordered his small troop to remount and patrol the large gardens of the bungalow.

'I think we should retire upstairs,' Peter suggested. It seemed best to defend the house from high ground. He had enough military experience from the Crimean campaign to understand such tactics, despite the fact he had been an army surgeon.

Through the windows the light of the numerous fires lit up the rooms. The smell of the burning timber drifted to them. They could hear the shouts of the mobs rampaging through the compound, accompanied by occasional small-arms fire. Peter looked to his wife, fearing she would be terrified, but instead she was calmly loading one of the shotguns. When he glanced at Lieutenant Craigie's wife he saw that she was also composed. They gave Peter confidence and he wondered not for the first time why it was thought by society that women were incapable of remaining calm under such conditions.

Lieutenant Craigie spoke quietly to Scott. 'I think I should take an escort of some of our men back to the barracks to see if I can convince the others who are undecided that they should side with us,' he said.

'It's a damned dangerous thing to do,' Scott said. 'You will have to fight your way through the mob, but I agree that our only hope of survival is to gather a stronger force until we receive help to quell this rebellion.'

Scott watched the young officer walk over to kiss his wife, before organising an escort party. It was the kind of courage displayed by Mr Craigie that would surely overcome the rebellion, Scott thought. He stepped out onto the upstairs veranda with a shotgun and was spotted by the mob on the opposite side of the street setting light to a house. They cried out and ran at the wall of the compound with fire brands, but Scott levelled the shotgun at them and they retreated. Scott knew that it was only a matter of time before they succeeded in burning the house, given their sheer weight of numbers.

Peter joined him on the veranda. 'There is a small Hindu shrine not far from here,' he said. 'Alice and I visited it a couple of days ago. It has thick walls of stone and is set on high ground with only one entrance. It is like a small fortress, and I suspect impervious even to artillery fire and arson.'

'I know the place you mean and it is a good plan. We will need to get our guns and ammunition across open ground to reach it,' Scott said. 'We will wait an hour to ensure that Lieutenant Craigie knows where we are.'

The two men remained on the veranda, using it as an observation post. Craigie's loyal troops continued their patrols, discouraging the looters from getting too close, but they reported the mobs were growing larger in numbers and better armed, having captured weapons from the regimental armouries.

Lieutenant Craigie returned and he had in his possession the regimental colours discarded by the mutineers. 'We had no luck convincing the remainder at the barracks to join us,' he said. 'And we had to fight our way back. The situation appears to be growing grimmer by the minute.'

Scott told him of their plan, and he agreed it was their only hope to hold out until reinforcements arrived.

Scott stared down at the tattered colours lying on the floor of the house, thinking bitterly that the mutiny had forever disgraced them. However, his main focus now was on reaching the Hindu shrine. He would order his troopers to continue patrolling while the European civilians in his charge took shelter inside the shrine. Scott gathered together his charges and briefed them on the plan. They nodded grimly and all available weapons and ammunition were gathered.

While Scott's troopers held back the rioters, he and the others made a dash for the shrine. The women carried bundles of essential supplies, whilst the men carried the guns. Under cover of darkness and away from the light of the fires they made their way to the relative safety of the shrine, climbing its stone stairway to the interior. Scott was pleased to see that the massive stone walls had slits through which they could fire on any Indian rebels attempting to assault the building. It was dark in the small room but its stoutness made them feel safe for the moment.

Peter took up a position in a corner with a loaded shotgun, as did Alice at another. They could still hear the frenzied and chilling cries of the mob swirling through the European compound.

One of the patrolling sepoys reported to Scott, telling him of the atrocities they had observed. He held a bloody cloth found on the body of the pregnant wife of an officer hacked to death in one of the houses which was now well alight. He said he had observed similar mutilated bodies of European men and women throughout the compound – one, a little girl whose head had been cleaved with a sword. The roll of horror continued.

'The soldiers are leaving Meerut and advancing towards the city of Delhi,' the Indian cavalryman said. 'But the mob remains, still searching for Europeans to kill. However I do not think they have the stomach to attempt an attack on the sacred place.'

Scott was reassured by this news but shocked by the extent of the rapidly spreading massacre of the European civilians in Meerut. He strained to hear the sound of rescuers arriving, but there was no sound except the roar of fires and the blood-curdling shouts of the rampaging mobs.

'That poor woman,' Alice said. In such a small space it had been impossible not to overhear the sepoy's report. 'Murdered with her baby still inside her.'

'We are still alive,' Peter said. 'And help is sure to come.'

'There is something I was going to tell you this evening, but matters changed all that,' Alice whispered, looking up into Peter's face. 'I think I am with child.'

Peter's first thought was that in the midst of death came life. He was both overjoyed and deeply fearful of their fate.

ELEVEN

He was a portly middle-aged man with watery eyes, clean-shaven save for a neat moustache. Charles Forbes sat in the modest office in London and wondered if this man, the subject of a short essay by Charles Dickens titled, *On Duty with Inspector Field*, was as good as many said. The retired head of detectives from the Metropolitan Police was now a private investigator and, it was said, not much liked by his former employer.

'Inspector, I have a case for you,' Charles said, and the man on the other side of the desk lifted his corpulent forefinger.

'Mr Forbes, I am no longer an inspector. You can call me Mr Field,' Charles Field replied in a gravelly voice.

'Mr Field, I am prepared to pay generously for your services in tracking down a man who goes by the name of Ian Steele,' Charles said.

'Does this man owe you money, Mr Forbes?' asked the famed former police detective.

'No, but I think he is involved in some kind of fraud against my family. I am not sure of the details, but I feel that if you are able to locate him, all will be revealed. As far as I can ascertain, this Mr Steele was staying at a private gentlemen's club on Pall Mall and has since disappeared. My informant told me he was in company with another man of his age who has an American accent. The two seem to be travelling together.'

'Do you have a description of this Mr Steele?' Field asked.

Charles reached into his pocket and produced a photograph of Samuel and Herbert standing side by side in their best dress regimental uniforms, hands resting on sword hilts. It had been taken in a studio at Alice's insistence. Charles had taken the photograph of the two grim-faced men from its frame and now he handed it to the private investigator.

'Which one is Mr Steele?' Field asked, staring at the photo.

'This is the queer bit,' Charles said. 'The man on the right is supposed to be my brother, Captain Samuel Forbes, but he is identical to the man purporting to be Mr Steele.'

Field looked sharply at Charles as he leaned back in his chair. 'Do you think this man in the photo may be an imposter?'

'Mr Field, I cannot be certain, but there is a strong possibility. If so, it has grave implications for the Forbes name. I trust that my generous fee for your services will also buy complete confidentiality.'

'I am aware of your family's social position, Mr Forbes. This is a delicate matter, not least because your father has a seat in the House of Lords. Who is the younger man in the photograph?'

'He was my youngest brother, Herbert, who was tragically killed in the battle for Sebastopol.'

'I am sorry to hear that, Mr Forbes. He looks like a fine young gentleman.'

Charles nodded and pretended to look sorrowful for his brother's death.

'How will you track down this Ian Steele?' Charles asked.

'I have an assistant, Mr Ignatius Pollacky, known to most in the business as Paddington Pollacky. Between us we will find this Mr Steele. I will require a gesture of good faith from you before we commence our investigation, Mr Forbes.'

'Certainly,' Charles said, and placed a small pile of paper currency on the private investigator's desk.

'Very generous,' Field said, counting the notes. 'I can assure you your money has been wisely invested.'

★

Charles Field had once aspired to be an actor on the stage, and as such used acting skills and disguises to pursue his role as a private inspector. The doorman at the gentlemen's club nominated by Charles Forbes did not question the portly well-dressed man with the expensive top hat and cane.

'I am seeking the whereabouts of a dear friend, a Mr Steele, who informed me that he was staying here,' Field said.

'I am afraid Mr Steele and his American friend booked out of the club some days ago,' the doorman replied.

'Damn!' Field said. 'I was to pass on an amount of cash for him for his stay in London.' Field reached into his pocket, producing a pound note. 'It is important that I locate Mr Steele as he may find himself short on funds.' Field passed the pound note to the doorman, whose face lit up with surprise and greed. He took the note and quickly pocketed it.

'I am afraid that Mr Steele did not leave a forwarding address, but I do know that he will return to pick up his mail very soon.'

'How soon?' Field asked.

'I am unable to say,' the doorman said. 'Could I contact you once he returns?'

Field frowned. He knew that he could stake out the club, but that would require him and Pollacky doing long shifts. 'Are you able to send someone to inform me the moment Mr Steele arrives and possibly find an excuse to keep him here?' Field asked, peeling off another pound note.

'I can do that, sir,' the doorman said.

Field presented him with a card inscribed with his office address. He was not mistaken in the look of avarice in the doorman's eyes and he knew the man would comply with his request. Mr Steele was as good as found.

*

It was just after midnight and a relief force had still not arrived. Scott consulted with Lieutenant Craigie and it was decided that they would have to get the women out of this dire situation. A mob of mutineers and their civilian supporters were gathering outside the shrine. Being besieged was not an option for the Canadian officer of the East India Company, and already a handful of the supposed faithful troopers had deserted.

Earlier, Scott had noticed a carriage nearby that was still intact, its horse in harness. That was their best hope.

'We need to get as far from here as possible and head north towards our outlying picquet lines,' Scott said. 'Peter will go in the carriage with you two ladies, and he will be armed. Mr Craigie and I will ride escort beside the carriage.'

None disagreed with the desperate plan as they all realised that if they did not escape under the cover of darkness, they would likely not escape at all.

When the carriage was secured Alice and Mrs Craigie stepped into it, Alice carrying one loaded shotgun whilst Peter held another. They could smell the acrid smoke and hear the crackling of the burning buildings. The few remaining loyal troopers formed a column of ten men behind the carriage and Scott and Lieutenant Craigie took up positions either side of it, their swords drawn.

They were ready to move when a large group of civilians surged out of the darkness, brandishing clubs and ancient curved swords. They were accompanied by a handful of mutinous cavalrymen. Scott could see the mob hesitate when they saw that the Europeans were defended by a column of troopers.

'Charge!' Scott yelled, and the native soldier assigned as carriage driver whipped the horse into a fast trot as the loyal troopers screamed war cries. The mob scattered as the carriage came on at full speed, and the cavalrymen slashing with their sabres swept through those members of the mob who had been slow to retreat.

Scott led his party out of the gates of the European compound until they came to an open plain, which to their relief was deserted. The carriage slowed, as did the horsemen accompanying it.

'A port fire!' Mr Craigie said when a faint light was seen in the distance. Both officers recognised it as the signal light used by the British army to indicate a small bridge over a gully.

'We will need to be very careful,' Scott said. 'If it is our men, they will be suspicious of our approach. You and I will go first.'

The two men kicked their mounts into a gallop and screamed at the top of their voices, 'Friend! Friend!'

They came to a stop before the bridge and could see an artillery cannon covering the route they had come from. Beside the artillery piece was a subaltern who recognised the two riders.

'Thank God you identified yourselves,' he said as Scott dismounted. 'I was on the verge of giving the order to fire at your party.'

'I am glad you kept your head, then,' Scott said. 'I will have my party join you. We have women and a few sepoys who have remained loyal.' He looked around and even in the dark could see the faces of British troops. Scott knew that for the moment they would be safe in the British lines north of Meerut. The sun was yet to rise and what lay ahead was an unknown.

Peter helped Alice and Mrs Craigie from the carriage and they were ushered to a small hut not far from the bridge where the women could sleep overnight.

'I have not had the opportunity to say how happy I am at your news,' Peter said, holding Alice's hand. 'Now I have two people to protect.' He would have loved to hold his wife in his arms, but public demonstrations of affection were not the done thing. Instead, he gave her a peck on the cheek before she entered the hut.

Peter left Alice and joined his brother in animated conversation with an officer of Scott's own rank.

'Why the devil did we not pursue the mutineers on their way to Delhi?' Scott was demanding. 'We have the men and guns to teach them a lesson before they get themselves organised.'

'I am of the same opinion,' the other officer said. 'But the general's orders are to remain here and gather our forces.'

Peter could see that Scott was fuming. His once clean uniform was covered in black soot and partly torn at the shoulder. Scott shook his head and the other major walked away.

'Not good news,' Peter said.

'Not good news,' Scott sighed. 'We have also learned that many from our compound fled before the mutineers marching to Delhi. In my opinion it is our duty to mount a rescue of any British survivors. If I am able to get permission, I would value your service with us, although it will mean leaving Alice.'

'Of course, brother, I would gladly be of service,' Peter said. 'I am sure that Alice will be safe here, and I will explain the situation in the morning.'

'Please be careful,' Alice pleaded with him the next day, touching his unshaven face with her hand. 'Remember, you have two of us to return to.'

When Peter looked at his wife he was almost overwhelmed with love for her. He understood now that she and the baby growing inside her were the centre of his universe. Yet he knew that he had a duty to others with his skills as a healer.

Peter swung himself onto the mount that had been prepared for him. A rudimentary medical kit had been put together from scrounged instruments, whilst his shotgun had been slipped into a carbine case attached to the saddle. Scott's force numbered around fifty mixed British and Indian troopers and included Lieutenant Craigie. They prepared to ride south towards Delhi in a possible rescue mission.

Alice waved to Peter as he rode away and he wondered with a heavy heart whether this would be the last time he saw the angelic face of his beloved wife.

On the first day they passed through several villages, and each time they received a sullen reception from the locals. At the second village one of the less hostile inhabitants quietly sidled up to Scott, informing him that a large party of Europeans had fled south through their village. There were both men and women who had escaped the massacre at the compound. There were also some men in military uniform who had acted as protection to the party of escapees.

On the eve of the second day the rescue party reached a mud-walled town with a big wooden gate barred to them. Scott knew he and his men were wearing the same grey uniforms as the mutineers, and he suspected the villagers feared they were the deserting East India troops wishing to enter in order to loot, rape and kill.

Scott, Peter and Lieutenant Craigie rode up to the gate. When the faces observing them from a parapet registered that they were European, their expressions changed from fear to relief. The gate was swung open and the trio were led to a mud-brick house that was the home of the town headman.

An old bearded man sat in a chair out the front of the house, an ancient firelock musket across his lap. Lieutenant Craigie addressed him in the dialect of the region, and he responded.

'What did he say?' Scott asked.

'He bids us welcome and says that amongst his people, he has hidden those who escaped from Meerut. He has sent someone to fetch them and reassure them that help has come.'

In minutes bedraggled men and women appeared from the various houses, cheering at the sight of the three rescuers. Amongst them were the wives of officers, some of whom had been killed during the initial stages of the mutiny. Scott also recognised a couple of fellow officers, and even a colonel.

Oxcarts were organised for transport of the civilians back to the British lines north of Meerut, and Scott ensured that the town's headman was paid for supplying the carts and oxen, as well as food for the travellers and grain for the oxen. Just after dark, they moved out of the town, the cavalrymen riding on the flanks and in front to prevent any attack. By the next evening they arrived and were directed back to Meerut, which had been recaptured, and temporary accommodation erected to house the survivors.

Peter flung himself off his horse, searching for Alice to tell her that he had returned, safe and well. He was directed to a semi-burned house in the compound where an Indian servant girl with a worried face greeted him. She spoke some English and as Peter was about to step inside, she stopped him.

'I sorry, Doctor,' she said with tears welling in her eyes. 'The mistress sick. She lose baby.'

With a feeling of dread Peter stepped inside to find Alice lying on a small bed, deathly pale, her skin clammy.

'Oh, Peter, I am so sorry,' she said, breaking into a sob. 'Our darling baby is gone.'

Peter fell to his knees beside the bed, gripping his wife's hand. He looked closely at Alice's face and his grief for their loss was worsened when he saw something else in her face. As a medical practitioner he had seen it many times before.

Alice was in the deadly grip of cholera.

TWELVE

It was the last month of springtime in London and the weather was warming. Ian spent most of his time at the regimental barracks overseeing the training of his company, although he knew the tradition of allowing the senior non-commissioned officers to look to the routine of managing the troops. His company, however, had come to learn he was an officer who took seriously his role as their leader, and although his training was rigorous, they also knew he cared for them. That endeared the Colonial to them.

It was the end of the day at the barracks and Ian prepared himself to return to his club for the evening. He was in his dress uniform when he took the salute at the gates of the regiment and walked onto the busy street outside.

Ian had hardly taken a step beyond the gates when he felt his heart skip a beat.

Ella!

The beautiful young woman stood smiling uncertainly at him as she held a parasol above her head. Behind her was an expensive covered coach drawn by two fine horses, a well-dressed driver on the seat.

'Hello, Samuel,' she said.

'I was told by your father that you were in America,' Ian said, hardly believing his eyes or trusting his feelings. 'How is it that you are here?'

'I was rejected by the medical schools in New York,' Ella replied, 'so I have returned home to London.'

'It is good to see you, but you have my sympathy for your failure to obtain a place in medicine. I know how much it meant to you. I am truly sorry,' Ian said. 'How did you know to meet me here?'

'It was not hard,' Ella said with a laugh, and Ian thought he was hearing the sound of an angel. 'People have said that you are an officer who spends his time with his men. So I am here, Captain Forbes . . . Samuel.'

'I am at a loss for words,' Ian said gently, fighting off an almost overwhelming desire to take her in his arms.

'I thought we might take tea at that little shop where we used to meet,' Ella said. 'My carriage can take us there.'

'You can tell me all about your adventures in New York,' Ian said, taking her arm.

He assisted her into the carriage and took a seat beside her. The simple fact that he could smell her perfume and knew that mere cloth separated their bodies caused him rich and complex feelings. He felt like a young man again, full of hope and possibility.

Both remained silent during the short trip to the fashionable street of coffee shops and milliners. It was as if they were happy simply to be in each other's company.

The tea shop was almost empty. Ian ordered tea for two

and sat down opposite Ella. She reached across the linen-covered table and took his hands in her own. Ian knew that this was the time to explain that as delighted as he was to see her, there could be no future for them. But her large eyes were gazing into his own and he suddenly forgot all logical reasons for restraining his feelings for her. He knew he could easily fall in love with this woman almost a decade younger than he.

'I could never forget you, Samuel,' Ella said. 'Even in New York I would think about you day and night. I would dream that I was in your arms and that we were planning a life together.'

Ian frowned. 'I must confess that you have always been in my thoughts too,' he said. 'I would be under the stars in the silence of the Mesopotamian desert and I would see you there. Before we went into battle you were always my last thought. But I also know that your father could never accept me. I am not of your faith.'

'Is that all you fear?' Ella asked as the china cups and teapot were placed on the table by a young woman in a spotless dress. 'We could leave England and go to one of the colonies to start a life together. I know you spent some time in the Australian colonies; we could go there where no one would care where we came from. My mother left me a substantial inheritance and I am independent of my father's money.'

'It is a wonderful dream, but I am a soldier.'

'You could sell your commission,' Ella said. 'You are an intelligent man and I know you would be capable of finding other work.'

'I cannot tell you why – and please don't ask me the reason – but I must serve seven years more as an officer with the regiment,' Ian said. 'There are just too many reasons against us being together.'

'Do you love me?' Ella asked tearfully, trapping Ian in a position from which he could neither retreat nor advance.

'My feelings for you are not the issue,' he said gently. 'You are a beautiful and intelligent young woman and any good man would wish to spend his life with you. In another seven years I will be in a position to resign my commission, but until then I am not the master of my own destiny.'

'I cannot believe that,' Ella replied, wiping away her tears with a delicate lace handkerchief. 'You do not love me.'

Ian desperately wanted to tell her that this was not true, but he could not reveal the truth to her. All he could do was reach out and hold her hand. He felt awkward and uncertain. Facing the Russians had been easier.

'I think you should return home,' Ian said, and Ella withdrew her hand angrily.

'I do not understand you.' She flared. 'I can see the desire in your eyes and yet you push me away. I never wish to see you again, Captain Forbes.'

Ella rose from the table and hurried outside to her carriage, leaving Ian caught up in a storm of emotions. It was obvious that she loved him, and he knew he loved her, but circumstances had conspired to separate them. Beyond the cosy tea house, the drums and bugles were even now calling him to yet another bloody campaign in a far-off country.

★

Dr Peter Campbell wrung out the wet cloth and applied it to his wife's fevered brow. Alice was drifting in and out of consciousness and Peter fought back the tears as he desperately sifted through all the medical knowledge he possessed for something that might save her life. So many times he had watched patients with cholera die – and yet he had seen others miraculously live.

He remembered how the Khan had called his wife the daughter of the goddess, Kali, the ultimate warrior. Alice had to fight like Kali, and he whispered in her ear, 'Daughter of Kali, I need you. Fight this thing with every breath you have.'

It was hardly logical, but Peter was desperate. Suddenly, Alice reached out to grip his hand and squeeze it. His hopes soared. She was alert enough to hear his voice.

'Fetch boiled water laced with sugar,' Peter ordered the Indian servant girl hovering in the room. 'Bring more clean cloths.'

When the servant girl reappeared with the water she was accompanied by Scott.

'How is Alice faring?' he asked in a concerned voice.

'I pray that she is fighting this insidious disease with all that she has,' Peter replied, looking up at his brother dressed in his dusty field uniform. Scott took a chair a short distance from the bed that Alice occupied.

'The word is filtering through that the mutiny has broken out across all of India. Unit after unit is deserting to form a rebellion in an attempt to declare independence from the East India Company. We are going to need reinforcements from England,' Scott said wearily. 'Your services here as a surgeon will be badly needed in the days ahead.'

'As soon as Alice recovers and is well enough to travel, I intend to get her out of India and home to England,' Peter said. 'There are other surgeons in the Company.'

'Not as good as you, little brother,' Scott said gently, and Peter was surprised to hear Scott finally praise him for his medical expertise. It caught him off-guard.

'Think about it,' Scott said. 'When Alice recovers, we can endeavour to have her return to England, but I know that she would want you to remain to minister to the sick and wounded here.'

Peter considered that the loss of their baby was bound to haunt his wife and it was his duty to be by her side to provide comfort. But he was also a surgeon and many lives might be saved in his hands. It was a dilemma, but his wife's welfare was his priority.

'I will think on your proposition,' Peter said, deciding to keep his options open and returning his attention to Alice, who still lay in a fevered state. Peter knew that the next few hours were critical and also that the odds were against her surviving the deadly disease. He had been a witness to this terrible death countless times. Tears streamed down his face as he held Alice's hand, feeling utterly helpless.

★

The doorman at the Pall Mall gentlemen's club had his plan in place. He had paid a couple of street urchins to hang around the entrance, ready to deliver a message to Mr Field. Early one morning, a man arrived and requested any mail addressed to a Mr Ian Steele. The doorman recognised the man as Steele's travelling companion.

The doorman passed a small pile of letters to James, who thanked him and quickly departed, leaving no time to detain him. The doorman quickly summoned one of the boys, instructing him to follow the man and report back where he went, whilst the second boy was to run to Mr Field's office and fetch him.

It did not take long for Field to arrive in a hansom cab. Both men waited and finally the breathless young lad returned, delivering his news. He had followed the man to an expensive boarding house only three blocks away. Field tipped the boy a few pennies and asked him to take him to the residence, which he duly did.

''E's in there, mister,' the boy said, pointing at the building. 'Saw 'im go in with me own eyes.'

Field dismissed the boy, who ambled away, gripping his precious pennies.

Field noted the address and mulled over whether he should enter to confirm that Mr Steele was inside. He decided against this in case the man turned violent. No, he would return with his partner, Paddington Pollacky, and armed with coshes, they would enter the building together.

★

'Water.'

The croaky voice brought Peter out of his dozing slumber beside Alice's bed. He sat upright in the chair then rose to lean over his wife.

'Alice, my darling, did you ask for water?'

'Yes,' she replied in a weak voice, and Peter observed that the fever appeared to have broken, although Alice lay still against the sweat-drenched pillows.

Peter bade the servant girl fetch clean, boiled water laced with sugar. When the water arrived he helped Alice sit up and sip the drink. She slept again and when she woke seemed brighter and stronger.

'As soon as you are well enough to travel, we will leave for England,' Peter said. 'My brother has asked me to remain as surgeon to the Company, but I will be informing him that getting you home comes before anything else.'

'Peter, my love,' Alice said, her voice sounding faint and shaky, 'Scott is right. You must stay to be of help to so many who will need your skills. I wish to remain at your side until this terrible situation is resolved.'

Peter frowned. His love for this truly marvellous woman grew by the day. 'It is too dangerous for you to be here,' he protested. 'I could never live a day if anything were to happen to you.'

'It already has, and I am still here,' Alice replied with a wan smile, reaching out for her husband's hand. 'I am so sorry that I lost our child,' she continued in a sorrowful voice.

'It was not your fault,' Peter said, gripping her hand. 'Such things are in the hands of God, my love. Do not blame yourself.'

Peter was about to assist Alice from the bed, intending that she be helped to wash by the servant girl, when Scott arrived. His face broke into a beaming smile when he saw that Alice had begun her recovery.

'Your brother has agreed that we should help in any way we can,' Alice said, and Peter looked at her in sharp surprise.

'Good,' Scott said. 'Because very soon we will be marching on the mutineers to give them a taste of cold British steel and lead.'

THIRTEEN

The knocking on the door of James and Samuel's rooms in the London boarding house was loud and urgent.

The men glanced at each other and James went to the door and opened it a fraction. He peered through the small gap and was taken aback to see the rough bearded face of a very large man.

'Who are you?' James asked, just a little fearful of the ferocious-looking man.

'Captain Forbes asked my boss to keep an eye out for you,' the man answered. 'I need to tell you that you have been recognised and that you have to leave London.'

James was slightly confused.

'Let the gentleman in,' Samuel called, and James opened the door.

When the man entered the room, it was his turn to be shocked by what he saw: a man dressed in women's clothing!

For a moment he stood blinking in silence. Egbert Johnson was an enforcer for Ikey Solomon, and his face reflected the scars of his work collecting debts from other hard men.

'Cor blimey!' he uttered. 'What is going on?'

'You mentioned Captain Forbes,' Samuel said, ignoring the question. 'You said he has hired your boss to look out for us.'

Egbert recovered his composure, staring at the man in women's clothing. 'My employer is Mr Solomon, and he had me keep an eye out for you two. I was watching this place when Field turned up and gave it the once-over.'

'Who is this Field chap?' Samuel asked.

'He's a private investigator, and a good one. I can only think that he was looking for you two. No other reason he would show any interest in this place. Which one of you is Mr Steele?'

Samuel identified himself and introduced James.

'You ain't got much time to get your stuff together and get out of here,' Egbert said. 'Matter of fact, that dress you are wearing might be a good idea when we get out on the street. Less chance of you being recognised.'

Samuel and James had to accept that the man was working in their interests so they quickly packed their possessions. They had been preparing to travel to Kent, to Herbert's memorial – hence Samuel's disguise – but their plans would have to change.

'What do we do now?' Samuel asked when they were ready to depart.

'I go downstairs and hire a hansom cab to take you to a place Mr Solomon has near the docks. You should be safe there for a while.'

Egbert departed, leaving the two men alone.

'Who is responsible for finding us?' James asked.

Samuel slumped on the bed. 'Don't ask me how I know, but I suspect my brother Charles has a hand in this. Somehow my visit to London has got back to him, which can only mean Charles suspects Ian is an imposter.'

'If your theory is correct, we need to get away from London and return to New York,' James said, pacing the small room. 'To remain will only put Ian's freedom in jeopardy. Your contract with him will have little bearing on his defence if he is arrested.'

Suddenly they heard the heavy thump of boots on the stairway. The door opened and both men were relieved to see Egbert appear.

'The good news is that I got you a cab downstairs and the driver has instructions to take you to the address at the docks. The bad news is that I just saw Field and another man turn up at the end of the street and they're coming this way.'

Samuel and James followed Egbert downstairs to where a hansom cab awaited. Samuel cast a quick look at the two men approaching and recognised his brother, Charles.

'Get in!' Egbert hissed as Field and Charles were a mere fifty paces away, hurrying towards them.

Charles Forbes glanced at the man and woman boarding the hansom cab but returned his attention to the entrance of the boarding house.

The hansom cab moved away, leaving Egbert on the footpath. He saw Field and the stranger enter the boarding house and grinned through his thick black beard. It was obvious that fortune had been on his side today. Mr Steele – or whoever he was – had been made up so well as a woman that under other circumstances he might have been propositioned by the men in search of carnal pleasure. Egbert shook his head in disbelief and continued back to his employer's office.

★

It was a glittering night of pomp and ceremony. Ian sat in the centre of the long table whilst Colonel Jenkins sat at the head. Candles threw their flickering light over the colourful uniforms of the officers, and the food and wine flowed. Ian noticed that there were a few new officers posted to the regiment, and they stared enviously at those more senior officers sporting the medals of their campaigns.

Beside him sat a young newly commissioned lieutenant.

'Sir, I believe that your company was involved with General Outram's river expedition in Persia,' said the lieutenant. 'You were most fortunate as the rest of the regiment was left out.'

'The regiment was required to remain at our depot and guard against a possible Persian counterattack at Bushehr,' Ian defended.

'Oh, I am hoping that we see some action in the near future,' the young officer sighed.

'I think you will,' Ian replied, suspecting what would be announced tonight.

When the president of the mess committee banged the gavel on the table, all fell silent. On cue, Colonel Jenkins rose to his feet.

'Gentlemen, no doubt you have been following the tragic events in India in *The Times*. It is with great pleasure – and honour – that I announce our regiment has been ordered to India to assist the East India Company in putting down the mutiny.'

Before he could continue, a roar of approval went up around the room as the officers banged the table with their fists and forks. Jenkins smiled, waiting for the outpouring to die down, then raised his hand to quell the boisterous cacophony.

'We are to ready ourselves and will be departing these

shores late June,' he continued. 'Gentlemen, a toast to our Queen.'

All officers rose to their feet, lifting their goblets of port wine. 'The Queen!' they chorused, and those of major rank and above added, 'God bless her.'

The royal toast over, the men resumed their seats and an excited chatter broke out amongst them.

'Sir, what exciting news!' the young officer sitting next to Ian exclaimed. 'A chance to prove oneself.'

Ian could see the radiant expression on the young man's face and was momentarily reminded of Herbert. Would this young man share the same fate as Herbert, dying before his life had even begun? Ian well knew that luck was about the only real decider on the battlefield. Maybe this time his own luck would run out.

★

The Indian soldier tried to resist the agonising pain from his knee, shattered by a lead ball from a mutineer's musket. Beside him an ashen-faced British cavalry officer slouched in a chair, clutching his chest.

Dr Peter Campbell had converted a room in the Meerut house he had been allocated and set it up as a makeshift surgery, and it was to this that Scott had had the two wounded men transported.

'We clashed with a rather large party of mutineers about three miles away,' Scott said. 'Captain Lockyer was shot in the chest.'

The wounded sepoy lay on the floor bleeding, but Peter knew the officer would have to be examined first. He carefully removed the captain's jacket until his bare chest was exposed and he could see the entry wound of the musket ball on the man's lower right-hand side. There was little bleeding and when he ran his hand around to the man's back he found what he was looking for. An exit wound.

'The captain is fortunate,' Peter said, looking up at his brother. 'The projectile has entered his chest just under the skin, travelled along his ribs then exited. It has not hit any internal organs, so the task now is to ensure he does not get an infection.'

A look of relief swept Scott's face. 'Thank God,' he uttered. 'Captain Lockyer, you will be back in the saddle before you know it.'

Captain Lockyer groaned but flashed a weak smile, and Scott summoned a couple of sepoys to assist him next-door to a room that was to be used as a makeshift ward.

Peter turned his attention to the badly wounded sepoy.

'Help me get him onto the table,' he said to Scott, and both men lifted the soldier onto a stout wooden table Peter had procured. The two sepoys returned and looked uneasy at the sight of their comrade lying on his back on the table, moaning in pain.

Peter rustled through the bag of medical supplies he had been able to scrounge and noted that they were from the Napoleonic wars. Still, he had the basic tools. He retrieved a canvas ligature with a screw-like apparatus on top and applied it above the shattered knee, using the screw lever to apply pressure, cutting off the blood flow to the lower leg. He had been unable to find any form of anaesthetic, so he knew that the operation would have to be carried out without pain relief.

'Get your men to hold the soldier down,' he instructed as he retrieved a crescent-shaped blade from the medical kit. The men obeyed Scott's instruction and grasped the patient. Peter was about to commence cutting when Alice appeared in the small room.

'Alice, this is no place for you,' Scott said, spotting her first.

Peter turned to his wife. 'You should be resting,' he said. 'Scott is right. This is no place for a lady.'

'Why not?' Alice retorted defiantly. 'After all, it was you who praised the nurses in the Crimea, and I am sure they were witness to such sights. I am the wife of a surgeon and it is my place to assist my husband in any way I can.'

Scott and Peter looked at each other, and Scott shrugged his shoulders. It was hard to counter her argument.

'I warn you,' Peter said, 'what you are about to assist me with is very unpleasant, and if at any stage you find it overwhelming, promise me you will leave the room. You will be no use to me in a dead faint on the floor.'

Alice nodded and Peter could see how she paled at the sight of the wicked-looking blade in his hand.

'What should I do?' she asked, and Peter instructed her to assist the two sepoys, one holding the legs of their wounded comrade, the other his upper body. Scott also stepped in, although Peter could see that he did so somewhat reluctantly.

'This is the glory you soldiers inflict on one another on the battlefield,' Peter said. 'Alice, make sure that the leg is held firmly.'

Peter bent down, placing the curved blade under the leg, and with a deft movement cut a neat circle around the leg above the knee, opening up the skin. The wounded soldier arched and screamed, unnerving his comrades. Peter did not hesitate but grabbed a tenon saw, pushing down hard on the bone, and began sawing with less pressure on the forward stroke. He glanced at Alice. She had gone deathly white but remained holding the leg firmly against the patient's desperate kicks. Blood sprayed all around and Alice's white dress was splattered with red.

The saw did its job and the leg came away in Alice's arms, causing her to stagger backwards under the unexpected weight of the limb.

'Just drop it on the floor,' Peter said as he continued his post-operational procedures to seal the wound before releasing the ligature clamp. The sepoy had mercifully fainted under the pain of the amputation and lay still on the blood-covered table.

'Get him to a bed,' Peter ordered. 'If he does not get an infection within the next twenty-four hours he may live.' Peter wiped his bloody hands on the apron he was wearing and tossed the tenon saw in a washbasin of water.

Alice stood in the room, the colour returning to her face. Peter went to her and placed his hands on her shoulders whilst Scott supervised the removal of the patient from the makeshift operating theatre.

'Are you unwell?' Peter asked gently and Alice shook her head, though he could see that the amputation had been a shock to her.

'You were so skilled in the way you carried out the removal of the poor man's leg,' she said. 'I know that I can assist you in such future operations.'

Peter knew now that his wife was a lot tougher than most men would ever credit. He would need her by his side as his surgical assistant, despite the protests of his European colleagues that medicine – especially surgery – was beyond the capabilities of the weaker sex. The Indian mutiny was growing worse by the day, and their lives were in real danger if British forces did not arrive soon from England. Many more men would pass through this ill-equipped surgery before then, and Peter would need Alice's help if he had any hope of ministering to them all.

FOURTEEN

It was a truly impressive gathering in London's Hyde Park. One hundred thousand civilian spectators watched as a huge military guard of honour wearing red uniforms formed up on foot and on horseback.

Ian stood beside Molly Williams, who was holding her dainty parasol against the morning sun of the London summer. Only a few scattered high-flying clouds broke the brilliant blue of the sky.

At the centre of this great formation sat the Queen on a magnificent horse. Ian had a clear view of her and thought how short she was but still attractive. Standing beside the mount was the tall and handsome Prince Consort, husband of the Queen.

'I can't see him,' Molly said anxiously.

'You will,' Ian reassured.

On a dais draped in a red cloth, attendants to the Queen

held platters laid out with the newly issued medals the monarch had instituted and named in her honour. Then the line of recipients marched forward, and each of the sixty-two medals was pinned on a soldier or officer's chest as the Queen leaned down from her horse.

'Sergeant Curry!' Conan's name was called and Molly raised up on her toes to witness this historic moment. She could not hear Queen Victoria utter the words as Conan halted smartly, saluted, standing rigidly at attention.

The spectators politely clapped their appreciation, and Conan saluted one more time before turning and marching back to the ranks of the regiment. Ian noticed how the Prince Consort bowed to each of the men receiving the new medal of the Victoria Cross, a medal cut out of the barrel of a Russian artillery gun captured at the fall of Sevastopol. Ian's recommendation for Conan to be awarded a medal for bravery had been countersigned by General Outram whilst in Persia.

When the ceremony was completed, the gathered military units presented their salute to the Queen as she rode off the temporary parade ground. Military bands struck up tunes to entertain those civilians remaining to enjoy the beautiful summer's day.

Eventually Conan and Corporal Owen Williams made their way through the crowd to join Ian and Molly.

Molly ignored all social protocols and flung herself into Conan's arms, kissing him.

'Congratulations, Conan, but I should parade you for being out of uniform,' Ian grinned.

'Sir?' Conan queried with a confused frown.

'You should be wearing the rank of sergeant major now, not sergeant. Your promotion has been approved. I should also have you charged, Corporal Williams. You can use

Conan's sergeant chevrons as he will no longer be needing them. Congratulations, Sergeant Williams.'

It took a few seconds for Ian's words to sink in, and then both soldiers broke into grateful smiles. Promotion meant better wages.

'Thank you, sir,' Owen replied, and Ian shook both soldiers' hands. 'No doubt the three of you will be off to celebrate. I know Colour Sergeant Leslie is lining up ales at the pub near our barracks, and he told me that you will be paying.'

'Thank you, sir,' Conan said. 'I am not sure even our promotion will afford us the payment for so many ales.'

'I know you both have a little gold stashed away, and I am sure it could be put to good use this day,' Ian said. 'Molly, I am commissioning you to ensure your brother and Sergeant Major Curry behave themselves.'

Molly leaned forward and kissed Ian on the cheek. 'Thank you, sir, for all that you have done for my Conan and my Owen. You have made good men out of them.'

Ian shook his head. 'They did that themselves,' he replied gently. 'Go now and enjoy this very special day.'

Ian stepped back and saluted Conan. 'New rule in the army,' he explained. 'Even an officer must salute an enlisted man if he is wearing the Victoria Cross.'

Conan returned the salute. 'It is you who should have been awarded the medal for all that you did for us in the Crimea. But I know while our colonel is in command he will never recognise your courage.'

Ian did not comment but he knew Jenkins hated him and, he suspected, wished to see him dead.

'Go off with you,' Ian said and the three disappeared into the crowd to make their way to the pub.

Ian stood for a moment amongst the dispersing crowd of

ladies in long white summer dresses and gentlemen in tall top hats and suits.

'Congratulations, Captain Steele,' a familiar female voice said behind him.

He turned to see the beautiful face of Lady Rebecca Montegue. She was standing a few paces away, wearing an elegant summer dress and holding a parasol. Rebecca was the living image of her twin sister, Jane. The two girls had been separated just after they were born and Rebecca had been adopted by the wealthy Montegue family, inheriting the titles and estates of the now deceased Lord Montegue. It was Jane who had revealed Ian's secret to her sister.

'Oh, have no fear, Captain Steele, I have never broken my promise to keep secret your identity,' Rebecca said with a sweet smile. 'I am only here to congratulate you on your recommendation for Sergeant Curry's medal. I know Clive attempted to have your report quashed but was overruled by General Outram.'

'Thank you, Lady Montegue,' Ian replied.

'There is no need for such formalities between us, Ian,' Rebecca said. 'After all, under other circumstances you might have been my brother-in-law. Have you learned anything concerning my sister's disappearance?'

'Nothing,' Ian said. 'I am forced to confront the idea that someone may have murdered Jane.'

'I suspect that you are correct,' Rebecca said sadly. 'I have terrible dreams of a ring of small stones on a hilltop near my sister's village. The place we first met, when you thought at first I was Jane. I suppose that is because Jane had a spiritual connection to that old Druid place of worship.'

'Strange,' Ian frowned. 'I have a similar dream that troubles my sleep,' he said. 'It is as if Jane haunts that desolate place.'

'I suspect, though, that you do not believe in ghosts, given you have demonstrated what a practical soldier you are,' Rebecca said. 'I do not believe that those we love come back to haunt us either, but I have faith that you will discover who is responsible for my sister's disappearance.'

'I have no real leads, although I suspect Charles Forbes,' Ian said.

'If Charles knew that my sister carried your child, that may have been enough reason to kill her,' Rebecca agreed.

'I have considered that,' Ian said. 'But I cannot exact revenge without evidence. If I do prove Charles is her murderer, I will ensure he is slain.'

'You will be my angel of vengeance,' Rebecca replied, then changed the subject. 'There is to be a ball at my estate the week before Clive's regiment steams for India. Your name will be on the invitation list, and also that of the charming young girl you escorted to my last ball.'

'I am afraid Miss Solomon and I are not on speaking terms,' Ian said gloomily.

'That's a shame, I thought you made a very handsome couple,' Rebecca said.

Ian did not wish to discuss his relationship with Ella. 'It is well known that you have often been seen in the company of Colonel Jenkins. Do you intend to wed him?'

'It is presumptuous of you to ask me such a personal question,' Rebecca replied. 'But as you occupy a rather unique place in my life, I will tell you that I do intend to accept Clive's offer of marriage when he asks.'

'Why?' Ian asked.

'Because he is a man I will one day guide to becoming the prime minister of England. We both know Clive does not have what it takes to lead men in battle, but he does have the acumen to become a politician of renown, particularly if his family fortune is married to mine. Ah, I see that Clive is just over there.' Rebecca and Ian turned to see Jenkins standing with a group of senior officers some yards away. 'I will bid you a good morning, Captain Forbes. Do not forget my invitation. I look forward to seeing you again.'

Rebecca strolled away, leaving Ian alone to ponder their meeting. He understood that his real identity was known to a woman who could easily expose him, and yet she chose to protect him, despite her alliance with one of his most hated enemies. It was apparent Rebecca Montegue liked to play games, but Ian was perplexed by her attraction to Clive Jenkins, if indeed that was what it was. He knew one thing, and that was that the invitation to her ball was more an order than a request. Ian groaned. He had never liked the pomp and ceremony of the English aristocrats; he was more at home in the field with his infantry company. He watched as Rebecca laughed with the high-ranking officers and placed her gloved hand on Clive Jenkins' arm. He could not understand how twins could be so similar in appearance and yet so different in character.

★

Sergeant Major Conan Curry lay on the double bed in Molly's room above her shop. Colour Sergeant Paddy Leslie had organised a huge celebration at their favourite pub – at no small cost to Conan and Owen. The ale had flowed and tankards were repeatedly raised in toasts. Predictably, it had ended in a brawl when a group of engineers entered the establishment, but no one could remember why the fight had started. The regimental men were able to extract themselves before the constabulary arrived, and now Conan lay beside Molly.

'You were a disgrace, Conan Curry,' she said, but without

venom. 'Captain Forbes would have been ashamed of you and Owen if he had been present. The captain has been very good to you both.'

Conan groaned. One of the engineers had been a big, powerful soldier who had connected a heavy blow to Conan's jaw and he had lost a couple of teeth. Or perhaps the drunkenness was turning now into a hangover. 'Captain Forbes and I go a long way back,' he slurred. 'All the way to New South Wales when he was the village blacksmith, and me and my brothers did a bit of bushranging.'

'What are you babbling about?' Molly scoffed. 'How could you know Captain Forbes before you enlisted?'

Conan paused. The ale had loosened his tongue. On reflection he felt that in the privacy of the bedroom nothing he said could do any harm. And this was Molly, the woman he loved, and someone who could be relied upon to keep the captain's secret. 'He is not Captain Forbes,' he admitted. 'His real name is Ian Steele and he has fooled the Forbes family into believing that he is one of them.'

Shocked, Molly hardly believed Conan's confession. Were these simply drunken ramblings?

'Are you saying that Captain Forbes is an imposter?' Molly asked.

'Ian Steele is the best man I have ever known, and the boys would follow him into hell if he asked,' Conan said, gripping his head in both hands. 'You cannot tell anyone what I have just told you.'

'You know that I love you, and anything you tell me within these walls remains a secret between us.'

'You swear?' Conan demanded, realising that he had said more than he should.

'I swear on my love for you,' Molly replied. She was mesmerised as her lover went on to tell her about the history of the real Ian Steele. Conan even confessed to his role in the robbery that had resulted in the death of Ian's mother. Molly did not speak a word as the tale of the contract between English aristocrat and colonial blacksmith unravelled.

'So there it is,' Conan concluded. 'Now I need to get some sleep because it will be my duty to parade the company for inspection in the morning.'

Molly rested Conan's head in her lap as he fell into a fitful sleep. She was secretly pleased to learn that Ian was not the brother of Charles Forbes, who had once attempted to rape her when she worked for the Forbes family at their manor in Kent. Conan had told her that the men in the regiment had given Ian the nickname of 'the Colonial' and she thought, *If only they knew.*

The fact that Conan had confided the secret to her only made her love the big Irishman even more. They had all come a long way from the slum tenements of the inner city since the day Conan and Owen were on the run from the law and had to enlist in the British army to avoid arrest by the London police. War in the Crimea had financed her business enterprise with Russian loot, and after this last campaign, Owen had produced a small fortune in gold coins. Whoever Captain Ian Steele was, it only mattered to her that his deception had brought them good fortune.

His secret would always be safe with her.

*

The cross-Channel steamer to Calais had been part of the ruse to ensure that Samuel and James were not spotted leaving on a clipper sailing for the Americas. Ikey Solomon had been sure that private investigator Charles Field would be keeping a close eye on all the New York–bound vessels with the hope of intercepting his target. New passports in new names had been procured for the two men, so from France they would be able to book a passage home. As they waited to embark, they would have the chance to take in the sights and pleasures of Paris. This they did before eventually taking berth on a ship to the United States two weeks later.

However, the clipper had hardly left Calais to sail south when it was hit by a furious Atlantic-born gale, forcing it to seek shelter at the English port of Dover and remain there whilst substantial repairs were made to its sails and rigging.

James and Samuel shared a small but clean first-class cabin, and though a little perturbed, James was not overly concerned that they were once again in British waters. After all, the odds were low that any of Charles' paid inform-ants would suspect a ship leaving from a French port could be their means of escape. If anything, they would be still watching ships *departing* English ports. They simply had to lie low and wait it out.

James poured gin for himself and Samuel into tumblers.

'Well, I did not expect to be back in England so soon, and I must say that I already miss the beauty of Paris.' James noticed Samuel gazing through a porthole at the wharves and docks of Dover. The gale had abated and the sun was shining in the early morning.

'Do you know, we are only a short carriage ride from our manor's chapel,' Samuel said, accepting the glass of gin.

'You aren't thinking of going ashore,' James groaned, aghast. 'We were damned lucky to get out of London.'

Samuel turned away from the porthole. 'We are safe, dear James,' he said. 'I could easily visit my brother's memo-rial and be back before the ship sails again.'

James pulled a face that displayed his frustration. 'I beseech you to reconsider yet another of your lunatic aspirations. We will not be safe until we are on our way back to New York.'

'I am sorry, James, but the opportunity is too good to ignore. It is as if this unforeseen deliverance to Dover has been granted me by God. Nobody would suspect we are here. You know how important it is for me to honour my little brother's death.'

'I doubt that you believe there is a God,' James scoffed. 'But your goddamned stubbornness will bring us undone.'

'I do not request you to accompany me,' Samuel said, taking a long swig of the gin. 'I would never put you at risk.'

James stepped forward, placing his hands on Samuel's shoulders. 'Despite your insanity, you know I would never allow you to face danger alone. If you insist on a visit to your brother's memorial, I will be going with you.'

Samuel had hoped that James would insist on accompanying him. He did not want to be parted from him. Since Jonathan, he had recognised that James was the only other man he would ever love in his life.

'Thank you, dear James,' Samuel said, tears welling in his eyes. 'We will arrange to leave immediately and be back before the ship sails.'

When Samuel turned to pack a few items, James shook his head, hoping that his lover was making the right judgement. Somehow he had his doubts.

*

Ian was announced on arrival in the magnificent ballroom at Lady Rebecca Montegue's manor just outside London. It was a dazzling affair of colourful military uniforms, glittering gowns and jewellery and a multitude of candles flickering soft shadows on the guests both military and civilian. Ian noted that all the officers of his regiment were in attendance, which was not surprising as the invitation had described the event as the farewell ball for the regiment before it steamed to India. He wore his own dress uniform and blended in with his military colleagues.

Ian took a coupe of champagne offered him by a servant wearing an old Georgian wig and equally ornate dress uniform.

'Here, sir, your dance card,' the servant said, passing Ian a slip of paper.

Ian hardly looked at the card, slipping it inside his dress jacket. He took a sip of champagne and glanced around at the guests already on the polished timbered floor for a quadrille. The regimental band struck up and Ian expected they would play until midnight when the guests broke for supper. He knew he would be bored by then as he had come alone, as prescribed by the invitation.

He saw Rebecca enter the dance floor on the arm of Jenkins, and he swallowed the last of his drink, looking around for a servant to replenish his empty glass.

As he did so, his eyes fell on a sight that almost caused him to drop the crystal coupe. 'God almighty!'

It was Ella, standing alone on the other side of the dance floor. She was holding a small fan and wearing a voluminous silk dress drawn in tightly at the waist, her shoulders bare. She appeared a little bemused and when she turned her head and caught sight of Ian, her expression mirrored his amazement.

Ian made his way around the tables to her.

'Ella! What are you doing here?' he asked.

'I would ask the same of you,' she replied. 'I was assured by Lady Montegue that you would not be attending tonight. That is the only reason I accepted her unexpected invitation.'

'Did your invitation specify that it was for you alone?' Ian asked, a suspicion forming in his mind.

'Yes, it did,' Ella replied, and Ian broke into a crooked grin.

'That is no accident,' he said, and remembered the dance card in his jacket. He retrieved it and saw his and Ella's names inscribed for a waltz following the quadrille. The quadrille had now finished and when the floor was clear, the bandmaster announced the next dance was a waltz.

'I believe this is our dance,' Ian said, taking Ella's elbow to escort her onto the floor.

He placed his arm around her waist and they stepped off in time to the rhythm of the music.

'I said that I would never see you again,' Ella said. 'Has fate brought us together tonight?'

'No, not fate but the scheming of Lady Montegue,' Ian replied. 'But I cannot think of a more beautiful woman to be in my arms right now.'

Ella blushed, tightening her hand on Ian's. It was said that the waltz was a licentious dance, leading to fornication, and for a moment Ian hoped that was true. With this beautiful young woman in his arms, floating across the polished floor together, his attempt to distance himself from her was forgotten.

'*I wonder, by my troth, what thou and I Did, till we loved?*' Ian said softly.

'*Were we not weaned till then?*' Ella said, looking into Ian's eyes. 'You are certainly a man of many surprises, Samuel Forbes. John Donne, "The Good Morrow". I would not expect a man whose life is devoted to soldiering to understand the pure romanticism of such a poem. I think we both understand its meaning, do we not?'

Just then the music stopped and the dancers left the floor. Ian was about to say something when he saw Rebecca gesturing to him. He escorted Ella to a table where some of the younger officers of the regiment were engaged in sipping claret and smoking cigars.

'Look after this lady, gentlemen,' he commanded as he pulled out her chair. 'I will be returning.'

The young officers said they would be delighted, and as Ian walked away he wondered if leaving Ella alone with those handsome and eligible men was such a good idea.

'I am pleased to see that you have been following your dance card,' Rebecca said with a smile.

'You planned this,' Ian said without any rancour. 'Why?'

'Let us just say that I learned that you have dealings with Miss Solomon's father and that he is a man with a formidable reputation for getting things done. I also remember that you escorted his daughter to her debut ball and he was very grateful. I gather that you have been seen many times in her company since, and when I look at the young lady, I can see why any man would risk the ire of Ikey Solomon. But he would have to be a very brave – or foolish – man to do that, and I know you are not foolish. You must have strong feelings for Miss Solomon. I ask that you escort her home after the ball. I promised Mr Solomon you would do that for him.'

'Good Lord!' Ian said. 'Jane was never this conniving.'

'It is because of my sister's memory that I have courted favour with Mr Solomon,' Rebecca replied. 'When the time comes for justice to be dispensed, I know he will be able to assist. Besides, if Clive does one day become prime minister, it will not hurt to have Mr Solomon as a discreet friend.'

Ian stared at Rebecca. 'I do hope I never get on the wrong side of you, Lady Montegue.'

She smiled warmly. 'I should also mention that when you escort Miss Solomon home, it will be in her carriage. Mr Solomon has arranged this with his man, Egbert.'

Egbert. Ian knew the employee as a tough and dangerous thug. Thoughts of the remainder of John Donne's poem melted away. Egbert was more than capable of breaking bones with his bare hands. He was almost as dangerous as Rebecca Montegue. She was one of the most manipulative people he had encountered but he respected her strategic mind. Ian almost felt sorry for Colonel Clive Jenkins in the hands of his future wife.

'You know,' Ian said, shaking his head, 'you would be a far more suitable commanding officer of our regiment than Colonel Jenkins. You have a fine head for tactics.'

'Ah, but it is well accepted that we ladies are simple, weak and frivolous creatures. It is not in us to be leaders, but simply the bearers of children and keepers of the house.' She gazed guilelessly at him.

Ian smiled broadly. He was not fooled for a moment.

FIFTEEN

The hulking man in the driver's seat of the carriage watched Ian like a hawk.

Ian helped Ella onto the carriage seat and sat opposite her for the journey to a small but comfortable cottage Ikey owned as his country retreat, away from the smog and slums of London. Ian ached with the desire to hold Ella and lie with her naked in a big comfortable bed and remain there forever in her arms. He knew by Ella's response to Donne's poem that she, too, wished to be with him. Of course, Egbert's presence ensured that would not happen. Ian did not doubt that if he had acted in an inappropriate manner towards Ikey Solomon's chaste daughter, he would likely not make it back to London alive.

Not even a kiss passed between them as Ian walked her to the door. The subtle, hidden touch of their hands was their only physical contact under the watch of eagle-eyed

Egbert. The touch was like an electric shock to Ian, who had experienced such a thing as a young man at a travelling show where a man demonstrated this new thing called electricity. Now he felt it again and knew the most important thing in his life was to be with Ella, regardless of the consequences. After all, within days he would be steaming to India and there his life might come to a brutal end at any moment.

'Excuse me for a moment, my love,' Ian said, and returned to Egbert in the carriage.

'Bert, I need a couple of hours alone with Miss Solomon,' Ian said, reaching into his trouser pocket.

'I have my orders from Ikey,' Egbert growled. 'You are to return with me now.'

Ian opened his hand, revealing a sparkling diamond he had retrieved when his company had looted a Russian baggage train in the Crimea. He always carried the precious gem for luck and considered it might prove to be so now.

'I appreciate your loyalty to Ikey but I am leaving for India very soon and would like to have a couple of hours in the company of Miss Solomon. She is agreeable to this, I assure you. This diamond is worth more than a working man's lifetime of wages and I think that you deserve it.'

Ian could see Egbert eyeing the glittering stone with intense avarice and awe. Loyalty to Solomon and greed seemed to battle inside him.

'As you are steaming for India, Captain Forbes,' Egbert eventually said, 'I can understand that you might wish to speak with Miss Solomon, but Ikey must never know about it.'

'That goes without saying,' Ian said, passing the diamond to Ikey's henchman.

'Two hours and I will be back, Captain Forbes,' he said, and flicked the reins to urge the horse forward. When he was out of sight, Ian returned to Ella.

'Do you want this?' he asked, and she nodded.

Hand in hand they walked through the cottage door.

What followed in the next couple of hours was worth all the diamonds Ian had ever possessed. He had almost forgotten how love could be expressed in such a physical way, with such joyful passion. All too quickly, however, their time together was over.

'It is time for me to leave,' Ian said reluctantly, rising from the bed and beginning to dress himself.

Tears began to stream down Ella's face. 'I can never love any man as I love you,' she said. 'Please come back to me safely and then we will be together always.'

Ian did not reply. He was acutely aware that war gave no guarantees.

He kissed Ella tenderly and then walked out into the darkness. Egbert was waiting for him, and Ian climbed aboard the carriage to return to London.

★

The regiment marched down to the wharf in the early evening. Their departure did not attract as much attention as when they had sailed to confront the Tsar's army in the Crimea. This time a scattered crowd of civilians lined the streets and urchins fell in behind the columns of soldiers marching to the beat of drums and the sound of trumpets.

Ian led his company and glanced from the corner of his eye to see if he recognised anyone amongst the gaggle of spectators. He hoped to see Ella, but by the time they arrived at the ships he hadn't sighted her. He spotted Molly, here to see Conan and Owen embark on the troopship.

When Ian had overseen his company boarding the ship, he clambered up the gangway to stand at the railings beside Conan and Owen. They had become a recognised trio in the company and many speculated about this. The old hands who had served in the Crimea and Persia with Ian's company soon set the newcomers straight. The trinity of the three men – two senior non-commissioned officers and a commissioned officer – brought the company luck.

Below them they could see Molly looking up at them with a tear-streaked face. She was waving a handkerchief and mouthing words drowned by the din of the wharf and the music of the regimental band playing the Scottish tune of 'Auld Lang Syne'. Soldiers on the ships and those waving farewell on the wharf joined in the singing.

Then Ian saw Ella.

She was not singing but staring up at him with a sad face. He saw her mouth some words and did not have to be a lip-reader to understand that she had said she loved him. He felt a lump in his throat and waved to her just as the ships slipped their ropes, taking advantage of the tide. It was like a recurring dream, Ian thought, as Ella became a small figure amongst all the wives, mothers, lovers, sisters and children saying goodbye to their soldier husbands, sons, lovers and brothers.

Ian made a vow there and then: if he returned from this campaign he would confront Ikey Solomon and declare his love for the formidable man's only daughter. He knew that could prove more dangerous than facing a battleline of well-armed enemy sepoys.

*

Major Scott Campbell sat astride his horse, gazing at the camp of white tents before the formidable walls of the Indian city of Delhi. Their own camp looked so insignificant compared to the expanse of the walled city. Forces composed of sepoys loyal to the Queen and British soldiers of the East India Company were here to take Delhi back from the Indian rebellion. Scott knew that his brother and sister-in-law had taken up residence in the British lines and he worried for their safety. As such, he had chosen to ride out to reconnoitre a position to the right rear of the British lines where their forces were thin on the ground.

Scott rode a mile and brought his horse to a halt. Observing a dust cloud rising on the horizon, he retrieved a small telescope from his pack. In the view he could see a tiny figure on a horse galloping at full speed towards him, and beyond the horseman Scott could see the tiny figures of enemy cavalry that had somehow got behind the British lines.

Scott pulled his horse around and set off at a gallop to return as fast as he could to the camp. He rode hard, his mount in a lather when he reached the lines. 'Saddle, boots and mount up!' he yelled. 'The enemy is upon us!'

Immediately cavalrymen tumbled from tents, throwing saddles on their horses and snatching weapons. Scott waited only a short time until a small force was ready for action, and suddenly realised that Peter was at his stirrup.

'What is happening?' Peter called up to his brother.

'The devils must have filed across the causeway behind us and formed up. They are coming in force.'

'I am coming with you,' Peter said, brandishing his big six-shot revolver.

'You need to stay and protect Alice,' Scott shouted down at Peter.

'If we don't stop them before they reach the camp we will all be finished,' Peter replied, comprehending the gravity of the sudden attack.

'Grab a horse and hurry then,' Scott said. Peter rushed to the horse lines, threw a saddle on a mount and quickly joined his brother. As soon as he did, Scott ordered the advance and the defending force set off to meet the attack.

They rode for a half-mile with outlying cavalrymen acting as picquets. When Scott spotted the dust cloud and the mutineer cavalry formation that had caused it, his heart sank. He guessed that his own meagre force was outnumbered at least four to one. He withdrew his curved sabre, held it aloft and roared, 'At a gallop, charge!'

The line of mutineer cavalry was taken aback by the absolute madness of such a small force galloping towards them, screaming their war cries, and the line halted before turning to fall back.

Scott had expected they would crash into the attacking force and be annihilated, but his bold move had unsettled the attacking enemy. Each of the British and loyal Indian cavalrymen knew his business and singled out their foe for combat as the enemy retreated. The British sabres descended, inflicting terrible wounds as the razor-sharp blades sliced through arms, shoulders and heads.

Peter kept close to his brother, who was locked in battle with a mutineer, slashing and parrying his opponent's desperate attempts to defend himself. The horses crashed together and whinnied their confusion. Peter suddenly noticed that the Indian cavalryman had taken advantage of an opening in his brother's defence and was on the verge of delivering a death blow. Peter was only feet away, fighting to control his panicked mount. He brought up his heavy revolver, firing at almost point-blank range at the head of the man about to kill his brother. The shot was true and the mutineer slumped from his horse, slamming into the hard and dusty ground below.

Scott swung around to see the smoking revolver in Peter's hand, realising that his brother had just saved his life.

He nodded his appreciation and spurred his mount towards a group of fleeing enemy. Peter followed and they went in pursuit of the larger force now attempting to retreat to a causeway. In their panic the enemy had milled into a confused mass, all attempting to cross the narrow causeway at once. The smaller British force took advantage of their disorganisation, and the slaughter continued at the entrance to the causeway in close-quarter killing.

The frenzy of battle had overtaken Peter's senses and he picked out an enemy lancer who wheeled around to confront him. Peter raised his pistol, firing two shots which missed, and suddenly the enemy horseman was on him. Peter felt the lance pierce his side, dragging him from his mount, and he crashed onto the earth, winded. He could taste dirt in his mouth and felt the lance being withdrawn from his body. Peter screamed his pain and realised that he had lost his pistol in the fall. He looked up to see the mutineer cavalry lancer rearranging his blood-tipped lance for a second strike.

Knowing he was about to be skewered, Peter experienced more regret than fear. His last image was of Alice's face. The look of triumph on the enemy lancer's face suddenly evaporated as it was smashed by a bullet. From the corner of his eye, Peter could see his brother's arm holding his own revolver, smoke drifting from the end of the barrel.

The lancer toppled from his horse, and Scott reached down from his own mount to grip Peter's outstretched hand.

'Get on your horse, old boy,' he yelled above the terrible din of men screaming, horses neighing and the metal clash of swords and sabres.

Despite the pain, Peter dragged himself into the saddle and scooped up the reins. The exhausted British force fell back into a disciplined formation as the remainder of the enemy cavalrymen retreated across the causeway, galloping back to the protection of the great walls of Delhi.

Peter realised how thirsty he was as the dust choked his throat and the adrenaline of battle began to seep away. Even Peter could see there was no sense in pursuing the survivors of the fierce battle. The retreating force still outnumbered them; if they attempted to finish the mission, they would have to file across the causeway, and the enemy might suddenly find the courage to fall into a formation to counter them.

'How bad is your wound?' Scott asked, seeing the wet, dark patch on his brother's left side.

'I will have to make my examination when we return to our lines,' Peter grimaced.

Scott gave the order to withdraw, and the weary column fell into a march after reclaiming their own wounded from the battlefield. Within the hour, Peter sat in his tent with his blood-soaked jacket on a chair beside him. Alice was fighting back her tears while chiding her husband at the same time.

'It is not your role to fight like your brother,' she said, washing the two-sided jagged wound from which blood still oozed. 'What insanity persuaded you to go with him?'

'I could see that our plight was desperate, and Scott needed every man he could muster to ward off the attack on the camp. I knew we must stop them from getting to our lines. It was our only hope.'

'But you are not a soldier. You are a surgeon,' Alice countered.

'I wear the uniform of a British officer, albeit without any commissioned rank. I am both soldier and surgeon,' Peter replied.

Alice reached for a glass bottle of antiseptic and with

it swabbed the open wound. The liquid burned and Peter groaned in pain.

'What do I do now?' Alice asked, wiping her bloody hands on an apron around her waist.

'You will have to sew it up,' Peter answered through gritted teeth. 'I know that you used to sew when we were in London, so I will leave the choice of stitch to you.'

'We have no anaesthetic,' Alice protested.

'Never mind. Just sew.'

Alice selected a needle that Peter insisted be placed in boiling water. When it had cooled she threaded the needle and began to sew the wound. Peter broke into a sweat but did not utter a word. When the task was completed Alice stood back to admire her work.

'You have done well,' Peter said hoarsely, reaching for his bloody shirt and jacket. 'I could never have imagined in my wildest thoughts that you and I would be spending our honeymoon under the current dire circumstances.' He reached across to touch his wife on the cheek. 'I could never have dreamed how very competent and courageous you are. I do not deserve you.'

A wry smile crossed Alice's face. 'I doubt the good ladies in London at their tea parties would be entertained by my adventures in India. Many of them would consider me a traitor to our gender.'

'True, my dear. Ladies do not shoot man-eating tigers, carry guns or act as assistants in surgical operations – let alone sew up their husbands!'

They both laughed.

'It is time for you to rest, Dr Campbell,' Alice said sternly. 'That is an order from a wife who has still not forgiven you for riding out with your reckless brother.'

Peter slid from the bench and took Alice in his arms.

'Mrs Campbell, I love you just a bit more every time I wake to see a new day.'

★

The troop transport had reached the southern tip of Africa and anchored at Cape Town for supplies.

Colonel Jenkins sat opposite a staff officer of major rank in the sweeping room adorned with the portraits of former governors and a young Queen Victoria at Government House. He was mystified as to why he had been called to this special meeting before the one scheduled for all officers of the expeditionary force steaming for India.

'Sir, a telegram has been received from the general staff in India,' the smartly dressed officer said. 'We have been requested to supply a rifle company in a rescue mission once the force reaches India. It is your regiment that has the honour of supplying that company.'

'Who is behind the request, Major?' Jenkins asked, suspicious about why his regiment had been singled out for what was likely a dangerous mission.

'General Outram, sir,' the major replied. 'It appears he is aware of your regiment from the Persian campaign.'

'Is the mission considered risky?' Jenkins asked.

'I must be honest and say it is,' the major said. 'It will be deep in territory overrun by the mutineers in the Bengali region. It was decided to risk only a single company should things go wrong in the rescue attempt.'

'I have an officer who is suited to this request. A captain already known to the general, one Captain Samuel Forbes. I know that Captain Forbes will jump at the opportunity to lead his men into such a venture.'

Jenkins was delighted. The pact he had made with Charles Forbes during the Crimean campaign still stood.

It had been settled that if Jenkins could ever place Captain Samuel Forbes in a situation that got him killed, Jenkins would be richly rewarded. But Clive Jenkins did not even need the substantial bounty, as his hatred for the man was such that he'd send him to his death even if he was not to be rewarded. He vividly remembered the slights he had endured when he had been under Samuel Forbes' command during the Crimean campaign. He grudgingly accepted that Forbes was an outstanding officer, but he was also a living reminder of Jenkins' own cowardice. One way or the other the captain must die, and here was the perfect opportunity.

'If that is all, Major, I will inform Captain Forbes of his mission,' Jenkins said, rising from his chair.

'There is just one other thing before I pass on detailed instructions, sir,' the major said, holding a thick package of sealed papers. 'This mission is considered to be top secret and not to be communicated to anyone else. When Captain Forbes has taken in the contents of the mission, as outlined in these orders, the papers are to be destroyed.' He passed the package to Jenkins, who smiled warmly. In his hands he held Captain Samuel Forbes' death warrant.

SIXTEEN

I an stood in the cabin of the expeditionary force's flagship. He saluted Colonel Jenkins who was sitting behind a small desk.

'Sit down, Captain Forbes,' Jenkins said, waving to a chair adjacent to the desk. 'I have summoned you here to discuss a mission assigned to our regiment by General Outram.'

Ian was pleased to hear the name of the British general he greatly admired. Whatever the mission, he knew it must be important. On the table, Ian could see a bulky brown envelope that had been closed with a seal. Jenkins fingered it for a moment, inspecting the seal, then he pushed back his chair and stood, his head almost touching the wooden ceiling of stout ship's timbers. Both men could feel the motion of the vessel rolling on the southern seas.

'I have volunteered your company to rescue a very important man to the Empire. He is the Khan of the Bengali district, and he and his family are currently hiding out in a coastal village – as you will see when you examine the documents the general's HQ has provided. From what is known, the area is heavily infested with mutineers. It will be your job to get the Khan and his family safely to one of our warships, and from there he will be taken to London. The details are in here,' Jenkins said, and finally handed the sealed packet to Ian. 'Needless to say our meeting is strictly confidential. At the appropriate time, and not before, you will brief those included in the mission. When we reach port in India, you and your company will be transferred to another ship bound for the Bengali coast. You will destroy the contents of that packet when you have perused them.'

Jenkins sat down again and busied himself with the papers on his desk. 'Good luck, Captain Forbes,' he said without much conviction. 'If you have any questions, you know where to find me.'

'Very good, sir,' Ian replied, then he stood and saluted.

He returned to the cabin he shared with his company second-in-command, Lieutenant Ross Woods, who was a man in his forties without the financial means to purchase a captaincy. He was an experienced officer, however, and Ian was pleased to have him in his company.

Ian opened the envelope and laid the papers on his bunk to examine them in detail. He was reassured to see that he was to confide the mission to his senior NCO and whoever he appointed as his second-in-command for the actual operation ashore. Ian had already decided that employing a few chosen men of his company would be the best way to track down and extract the Khan from India. He knew that he could trust Woods to assume command whilst he and his selected men went ashore.

When Ian was satisfied that he had taken in all the intelligence the report provided, he carefully folded the papers, securing them in a small locker for which only he had a key. He would dispose of them later. Then he made his way to the deck of the ship where he knew he would find his company sergeant major.

'Sarn't Major, a good evening to you,' Ian said, joining Conan at the railing. The seas were calm and fluorescence followed the wake of the steamship.

'Evening, sah,' Conan replied, tapping his pipe on the rail. 'A grand night it is.'

'You may not think so after what I am about to tell you,' Ian said. 'Our old friend, General Outram, is requesting that a company from the regiment carry out a very secret and rather perilous mission when we get to India. Colonel Jenkins has chosen us to undertake that mission.'

'I am not surprised,' Conan grinned. 'Considering how our illustrious colonel would like to see you dead.'

'That may be so,' Ian agreed. 'But it also puts the lives of my men in harm's way. That includes you. I may have a way to exclude you from the mission.'

'Sir, you and I will come to blows if you leave me out,' Conan said with a pained expression. 'You will need me, and Owen. It's in our Celtic blood to fight.'

Ian stared at the calm seas under a rising moon and felt humbled by Conan's willingness to stand by his side. 'Maybe there will be a way to minimise the risks to the company. I will need time to figure that out. Mr Sinclair will act as my second-in-command in the mission.'

'Captain Sinclair's brother?' Conan queried. 'He has not seen any action. Do you think he is a wise choice, considering that we lost his brother at the Redan?'

'I have a feeling Mr Sinclair will acquit himself well,' Ian replied. 'He has to start somewhere, and I know if you keep an eye on him he will be as safe as any soldier can be.'

Conan nodded his understanding.

'I forgot to mention that there is one other very important reason why Mr Sinclair should accompany us,' Ian added. 'He speaks the Indian language. According to his record of service, Mr Sinclair studied the language at university before taking his commission. It seems he also had ideas of joining the honourable East India Company but decided on the army when Miles was killed. He is keen to use his language skills when we get to India.'

'What about Owen?' Conan asked.

'Sergeant Williams will remain with the company and assume the temporary role of CSM in your absence,' Ian said.

'We will miss his canny knack of finding things that sparkle and gleam,' Conan chuckled, plugging his pipe with tobacco.

'Look at it this way,' Ian said with a wry grin, 'if we fail and don't come back, he will get extra pay for your job as the future CSM.'

'The bastard,' Conan said without rancour as both men continued to gaze out at the silver path the rising moon cast on the ocean.

★

James reluctantly accompanied Samuel to the Kentish village not far from the Forbes country manor, taking a hired carriage north-east of Dover Port and booking into lodgings on the outskirts of the little community.

The next day Samuel dressed in his best suit and top hat and informed James that he would go to the village church to visit the memorial to his brother, Herbert, who had been killed in the Crimean War. Ian had said that Sir Archibald had commissioned a stained-glass window in honour of his youngest son's memory.

James expressed his concern but let his love for Samuel silence his fears.

Samuel left in a hired carriage and journeyed the short distance to the church. It was typical of so many English churches, with its graveyard bearing headstones weathered by the years, and a flower garden carefully tended by the parish priest.

Samuel walked towards the arched entry and was startled when a voice said behind him, 'Good morning, Captain Forbes.'

Samuel turned to see a man dressed in gardening clothes and guessed he was the parish priest. When he did so he noticed a sudden expression of puzzlement on the man's face.

'I am afraid that you have mistaken me, sir,' Samuel said, his heart beating hard in his chest. 'I am John Wilford from London.' Samuel used the name on his forged identity papers.

'Oh, I am sorry,' the Anglican priest said, wiping his hands on a dirty cloth. 'It is just that you bear an uncanny resemblance to a Captain Samuel Forbes, but I realise that I must be mistaken as the last I heard of Captain Forbes and his regiment was that they had been sent to India to sort out that terrible mutiny. May I offer you a cup of tea? I am Father Ogilvie.'

Samuel felt his heartbeat slow with relief. 'I thank you for your kind offer of hospitality, Father, but I am a sight-seeing visitor to your parish and do not have long to see all the local attractions.'

'I would hardly describe my church as a tourist attraction,' Father Ogilvie smiled, 'but I do have a loyal parish on Sundays for services. Even Captain Forbes' father,

Sir Archibald, attends on a regular basis since the unfortunate death of his youngest son.'

The mention of Sir Archibald's name caused Samuel a flood of memories of a young man many years earlier left at the gates of a regiment, armed with a commission he never wanted and began to hate when he faced his first battle in New Zealand against the fierce Maori warriors.

'I believe there is a memorial to Herbert's death in the church,' Samuel said.

'How is it that you know the name of Sir Archibald's son?' the priest asked. 'I thought you were a visitor to our little village.'

Samuel felt the cold sweat of fear when he realised his slip. 'Oh, I overheard the local people mention it at the tavern,' he replied, his hands suddenly clammy. He could see that the priest was staring at him, pondering Samuel's answer.

'If you accompany me I can show you Herbert Forbes' memorial window,' Ogilvie said, and Samuel followed him inside to a large, colourful stained-glass window through which the sun streamed, illuminating a red-coated soldier being taken to heaven by two winged angels. Underneath the glass was written Herbert's name and the place and year of his death. Samuel gazed with reverence at the expensive window dedicated to his brother.

'It is certainly impressive,' Samuel said.

'Sir Archibald did not spare any expense in having it crafted,' Ogilvie said. 'As a matter of fact, he will be arriving here very soon for a meeting with the church council.'

'Thank you for showing me the memorial window, Father,' Samuel said, startled by the news of Sir Archibald's imminent arrival. He was the last person Samuel wished to encounter; his father would not be so easily fooled as the parish priest. 'I must leave now.'

Samuel walked quickly out of the church, replacing his top hat and striding towards his carriage. He had hardly gone a few steps when the rattle of a second carriage sounded outside the church gate only a few paces away. As Samuel feared, it was a fine carriage drawn by two thoroughbred horses and driven by a uniformed servant. In the open back in a leather seat was a white-haired man with a face flushed red by the summer sun. Beside Sir Archibald sat his eldest son, Charles. Samuel's first impression was of how old Sir Archibald had grown since he'd last seen him at the gates of the regiment. Samuel prayed that he would reach his carriage before either man noticed him. He was relieved to see that Sir Archibald was being helped from the carriage by Charles, who handed his father a walking stick, ignoring Samuel altogether.

Samuel kept his face down and climbed into the carriage, giving the driver instructions to return to the village immediately. As the driver prepared to depart, Samuel could just make out the conversation between the three men, and felt his blood run cold when he heard Ogilvie remark that he had just had a visitor who bore a remarkable resemblance to Samuel and knew of Herbert. From the corner of his eye, Samuel could see the outstretched arm of the priest pointing to him and Charles turning to stare right at him.

★

The puff of smoke rising from the walls of Delhi heralded a large mortar being fired at the low rise where Scott and Peter stood, facing the formidable city walls.

'Time to seek cover,' Scott said and they both stepped behind a large rock. Seconds later the mortar bomb exploded a short distance from them, spattering the rock with red-hot metal and loose stones.

'They had the right angle but not the right range,' Scott said, standing and brushing down his uniform. 'Well, time to return to camp and see if that grain merchant has arrived,' he decided, striding towards their horses which were grazing on lower ground.

The British operation could not really be called a siege as the British forces were spread around only one area of the city's walls, and the mutineers were able to have reinforcements arrive elsewhere on a daily basis to fortify the city. The mutineers had concentrated their army within the city's great walls in an attempt to confront their enemy, and the commanders of the British forces could only wait and pray that reinforcements would arrive before any serious effort to take the city was made.

'Look!' Peter said, pointing to a gateway in the city wall. Scott swung around in the saddle to see a large column of Indian cavalry accompanied by infantry flowing across the plain towards the camp.

'Go!' Scott shouted as he dug his stirrups into his mount, forcing it into an urgent gallop towards the fortified lines defending the village of white army tents. The mutineers were mounting a large-scale attack on the camp, and Peter knew where he must be when the fighting commenced. Within minutes he flung himself from his horse inside the British camp. Both horse and rider were bathed in sweat from the hard ride under a fierce sun.

Already Peter could hear the roar of the defending British cannons pouring canister shot and high explosive into the waves of approaching enemy infantry.

Peter ran to a tent, flinging open the flap to see that Alice was already laying out his surgical instruments and ordering servants to fetch buckets of water, anticipating the flow of wounded from the battlefield.

'The Sikhs and Gurkhas have taken up their posts,' she said to Peter as he stripped away his officer's jacket and grabbed an apron that had been washed but still bore the stains of blood from previous surgeries. This had not been the first attack on their camp, and each time the casualties on their side whittled down their numbers. Reinforcements had to come soon or the mutineers would surely wipe them out.

Peter quickly surveyed his instruments and medicines, assessing what he had to work with. He glanced up at his wife who, although grim-faced, appeared to be as composed and ready as he. She was now his main nurse and assistant during surgery, for which she showed a genuine flair and interest. It was a shame, he felt, that women were not cut out to be surgeons. It was simply a law of nature, he explained to Alice, but privately he doubted his own convictions when he watched his wife stitching and dressing wounds. He admitted to himself that he could not have done better.

The crackle of rifled muskets and the blast of cannons filled the air around the camp. Within ten minutes the first of their patients was carried to them on a stretcher. He was a British captain whose face had been smashed by a musket ball. Blood streamed down his jacket as he was sat up on the operating table, once a stout wooden dining table.

Peter examined the officer's face but could only see an entry wound when he splashed water over the injury. He could see that the ball had smashed out the man's teeth.

'I think he has swallowed the ball,' Alice said, peering over Peter's shoulder.

'I think you are right,' he said, turning to Alice. 'Could you attend to his wound?'

Alice took the officer by the elbow, assisting him to a corner of the tent just as another casualty was littered in by two Sikh soldiers. This soldier had a stomach wound and was groaning in agony as he was laid out on the table. And then another wounded man was brought in, and Alice calmly began to organise that the wounded be laid out on stretchers in front of the tent. She went from one to the next with soothing words of comfort, a canteen of water, and an eye for who most needed her husband's surgical skills next. Those with lesser wounds she tended to with disinfectant and bandages.

The day drew on until eventually the roar of cannons and musketry died down as the mutineers withdrew from the battlefield. Outside Peter's surgery tent, amputated arms and legs had piled up and were covered by a swarm of fat feasting flies. The soldiers with the stomach wounds were inoperable and Peter used his meagre supply of opiates to ease their agony until death took them.

The sun was setting on the dusty horizon when Peter and Alice sat, exhausted and covered in drying blood, on a bench outside the surgical tent. Soldiers had been recruited to minister to the needs of the wounded and to carry away the bodies of the dead.

Peter took Alice's hand as they gazed with vacant eyes at the peaceful stars above. 'It will not always be like this,' he said in a tired voice. 'One day we will return to a sane life in London.'

Alice chose not to reply. She felt Peter would not understand that she felt exhilarated by her role helping the wounded. This experience was so far removed from the tedious garden parties and balls that would have made up her social calendar had she been at home in England. Here, what she did was as important as the role of any man, and it gave her life new meaning. Alice was in no hurry to return to her uneventful life in London.

SEVENTEEN

'That man who just left, Father Ogilvie, do you know him?' Charles asked.

'A Mr Wilford,' Ogilvie replied. 'A nice gentleman on a holiday visiting our parish. It was interesting that he knew of the window dedicated to your brother, Herbert.'

Charles took in the information and swore under his breath. Sir Archibald looked at his son with reprobation.

'What is it, Charles?' he asked.

'Did you not see the man who just departed?' Charles asked his father.

'No, I was talking to Father Ogilvie.'

'Well, if you had, you might have been looking at the Samuel we both once knew,' Charles said.

'Samuel is with the army in India,' Sir Archibald answered, confused at Charles' statement.

Charles thought hard for a moment. 'What if the man

you think of as Samuel is an imposter, someone who has conspired with the true Samuel to take his place in the army? Samuel always hated being in the military. What if he has found someone to take his place and complete his ten years of service so that he is able to claim his share of the Forbes estate?'

'Don't be foolish, Charles. What man would take Samuel's place and risk his life in such a manner? No, it is ridiculous. Besides, when Samuel returned to London it was obvious that he knew too much about the family's secrets to be an imposter. It would take a very intelligent man to be able to fool me.'

'You know, I have heard from officers in the regiment that the men call Captain Forbes "the Colonial". What if Samuel met a man with a striking resemblance to him whilst in New South Wales? It is possible that they made a pact to swap places. I say that the man you think is Samuel is an imposter, and that the real Samuel was just here.'

'It sounds preposterous to me,' Archibald said with a frown. 'You will need to provide evidence. Go and meet with the man who just left.'

'I will do that,' Charles said, and turned to Father Ogilvie. 'Did Mr Wilford say where he was staying in the village?'

'I am afraid not,' Ogilvie replied. 'There is only the one tavern in the village, so my guess is that is where you will find him.'

'Father, I will take our carriage and go immediately to the tavern.'

Without waiting for a reply, Charles strode to the carriage, instructing the driver to take him to the village tavern and leaving a befuddled Sir Archibald in his wake.

★

'There's no Mr Wilford staying here, Mr Forbes,' the tavern keeper answered. 'He might be staying at the boarding house on the northern side of the village, though.'

Charles hurried back to the carriage and directed the driver to the boarding house, where the landlady told him that a Mr Wilford and his travelling companion had just fifteen minutes ago paid their bill and left. She did not know where they were going and Charles guessed it was probably London. He knew there was no sense in pursuing them – in this parish there were too many byroads heavily covered with trees that could easily hide a small carriage.

Charles decided he must return immediately to London and make contact again with Mr Field. The truth about Captain Forbes was about to be uncovered and so, too, what Charles was convinced was his brother's fraudulent attempt to claim his inheritance. He smiled grimly as he returned to his coach. He was on the verge of exposing an ingenious plot to defraud the family fortune.

*

Samuel and James, both wrung out after their headlong flight from the village, arrived in Dover and went straight to the wharf where their ship was docked. To their horror there was no sign of it. The ship had sailed!

When they asked around the wharves they were informed that the vessel's repairs had been completed and it had sailed some hours earlier.

'What are we to do?' James asked in despair.

'We have no choice but to continue to London and make contact with Mr Solomon,' Samuel said, staring at the vacant space where their ticket to safety had been waiting for them.

'I had a bad feeling circumstances would not be in our

favour when you chose to visit your brother's memorial,' James said bitterly. 'Luck has not been on our side.'

'I am sorry, dear James,' Samuel said sadly. 'I suppose my stubbornness has brought us to this place. I should say that you warned me it would.'

'Too late for recriminations,' James replied in a resigned tone. 'Pray that Mr Solomon is disposed to assist us once again.'

★

It was at Ceylon that Ian's company was transferred to another steamship. His men boarded, mystified as to why they were being separated from the regiment. Only Ian, Conan and Lieutenants Woods and Sinclair knew the reason as their ship raised its anchors and steamed alone on a northerly route along the east coast of India.

The ship, disguised as a merchant vessel, was not heavily armed but did carry a detachment of Royal Marines. As the ship approached the delta of West Bengal, Ian felt it was time to gather his company of riflemen on deck to brief them on their mission. It was a viciously hot, cloudless day.

'Men, no doubt you have been wondering why you were chosen to join this ship whilst the regiment remained behind to travel to Calcutta. I can tell you now that Colonel Jenkins has chosen us for a mission to save an Indian prince of strategic importance to England. Because of the sensitive nature of what we will be doing, it has remained a secret until now. Very soon, the ship will anchor off the coast and you will be further briefed on your role in this operation. For the moment you remain with the ship under the command of Mr Woods. That is all I can tell you at present, but be assured, we will bring honour to the regiment and the Queen.'

One of the soldiers in the ranks raised his voice and called, 'Three cheers for the Colonial and the Queen.'

The cheers erupted and Ian was touched by his men's sentiments. He noted that cheers had not been offered for Colonel Jenkins.

'Sarn't Major, fall out the parade,' Ian ordered and Conan stepped forward, saluted and turned to dismiss the infantrymen back to their allocated duties.

Ian made his way to the bridge to find the ship's captain, a burly Scotsman with a gingery beard and ruddy complexion. Ian saluted the superior rank of the British naval captain.

'Well, Captain Forbes, as per orders from the Admiralty, we will drop anchor tonight about a mile from the coast. I have been able to secure all the stores you require for your mission. I will arrange to have them taken to your cabin.'

The captain ordered a young naval sailor to carry the bundle of garments to Ian's cabin, and Conan and Lieutenant Sinclair met him there.

'Gentlemen,' Ian said, pulling apart the bundle of native Indian clothing and revealing six revolvers and three wicked-looking American Bowie knives. 'This is our uniform and our weapons for the task ahead.'

Conan lifted one of the heavy Colt 1851 Navy revolvers from the bundle of clothing. 'I have always wanted one of these,' he said with pleasure.

'You get to have two of the Colts each,' Ian said. 'They are ideal for what we have to do.'

The two men picked through the clothing and dressed with advice from Lieutenant Sinclair, who was something of an authority on Indian customs, clothing, culture and language – at least from an academic point of view. Each man was able to conceal the weapons he carried, as well as the ammunition required. They then applied dark polish to their faces and hands, the only flesh exposed when the clothing was adjusted. To all intents and purposes, and if no one looked too closely, they could pass as Bengali locals. Ian had ensured that he had a good supply of rupees with him in a leather pouch.

A knock on the door of the cabin alerted Ian and his team of two that it was time to commence the dangerous mission. The Indian prince was somewhere ashore in a village not far from the coast. All Ian had was a map drawn up by a member of Outram's staff who was familiar with the area, and intelligence that was six weeks out of date. For all Ian knew, the prince and his family had been discovered by the mutineers and murdered.

They followed a marine officer above decks and were pleased to see that heavy storm clouds had masked the half-moon. Six marines sat in a landing boat waiting to ferry their passengers ashore. Ian, Conan and Lieutenant Sinclair clambered over the side on a rope ladder to join the men who would row them towards the faint lights of the coastal village a mile away. It was just after midnight and Ian experienced both exhilaration and fear for what lay ahead.

The tide was running in and the clinker-built wooden landing boat made good progress through a shallow surf, beaching on a muddy bank covered by scrub trees. In the distance they could see a fishing hut with a lantern burning in the window.

'Good luck, chaps,' the marine officer whispered. 'Better you than me.' With that, the marines hauled their boat off the mudflat, turning to row back to the ship which would withdraw out to sea beyond the horizon.

A soft wind blew through the long jagged grasses of the mudflats, and when the gentle slap of oars on water disappeared from hearing Ian realised just how alone they were in a hostile environment where wits and daring alone would have to carry the day.

'We take a chance and make contact with the natives in that hut ahead of us,' Ian said softly. 'Are there any questions?' Both men shook their heads, and the three trudged across the sticky mudflat until they came within paces of the small hut with its single door and window. Crouching behind a rack of fishing nets, Ian gave his last directions.

'We enter without displaying our pistols,' he said softly. 'Mr Sinclair will inform those inside that we mean them no harm, and request that they allow us to remain during the day. I will creep up and see who is in the hut.'

Ian made his way to the window to peer inside. Conan could see that the young officer was trembling and he recognised the fear.

'It's all right, sir,' he said. 'Captain Forbes and I have done this sort of thing before in the Crimea. The captain gets us safe home every time.'

Harry Sinclair could see Ian signal to them to approach the hut. The three stepped inside, startling a man sitting on the earthen floor mending a net. Beside him lay a woman under a blanket. Ian raised his finger to his lips to signal silence to the terrified man, now frozen with fear. Harry Sinclair said something that seemed to confuse the man, and his wife woke with a start, staring with petrified dark eyes at the three strangers.

Harry repeated his words and the man moved his head to indicate that he did not understand him. Frustrated, Harry turned to Ian.

'I'm sorry sir, but this man must speak a dialect I am not familiar with,' he apologised.

'That is not your fault, Mr Sinclair. I think I have the

universal language solution,' Ian said and reached under his baggy clothing to produce the leather purse. He retrieved a generous handful of rupees, offering them to the man, whose expression was a mixture of puzzlement and avarice. 'For you,' Ian said, pressing the coins into the man's hand. The universal language appeared to work as they could see some of the fear evaporate and composure return.

The man turned to his wife and said something.

'I think I understood some of his words,' Harry said triumphantly. 'I think he said we are crazy bandits who give away money rather than steal it!'

'See if you can tell them that we mean them no harm – unless they tell others that we are here. If they betray us, they will be killed,' Ian said.

Harry was able to get the message across and the man knelt, grabbing Harry's hands and babbling his gratitude.

Satisfied, Ian turned to Conan and Harry. 'We remain inside this hut until night comes again, and when it does, we set out on the next leg of our journey. According to the orders I received, we should meet a European contact in the next village who appears to have some protection against the local mutineers.'

While they waited out the day, the man left the hut and returned with water and food for his uninvited guests, reassuring Harry that he had informed no one of their presence.

The men spent the day cleaning their revolvers, ensuring that the powder loaded in the chambers was dry and that the fulminate percussion caps were secured on the nipples at the rear of each loaded chamber.

Ian had learned from the Bengali fisherman that the next leg of the mission would take them across a plain past a few scattered mud huts to a small village. They would travel that night knowing time was critical as the naval ship would return in forty-eight hours, sending a boat ashore under the cover of darkness to pick them up from the mudflats.

Evening was coming to the tropics, and as Ian prepared to move out he was suddenly alert to the noise of a party of men moving in their direction. Ian peeked out through a crack in the wall and felt his heart skip a beat. He could see a group of ten well-armed men moving towards them. Had they been betrayed?

EIGHTEEN

'What do we do, sir?' Harry asked.

'This reminds me of an incident when we were in the Crimea,' Conan said with a grim smile, unholstering his pistols.

'Ask the fisherman if he knows who the men are, Mr Sinclair,' Ian said.

Harry turned to the terrified fisherman and spoke with him.

'He says the men are bandits well known on this part of the coast. They take what they want – and that includes the women.'

'So they are not sepoy rebels,' Ian said. 'We have only one choice and that is to kill them all and let none get away. We have surprise and firepower on our side.'

'Do you mean we fight them?' Harry asked, open-mouthed.

'I strongly suggest you unholster your pistols, Mr Sinclair, and prepare to use them,' Ian said, pulling back the hammer of his Colts. 'We burst out on my order and start shooting as fast as we can until they are all dead. Any questions?'

The husband and wife clung together, huddled in the corner of the hut with absolute fear written on their faces. Ian took another peek at the approaching party of bandits, noting that they were armed with ancient muskets and long knives. They appeared relaxed and were even joking together as they came within ten paces of the hut. One of the men called out, and Ian guessed that he was the leader of the party.

'He is calling to the fisherman to come out with his wife,' Harry whispered, his trembling hands gripping his pistols.

'Get ready,' Ian said softly. 'Now!'

Ian was the first to burst out from behind the flimsy door, firing as he did so. Conan quickly followed, and behind him, Harry. Ian's first round brought down the bandit who had called out, and the man fell backwards as the .36 calibre lead ball took him in the chest. Such was the surprise of the attack that the rest of the party were momentarily frozen in their confusion, and Conan's rounds caused others to topple as each ball found a target. Only one man was able to raise his musket and fire wildly. A round from Harry took him out, and within seconds the sandy stretch in front of the hut was covered in bodies. Satisfied that the ten men were dead, Ian quickly reloaded, as did Conan.

'Time for us to get moving,' Ian said as the fisherman tumbled from the hut to stare wide-eyed at the mass of bodies in front of his hut. He spoke rapidly to Harry.

'What is he saying?' Ian asked.

'He is thanking us for saving him and his wife, and he says he will tell anyone who asks how they were killed that it was another bandit gang known in this district.'

The fisherman grasped Ian's knees, tears in his eyes, babbling his thanks, and Ian felt that the man could be trusted to keep their secret.

The trio checked their clothing and faces to make sure their disguise still held, then used the falling darkness to follow their course to a village a couple of miles away. They were to make contact at a specific house at the edge of the town marked with a painted red crescent on the door. Ian had Conan and Harry run for a while, then walk, followed by another run to put distance between themselves and the coast.

After a couple of exhausting hours he ordered a stop two hundred yards short of the village. They slumped to the grassy earth, getting their breathing under control. Each man took a long swig of water from his canteen, and after a few minutes Ian turned to Conan and Harry. 'I will leave you two here and reconnoitre the village. If I don't return, you are to make your way back to the coast and await the navy's pick-up.'

Harry and Conan accepted the order and Ian stood and walked towards the village.

'We had a close call back there,' Harry said. 'We were lucky to survive.'

'Luck is when you are charging the enemy across no-man's-land,' Conan said. 'Musket balls and grapeshot do not discriminate. At the hut, Captain Forbes knew exactly what he was doing and he decided the odds were on our side.'

'My brother always spoke highly of Captain Forbes,' said Harry. 'Said that he was born to be a soldier.'

'If you only knew,' Conan chuckled. 'There is more to Captain Forbes than any man will really know.'

They peered into the night until the darkness completely swallowed the figure of Ian Steele making his way cautiously into the village.

★

Far away in England Charles Forbes was once again in the private investigator's office.

'The man that I wish to meet is now going under another name,' Charles said. 'I would presume that this Mr Ian Steele has had help to forge a new identity.'

'Quite so,' Field answered. 'Whoever your man is, he must have contacts in London who have been helping him.'

'The man I seek I suspect to be my half-brother, Samuel, using the fictitious name of Ian Steele or John Wilford. It is vital that I confront him.'

'May I ask why?' Field asked.

'I think Samuel has hired a man to substitute for him in my grandfather's regiment. By doing so, and if this man completes ten years' service, Samuel will be able to claim his equal share of the family estates. As you can gather, he is doing this by fraudulent means, and if I can prove this he will no longer have a claim.'

'Ah, money,' Field said. 'One of the principal reasons for murder – along with love and revenge. I pray that you do not wish to do your half-brother any mischief when we find him.'

'Nothing of that nature will be necessary,' Charles said. 'Samuel will be exposed before the law and the matter of his inheritance curtailed.'

'That is good because I will not be party to anything unlawful. I know of a forger who may have assisted this man.'

'Who might that be?' Charles asked.

'A fellow by the name of Ikey Solomon. Our paths crossed when I was with the police. He has a somewhat fearsome reputation in the city's underworld and it is not wise to get on the wrong side of him. He has an office not far from here, and for a few pounds might be willing to discuss the matter with us.'

'I am prepared to pay if you think he could help us,' Charles said.

'If that is so, we might be able to meet with him now if that is convenient to you,' Field said and Charles agreed.

The office was within walking distance and the two men found themselves confronted by a burly and dangerous-looking man at the entrance to the building.

'Hello, Egbert,' Field said. 'I see that you are still working for Ikey.'

'Mr Field,' Egbert said with a note of respect. 'What brings you here?'

'I have a financial matter to discuss with Mr Solomon,' Field said. 'If you would do me the courtesy of taking me to him.'

Egbert told them to wait, then after a couple of minutes returned to usher them inside. It was obvious that the former detective inspector still had a reputation amongst London's underworld.

Egbert knocked on a door and a voice bade them enter.

Field stepped inside first, followed by Charles and Egbert.

Ikey did not bother to rise from behind his desk. 'Detective Inspector, a pleasure, I am sure, that you should visit my humble establishment. What can I do for you?'

Although he had not been offered a chair, Field found one, sat down and placed his hat on his lap. 'Ikey, I would like to introduce you to Mr Charles Forbes. He has a proposition for you that comes with a generous financial reward.'

'Charles Forbes,' Ikey said. 'Are you any relation to Captain Samuel Forbes?'

'Do you know my brother?' Charles asked, surprised that the Jewish businessman with the dangerous reputation would know Samuel, as Ikey belonged to a class of people no member of the Forbes family ought to mix with.

'I do. A fine gentleman.'

'What if I said that the man you think is my brother, Samuel Forbes, is an imposter?' Charles said, and noticed Ikey Solomon shift in his chair.

'I am sure you must be mistaken, Mr Forbes,' Ikey replied mildly.

'The brother I knew was a shy dreamer who desired a life as a poet. Does that sound like the man you know as Captain Forbes?'

Ikey did not respond to the question but leaned forward towards Charles. 'I was informed that you came here with an offer to pay me generously for my services,' he said. 'Tell me what you want.'

'We want to know if any of your acquaintances have been involved in forging identity documents for one John Wilford,' Field said. 'If you do, Mr Forbes will pay for that information.'

'Forgery is a serious crime, as you well know, Mr Field,' Ikey said. 'I am an honest businessman.'

'Mr Forbes is prepared to pay well,' Field reminded him. 'I am sure as a businessman in this part of the city you must have heard something about such criminal people.'

'I am sorry, Mr Forbes,' Ikey said. 'I cannot help you. Mr Field has the wrong man for such information.'

Field rose from his chair, replaced his top hat and gestured to Charles to follow him.

'We will bid you a good day, Mr Solomon,' Field said,

walking to the door with Charles in tow. 'If you do come across such intelligence in the future, I am sure Mr Forbes' offer will still stand.'

Ikey did not get up as the two men left his office. He frowned. Was the man he knew as Captain Samuel Forbes an imposter? If so, he had allowed his one and only precious daughter to be escorted to a ball by the man. It was time to make his own enquiries into Captain Samuel Forbes – whoever he was.

★

On the street, a small shower promised to become a heavy downfall. Charles and Field hurried back to the private investigator's office.

'Well, that proved to be fruitless,' Charles said irritably.

'I would not be so sure of that,' Field said. 'My copper instincts tell me that it is Ikey who is helping your brother, and who is in contact with the man you consider a charlatan. We learned all that without you having to spend a penny of any reward. At least I have a point to work from, but I must caution you, Mr Forbes, it will be expensive to bring to heel the two you believe are defrauding your family.'

'Money is not a consideration, Mr Field. The honour of the Forbes name is at stake,' Charles said in the most righteous tone he could muster.

'Ah, yes, family honour,' Field echoed with a knowing smirk.

★

Ian could hear the occasional barking of the village dogs that prowled the empty streets and lanes. He crouched, counting the buildings as per the sketch map he carried, until he settled on one that bordered the flat grass-covered plain from which he was making his observations. Amongst Ian's briefing was the information that his contact was a former Russian army officer. Ian was baffled by this as it was well known that the Tsar of Russia had ambitions to control the Indian subcontinent. Why would a former Russian army officer be assisting the British? Ian shrugged and crept forward to the mud-walled house, pistols in hands, to see the red crescent sign on the door.

Very gently he eased open the door, but it still creaked on it rusty hinges. Every nerve in his body was on edge.

'Hail Caesar,' Ian said, the code to be used to identify himself to the contact.

'*Et tu, Brute*,' a voice said softly from within the darkness of the tiny house.

Satisfied at the response, Ian stepped inside the hut, pistols raised. A light flared from a lantern. It took a few seconds for his sight to adjust and when it did he found himself mere paces from the Russian, who was pointing a British-manufactured revolver straight at him. The two men stared into each other's faces and the shock was mutual.

'You!' Ian hissed.

The Russian nodded incredulously.

NINETEEN

By the dim light of the lantern the two men faced each other, pistols drawn.

'I think I wished you well the last time we faced each other in the Crimea,' the tall, handsome man said with a slow smile, lowering his revolver. 'It is like an act of God's humour that we should meet again under these circumstances.'

Ian lowered his guns. 'I must apologise but I have forgotten your name since we met during that truce,' he said. 'I am Captain Samuel Forbes of Her Majesty's London Regiment.'

'I remember your name, Captain Forbes. I am Count Nikolai Kasatkin, formerly of the Tsar's army,' the Russian said without extending his hand. 'I presume by the code you gave that you are on a mission to retrieve the Khan and his family.'

'I am,' Ian said. 'The rest of the rescue party is a short distance from here, but first I am curious as to why a representative of the Tsar should be found in India when we well know that the Tsar has ambitions for this part of Her Majesty's Empire.'

'Good question, Captain Forbes, and I think it is worth an honest answer. I am working for the British Foreign Office, not for the Tsar. My allegiance has changed for personal reasons. One might say that an indiscretion in Moscow is not forgotten when one is a Jew, and as far as the Tsar's government is concerned, I am here to negotiate a deal with the Khan for a precious metal both Russia and England need for waging war.'

'What metal?' Ian asked.

'Lead,' Nikolai replied. 'The Khan has maps to potential rich lodes of lead in his district and is prepared to sell to us at a reasonable price. I was selected by my former masters to make contact as I speak the Indian language. It gave me the opportunity to correspond with friends in England I knew as a young student at Oxford. That was before we faced each other in that terrible war that cost us the Crimea.'

'I cannot see how an officer of the Tsar would turn traitor,' Ian said.

'I am a Russian but I am also a Jew, and my people are being persecuted in Russia. I have been granted British sanctuary on the condition that I use my position to encourage the Khan to go with us to England, where he can be convinced to turn over his mining rights to the East India Company. It is really the board of the East India Company that I deal with in this matter.'

'Never let a little mutiny get in the way of business,' Ian said with a wry smile. 'So, you and I find ourselves in this place at this time to assist the Company in rescuing a future trading partner.'

'It seems so,' the Russian count replied with a faint smile. 'Upon a successful outcome to our mutual mission I will able to purchase property discreetly through contacts in the London Jewish community.'

'One of those contacts would not be a man by the name of Ikey Solomon, would it?' Ian said on a hunch, and saw utter surprise cross the Russian's face.

'How do you know Ikey Solomon?' he asked.

'I have had dealings with the man in the past,' Ian replied.

'I have never met him,' Nikolai said. 'Is he a good man?'

'He is – if you don't cross him,' Ian said. 'Now, I will signal to my men to join us.' Ian stepped outside with the lantern and waved it gently and was soon joined by Conan and Harry.

They stepped inside the hut and eyed the tall stranger with suspicion.

'Count Kasatkin, this is Sergeant Major Curry and Lieutenant Sinclair, both of my company.'

'It is just the three of you,' Nikolai said, shaking his head. 'I was expecting at least a regiment to carry out the task of rescuing the Khan and his family.'

'You were allocated a company of my infantrymen but I decided that it was more discreet to use only the three of us, considering that this can be considered hostile territory and a large force of red-coated infantry would have drawn more attention than would be comfortable.'

For a moment the Russian pondered on Ian's choice. 'Probably a wise tactical decision,' he finally replied. 'I have been able to remain alive amongst the population because some of the leaders of the mutiny in this area believe I am here working for the Tsar to supply them with arms and ammunition. So for the moment I am safe, but I fear the mutiny leaders grow suspicious as I have not been able to fulfil my promise to provide arms. They watch me closely, but at night they prefer to remain at their camp outside the village.'

'Sir, what is going on?' Harry asked, confused that a Russian would be in league with them.

'Trust me, this man has his reasons to be on our side,' Ian said. 'If not, we will kill him.'

The count raised his eyebrows but smiled grimly. 'Another sound tactical decision, Captain Forbes,' he said, producing a bottle of clear liquid. 'Vodka,' he added, taking a swig, and handing it to Ian. 'We toast the success of our mission.' When Ian had taken a swig, he handed it to Conan and then on to Harry.

When the bottle was returned to Nikolai he raised it. 'Another toast to the friends who lie in the earth of the Crimea – Russian, British – and maybe even the French.'

The men drank another toast and then Nikolai placed the bottle on a rickety table. The room was bare: a wooden table, chair and what looked like a bed on the floor. It smelled of cattle dung, smoke and aromatic spices. It had only one entrance and a small open window for ventilation.

The count laid a small sheet of crumpled paper on the table and pulled the lantern closer. The rescue party gathered around the sketch map of the village.

'The Khan is living under the disguise of a Bengali merchant in this house,' the Russian said, pointing to a place on the map. Ian could see that it was on the other side of the village, and marked nearby was the mutineers' camp. 'I have made contact with him under the guise of purchasing goods, and he is aware that we will be coming for him at any moment. We reach him and take him, his wife and young son with us to the rendezvous point I presume you have established, Captain Forbes.'

'We have a place established on the coast and a plan for evacuation,' Ian said, gazing at the map and taking in all the places marked on it.

'Given the way you are disguised, we should not attract undue attention in the village,' Nikolai said.

Ian turned to Conan and Harry. He could see the fear on the young officer's face. 'Are you up to this, Mr Sinclair?' Ian asked.

'I am, sir,' Harry answered. 'But I must admit that I am a little fearful.'

'Good,' Ian said. 'As Sarn't Major Curry will tell you, he felt the same way when he won his Victoria Cross.' He grinned. 'It is time to go, so check your arms.'

The four men stepped cautiously from the hut. There was no moon and the village was silent, with the exception of a baby wailing a short distance away and a mother softly crooning to her child. Ian prayed that nothing would go wrong as they filed down a narrow street, revolvers at their sides.

★

Alice sat by Peter's bed, swabbing his brow with a damp, cool cloth. The fever racked his body and he glistened with sweat. Outside their tent before the walls of Delhi, she could hear the crash of cannon and the rattle of rifle and musket fire in the distance. Peter had come down with a fever earlier in the day, and was delirious before night had fallen. From all that she had learned, Alice suspected he did not have cholera but some other form of illness. Whatever it was, it caused him to alternately shake as if freezing and sweat and heat up as if on fire. Alice prayed that the fever would break and her beloved husband would recover.

The servant girl hovered at the edge of the bed, and Alice instructed her to fetch more clean water. The girl hurried away and when she returned Alice looked up to see a blood-stained Indian soldier of the Company with her.

'What is it?' Alice asked.

'Missus Alice,' the soldier said. 'We need the doctor master. Many wounded.'

Alice glanced down at Peter, who was tossing and turning deliriously. 'The doctor is not well,' she said.

'Please, missus doctor,' the blood-soaked soldier said. 'We need doctor. All doctors busy.'

Alice stood from her chair beside the bed and handed the wet cloth to the servant girl. 'Keep washing down the master.' The girl nodded her understanding. 'I will go with you, soldier,' Alice said and saw the expression of relief on the man's bearded face.

They crossed a pathway between the tents until they came to Peter's field surgery. Already Alice could see the red-coated soldiers lying on litters outside the tent, whilst other soldiers attempted to tend to them with water canteens and encouraging words. They were all Sikh and Gurkha soldiers who had manned the lines against the enemy pouring out from the city walls in another attempt to destroy the British camp.

Alice could hear a soldier crying out in his agony, and she pushed aside the tent flaps to find a young Sikh soldier laid out on the improvised operating table. She could see that the bottom half of his leg had been shattered, a bone protruding as blood welled from the wound. Two of his comrades were holding him down and they looked to Alice when she entered. From all she had witnessed working alongside Peter, she knew that the leg must be amputated. For a moment she stared at the young man, realising that he would die unless the injury was treated.

The pleading look from the men who were holding down their comrade was enough to convince Alice she had no other choice. She must do something. She looked to Peter's tools of surgery. She remembered exactly how he went about amputations.

'Hold him down hard,' she commanded, then turned to the soldier who had fetched her. 'You, hold his leg.'

Alice took a clamp and affixed it above the wound to stem the flow of blood. Then she picked up the razor-sharp crescent-shaped cutting blade and leaned over the soldier.

'Hold him!' she said loudly in an attempt to stem her own fear.

Alice began cutting and the wounded soldier arched in his pain. As if in a terrible dream she continued with the operation, hardly aware of the sound of the leg thumping onto the earthen floor after she had used the tenon saw to cut through the bone. Within minutes it was all over and the man was taken off the table to be placed on a litter outside the tent.

Alice reviewed each wounded man who was placed on the table. She knew there was nothing that could be done for the stomach or head wounds. She instructed the men who had remained after the first amputation to have these cases taken outside, to a separate tent, and asked for them to be tended until their agony was finally over. From some of the wounds she was able to retrieve musket balls and then quickly stitch the flesh and apply antiseptic solution. Before she finished, she carried out two more amputations. It felt to her that she almost always knew exactly what she was supposed to do, and that her hours of carefully observing

Peter at work had paid off. She had been able to detach herself mentally from the awful work of cutting, sawing and stitching throughout the night. She had had no time to think about Peter's condition, and she wondered now whether he had recovered or, God forbid, grown worse.

Exhausted physically and emotionally, and soaked in blood, Alice stepped out of the tent to see the first rays of the sun on the horizon. Her hands were trembling now but they had been steady and certain during those terrible hours of surgery. Around her were the litters waiting to be carried to the recovery tent. A wounded soldier who had only required her to stitch his bayonet wound stood nearby and went to her, falling to his knees and taking her hands in his own. He said something Alice could not understand, but his gesture said it all. He was thanking her for helping him, for helping them all. She smiled weakly down at him in her own appreciation for what she had done that night under the light of a single lantern.

'Good God!' a voice boomed, and Alice recognised it as one of Peter's fellow army surgeons. 'Your husband has done a fine job with the amputations,' he said as he strode towards her. 'I have just seen them come into the hospital tent. Where is Dr Campbell?'

'I am afraid that my husband is not here,' Alice said, pushing back her hair with a bloody hand. 'He is in our tent with a fever.'

'But, but . . . who operated on the Sikhs who were brought to his surgical tent?' asked the surgeon, confused, looking around as if expecting to see another doctor step forward.

'I did,' Alice answered defiantly. 'It was either that or let them die.'

For a moment the British army surgeon simply gaped at

her as if she was something from an alien world. 'Damn it, Mrs Campbell, please do not jest. Who really carried out the surgery?'

'As I said, Doctor, I did,' Alice answered.

'But you are not a qualified surgeon,' the man said. 'You are a woman.'

'Pure necessity, Doctor,' Alice said, standing her ground. 'Now, I need to wash and change my clothes.' She walked away and the surgeon stared after her in utter disbelief.

When Alice returned to her tent she saw with joy that Peter was sitting up on the edge of the bed. He still looked pale and weak, but he smiled at her – until he saw the blood.

'God almighty!' he exclaimed in shock. 'Are you hurt?' He rose shakily to his feet to take his wife in his arms.

'It is not my blood, my love,' Alice said. 'It is the blood of the men whose limbs I amputated during the last few hours.'

Peter sat back down hard on the bed, almost faint at her statement so casually delivered.

TWENTY

The four men moved cautiously through the village, ever aware of how important it was to reach the coast before first light.

'How far?' Ian whispered to Nikolai, who was leading their party.

'Just around the corner of this street,' he answered.

They turned the corner, and Ian felt his heart skip a beat. He could see two armed men standing by the house Nikolai identified as the Khan's residence. He thought from the arms they carried and the uniforms they wore that they were probably mutineers from the nearby camp.

'What do we do?' Harry whispered.

'We get rid of them,' Ian replied.

'But if we shoot them, it will alert the camp nearby,' Harry said.

'We don't shoot them,' Ian replied, drawing his razor-sharp

Bowie knife from under his clothing. 'We cut their throats.' He could see the young officer recoil at the idea.

Conan slid out his knife, waiting for Ian's instructions.

'I will distract the men,' Nikolai said, 'then you can dispatch them.'

Nikolai stepped out and walked towards the two men, who were engaged in conversation. As he emerged from the shadows the two former sepoys raised their rifled muskets to challenge him. Nikolai said something in their language and there was a small burst of laughter from the two armed men. It was obvious that they knew him, and he was able to position himself so that they turned their backs to the waiting assassins. Ian and Conan moved forward stealthily in the dark and were on the two guards before they could react. Ian placed his hand over his man's mouth and nose and brought his knife blade across his throat. The blade bit, and the man hardly had time to struggle before Ian could feel the hot blood splashing his arm. Conan had carried out a similar manoeuvre on his selected target. When the bodies ceased twitching, they let go of the dead men, who crumpled at their feet.

'What do we do with them?' Nikolai asked.

'We drag them inside the Khan's house so they are out of sight. Hopefully they won't be missed for a while, which will give us a chance to put distance between us and the mutineers.'

Nikolai knocked loudly on the door to attract the attention of those inside.

A candle flared and the door opened cautiously. Then it was opened wide and the three men tumbled through with Harry hurrying across to the house to join them. In the candlelight Ian could see that this house was relatively comfortable and clean, with ornate rugs on the floor. He could see the horrified expression on the face of a pretty young woman clutching a boy to her, and Ian realised that both he and Conan were soaked in blood.

'This is the Khan,' Nikolai said, introducing a tall and handsome young man with a regal bearing. 'This is Captain Forbes of the British army. He is here to get us to the coast and onto a British warship.'

'Then we must go quickly,' the prince said. 'We already have our few possessions packed.'

The Khan threw two bags on his shoulders and said something to his wife, who picked up a couple of smaller bags. With the small family outside, Harry and Conan dragged the bodies of the mutineers into the house and shut the front door on them.

'Let's go,' Ian said, withdrawing his two Colts in case they had to shoot their way out of the village. He was pleased to note that the residents appeared to be asleep and undisturbed by their activities.

They hurried through the streets and alleyways in the pitch dark until they came to the grassy plain on the edge of town. They would be walking towards the rising sun. Ian took the lead, navigating with his compass. By sunrise they were on the outskirts of the fishing village and Ian supervised positions in a ditch for them to hide. All they had to do now was wait till evening when the warship would stream into the coast and retrieve them.

*

'I have just come from a meeting with my commanding officer,' Major Scott Campbell said, pacing the small space of the tent his brother shared with his wife. Alice was currently absent from their quarters, tending to sick and wounded soldiers at the hospital tent. 'Alice has caused somewhat of a furore.'

'I half expected that,' Peter sighed as he filled his pipe with a plug of tobacco. 'I have returned from examining the men she operated on and, without exception, they are all recovering well.'

'But Alice acted as a surgeon without any qualification to do so,' Scott exploded. 'She is a woman. What if she had botched the amputations?'

'I have been a surgeon for many years past and cannot even remember how many limbs I have removed. What I saw of her work was as good as any qualified surgeon I know, maybe better. God knows how she was able to do what she did. Call it a miracle or, God forbid, admit that women are able to carry out the tasks of a surgeon. In a sense, Alice has been learning the art of amputation from assisting me. I do not say that qualifies her to be a surgeon, but with me bedridden with fever that night, I feel she had no other choice. Those men she operated on are still alive today thanks to her intervention – qualified or not.'

Scott ceased pacing and rubbed his brow in frustration. 'I accept what you are saying is true, brother. Alice is truly a remarkable woman, but the instruction from my commanding officer is that what she did will never happen again. I need your word Alice will never pick up an operating saw again. Give me your word and I will relay that to my commanding officer so that the matter is taken no further.'

'I will promise that Alice will not carry out any further surgical duties – other than assisting me during operations as a nurse would,' Peter said reluctantly.

Scott nodded, then bid his brother a good morning and left the tent. He was startled to see Alice standing outside and he muttered a hasty greeting and strode off.

Alice stepped into the tent.

'I have the feeling from your annoyed expression you heard the conversation with my brother,' Peter said wearily.

'I did,' Alice replied angrily. 'How stupid you men are!' she exploded. 'Would it have been preferable to have let one of the Sikh soldiers chop off limbs simply because he was a man? Or perhaps I should have left those men to die even though I had the skills to save them?'

'I am very proud of the work you did,' Peter said, walking to Alice and embracing her. Any doubts he had had that women were capable of being surgeons had long been dispelled. 'But we live in an age that cannot accept that a woman such as yourself is as capable as any one of us men. So for the moment I have had to promise the army hierarchy that you will not indulge in surgical procedures again.'

'Is stitching wounds a surgical procedure?' Alice asked sweetly.

'Well, technically, yes,' he replied. 'But if you do it out of my sight, I cannot chastise you for it, can I?' Peter grinned, knowing that the woman in his arms was incapable of following the rules of Queen Victoria's England.

★

The sun blazed down on the ditch but Ian was satisfied his party was hidden from the sight of the people in the coastal fishing village. The last of the water in the canteens had been drunk, and neither Ian nor his men had had much sleep since they had stepped ashore for the rescue mission. They dozed intermittently, gazing up at the blue skies now filling with great billowing thunderhead clouds.

Ian found himself sitting beside the Indian prince, who was staring across the shimmer of heat just above the tops of the long dry grass.

'I am curious as to why you would be fleeing your

home,' Ian said. 'I imagine you had a palace like most of the local royalty.'

The Khan turned to look at Ian. 'I have, and as soon as this mutiny is suppressed I will return to it.'

'According to the count you were about to negotiate a contract to sell lead to the Russians. Why would you wish to seek sanctuary in England?'

'I never considered trading with the Russians. The count approached me with the offer and I refused. It was then that he revealed himself to be an agent for the British. He explained that he had left Moscow under the guise of making a deal with me. He wanted to test my loyalty to the Queen, our Empress, and thanks to the wise hand of Allah, may His Name be blessed, I was able to prove my faith in the East India Company. At the same time the Sikhs in my realm wanted me dead. The count was able to put together a plan to smuggle myself and my family to a safehouse, which is where you found us. He has made contact with your General Outram to get us to England where I will sign my lead rights over to the East India Company. A small cost to save my firstborn son and the future heir to my kingdom.'

'You must be worth your weight in lead,' Ian grinned.

The Khan smiled at Ian's joke. 'You appear to be a very competent British officer,' he said. 'When I get my land back, I would like you to be a guest at my palace.'

Ian was touched by the offer and felt a great respect for the Indian prince. 'I would be honoured,' he said.

'I have met many remarkable English people,' the Khan continued. 'I recently met an Englishwoman who shot one of our fierce Bengal tigers as it was about to attack her. She has the spirit of the goddess Kali in her. Mrs Alice Campbell.'

Ian looked sharply at the Khan. 'Her husband's first

name is Peter,' he said, and now it was the Khan's turn to look surprised.

'Do you know Mrs Campbell?' he asked.

'She is my sister,' Ian replied. 'Do you know where Alice and her husband are now?'

'They travelled to Meerut with the doctor's brother, Major Campbell. That is all I know. I can see that Allah moves in mysterious ways and has guided my family under your protection.'

Ian knew that a bloody mutiny had occurred at Meerut and many Europeans had been slaughtered. He felt sick to the stomach.

The Khan saw Ian's stricken expression. 'My friend, I would not fear for the fate of your sister. She has the spirit of the tiger in her and no enemy can hurt her. You will meet with her again.'

Ian nodded his appreciation but still felt sick with apprehension.

'Sir!'

Ian turned to Harry who was peering above the top of the long grass. 'Yes, Mr Sinclair, what is it?'

'Sir, I can see a large cloud of dust on the horizon, as if raised by a number of horses.'

Ian scrambled to his knees and saw the dust rising slowly in the hot, humid air. He calculated the distance to be about a mile from their present position, and from his long experience calculating numbers of troops he guessed a party of at least fifty men on horseback.

Conan was beside Ian in an instant. 'Do you think it is the men from the village camp?' he asked anxiously.

'Could be,' Ian said, his mind already racing to find a plan of action. 'They will be on us within the next half-hour. I doubt this ditch will conceal us from them.'

'We are outnumbered and outgunned,' Nikolai said grimly.

Ian sighed and sat back down in the ditch. 'Our options are limited,' he said. 'We either stand and fight, which will mean they eventually overwhelm us. Or we surrender and put our trust in being taken prisoner. I doubt that is really an option because of what will be a slow death at their hands. There is no sense retreating to the mudflats when we don't expect to see our fellows until dusk.'

'We have faced worse odds before,' Conan said. 'Remember how we were trapped in that villa in the Crimea and it looked impossible that we would get out alive?'

Ian remembered, appreciating Conan's faith in his ability to find a solution to this dire situation.

'Mr Sinclair, you and the count must escort the Khan and his family back to the fishing village and hide until the retrieval boat arrives.' Ian turned to Conan. 'I am afraid you and I will have to remain here in the ditch and put up a show to delay whoever is coming our way.'

'That is as good as suicide, sir,' Harry protested. 'It should be me who remains to delay the enemy, not Sergeant Major Curry.'

'You obey orders, Mr Sinclair,' Ian said firmly. 'Your duty is to ensure our guests leave the country safely and our mission is completed.'

'Sir, I –' Sinclair began.

'Do it now, Mr Sinclair,' Ian commanded.

'I will remain with you, Captain Forbes,' Nikolai said quietly. 'But I will trade my pistol for Mr Sinclair's two Colts. I am sure that Mr Sinclair, as one of your officers, is more than capable of escorting the Khan and his family to safety.'

Ian frowned at the Russian. 'It is not necessary to remain,' he said. 'There is no sense in us all getting killed.'

'I was at the Redan the day you British stormed it and I thought that was to be my last day on this earth,' Nikolai said. 'Maybe we will triumph today. It could not be as bad as those final weeks at Sebastopol.'

'Sarn't Major Curry and I were also at the Redan,' Ian said with a tone of respect. 'We all survived those terrible days, so you may be right, Count Kasatkin.'

Ian extended his hand and the Russian took it.

'Go, Mr Sinclair, and raise a tankard to us if we don't make it,' Ian said, and the young British officer scrambled with the Khan and his family from the ditch, looking back once to see the three remaining men facing the long rows of mounted figures that could be discerned ahead of the dust cloud.

Ian checked his pistols, as did Conan and Nikolai.

'What I would give for my old Enfield right now,' Conan grumbled. 'I could be picking off the bastards long before they reached us.'

Ian could now see the figures on horseback, noting that they appeared to be cavalry.

'We have to wait until they are almost on top of us before we commence firing,' Ian said. 'That will give us the best chance to make every shot count and maybe make them think twice. We will spread out. A distance of around ten yards apart to give us more frontage.'

Conan extended his hand. 'Ian,' he said. 'We have come a long way from the bush of New South Wales, and in the short time we have served together, it has been an honour.'

Ian accepted the gesture, growling, 'We're not dead yet, Curry.' Deep in his heart Ian knew that was not true, as the extended line of enemy cavalry came close enough that he could see their bearded faces and the sun shining on their sabre blades. They were dead men for sure.

TWENTY-ONE

The three men crouched in the ditch as the cavalry approached at a steady pace. Ian could see that they were well trained, and a half-dozen rode ahead of the main body as a screen. He knew they might prevail for a short time, but soon enough the enemy would outflank them and a slashing blade would end their lives.

'Wait until they are almost on top of us before firing,' Ian called as a reminder.

Each man, armed with two Colt pistols chambered for six rounds, could certainly provide a devastating initial output of firepower.

Then the advancing six men on horseback were only ten paces away. Ian could see that they were not expecting any resistance from the party as their sabres were still sheathed.

'Now!'

The three men rose from the ditch, startling the enemy cavalrymen. Ian levelled his pistol and fired two shots at the horseman nearest him. He toppled from his horse, which reared, leaping the ditch to gallop riderless towards the fishing village. Ian quickly switched his aim to one of the enemy desperately scrabbling for his sword, but another two well-aimed shots brought him down.

From the corner of his eye, Ian could see that Nikolai and Conan were having the same success and only one of the riders was able to wheel about, galloping back to the main body of enemy some three hundred yards away.

Ian noticed Conan standing over one of the men he had shot. He bent down and pulled off an Enfield rifled musket the man had slung across his back. It did not have a bayonet but Conan ripped the spare ammunition from the dead body.

'Now I will teach the buggers a lesson in marksmanship,' Conan said.

Nikolai recovered a sabre, and Ian immediately reloaded as he watched the cavalrymen milling about in the distance. A flash of lightning startled the three men, and Ian immediately thought that the mutineers must have a cannon. But fat droplets from the darkening sky alerted him to the fact that a heavy storm was closing in on them.

'Brings back memories,' Conan muttered to Ian as he levelled the Enfield on the distant cavalry formation.

'Can you make out the leader?' Ian asked, squatting beside Conan as the rain began to fall.

'I think so,' Conan said, squinting down the sights and steadying his aim. He squeezed the trigger and a second later they had the satisfaction of seeing a rider fall from his horse. It seemed to unsettle their enemy, who withdrew a couple of hundred yards.

'Damn!' Conan swore. 'I missed the bugger – I was aiming for the man next to him.'

'It does not matter,' Ian said with his hand on Conan's shoulder. 'You have made them think about withdrawing out of range and now we have a little time as they get organised.'

'What do you think will be their next move?' Conan asked, already reloading the rifled musket.

'As they appear to be trained cavalrymen, I suspect that they will attempt to flank us. Maybe even launch a frontal attack to distract us as they manoeuvre to the flanks. Whatever they do, I doubt we will be able to hold them off for long,' Ian answered grimly.

Ian's prediction proved correct as the three defenders watched the formation split into three parts. Two large parties wheeled away from the centre to ride in a long arc on either side of the ditch. Nikolai stuck the blade of his captured sword in the earth, waiting with his twin revolvers, whilst Conan levelled the deadly rifled musket on another target. The rain was increasing in its ferocity but it would not save them from a swinging sabre when the enemy finally charged the ditch again. Ian knew that there were no such things as miracles and he wondered how he would die – by bullet or sword. His greatest regret was that he would not have the opportunity in this life to be with Ella Solomon again.

★

Five boats arrived early on the mudflats, three manned by Royal Marines and two loaded with a small group of men from Ian's company. Harry Sinclair stood beside the Khan and his family, waving frantically in the rain. He was seen and the boats beached on the mudflats nearby. Harry recognised Lieutenant Ross Woods and Sergeant Owen Williams as they disembarked from one of the boats.

'Good to see you, old chap,' Ross said when Sinclair approached him with the Khan and his family. 'It appears that you were successful in your mission.'

'There is not much time. We have to go back and fetch Captain Forbes,' Harry said.

A Royal Marine captain approached. 'Time to go, gentlemen,' he commanded.

'Sir, my commanding officer and the company sergeant major are just a few hundred yards behind this cluster of fishing huts. They are pinned down by a force of around fifty sepoy cavalry,' Harry said. 'We need your men to assist us in getting Captain Forbes back to the ship.'

'I am sorry, Mr Sinclair, but my orders are to rescue our esteemed guest, not to chase after anyone left behind. It is too risky.'

'Sir,' Harry pleaded, 'they are close by. I request that I take command of the men of our company who are with you.'

'My orders instruct me to take our guests aboard so that we can steam away before the rains become heavier. That is why we are early,' the marine captain reiterated. 'I am sorry, Mr Sinclair.'

'I have temporary command of the company,' Ross intervened, 'and my orders are that we go in search of Captain Forbes.'

'You will do so on your own, as my orders are that we return to the ship immediately,' the marine captain snapped.

Ross stared with contempt at the higher-ranking officer, turning his back to address the handful of men from the company still in the boats. 'Company, fall in!' he barked and the riflemen clambered out of the boats, assembling in their ranks on the mudflats.

'Lead on, Mr Sinclair,' Ross said, drawing his sword and pistol. 'Take us to Captain Forbes.'

Harry flashed a smile of gratitude, then set off through the village in the heavy rain with Lieutenant Woods and the contingent of twenty infantrymen following. But when Harry looked back he was surprised to see that the marine captain – with a contingent of twenty Royal Marines – was following them.

★

'Here they come!' Ian shouted unnecessarily as the formations galloped towards them, yelling war cries to bolster their courage.

The three men were now back to back in a triangle, as they had more chance of living for a short time in a formation of all-round defence. The thunder of hooves was muted by the noise of the storm, but the spectres of death appeared through the sheets of rain.

Conan fired a shot at the cavalrymen charging from the flank and was satisfied to see a man fall from his saddle. He dropped the rifle, which he would wield as a club when his pistols were emptied.

Ian raised his pistols at the group charging from the front, taking careful aim, knowing there would be no time to reload when the enemy arrived. A horseman was on him and the blade slashed down. Ian felt the stinging tip shred through his coat jacket, slicing his flesh in a shallow wound. In desperation, he fired both his pistols at the cavalryman who was swinging his mount around to make another pass. The shots found their mark and the horseman slumped in the saddle as his horse galloped away.

The Russian count had emptied his pistols and was standing with the captured sabre, waiting for one of the enemy to attempt close-quarter combat.

Ian knew that the ditch would soon run with their blood

and he had one final thought of Ella. Oh, how he desired to hold her one last time. The three waited for the cavalry to swamp them once and for all. Conan held the captured musket by the barrel to use it as a club, and Ian held his Bowie knife in a futile gesture of defiance. The thunder of hooves was loud enough that even the drumming rain could not conceal the terrifying sound.

They were only seconds away when Ian swore he heard the sound of nearby thunder. Momentarily confused, he watched the Indian mutineers and their horses crash into the earth as if hit by lightning. The sudden and unexpected interruption to their attack caused the surviving enemy to pull on reins, turning in confusion to confront the new threat. A second devastating volley tore into the sepoy horsemen.

'There!' Conan shouted above the roar of falling rain and gunfire. 'Over there!'

Ian swung around to see the dim outlines of kneeling men firing in their direction, whilst a second rank was standing, ready to fire whilst the kneeling rank reloaded.

'It's our boys!' Conan whooped as the cavalry broke formation to seek safety away from the deadly fire.

Miracles did happen after all, Ian thought as the riflemen advanced in line towards them with Lieutenant Woods in front, followed by Lieutenant Sinclair.

'Just like the old days in the Crimea,' Conan said, a grin from one side of his bearded face to the other. 'Ian Steele, you must be the luckiest man alive.'

'Not luck, Conan, a bloody miracle this time,' Ian grinned. 'The miracle is the boys of our company and, it appears, a few Royal Marines to boot.'

Harry hurried over to Ian. 'Sir, are you wounded?'

Ian was puzzled and then realised blood was pouring down the sleeve of his jacket. 'Nothing a few stitches won't fix,' he replied, examining the wound to his upper arm. He could see that the blade had not penetrated very deep and he tore off his sleeve to bandage the laceration. 'I must express my gratitude to you for coming back for us, Mr Sinclair,' Ian continued. 'I presume that you were able to get the Khan off the beach first.'

'Yes, sir, we were,' Sinclair replied.

'Well done, Mr Sinclair. Your brother would be proud of you,' Ian said.

'Sir, he once told me of how you would draw the Muscovites towards your position and then have the company ambush them,' Sinclair said. 'I simply used your tactics against those savage scoundrels as you would have.'

Ian did not have the heart to correct his junior officer. Those times were the result of Herbert's quick thinking, not Ian's. Maybe Herbert was now his guardian angel.

The marine captain approached. 'I say, old chap, you seem to have an uncanny loyalty from your officers and men,' he said to Ian. 'I wonder if my men would do the same for me under such circumstances.'

'It is the way of our regiment,' Ian said. 'We are all brothers, regardless of rank.'

'Mr Ross led me to disobey my orders and intervene here,' the marine captain said, gesturing to the scene of carnage where the ditch ran red with the blood of the mutineers and their mounts. 'But I realised that if Mr Ross was going to be successful, he would need the assistance of the Queen's Royal Marines.'

'I thank you for that,' Ian said, extending his hand. 'Maybe one day we will be in a position to assist you under similar circumstances.'

Around them in the torrential rain, wounded horses whinnied pitifully and wounded mutineers moaned. The

Minié bullets had caused horrific injuries, and already Lieutenant Ross was supervising the shooting of both wounded horses and enemy combatants. To the soldiers carrying out the shootings it was an act of mercy and not barbarity.

'It is time that we left and returned to our rum ration,' the marine captain said.

Ian heartily agreed as he attempted to bring his suddenly shaking legs and hands under control. He realised that they had probably been mere seconds from death before the timely intervention of the small but lethal British contingent.

Ian turned to the Russian count. 'Are you coming with us?' he asked.

Nikolai nodded. 'I do not think I will be welcome back at the village and your government has promised me sanctuary. I think it is time for me to leave India behind and travel to London.'

★

Aboard the warship steaming south, Ian gratefully accepted the tin cup of rum from Conan. The decks were lashed by monsoonal rain and the ship wallowed in the rising sea, but Ian did not care that he was soaked to the skin as he stood gazing back at the distant coastline cloaked by the night.

'Another close-run thing,' he muttered as he raised his tin cup to drink the dark liquid.

'Luck of the Irish,' Conan said, swallowing his ration.

'Sir, the Khan would like to see you below decks,' a soldier of the company said, miserable that he had been forced to go above into the storm and be drenched to the skin.

Ian glanced at Conan with a questioning expression and followed the soldier below, attempting to shake off the wet and make himself presentable. He was brought to a cabin that had once been occupied by the ship's captain. The soldier knocked and the Khan bid them enter.

Ian stepped inside the cabin which was just large enough to accommodate three people. He saw the Khan's wife sitting on the bunk with her son beside her, and the Khan standing by a desk.

'Captain Forbes, I requested your presence to thank you. I know that your decision to remain behind was one that the odds said you would not survive. You did that to ensure that my family and I survived. Such an act of courage should be recognised. In your army I believe the Queen has issued a new medal, the Victoria Cross, which I believe you have truly earned. But I do not have the power to grant you the medal.' The Khan reached into one of the leather sacks he and his family had carried with them from the village. When he pulled his hand out Ian could see the sparkle of red rubies and green emeralds under the light of the lantern swinging from the ceiling.

'These are for you, Captain Forbes,' the Khan said, offering the precious stones.

'I was only doing my duty, sir,' Ian said, transfixed by the beautiful sparkling gems. 'I do not expect any financial reward for carrying out the Queen's commands.'

'Please take them, Captain Forbes. My son is worth more than every stone I carry with us. If you, Sergeant Major Curry and Count Kasatkin had not offered to stay behind, we may not have survived. I will personally thank your sergeant major and the count in turn. Consider the rubies and emeralds my medals to you in recognition of your bravery.'

The Khan dropped the precious stones in Ian's hands.

'Thank you, sir,' Ian said with genuine gratitude. 'It is not necessary, but gratefully accepted.'

Ian left the cabin gripping the cold stones in his hand. Only hours earlier he had not believed he would live out the day, and here he was with a small fortune of emeralds and rubies! He had always dreamed of fame and fortune. War had provided him with fortune and a certain degree of fame amongst the men of the regiment. But what lay ahead when his company re-joined the regiment in India? Fame and fortune would not save him on the battlefield. More importantly, what had been the fate of his beloved Canadian friend, Dr Peter Campbell, and Alice, Peter's wife and sister of the real Samuel Forbes?

Ian met with Conan on the deck. 'Did the Khan reward you?' Conan asked.

'He did, and he will also reward you with riches well beyond anything the army can pay you in the next ten years,' Ian replied, displaying the handful of glittering stones. 'We will split the money we receive four ways, as is our custom.'

'Four ways?' Conan queried.

'Yes, a share will go to Molly,' Ian replied.

'Yes, it is only fair,' Conan agreed. 'Our situation may look dire from time to time, but at least I am making more money as a soldier in the Queen's army than I would have made back home in a lifetime of robbing travellers.'

Ian grinned. 'Soldiering has made an honest man of you, Conan Curry.'

TWENTY-TWO

Samuel felt trapped. He had come so close to being exposed by Charles and now, hiding out in yet another London boarding house with James, he knew that they must get out of England. This time their accommodation was less salubrious but cash payment meant no questions as to their identities.

The room he shared with James felt like a prison cell. It was barely an attic but it was a place that would not attract Charles' attention as it catered to workers from out of London and not those of aristocratic breeding.

'We have to do something,' James said. 'I think I will go mad if we remain in this place.'

'There is nothing stopping you from returning to New York,' Samuel said, pacing the small room. 'My brother is not hunting you.'

James walked over to Samuel. 'You know I would never leave you,' he said gently. 'We face this situation together.'

Samuel smiled sadly, touching James' cheek. 'I love you and it pains me to see you caught up in a mess of my making.'

'I think our best option to leave England is for us to make contact with that Jewish man. He seems to have the ability to help us.'

'Mr Solomon,' Samuel said. 'I do not completely trust him. He is a criminal whose main ambition in life is to make money. He has no reason to be our friend.'

'If money is his friend, I can pay,' James replied.

Samuel slumped on one of the single beds and sighed. He knew James was right. They were trapped and the dubious Jewish businessman was their only hope.

★

Charles Field had been paid enough money by his generous client, Charles Forbes, to hire a network of immigration officials at London's seaports, and even a round-the-clock surveillance of Ikey Solomon's office. Like a spider at the centre of a web, Field was able to respond to any filament that might vibrate, indicating the fly had been caught. He had no personal animosity to the man he hunted; it was purely business. But he did have a personal stake in the case. Ikey Solomon had always been able to thumb his nose at the police, and Field, when he'd been a detective inspector, had repeatedly failed to have him put away. Here he was presented with an opportunity to catch his old adversary in the illegal act of aiding and abetting a man falsely pretending to be someone else. Catching Ikey Solomon would be the icing on the cake of an already highly lucrative case.

★

Samuel and James arrived in the afternoon at Ikey's office and were met at the door by Egbert. They explained that

216

they wished to speak with his boss and were prepared to pay for the consultation. Egbert left them and went upstairs while Samuel and James remained nervously on the street, glancing at the people passing by.

'Mr Solomon says he will see you,' Egbert said and the three men climbed the stairs to the office. They were ushered in and found Ikey standing by a window peering out over the city's rooftops. Smoke spouted from the many chimney and a lay like a blanket across the city.

'Gentlemen,' said Ikey, turning around. 'I did not expect to see you back in London after all my hard work in assisting you to leave for New York. I have since had a visit from a Charles Forbes purporting to be your brother, and my old friend, Inspector Field. Why are you trying to pull the wool over my eyes, Mr Steele? I am not a man who has much patience for people lying to me.'

'It is a long story, Mr Solomon,' Samuel said. 'I am sure you are a man who is too busy for stories, but if you help us leave England once again – a kindness we will pay for generously – I can promise we will not return.'

'The man who recommended my services to you, Captain Samuel Forbes, is a man I thought I could trust in a world of lying scoundrels. But is it true that you are the real Samuel Forbes and that he is in fact Mr Ian Steele?'

'Would it matter if it were?' Samuel countered.

'I need you to be straight with me,' Ikey replied. 'As I said, I do not like being lied to.'

'I can vouch for the integrity of Ian Steele, the man you know as Captain Forbes. I assure you the reason he and I switched places is quite separate from our dealings with you,' Samuel said. 'Now, my friend and I need to get out of England as soon as –'

Suddenly Egbert burst through the door. 'Mr Solomon,

one of those kids hanging around across the street has run off.'

'Gone to get Mr Field, no doubt,' Ikey said. 'You don't have much time,' he said to Samuel and James, 'and you won't be leaving through the front entrance.' He leaned over his desk and scribbled something on a piece of paper, thrusting it at Samuel.

'This is the person you will contact in the future if you require my services,' he said. 'Do not attempt to contact me here. I do not wish for any more attention from Inspector Field. Now, follow me.'

Samuel slipped the scrap of paper into his trouser pocket and hurried after Ikey. He and James were led down a hallway with empty offices either side until they reached the end, where Ikey seemed to magically make the wall slide sideways, revealing a set of steps down into the dark.

'Go down there and follow the tunnel until you get to a fork, then turn left. This will take you out behind this building to an empty warehouse. You can then leave without being seen on this side of the street.'

Samuel and James did not question Ikey, who quickly closed the sliding door behind them, throwing them into pitch blackness. Very carefully, the two men inched down the steps, touching the wall for balance as they went. In the dark they could hear rats scurrying away from their footsteps. It was obvious that this was a last-measure escape route from Ikey's building and rarely used. It stank of sewage and must. A dim light glowed ahead from an overhead manhole in the street, and when they came to the fork they took the left-hand turn and found themselves inside a small warehouse frequented only by pigeons and spiders.

'This way,' James whispered.

They walked to the door which led out onto the street. It took a few moments to orient themselves but both men walked casually along until they located a familiar side street that would direct them back to their lodgings.

When they were safely in their attic room, Samuel removed the slip of paper from his pocket. He read the name of the middleman who was to be their contact with Mr Solomon. But it was not a man, Samuel noted with surprise. It was a woman by the name of Miss Molly Williams, confectioner.

★

Henry Havelock, now a general in the Queen's army, had received the telegram that Cawnpore had fallen to the rebels and that the majority of the British civilians – men, women and children – had been massacred by sepoy troops. Those who had survived the initial slaughter under a flag of truce were rounded up and ordered to be killed. But even the mutinous Indian soldiers refused to carry out the order, so butchers were employed to kill the surviving civilians, dismembering the bodies as they would sheep or goats.

The general had a secret fund to pay local spies, and his intelligence service was a well-oiled machine. He pored over one report from a loyal Indian shopkeeper who provided his staff the mutineer's numbers and dispositions in the Cawnpore region.

'Sir, Captain Forbes is outside as you requested,' a major of his staff said through the tent flap of Havelock's field HQ.

'Bid him enter,' Havelock said, pushing away from the field table and standing to receive Ian.

Ian stepped inside, saluted smartly and stood to attention.

Havelock thrust out his hand, surprising Ian.

'My hand in gratitude is about all I can offer you, Captain Forbes, for successfully rescuing the Khan.'

'I was doing my duty, sir,' Ian replied as he let go the firm grip.

'I have been informed by General Outram that you continually prove your courage and resourcefulness. It should be you commanding your regiment and not that popinjay, Jenkins. As it is, I will be sending your regiment in the advance on Cawnpore. Colonel Jenkins has been given his orders to help provide reinforcements there.'

'Sir, I can promise you that the regiment will gather glory in any contact we have with the mutinous sepoys,' Ian said.

'I know it will with officers such as yourself in command of the men.' Havelock sighed. 'I also have information on the welfare and whereabouts of the surgeon you wrote to my headquarters about. Dr Campbell and his wife are well, and with the contingent we have outside the walls of Delhi. I even heard a rumour that Mrs Campbell successfully carried out surgery, amputating limbs. However, I know that could not be true as she is a woman, and we both know such a gory procedure is beyond the sensibilities of a delicate English lady.'

Ian could see that the general had the hint of a smile on his face and sensed Havelock believed the rumours to be true. 'My sister is a remarkable lady, sir,' Ian said diplomatically.

'Last reports said that she and Dr Campbell have been carrying out their duties under rather arduous conditions, so hopefully we will recapture the city soon.'

'Sir, my gratitude for your enquiries,' Ian said. 'Cawnpore is on the road to Delhi, and I hope that I soon have the opportunity to meet with them.'

'First Cawnpore and then Delhi,' Havelock said with a nod.

Ian left the tent and marched back to the regiment's lines nearby where he was met by his company sergeant major whose gloomy expression said it all.

'Sir,' said Conan, 'the commanding officer desires to meet with you immediately.'

'How could I guess,' Ian sighed.

Ian made his way to the regimental HQ tent where he was saluted by the two soldiers on guard. A young officer appointed to Jenkins' staff stepped out of the tent and also saluted. Ian returned the salute.

'Sir, the colonel will see you now,' the young officer said, ushering him inside.

Ian saluted and stood to attention. 'Sir, you wished to see me?'

Jenkins rose from his desk and stood with his hands behind his back. From the scowl on his face Ian knew things were not going to go well for him.

'I have finished speaking with your second-in-command, Mr Sinclair, and your CSM about the mysterious rescue mission General Outram sent you on, and neither would divulge any information. They said they had been sworn to secrecy and only you were authorised to speak about it. As your commanding officer I am now ordering you to give me a full report on the matter.'

'Sir, with all due respect, I think you should first speak to General Havelock before I comply with your request,' Ian answered, and noticed the scowl on his commanding officer's face deepen.

'I am not about to disturb the general as he is a busy man,' Jenkins said in frustration.

'I am not sure of that, sir,' Ian said smugly. 'I have just come from his HQ and he had time to have a chat with me.' He knew his statement would take the wind out of Jenkins' sails.

'You are insolent, Captain Forbes,' Jenkins snarled. 'And you appear to have the luck of the devil on your side. I won't be forgetting your arrogant behaviour. You are dismissed.'

Ian saluted, turned on his heel and marched out of the tent with a smile on his face.

TWENTY-THREE

Samuel had developed a nervous tic at the corner of his eye, and the strain of remaining in the nondescript boarding house in London was taking a toll on his relationship with James. James had snapped that they may as well be living in a cage, and Samuel felt the guilt of having dragged him into this game of cat and mouse with his brother.

Right now James was out purchasing a newspaper, so Samuel wrote a note to inform him that he would be away for a short time. He did not want to cause the man he loved any more anguish if he should be caught.

Samuel slipped out of the boarding house, hailed a hansom cab and directed the driver to Molly's shop in a better part of London. As he walked through the door he was assailed by the pleasant scent of confectionary. Behind the counter, weighing out bags of boiled lollies, was a young woman, barely into her teens.

'Miss Molly Williams?' Samuel asked.

'No. The mistress is in her office,' the girl said with a pleasant smile.

'May I speak with her?' Samuel asked politely.

The girl looked him up and down. 'I will see if Miss Williams is taking visitors.'

She disappeared and a minute later returned. 'Miss Williams wishes to know who is requesting to speak with her and on what business.'

'I am an acquaintance of Mr Ikey Solomon and he gave me Miss Williams' name,' Samuel said, and the girl disappeared and this time returned with a young woman with a pretty face and firm figure. For a moment Molly stared at Samuel with a look of both confusion and recognition.

'You can come to my office,' Molly said. 'May I ask your name, sir?'

'Hubert Smith,' Samuel improvised.

Molly led him into a small office piled with stores for the shop. She closed the door behind them and gestured to a chair near her overflowing desk.

'You are not Mr Smith, but I suspect that you are one Samuel Forbes,' Molly said. 'Your resemblance to Ian Steele is remarkable.'

Samuel was taken off guard by this woman's recognition and the mention of Ian's real identity.

'How did you know?' Samuel asked.

'My man told me the story of how you and Captain Steele traded places,' Molly said. 'Captain Steele is a wonderful and remarkable man, and his secret is safe with me. Now, Ikey Solomon sent you to me for a reason.'

'I need some assistance to leave England,' said Samuel, 'and as soon as possible.'

'I see,' Molly said. 'It is well known on the streets that

224

you are being sought by Inspector Field's investigative service, and from my knowledge of Inspector Field, he is a man who always solves his cases.'

'I am a little confused as to how a lady of your standing knows the likes of Mr Solomon. You appear to be a successful person in your own business.'

'It is a long story, but I once worked for Ikey as his book-keeper, and he looked out for me, so now I try to repay that kindness by returning a favour when I can. Ikey is a good man, despite what some might say about him. Now, we should get down to business.

'Field is meticulous, so we have to presume he has all the ports covered with his spies.' Molly looked thoughtful. 'But probably not those ports in Wales,' she concluded. 'I know people there who can smuggle you aboard a ship leaving one of the Welsh ports, but you will need money.'

'We have money,' Samuel replied. 'Our fate is in your hands, Miss Williams.'

'I am not doing this for your sake,' Molly said. 'I am doing this to ensure that Captain Steele's real identity is not revealed. While you remain in England you put him in jeopardy. Come back to my shop tomorrow night after I close and I will have something arranged.'

Samuel thanked her and purchased a bag of Turkish delight on the way out. Feeling much relieved, he stepped onto the street and was fortunate to hail a passing hansom cab.

★

Havelock's intelligence service informed him that a leader by the name of Nana Sahib had emerged after the defeat of the Cawnpore garrison. The Moslem leader had declared himself Peishwa of the Mahrattas. This self-proclaimed sovereign had almost destroyed a smaller force of British soldiers under a Major Renaud's command as they advanced towards Cawnpore. Now he aimed to take the city of Allahabad and then advance on Calcutta where he would establish his Moghul dynasty.

The British general knew from reports that the self-proclaimed Peishwa had at least three and a half thousand well-trained sepoy infantry, reinforced with eager recruits, and had many artillery guns taken from the British. Opposed to his force were a mere four hundred British troops and three hundred untested Sikh soldiers, as well as a small force of irregular cavalry. Havelock's great fear was that the Sikh troops might desert when they made contact with the vastly larger enemy force confronting them. Major Renaud, who had survived the slaughter of his troops, knew he was faced with a terrible decision, but it was one that had to be made. Did he withdraw his outnumbered force, or would he command it to stand and fight?

The decision was made to stand and fight the superior force.

★

The blistering sun was taking a toll on Ian's men. This was the time of year when the sun would appear in the Indian skies between downpours of monsoonal rain to savage everything below with its blazing rays.

The column had trudged through a dismal landscape of stunted trees and shimmering plains with Ian at the vanguard of his company. Before they'd left, Colonel Jenkins had feigned great disappointment that only Ian's company and not the whole regiment would be joining the attack on Cawnpore, but the cowardly colonel's relief at avoiding combat was palpable. Rumours already abounded that the small force marching towards Cawnpore would encounter a large number of enemy and likely be massacred.

They had marched fifteen miles under the unforgiving sun and Ian could see that his company was flagging. The oxen carts creaked behind the column, filled with men struck down with heatstroke, and even the army medical staff begged the column's commander to rest the men. But Major Renaud chose to push on, until finally the sun set across the dreary plains of scrub and the men were given orders to pitch tents and rest.

Ian walked amongst his exhausted soldiers, sharing a joke here and there, asking about their health. He always received the same answer: they could go on. He sat down in a small copse of scrubby trees with a small fire to heat his water for his ration of tea. He was joined by Conan, who squatted down beside him.

'How do you think the men are holding up?' Ian asked, swishing the tea leaves into the boiling water with a twig.

'They would follow the Colonial into hell if he asked them,' Conan replied, producing his battered metal cup to share Ian's tea. 'The lads think that serving under you means they cannot be killed.'

'If only that were true,' Ian said wearily. 'I have orders that we strike tents just before midnight. Try to get a couple of hours' sleep.'

Conan rose with his mug of tea and walked into the night, leaving Ian alone with his thoughts. Ian was aware that his company was always singled out for the most dangerous missions, and wondered how his men would react if they knew that. He felt they were misguided to put so much faith in him to keep them alive. As he sipped his brew, he reflected on the seemingly hopeless task ahead when they eventually clashed with the superior Indian force.

At 11 pm, the column struck their tents and marched in under the light of the full moon, until about an hour later they were challenged by the picquets of the force they had come to strengthen.

This did not mean any rest for Ian's company, however, as the two small forces continued marching until the sun rose the next morning, when the order was to take an overdue rest before they encountered the enemy.

★

The blast of an enemy cannon shattered the morning.

Meals being prepared were quickly discarded as the order, 'To arms!' was yelled down the lines. Soldiers scrambled to snatch up their Enfield rifles and ammunition as senior NCOs harried them into battle formations. Ian grabbed his sword and revolver, falling in with his company. He ensured that he was standing conspicuously, his sword drawn, amongst the men in the first rank.

To his front Ian could see the dust rising as a large force of Indian cavalry charged their position. Conan was moving through the ranks, chiding some for not having percussion caps on their rifles, or not being properly dressed for battle. He knew his role was to act as Ian's guard dog in battle – and he did his job well.

'Sir, there are so many of the buggers,' a frightened young new recruit said.

'Then you can't miss when you fire, Private Cummings,' Ian said. He knew the name of every man in his company, and that alone seemed to settle the soldier down.

The sudden charge of enemy cavalry came to a confused halt, no doubt because they only now realised they were facing five regiments of infantry and eight artillery guns drawn up in perfect order. The Indian mutineers were well aware of how deadly the British army was on the battlefield when they were organised for combat, and they instinctively slowed in the attack.

Ian could feel the tightness in his stomach that he experienced before every battle. He was careful that his men not discern the slight tremble of his hand as he held his sword aloft. He knew they looked to him with blind faith in his ability to keep them alive and he did not want them to lose confidence just as they stepped into battle.

The Indian cavalry fell back and a couple of cannon were pushed forward, along with the Indian infantry.

'Steady, lads!' Conan roared down the ranks as they witnessed the smoke erupt from the mouth of the artillery pieces, and seconds later heard the sound. It was important that the British formations display a vision of resolute red-coated ranks to the Indian mutineers.

A junior officer from the task force HQ hurried to Ian. 'Sir, the general requests your company to occupy a copse to our front.'

Ian acknowledged the order and passed it on to his NCOs, who hurriedly arranged his company of riflemen to advance to the copse of trees Ian had indicated. Ian knew that they were being pushed forward to act as skirmishers, using the Enfield's range to inflict casualties on the enemy before they could come into range of the Indian smooth-bore muskets. Ian's company had only just arrived in position in the stand of trees and deployed into fighting formation when the Indian infantry charged their position.

Ian gave the order and a volley of well-aimed Minié bullets struck down the forward troops charging towards them in the trees. Ian trusted that his hours of training his men would lead them to fire and reload quickly. The first volley was followed by disciplined volleys, pouring the deadly and devastating bullets into the waves of advancing enemy infantry.

Gun smoke filled the still air like a London fog, partially concealing the plain to their front. Ian roared encouragement as the withering fire continued. Private Cummings was only feet away and Ian observed how calmly he fired and reloaded the long rifled musket. If the enemy came close enough, Ian knew he would have to give the order to fix bayonets, although this made loading the rifles harder. For the moment the well-aimed rifle fire was doing the job of slowing down the attack.

Above the constant loud crash of rifles, Ian could hear the blast of artillery not far away and knew it was British guns. The smoke continued to billow around the copse, obscuring the enemy to their front, but it was now Ian's job to defend the gunners from the mutineers as the artillery shells tore huge gaps in their ranks.

Conan was beside Ian, holding spare ramrods, and young Private Cummings fired off a shot. In his haste to do so he had left the ramrod in the barrel and it flew away like a spear.

'That will come out of your pay, Private Cummings,' Conan growled in the young soldier's ear. 'Take one of these.' Conan thrust the spare ramrod into the soldier's hand, who accepted it sheepishly.

'Sorry, sir,' Cummings said, cursing himself for his mistake.

Swamps either side of the hard ground to their front channelled the attackers, while the British cavalry used the strips of firm earth to advance.

Ian did not know how long his men continued to fire but suspected it was for at least ten minutes. He could see that the longer range of the Enfield rifled muskets was devastating the advancing infantry, and he sensed that the smaller British force was getting the upper hand. Thirst, smoke, noise and heat were Ian's impressions of the battle.

The artillery guns were being limbered and Ian saw them dragged further forward onto the firmer areas of the nearby swampy ground, to be unlimbered and put into action closer to the enemy forces, firing at almost point-blank range. They particularly targeted the brass and iron cannons of the mutineers, putting three of the Indian guns out of action.

Part of the enemy force was situated in a small village behind a cluster of garden enclosures made of mud bricks. The British artillery rounds smashed through the walls, killing and wounding anyone in their lethal path.

Ian noticed that the attacking infantry had withered away in the face of the deadly volleys of his riflemen, and he ordered a ceasefire to conserve valuable powder and shot. As he gave the order another junior staff officer appeared.

'Sir, the general has ordered an advance to the front,' he said breathlessly. 'Your company is to reinforce Major Renaud on a hill he has captured to our right.' Ian could see the British redcoats on the hill indicated by the staff officer.

'Tell the general we will move to Major Renaud's position now,' Ian replied, and the officer saluted and dashed back to HQ.

Ian turned to Conan. 'Sarn't Major, form up the company to advance to that hill over there,' he said, and Conan immediately issued the order. Platoon commanders and their senior NCOs expertly fell in and hurried forward. Ian observed the exhaustion of his men in the heat of the day. The fact that they had had little sleep the night before and no breakfast only exacerbated the situation. Still, they reached the hill held by Major Renaud, and Ian reported his arrival.

'Sir, what are your orders?'

'Good show, Captain Forbes,' the weary major replied, wiping his brow with the back of his cuff. 'We will have to advance through a swamp down there.'

Ian followed the major's outstretched hand.

'Company, advance to the front!' Ian bellowed, and the men stepped forward off the hillock into the swampy ground, moving towards the village of mud huts.

They were only yards from the first of the small walls when Ian saw the Indian artillery gun being wheeled into a position to fire point blank at his and Major Renaud's troops. Acting quickly, he drew his pistol and sprinted towards the crew of three Indians manning the gun. He was firing at such close range that his bullets took the lives of two of the enemy serving the gun. But the third man desperately reached to fire the upper hole on the cannon. Ian knew that the gun was probably filled with canister shot, an artillery round that acted like a giant shotgun for close-range defence. He leapt the wall with a strength he did not know he possessed, and before the taper could touch the hole, he had driven his sword into the man's chest. He fell and Ian fell on top of him. When Ian attempted to scramble to his feet, he was aware that Conan was beside him.

'You orright?' the sergeant major asked, helping Ian to his feet. 'Bloody stupid thing to do.'

'There was no time,' Ian gasped. His lungs felt like they were on fire. His company were pouring over the low walls and advancing towards the village.

'Fix bayonets!' Conan roared and the men paused to slide the long knife-like bayonets onto the end of their rifles before continuing the advance. All around them lay the dead and dying Indian mutineers. As Ian's company advanced they were able to clear the town of fleeing enemy without sustaining any further battle casualties. Ian noticed some of his men collapse, though, the victims of heat exhaustion rather than enemy action. But his priority was to clear the town, and he could not spare any soldiers to tend the sick.

Soon they were through the town, driving the enemy before them.

Ian ensured his men were in their battle formations when they broke out onto the plain on the other side of the village. It was then that he saw a large formation of Indian cavalry make a determined charge against their own outnumbered cavalry on the company's flank. He was acutely aware that should the Indian mutineers succeed, they could then attack along the flank of his own force and, at such close range, obliterate them. From the corner of his eye, he could see that the British artillerymen had been able to bring up a couple of guns and were already setting them up to fire into the Indian formation.

Ian was weak from the physical effort of battle and his throat was parched. Despite this, he bellowed his order.

'Riflemen, cavalry to the right. Form ranks!'

Above the din of the scattered firing and the triumphant shouts of the enemy, Ian's order carried, and at the same time the two cannons roared their defiance into the men and horses about to attack their own weakened cavalry.

The volley of rifle fire rippled along the rifles of the company line, bringing down both horses and men. The combined artillery and rifle fire proved to be too much for the Indian cavalry who only mere moments earlier had sensed an easy victory. In disarray, they turned and fled the battlefield. Off to their left, Ian could see the swirling tartan skirts of the Scottish infantry regiment break through. He knew then that they had done the impossible and won the day.

But at what cost?

TWENTY-FOUR

Already the familiar sickly sweet stench of death rose in the hot air from the already fly-covered bloated enemy bodies scattered about the battlefield. Ian barely noticed it anymore.

'I don't know how we survived,' Conan said, surveying the carnage of the battlefield. 'They had us outnumbered.'

'But we had the Enfield,' Ian said.

'Never in my wildest nightmares back home could I have ever imagined I would be standing here today wearing a bloody British red coat. My Irish ancestors will not welcome me to heaven when I die.'

'Put it this way, Sarn't Major, we don't get to choose where we are born – but we have a choice in where we die in the business of soldiering for the Queen.'

'That is not very cheerful.' Conan smiled under his thick beard. 'I am hoping to depart for the next world in a soft bed with Molly holding my hand.'

'Maybe that will happen,' Ian said. 'In the meantime, I need you to make a rollcall to see if any of our lads have been killed or wounded.'

'Sah,' Conan replied and marched away. When he returned with a long face Ian knew they had taken casualties.

'Two dead, sir,' he said. 'Struck down by the sun. I heard from an officer that we lost twelve all up to the effects of the sun – and none from enemy action. I also heard this is the first successful encounter with the mutineers.'

'Not for the twelve poor souls who will not be going home,' Ian replied.

'What is the name of this place?' Conan asked, his pencil poised to record their geographic location.

'Futtehpore,' Ian replied. 'But I doubt any will remember the name – except the men who were here today.'

The twelve soldiers who had succumbed to heatstroke were buried on the battlefield with military honours. Their graves were marked, but in time they would disappear forever in the Indian earth.

★

Alice Campbell stood gazing at the massive walls of the city they besieged. The sun was setting and she reflected on the moment. She was so far from the genteel salons of London and the gossip of her friends. Here she stood with the blood of her patients on her worn dress. The past was little more than a ghost and she knew she could never go back to being the protected and pampered young woman she had once been. In that moment she felt an affinity with Miss Florence Nightingale, who had ministered to the wounded of the Crimean War.

'Well, my dear,' Peter said, approaching his wife. 'I have some good news. A trader came through camp and for sixteen rupees I was able to purchase a dozen bottles of tar bund beer, and also a bottle of Harvey's Sauce, as well as a good selection of tinned foods. We shall dine in luxury tonight.'

Peter placed his hands on his wife's shoulders and stood for the moment also gazing at the massive and seemingly impregnable Delhi walls. 'A penny for your thoughts?'

'What becomes of us after this dreadful war is over?' she sighed. 'I do not desire to return to London and the family home.'

'We will do whatever it is you desire,' Peter said, gently turning his wife to face him.

'I wish to travel with you to see the world,' Alice said. 'I would like to see your Canada – and even the Australian colonies where my Uncle George has a sheep farm.'

'Is that all?' Peter asked with a twisted smile.

'No, I wish to travel to Africa, and to Egypt after that.'

'Well, Canada is achievable, but you must remember that I am a simple surgeon on a simple surgeon's income.'

'You are not a simple surgeon,' Alice said. 'I have been beside you when so many poor souls have been saved by your God-given skills.'

'But I have never shot a tiger.' Peter laughed, realising it had been a long time since he had laughed. 'Maybe we could hunt lion in Africa.'

'No, I will never again kill such a beautiful and noble creature. Sometimes the spirit of the tiger haunts my dreams,' Alice said sadly. 'After all that travel, I will be content to find some part of this world to settle down with my country doctor and raise a family.'

Peter did not reply but gazed at the great walls of the city which harboured a vast army of men ready to kill them at the first opportunity. He knew that they were still outnumbered and outgunned by the Indian mutineers, although word had arrived in the camp that General Havelock was having success against the mutineers just south-west of their current location. For now, all they had was the stark reality of the present. At least that promised a feast for dinner. For the moment, that was enough.

★

Charles Forbes was frustrated and angry. He forced himself not to pace in the private investigator's office but stood with his hands behind his back, glaring out a window at the smog hanging over the city.

'I am afraid at this stage, Mr Forbes, that our man has disappeared. If it is any consolation, I believe he and his companion are still in the city, as my contacts on the docks have not reported them attempting to leave London.'

'What if my brother is cunning enough to depart the country from another port?' Charles asked, turning towards Field.

'Ah, to prevent that happening you would have to be prepared to pay a lot more,' Field said. 'Your money would need to buy eyes and ears in every port in the British Isles.'

'I am prepared to pay,' Charles said.

'Then I will be able to put a watch on Scotland and Wales – as well as all our ports in England,' Field said.

'But if they identify my brother, how could you detain him if he attempts to leave from, say, a Scottish port?'

'I still have many contacts in my old job,' Field said. 'After all, this appears to be a case of fraud and the local constabulary can be enlisted to arrest the man you say is your brother. I have prepared posters from the photograph you gave me to be distributed across the country – with a cash reward for any information that locates him. Your brother's face is now familiar to many police constables and members of the public.'

For the first time, Charles smiled. 'I can see that my money will be well spent,' he said. 'There will be a generous bonus if you succeed.'

'I always do, Mr Forbes,' Field said. 'I always do.'

★

Samuel Forbes truly regretted not leaving England when he had had the opportunity. Now he felt like a hunted animal, and the tic at the side of his eye grew more persistent as he walked towards Molly's shop, where he was ushered into the back office.

'I have written to my cousin in Cardiff and he has agreed to help you, but he will require payment for his troubles,' Molly said. 'He will arrange a ship to take you to America.'

'I thank you for helping us,' Samuel said.

'I am doing this for Captain Steele,' Molly replied. 'You will need to be ready to take a locomotive train to Bristol this Friday, and then travel by coach to Cardiff,' she said, passing Samuel a piece of paper. 'This has all the information you will require to make contact with my cousin. From there he will be able to book you passage once you pay him. I will bid you a good voyage.'

Thanking Molly again, Samuel slipped the paper into his pocket.

Molly watched him depart and reflected on how strange life had become since the day a young colonial had first set foot in the rundown tenement she'd shared with her brothers, Owen and Edwin. Fate had brought them all together, and Captain Steele was enmeshed in their lives now. Edwin was dead – killed on the bloody battlefield of the Crimea – and the man she loved above all others, Sergeant Major Conan Curry VC, was far away in India, serving alongside Captain Steele. Molly was growing wealthy from the two shops she now owned, serving the finest confectionary to wealthy patrons. They had all experienced such a dramatic change in their lives, and at the centre of it all was the enigmatic Captain Ian Steele.

*

Rarely did Ian have personal contact with his commanding officer. As their animosity was mutual, he only found himself in Colonel Jenkins' presence at the officers' mess when they dined or at formal regimental briefings usually conducted by the regimental second-in-command, Major Dawkins, whom Ian respected for his competence. Whenever Jenkins had him summoned to his office, Ian knew he was in trouble of some kind.

Ian stood to attention in Jenkins' tent. He could hear the senior NCOs barking orders to the soldiers outside as they drilled, and the clatter of a field kitchen nearby. It was a very hot day and the sweat trickled down both men's faces.

'Captain Forbes,' Jenkins said, and Ian could see that he had an open letter on his desk. 'I have received disturbing correspondence from London that you may be an imposter.'

Ian could see the grim look of victory on Jenkins' face.

'May I ask who has levelled such a preposterous and malicious accusation against my good name?' he asked, feigning indignation.

'None other than your alleged brother, Charles Forbes,' Jenkins answered smugly. 'Now, I ask why such an honourable man as Charles Forbes would intimate that you are not who you say you are?'

Ian could feel the sweat trickle down inside his jacket and knew that somehow Charles had come into contact with Samuel in London.

'My brother has never liked me,' Ian replied. 'I suspect that this is his way of causing mischief. I would suggest that you write to my father, Sir Archibald, before this matter gets out of hand.'

Jenkins leaned forward in his camp chair and stared at Ian. 'I know that you are Outram and Havelock's golden boy, God knows why, but they will not always be around to protect you. I am being posted back to London to attend the newly established staff college there and I will make personal contact with Charles and ensure we sort out this matter. Until then you will remain with your company, but Major Dawkins, who will assume command in my absence, will be reporting to me on your conduct. That is all, Captain Forbes – if that is your real name. You are dismissed.'

Ian saluted and stepped outside the tent into the blast of Indian heat, experiencing the familiar trembling in his hands and the feeling his legs would give way. Somehow he made it back to his tent where he slumped on his camp bed, cursing Samuel for putting them both in this dangerous situation. At least he had General Havelock's tacit protection, and Jenkins had enough sense not to upset the brilliant general. However, when Jenkins returned to England he would certainly make contact with Charles, and if Charles had managed to find Samuel, Ian knew his time would be over as the Queen's colonial.

*

Samuel and James arrived at the Paddington railway station in the very early morning to purchase their tickets to Bristol. The train was scheduled to leave at 4.30 am and arrive in

Bristol at 10 pm. The two men were dressed in their finest suits, wearing expensive top hats and looking the part of first-class travellers. The fares were expensive but at least they would receive a private cabin with padded seats and windows through which to gaze at the passing countryside. As it was proving to be a warm day the windows would also provide a cooling breeze.

They carried only hand luggage, which meant they did not have to be separated from their bags by the railway porters. On each carriage roof sat a guard in the tradition of horse carriages, and the men could see that the Brunswick green train engine had an open cabin for the railway engineers, who would have to suffer any kind of weather they might encounter on the journey. Their own carriage was painted in chocolate and cream colours, with open carriages being towed behind for the third-class working men and women. The movement of the working class was driven by the massive coal and iron industries of the Welsh valleys, but the railways preferred to transport the wealthier patrons with money to spare, drawn to the tourist pleasures of Bristol.

Samuel and James boarded their carriage and settled opposite each other. 'At least we will be able to take in the scenery of my country before we depart England.' Samuel sighed, lighting up a cigar as the engine pulled out of the station, billowing thick, acrid coal smoke into the fading darkness of the summer morning.

'What if someone was loitering at the railway station to identify us?' James asked in a concerned voice.

'I don't think my brother has the means to have someone watching every train station in the country,' Samuel replied. 'I suspect he has the ports in London under watch, but our contact in Cardiff will be able to put us on a ship leaving the Bristol Channel, which is a long way from London and

Mr Field. I have arranged for us to be accommodated at a hotel in Bristol tonight, and tomorrow we take our journey to Cardiff on a coach, so just relax and take in our beautiful and historic countryside, old chap. There is nothing we have to concern ourselves with now.'

James tried to settle back in his seat but could not dismiss the nagging feeling that they were still being hunted.

TWENTY-FIVE

All had gone smoothly. Samuel and James had stopped overnight at a fashionable hotel in Bristol and the next morning purchased a fare on a coach to Cardiff, where they were able to find the address of their Welsh contact.

Samuel and James were disappointed to see that the Welsh town was a dirty, disease-ridden place thanks to the sudden industrialisation produced by its ironworks and export of coal. So many English and Irish workers had flooded the place that it had shantytowns filled with the desperately poor. Samuel knew his own family had shares in the new industries and felt a twinge of guilt when he took in the poverty of the workers and unemployed in the town bordered by the beautiful and rolling hills of Wales.

Molly's cousin lived in a tiny tenement house in a row of such places built by the big mining and industrial companies to house their workers.

The two men had walked from the coach depot with directions from those they met on the street.

Samuel knocked on the door and it was opened by a smallish man whose skin appeared to be ingrained with dirt. He was of an indeterminate age, balding, and his clothes were almost ragged.

'I am Samuel and this is James,' Samuel said. 'Your cousin, Molly, informed us that you would know why we are here.'

'Come in, sirs,' the man said, opening the door wide to allow them entrance. 'I know of your plight and have made preparations for you to ship out of Cardiff,' he said. 'My name is Kevin Jones.'

Samuel glanced around the tiny house. The strong stench of boiled cabbage filled the room. A woman with a wizened face and of similarly indeterminate age appeared. 'This is Mrs Jones,' Kevin said awkwardly, and Samuel's guilt increased at the sight of these malnourished people. He was aware that the rich, and he was one of them, lived off their poverty, making huge profits from their labour and enjoying lives of excessive luxury.

'I believe that you will require some payment now,' Samuel said, reaching into his coat pocket and peeling off a wad of English pounds. He handed them to Kevin, whose eyes widened at the amount.

'Sir, this is more than I agreed with Molly. It is very generous,' he said. He attempted to pass back an amount of the currency, but Samuel raised his hand.

'It is what I wish to offer for the trouble you have gone to in assisting us,' he said with a gentle smile, aware that James was frowning. Their supply of ready cash was diminishing, although they had more than enough money when they returned to New York.

'My wife can make us a pot of tea and you are welcome to share a meal with us,' Kevin said.

'I thank you for your kind offer,' Samuel said, the stench of the overcooked cabbage still in his nostrils, 'but James and I will take up temporary accommodation in one of your hotels until it is time for us to depart.'

'That will be later tonight, so you will not need to arrange accommodation in the town,' Kevin said. 'I have been able to get you both a berth on a coal ship leaving on the high tide. Here are your papers for the passage, which contain all the particulars of the ship, berth and time to board. It is steaming to a port in Canada, and from there you will be able to make your way to America. I hope that is to your liking.'

Samuel accepted the papers with thanks, hardly glancing at them, and asked, 'Do you recommend any establishment in town we might partake of an ale and meal before we depart?'

Kevin thought for a moment, suggesting the best place for a meal for gentlemen who were able to pay.

The two men thanked the couple again, and departed the tenement with directions to the hotel.

★

It was a chance in a million!

Ewen Owens stood amidst the tobacco smoke, staring at the two well-dressed gentlemen imbibing in the bar. Owen gripped his ale and shuffled closer to the pair, who appeared oblivious to him.

Ewen knew from the accent that one of the two men was an American, and the other bore a striking resemblance to the poster Ewen carried in his ragged coat pocket. It had to be Samuel Forbes. He tried to remember what he was to do next to claim his reward. Yes, that was it – Mr Field had instructed that the local constabulary were to be contacted to arrest Mr Forbes on a charge of fraud. But Ewen was afraid that if he left the hotel, the subject of the search might disappear into the crowded city.

Ewen knew that he must remain and observe the wanted pair and find out where they were staying. It was frustrating as he did not trust any of the other patrons to deliver a message to the local police. This was his prize, and he calculated that he could personally lead the constables to wherever the men were residing. Two hours went past and night was arriving. Ewen had used the last of his pennies to buy ale as he sat in a corner watching the two men as a hawk would a coop of chickens.

A bell rang and the two men finished their drinks and went into the dining room.

Ewen felt it was safe to leave and fetch the constables now, as the men would be occupied with dinner for a while.

★

'Samuel, I swear that man sitting in the corner was watching us,' James said when they entered the dining room laid out with fine linen and polished cutlery and already filling with well-dressed men and women.

'You are just being paranoid, dear James,' Samuel countered. 'We are safe in Cardiff.'

James turned and, walking to the door of the dining room, looked back at the bar. 'Don't you think it is strange that the man I observed left the hotel at just the moment we came in to dine?' he said. 'I do not wish to take any chances. I think we ought to leave now.'

Samuel was a little tipsy from the alcohol he had consumed over the last couple of hours. Maybe James was right, he pondered. He had made the mistake of being complacent before. Nowhere in the British Isles seemed to be safe from his brother's reach. 'Your instincts may be right, my dear,' Samuel said. 'I think it is time that we found a back entrance from this establishment and made our way to Mr Jones' residence.'

On the street the sun was setting over the smoggy town and already sinking behind the green hills. James and Samuel walked quickly towards the row of tenements, and when they reached Kevin Jones' house it was his wife who opened the door.

'My husband is not here,' she said, not inviting the two men into her house. 'He has gone to the docks.'

'Damn!' Samuel muttered. He was feeling more and more paranoid. The coal ship they were to take passage on was not due to depart for another two hours.

'James, I think that we should make our way to our ship and board early.'

'A goddamned good idea,' James agreed with relief. 'In my opinion, the sooner we are aboard the better.' James wanted to add that it had been Samuel's reckless and impulsive nature that had brought them to this point of fleeing like felons from the law, but he restrained himself. After all, aboard their passage to Canada they would be beyond Charles' clutches. They were mere hours from escaping both the British law and Charles.

★

Ewen led two uniformed constables and a sergeant to the hotel, but when they arrived they were told by the publican that the Englishman and American had left without dining. It seemed they had left the establishment via the kitchen door.

'Well, Owens, where do you think they have disappeared to?' the police sergeant asked irritably.

Ewen screwed up his face in frustration. The generous reward was slipping through his fingers. 'From what I understand, the two men are attempting to flee the British Isles. Maybe they have a berth on one of our ships departing tonight? I think we should go to the docks.'

'You had better be right, Ewen Owens, or I will consider doing you for wasting police time,' the sergeant replied. 'There are a lot of ships at the docks.'

'It would have to be one of the cargo ships steaming out of the country,' Ewen said. 'That narrows things down.' He knew the docks like the back of his hand and there was nowhere for the wanted man to hide.

*

In an elite gambling club in London, Colonel Clive Jenkins, recently returned to London from India, sat across the table from Charles Forbes, examining his hand of cards. The game was of secondary importance, however, a way of going unnoticed amongst the rakish gentlemen of the British aristocracy.

'Your brother is a hard man to kill,' Jenkins said quietly, staring at his cards.

'As I informed you, the man in your command is not my brother,' Charles said, and Jenkins looked at him sharply.

'Then who is he, old chap?' Jenkins asked.

'I have very strong reasons to believe that my brother has swapped roles with some unknown person, probably from the Australian colonies,' Charles said. 'However, I have just received a telegraph that the real Samuel Forbes has been sighted in Cardiff, and that the local constabulary will arrest him on fraud charges. When that happens, the imposter, your so-called Captain Forbes, will be revealed for who he really is. I am sure then you will be able to have him court-martialled. Does the army execute imposters pretending to hold the Queen's commission?'

'If what you say can be proved, Captain Samuel Forbes will definitely be drummed out of the army, but I doubt it will lead to his execution. He has friends on General Havelock's staff, and an impressive record of military service.'

'No matter,' Charles replied. 'As long as he is exposed.'

'It will be my greatest pleasure to have the man in my regiment paraded as an imposter and dishonourably discharged from the army,' Jenkins said. 'But what if he is killed before I return from staff college? Does the bounty still exist on his life, old chap?'

'A gentleman's agreement is to be honoured,' Charles replied, laying down his hand on the table with a smirk of satisfaction.

★

The Cardiff dock was a hub of noise and suspended coal dust. Lights illuminated areas where grubby men toiled to ensure the black gold was loaded aboard freighters, and the noise of metal chains and shouting workmen filled the early evening.

Samuel and James made their way towards the gangway of the ship that Kevin had named as their transport to Canada.

'Stop!'

The command rang out and was followed by a whistle blast. Samuel turned to see three uniformed policemen hurrying towards them, in the company of a civilian. It was obvious they were in deep trouble.

Already the appearance of the Cardiff constabulary had drawn the attention of the men working on the docks, and they paused in their labour to see what the excitement was all about.

'Stop those men!' the sergeant commanded.

'What do we do?' James asked in panic.

'We run,' Samuel said, and broke into a sprint.

Both men discarded their hand luggage to run faster, knowing that the most valuable items they had were the money belts around their waists which contained their supply of English banknotes. The situation looked hopeless when they reached the end of the wharf and turned to see the police only yards away.

'Jump!' Samuel said, grabbing James' arm and hauling him from the edge of the wharf into the dark water many feet below. They hit with a hard splash and disappeared beneath the murky salty water. Samuel was still holding James' arm as they descended into the depths. Samuel kicked out, desperately forcing his way to the surface, dragging James with him. James spat out a mouthful of dirty water when they broke the surface.

'I can't swim,' James gasped.

'I can,' Samuel spluttered, grateful he had learned when he was in the colony of New South Wales.

The weight of their shoes and jackets was dragging them beneath the surface, so Samuel quickly kicked off his shoes and struggled out of his jacket. He required all his strength to keep James afloat and when Samuel glanced up at the wharf he could see the faces of the police above peering down at them.

'You men, come to the shore immediately,' the sergeant yelled. 'You are to be arrested.'

'Like hell,' Samuel muttered to James, who bobbed in

the water while Samuel held him as best as he could with one arm. Drowning was fast becoming a possibility in the cold, filthy waters.

'We are going to swim around the bow of the ship to the other side where they cannot see us,' Samuel said in desperation. He knew they could not stay in the water for long, especially as night was beginning to fall, and if they did not drown they would be captured. It appeared that Charles had finally won. Samuel's greatest regret now was that Ian would suffer for his foolish desire to return to England. The situation was hopeless, but Samuel began swimming anyway, dragging James with him.

Somehow he was able to get them both to the far side of the hulking ship where they were hidden from the shore. But he could not find anything to hold on to, and he knew his strength was rapidly fading in the icy waters.

'I'll get you in,' came a voice from behind, and in the dim light Samuel could just make out a small rowboat with Kevin at the oars. Relief flowed through him. 'Just keep to the shadow of the ship.'

Samuel dragged James with him to the shadow, out of sight of the police on the shore. Kevin reached down and gripped James by the collar of his shirt as Samuel helped push him up and over the side of the boat. James struggled into the small craft, coughing up water. Using the last of his diminishing strength to aid him, Samuel dragged himself into the boat and slumped down beside James.

From the shore they could hear the shouts of the police trying to catch sight of them.

'Thank you,' Samuel finally gasped. 'I thought that we would drown. How is it that you became our guardian angel?'

'I was at the docks, and as soon as I saw what was happening with the peelers after you, I guessed you were in trouble. When I saw you jump into the water I ran to fetch a rowboat nearby, belongs to a friend of mine. I doubt you will be able to return to the wharf to board your ship, but all is not lost, boyos. I think I can still get you a berth. I am going to row out into the channel where the lights from the shore do not reach and take you to an iron ship that is ready to up anchor. Do you still have money?'

Samuel touched his money belt. His cash would be a bit soggy but it was still currency of the realm. 'I do,' he replied, and Kevin set out with a strong stroke, rowing the boat towards a well-lit freighter raising steam.

Samuel started to feel the night air chill his sodden clothes and beside him he could feel James shivering. After fifteen minutes they reached the side of the vessel, just as the anchors were rattling up the ship's side. Kevin called out and a rope ladder was thrown to the small boat below. He told the faces above that he needed to speak with the ship's captain about a couple of unexpected passengers prepared to pay well for a berth.

'I know the captain,' Kevin said, 'and if you mention my name while producing a generous amount of English pounds, I am sure he will find a passage for you both.' With that, Kevin extended his hand.

Samuel took it and hoped his firm grip conveyed his gratitude. 'We cannot thank you enough. I hope that we may meet again under better circumstances,' he said, releasing Kevin's hand and grasping the rope ladder.

Both he and James were able to clamber to the ship's deck, where they were met by a bearded sailor who looked more like a pirate. Nevertheless he identified himself as the ship's captain and said he had come down from the bridge to find out why his ship was being hailed by a man in a rowboat.

'Hope you got a bit of money to pay your fare,' he said.

'We do. Mr Kevin Jones highly recommended your ship,' Samuel said. 'Where is this ship bound?'

'First stop, Cape Town, and then the colony of West Australia,' the captain replied. 'Afterwards we steam to New South Wales to deliver our cargo. Have you ever been to the Australian colonies?'

Samuel just grinned.

The ship slid into the running waters of the channel, tooting its horn to indicate that it was departing on a long sea voyage, and leaving Ewen Owens on the wharf using language not acceptable in polite company.

Part Three

A Tale of Two Cities: Delhi and Lucknow

TWENTY-SIX

Alice stood on the stony ridge amongst the small encampment of army tents wearing a ragged dress stained with dried blood. The air was still filled with the stench of rotting bodies, but she barely noticed these days. If it was not raining, it was hot and humid, and the ground was a world of sticky, stinking mud.

As she stood gazing at the relief column approaching from the north, Alice saw horses pulling artillery twenty-four-pounder guns along a rutted track towards their camp. She had grown to know one artillery gun from another and had often stood beside her husband treating the results of their devastating cannonballs. Even so, it was cholera that remained the gravest threat due to the unsanitary conditions. Peter had insisted that water brought up from the stream be boiled before consumption, but Alice spent much of her time visiting those sick soldiers who had ignored her husband's advice.

Alice knew that these guns and the men marching beside them were coming to their aid. A frontal infantry assault on the impressive city walls was akin to suicide – the defenders outnumbered them and were well armed – but a combined infantry and artillery attack could make a breakthrough.

The mutineers had continued their forays against the British force on the ridge, but each attack had been repulsed by the mixed force of British soldiers and loyal Indian troops. Scott had informed Peter and Alice that the mutineers were being reinforced with what were known as Moslem *mujahidin*, holy warriors, and intelligence sources indicated that Delhi was to be established as a major centre in a resurrected Moghul empire.

'Impressive, aren't they?' Scott said, striding towards Alice. 'We now have six twenty-four-pounders, eight eighteen-pounder long guns, six eight-inch howitzers, and four ten-inch mortars. Enough artillery to concentrate on breaching the city walls. Alas, it will be the gunners, sappers and infantry who will lead the eventual attack on the town, but my squadron will follow up once they are inside the walls.'

Just then the explosive blast of British guns opened fire from the southern edge of the ridge.

'Counter battery fire,' Scott said. 'Our gunners are neutralising the closest enemy guns in one of the bastions outside the eastern city walls. We want the damned rascals to think that will be the direction of our eventual main assault.'

Suddenly, Alice doubled over and vomited, causing Scott to leap forward to her. She straightened up and wiped her mouth with the back of her tattered sleeve.

'Are you ill?' Scott asked, and his first thought was that he was seeing the onset of cholera.

'If being with child is an illness, then you could say so,' Alice said with a weak smile.

Startled, Scott could only blink his surprise. 'Does my brother know?' he asked awkwardly.

'Peter is aware of my condition,' Alice answered and Scott frowned.

'This is not the place for a woman who is with child,' he chided. 'As a medical man, my brother should know that.'

'It is a bit late now,' Alice smiled. 'Besides, for centuries women have borne children in times of war. Why should I be any different?'

'Well, let me extend my congratulations then,' Scott said gruffly. 'Let us pray that the birth comes when we are back in England.'

England, Alice thought. England was just a vague memory now, and this world of war was all she knew with its pestilence, death and dying.

Scott made his way back to HQ for a briefing, leaving Alice alone to listen to the guns roar and watch the smoke rise in the distance as the cannonballs found their mark. She was relieved that she could not hear the screaming of the men they hit – even if they were the enemy – and returned to her tent for a short nap before she joined Peter in his makeshift surgery. There were bandages to be boiled and rolled, surgical instruments to sharpen. There was a kind of simplicity to her life now, but she also thought about her pregnancy with great fear. Under these terrible circumstances, would she be able to carry the life within her to term?

★

Lucknow was now the objective of Havelock's small mixed force of British and Indian troops. First, however, the city of Cawnpore had to be taken from the rebels and the days of fighting in the surrounding countryside had taken a great toll on the Queen's soldiers. Bursting artillery fire, volleys of musketry and terrible bayonet charges under a fierce Indian sun had taken their share of lives in Ian's company at the walls of Cawnpore. But they had taken the city.

The British forces bivouacked on the Indian plain and sentries were posted. Ian's batman assisted him in setting up his tent in the meagre shade of some scrubby trees.

'I have the list of men reporting sick,' Conan said, passing Ian the company roll book.

'Cholera?' Ian asked, and Conan nodded. 'That bloody disease is taking a greater toll on our ranks than the mutineers,' Ian growled.

'The lads are still in good spirits,' Conan said. 'They trust you.'

'I fear that my decisions will one day cost them their lives,' Ian quietly admitted.

'They all took the Queen's shilling knowing that a soldier's life means the risk of being killed one day,' Conan replied.

Ian shrugged. How many times in the bloody hand-to-hand fighting for Cawnpore had he come close to death? He was fortunate that at night in his tent no one witnessed the feverish nightmares; the twitching, crying and sweating. These were the unseen wounds of a soldier exposed to combat.

Colour Sergeant Paddy Leslie approached, saluted and stood to attention.

'At ease, Colour Sergeant,' Ian said, returning the salute. 'You wish to speak to me?'

'Yes, sah,' Leslie said, glancing at Conan. 'It is a private matter.'

'I need to check on the lads settling in for the night,' Conan said and walked off.

'What is it?' Ian asked.

'It's about Sergeant Williams, sah. He has assaulted one of his men and is drunk in his tent.'

Ian was startled by the colour sergeant's revelation. He had always observed Owen's behaviour as a senior non-commissioned officer to be in line with the highest traditions of the service. He made his way to Owen's tent and found his friend sitting on an ammunition box, a bottle of gin in his hand. Owen looked at Ian through bleary eyes and remained sitting.

'Stand up, Sergeant Williams,' Ian barked.

Owen rose unsteadily to his feet in a semblance of attention, still holding the half-empty bottle of spirits. 'What is this that I hear of you assaulting one of the lads?'

'Dunno what you mean,' Owen slurred.

'Don't know what you mean, sir,' Ian said.

'Sir,' Owen added reluctantly. 'If that is what I should call you. I know all about you, *sir*. I know who you really are.'

'What are you talking about?' Ian frowned.

'Molly told me that your real name is Ian Steele and that you were once a colonial blacksmith. Between you and Curry, I reckon you have been cheating me on the loot. All you colonials are a thieving lot.'

Ian was shocked by Owen's revelation. How had Molly learned his secret? The suspicion that Conan must have told her crept into his thoughts. Who else knew? He could see there was a dramatic change in Owen, and it shocked him, but he did not understand what had caused it. It was as if he had a mental sickness – like those Ian had seen driven mad by the horrors of war.

'You well know that everything has been equally divided,' Ian said.

'What about the jewels you took when we were in the Crimea? You didn't share those with me and my brother.'

Ian acknowledged that he was right, but the Williams brothers had found their own small fortune in the Russian baggage train they had looted.

'We all collected valuables in the Crimea,' said Ian calmly. 'We have all contributed on an equal basis since then.'

'I don't believe you . . . sir,' Owen said, swaying on his feet. 'You and that colonial Paddy are working together against me. But it don't matter, because I know this war will get me killed anyway.'

'You have been reported for assaulting a soldier and here I find you drunk. No matter the circumstances of our friendship, I am obliged to have you punished in order to maintain discipline in the company,' Ian said.

'What are you going to do with me?' Owen asked.

'I am forced to have you stripped of your rank,' Ian said sadly. 'You have to get a grip, Owen, or you will get yourself killed. You will surrender that gin bottle to me now, and you will also remain in your quarters until you sober up.'

Owen hesitated but passed the bottle to Ian, who turned on his heel and stepped outside the tent. Colour Sergeant Leslie was hovering nearby.

'Make sure Private Williams remains in his tent until you deem him sober enough to join the ranks, Colour Sergeant,' Ian said, emptying the remaining gin on the dry soil of the Indian plain.

Ian found Conan supervising the cleaning of regimental kit and gestured him to follow a short distance away.

'You saw Owen?' Conan asked quietly.

'I am afraid something has happened to Owen,' Ian said worriedly, and quickly described to Conan the scene he had just witnessed. 'It is possible that the fighting has unnerved him. I have stripped him of his sergeant's rank rather than see him flogged before the regiment on a punishment parade.'

'From what the lads told me, Owen punched a soldier to get hold of the bottle of grog,' Conan said. 'Maybe the sun has got to him. A few of the lads have told me that they see Owen talking to himself – or to people he says are talking to him in his head.'

'I think the fighting and killing has got to him. Owen was never born to be a soldier. I know that because I convinced him to join up. At the time I thought we had little choice if we wanted to stay out of the hands of the peelers back in London. I think Owen resents me for making that decision.'

'How does he know my real identity?' Ian asked, staring directly into Conan's face and watching as he paled.

'I told Molly,' Conan said, stricken that he had broken his mate's confidence. 'She swore she would tell no one.'

'Well, it seems she told her brother. When I meet the Queen at a tea party, I may as well tell her I am an imposter, too. Although I am sure she already knows.'

'I'm sorry,' Conan said, truly repentant. 'Molly must have thought that as our friend, Owen already knew. I am sure both she and Owen will keep their mouths shut.'

'I hope you are right because Owen thinks that you and I are in a conspiracy to take his share of the war booty,' Ian said. 'Keep a close eye on him. He told me he thinks he will be killed in this campaign, and expressing such thoughts is likely to make him careless in what he tells people. He may think he has nothing to lose.'

'I'll kill him myself if he opens his mouth about who you really are,' Conan growled.

Conan stepped back, saluted and marched away, leaving Ian to ponder how hard it was becoming to remain Captain Samuel Forbes when so many people knew the truth.

★

Charles Forbes reluctantly paid out the last of the commission to Charles Field.

'I am sorry that you have spent so much on this search for your brother,' Field said as the pound notes were placed on his desk. 'He has proven to be a very resourceful man.'

'Do you know where the ship he escaped on was bound?' Charles asked.

'I was informed that the ship was carrying a supply of iron to South Africa, and its final cargo to the colony of New South Wales. From there I presume that your brother and his friend will take a ship across the Pacific to the United States.'

'New South Wales, you say,' Charles mused with a flicker of hope. New South Wales was where his uncle, Sir George Forbes, had a sheep property. Surely Samuel would not be able to resist visiting the man who was his real father.

Charles leaned back in his chair. 'Tell me, Mr Field, do you have contacts in the colonies?'

Field had finished counting the money and looked with surprise at his client. 'A detective I once worked with migrated to Sydney Town,' he replied. 'What do you have in mind?'

Charles removed a wad of currency from his pocket, peeled off some notes and placed them on the desk in front of Field.

'If you could get an urgent letter to your former colleague I am sure our business arrangement will continue, Mr Field,' Charles said, his determination to unmask the conspiracy stronger than ever. 'If your agent in the colony can prove that Samuel is actually in New South Wales, then that would mean the man serving in the regiment is an imposter.'

'The Australian colonies are a long way from here,' Field said.

'I have the exact details of where my brother is likely to be found. You know I am prepared to be generous and this is my advance on our venture.'

Field stared for a short moment at the money on his desk, then reached for it.

'I will endeavour to contact my man in the colony,' he said. 'But I do not promise anything.'

'My brother will feel safe and secure so far away,' Charles said. 'He will not in his wildest imagination think that I can reach across the ocean to him.'

Field stared at his client and could see the obsession blazing in his eyes. What else was this man capable of? He did not want to reflect on that any further; as a detective inspector he had once hunted murderers. He did not now wish to be employed by one.

TWENTY-SEVEN

The sound of artillery guns hardly disturbed Alice's sleep as they fired relentlessly day and night. Her baby had been conceived to the sound of their thunder, although now the gunfire was growing more intensive. Alice came awake under her mosquito net in the early hours of the morning and realised Peter was not beside her. This immediately made her think that something of great importance was occurring. She slipped quickly from the bed and dressed.

Bugles sounded and Alice could hear that the camp was coming awake with the jangle of saddlery and the neighing and snorting of cavalry horses. Men were shouting orders and outside the tent she could see the flaring lights of burning tapers.

Scott had informed her weeks earlier that the gunners had been directing a heavy bombardment on the enemy bastions outside the city walls in an effort to neutralise them before the inevitable assault on the city. The guns would also breach the walls, and then it would be up to the engineers, infantry and cavalry to finish the job.

Last night Alice had watched the columns of East India Company and British troops with their loyal Indian regiments moving out in grim silence. Scott had waved to her and shouted, 'Cheerio, old girl. Tell my brother I hope I don't meet him on his operating table.'

Alice had waved back, his ominous words echoing in her mind. It seemed that, one way or another, the fate of Delhi was in the balance on this day. A cold tremor ran through her and she hurried to the operating tent where she found Peter cleaning his surgical tools in boiling water.

'You should be resting,' Peter said when he saw her.

'I am not sick, Peter, I am pregnant, and I think you will need me when the sun rises on this day,' Alice replied firmly, looking to the pile of rags that would become bandages.

'I think you are right,' Peter said, wiping his wet hands on the apron he wore to absorb the blood. 'Scott told me that five columns have been organised to attack the city. He said not to worry about him as he was in the third column, acting as a liaison officer for the fifth column, for when the breaches had been made. He assured me that he would be safe. He said that they will be attacking from the north.'

Alice had grown very fond of her dashing brother-in-law, so different from her quiet husband, and if he was killed she knew she would mourn deeply for his loss.

'I will roll bandages and have tea and chapattis brought to us for breakfast,' Alice said, and then they fell silent as they prepared for the stream of wounded that would inevitably come once the attack commenced.

★

Major Scott Campbell sat astride his mount, frustrated by the delay. The assault had been scheduled for dawn, but the enemy had replaced some of the breaches with sandbags, and the British artillery was once again required to smash the hastily repaired fortifications.

He watched the first glimmers of the sun's rays creep above the flat horizon as his column waited behind a former residence of the old Moghul kings a quarter of a mile from the city walls to their south. Scott was not with his squadron, which had remained with the fifth column in reserve. The plan was that once the engineers and infantry had entered the city the cavalry would sweep in behind to help clear the narrow streets and alleyways of any resistance.

'It will be a damned hot day,' commented an infantry major sitting on his horse beside Scott. 'And I don't just mean the weather.'

The crash of artillery shells slamming into the city appeared to taper away and both men knew what that meant. The sun was now above the horizon and they had a clear view of the walls. Heavy smoke from the guns drifted on a light breeze.

'Well, old chap, this is it for me,' the British major sighed, dismounting from his horse and handing the reins to an Indian servant.

Scott also dismounted, disobeying his orders to act in a liaison capacity as he knew there were junior officers who could take this role. He cast about to see a lieutenant, pale faced and trembling.

'Mr Giles, you are now the liaison officer for the fifth column.'

'Sir,' the startled young officer replied. 'What do I do?'

'You remain in place close to the colonel, and he will direct you to carry orders to the fifth when required,' Scott said, and could see the expression of relief on the young man's clean-shaven face. The young officer would not have to go forward in what appeared to be a suicidal attack on the city.

The infantry major drew both his pistol and sword. Scott, who was not about to be left out of this chance for glory, did so too, although something inside told him that he was a fool.

'Welcome to the infantry, Campbell,' the infantry major grinned. 'Not as fancy as being astride a horse, galloping through the enemy ranks.'

Scott watched as the engineers moved forward to blow the Kashmiri gate open on the city's north wall. It was an extremely hazardous mission as the British engineer officers and Indian sappers would be under constant fire from the defenders on the wall when they carried the explosives forward. Under a withering fire, the British and Indian engineers were to place four gunpowder charges, reinforced by sandbags, concentrating the blast at the gate. The engineers advanced, and many were wounded or killed in the process of lighting the fuses, but their bravery was rewarded when the explosion demolished the gate.

Scott waited beside the infantry major, and a bugle sounded for the charge through the gap created by the courageous engineers. He surged forward, yelling at the top of his voice, brandishing his sabre and gripping his revolver. Men were falling before they reached the wall but Scott ignored the casualties mounting around him. The red haze of battle was on him as he panted and sweated under the heat of the early morning sun. Something whipped through his sleeve but Scott hardly registered the musket ball coming so close.

He stumbled over the rubble mixed with the smashed bodies of the engineers and found himself in the city, where the British force was met with further heavy fire from nearby houses. Scott realised that he was in the lead and had become separated from the infantry major. He cast around to see if any threats showed themselves and noticed the blood-soaked body of the major sprawled only a few paces away. The soldiers around their fallen officer hesitated, but Scott roared at them to continue the attack on the enemy, who were shooting at them from loopholes in the walls of the surrounding buildings. The men responded to his leadership, and Scott continued at a trot towards an alley which he suddenly realised was manned by four enemy infantrymen.

He whipped up his pistol arm and emptied his six shots into the four men. Two fell but the remaining two charged forward with bayonets fixed. Scott balanced on his feet and met the first bayonet lunged at him, deftly deflecting the sharp point from entering his belly. With practised skill he brought the razor-sharp sabre around to slice through the Indian's neck, severing his head from his body. A burst of blood spurted like a fountain from the headless man, soaking Scott. The second enemy soldier hesitated at the terrible sight. Scott did not pause and in a blurred movement sliced his sabre down on the sepoy's head, splitting it asunder. Four dead mutineers lay at his feet, but when he looked up he felt his stomach knot. From the other end of the alley he could see around twenty mutineers running towards him with bayonets fixed. He knew he could not fight his way out of this situation in the narrow confines of the alleyway. He was seconds from certain death when he felt himself brushed aside. A dozen red-coated soldiers pushed past him, levelling their rifled muskets at the advancing enemy. Well disciplined, they fired a volley, each bullet finding a target, and in some cases passing through one body to hit another. The attack was halted, and before the enemy could consolidate, the redcoats charged with fixed bayonets any mutineers still standing. The clash was bloody but brief. Men screamed, grunted, swore, and some even cried in the hand-to-hand fight to the death.

Scott quickly reloaded his revolver with powder and ball in a whirl of noise, heat, confusion and death. Smoke poured from burning buildings and muskets crashed all around. Chips of stinging stone spattered his face as stray musket balls hit nearby walls, but Scott hardly felt them. The red-coated soldiers retreated back to Scott, their faces and hands covered in blood. In all he counted eleven soldiers with two suffering wounds requiring a surgeon's knife.

'What now, sah?' a corporal asked, and Scott had to think. As a cavalryman, it would be simple: keep moving forward until they were through the enemy ranks.

'Get those two wounded men back to the surgeon. One man can assist them while we continue forward to capture the palace.'

'Very good, sah,' the corporal answered. He was an older man and Scott could see in his expression the years of service.

'What is your name, Corporal?' Scott asked.

'Corporal Welsh, sah,' the man answered.

'Well, Corporal Welsh, let us do some mischief to these mutineers.'

The corporal grinned under his face blackened by gunpowder. 'C'mon lads,' he said, turning to the private soldiers gripping their muskets and Enfield rifles. 'You 'eard the officer.'

Scott advanced down the alley with his loaded pistol and sabre. The soldiers followed, ready for the next encounter. As they advanced towards the royal palace, the other British columns entered the city, and also encountered fierce resistance. Many officers were killed, and some disorder ensued from a lack of leadership. At least Scott was able to provide leadership in his little sector of the battle, but he was starting to regret that he had not entered the city on his horse with his squadron. At least a horse provided him the mobility to escape the enemy, who were mostly on foot.

They broke out of the alley into a plaza where Scott could hear the crackle of musketry. When he scanned the open ground he saw the ranks of mutineers on the far side readying themselves to fire a volley at the British soldiers who had taken up a position in the open a hundred yards away. The mutineers were in the process of loading their cumbersome muskets but they had been previously trained by the British occupiers and knew their drills well.

Scott quickly appraised the situation, realising that his small force had not been noticed.

'Form a single rank!' he roared, and the well-disciplined redcoats fell quickly into a line slightly to the front and flank of the mutineers.

'Present! Fire!'

The soldiers stood, firing a volley into the mutineer infantrymen on the other side of the plaza. Their musket balls, and a few Minié balls from the Enfields, tore through the two ranks of the enemy. The volley caused confusion in the enemy ranks, and they discharged their muskets without properly levelling them.

'Ready bayonets! Charge!'

Immediately, Scott's small detail of redcoats charged across the open plaza. Yelling and cursing, they caused panic in the demoralised enemy ranks and the flashing bayonets of the British tore into exposed bellies, chests and throats as men cursed, cried and grunted their last breaths.

Scott brought his pistol up to a big, bearded Indian who was waving a large sword in the air. He thrust the muzzle into the man's face, firing as he did so. The heavy lead ball shattered bone, and flesh and blood splashed back into Scott's face as the man fell. Scott was almost felled by the body of an enemy soldier falling against him from a bayonet thrust in his chest. He stumbled but quickly regained his feet, glancing around for any immediate threat. He was pleased to see that the charge across the open plaza had succeeded, and only panting, shocked red-coated troops remained standing amongst the dead and dying Indian rebels.

'Sir, I must extend my gratitude to you for your timely intervention,' said a young lieutenant with a blackened face and blood-soaked uniform. Desultory fire was still coming from isolated enemy marksmen in the surrounding buildings. 'Lieutenant Johnson of the Foot Regiment, at your service.'

'Major Campbell, Bengali cavalry,' Scott replied, and suddenly registered his raging thirst. He reached for his water canteen on his belt and a searing pain shot through his left wrist.

Scott spun around in shock, noticing at the same time that Lieutenant Johnson had already issued orders for his men to take cover. Scott felt Corporal Welsh grip his jacket and yank him to the cover of a stone wall at the edge of the plaza, shielding him against other marksmen in the surrounding houses.

Scott stared down at his hand and saw his mangled wrist. Blood was flowing from the wound and pain coursed through his body.

'Here, sah,' said the British NCO. 'I will wrap your wrist.' He produced a clean linen cloth and commenced wrapping the wound, although blood quickly soaked the cloth. The pain was numbing Scott's mind as he fought off the desire to scream.

'Corporal, you take our men to join Mr Johnson's unit.

Leave me and I will make my own way back for medical treatment,' Scott ordered through gritted teeth.

'Sah, I can help you back to our lines,' the corporal protested. 'The lads will be all right with Mr Johnson.'

'Thank you, Corporal Welsh, but I can see your lads will need you, and I can walk,' Scott grimaced.

'Very good, sah,' the NCO answered. 'Good luck, sah.'

Corporal Welsh fell in with the main contingent of the advancing force preparing to clear the enemy from the houses around them. Their muskets were primed and their bayonets fixed for the inevitable hand-to-hand fighting.

Scott gripped his loaded pistol in his right hand and looked back to the mouth of the alley he had cleared minutes earlier. He knew that he would have to retrace his steps lest he become confused in the winding streets of the city. Around him he could hear the firing of small arms and artillery, and the shouts in English and Indian dialects of men using their last words in defiance of death. He was still experiencing a terrible thirst and slipped his revolver into the leather holster as he again attempted to retrieve his canteen. The water partly revived his body and when he had finished slaking his thirst, he carried on.

Scott stepped over the bodies of the mutineers he and his small squad had killed only minutes earlier, although it felt like a lifetime ago. When he reached the area before the breach in the wall he saw a red-coated soldier lying on his back, groaning as he held in his own intestines. Scott looked around and could see that the army had advanced, leaving the critically wounded soldier to his fate. Scott knelt beside the man and saw how young he was. He guessed he must have been around sixteen years old.

'I will get you to the surgeon, Private,' Scott said, ignoring the intense pain of his own wound.

'Too late for me,' the soldier said, staring up at the blue skies. 'Could you tell me ma that I died like a soldier?' He gasped and closed his eyes. Scott could see that his stomach wound was beyond medical care, and he would die in agony under the blazing sun alone.

'I will tell your family you died heroically storming the walls of Delhi,' Scott said, and while the young soldier's eyes were closed, he shot him in the head, ending his agony.

Scott rose and stumbled towards the smashed gate to leave the city.

★

By midmorning a steady stream of wounded was arriving at Peter's tent for surgery. The big, lead balls of the enemy's muskets caused horrific wounds, smashing bone as they entered the body. There were others with bayonet wounds and sword cuts, and Peter worked feverishly to amputate limbs that were beyond repair. Alice went amongst those waiting on stretchers outside in the blazing sun, carrying canteens of boiled water to quench their thirsts, and examined the extent of wounds, prioritising those she knew her husband might save.

Alice bent over one older soldier who had sustained a musket shot to the chest. She knew there was no sense in attempting to extract the ball, as bloody froth formed around his mouth and his skin had paled under his tanned, bearded face.

She felt the grip of his hand in her own as he stared at the vultures swirling in clouds over the camp. 'I'm slain,' he whispered, closing his eyes. Alice could see that he was dead, and slowly rose to attend the next man.

'I said I would be back.'

Alice turned to see Scott standing a few paces away, holding his arm. She could see the blood-soaked bandage around his left wrist.

'Oh my God!' she said, stepping towards him. 'How bad is your wound?'

'I am hoping that Peter can tell me,' Scott replied through gritted teeth, and slowly sank to his knees.

TWENTY-EIGHT

The two medical orderlies assisting Peter were older soldiers unfit for combative operations, and they carried the amputated arms and legs of soldiers out of the large surgical tent and discarded them in a pile outside. While Scott waited for his turn, he glanced at the tangle of limbs, wondering if his left hand would soon be added to the already stinking and decomposing flesh now covered with myriad crawling flies.

Scott stepped inside the tent, dread written in his agonised expression. Peter looked up from a patient whose life he could not save, and the orderlies removed the body from the table.

'I hope you have time to look to my rather minor wound,' Scott said, attempting a smile that turned into a grimace.

Peter could see the blood-soaked bandage and the blood dripping from it.

'Good God, old man!' Peter said, wiping his bloody hands on his apron. 'What have you done to yourself?'

Scott stepped forward, raising his arm so that Peter could examine the shattered wrist. Peter gently unwrapped the bandage to reveal the extent of the wound.

'I think it just needs a few stitches and then I will be able to join the lads again,' Scott suggested, but Peter knew better. He could see fragments of bone mixed with the pulverised wrist joint, all barely held together by a few strips of raw flesh. It was obvious that the wound was beyond repair and the hand required amputation.

'I need you to get on the table,' Peter said. 'The only way I can save your life is to remove your hand at the wrist.'

Scott looked with despair into his brother's eyes. 'Are you sure you cannot sew my hand back together?' he asked, and Peter shook his head.

'I promise it will be quick, and with further treatment you should recover well.'

Scott lay down on the table smeared with blood and Peter nodded to his two attendants who stepped forward and put their hands firmly on the cavalry officer's shoulder and arm. Peter fetched an extremely sharp knife, silently thanking God that from what he could observe he would not have to use a surgical saw to cut through bone.

Before Scott could react, Peter gripped the useless hand and, with a deft movement, sliced through the flesh that retained hand to arm. The hand came off and Scott let out a strangled cry of pain. Peter quickly passed the amputated flesh to one of the orderlies who discreetly placed it in a new pile of limbs collecting in the corner of the tent, awaiting disposal outside.

Peter quickly and expertly went about cleansing the open

wound with a mix of water and carbolic acid. His brother attempted to sit up.

'Take it easy, old boy,' Peter said gently, tears in his eyes. He had always thought he was immune to the terrible suffering of his patients, but this was different. This was his own brother who had always lived life to the fullest. Now he had lost his hand and his life would change forever.

Alice appeared in the tent.

'Alice will help you back to your quarters,' Peter said after bandaging the wrist. 'She will care for you until you have recovered.'

Alice helped Scott from the surgical tent to his own, and there made sure he lay down on his cot.

'I need some medicine,' Scott groaned. 'You will find it in my chest.'

Alice opened the lid to the big chest and saw a bottle of whisky on top of his kit. Alice removed the stopper and poured an amount into a tin mug, handing it to Scott.

'You should be drinking water and trying to sleep,' she chided gently.

He grinned weakly and took a long gulp of the alcohol. 'Leave the bottle by my bed,' he said, using his right hand to place the mug beside him and pouring another shot from the bottle.

'I will return whenever my duties allow,' Alice said. 'Your bandages will need to be changed daily.'

'You are an angel in my life,' Scott said. 'The best thing my brother ever did was marry you, and if he had not, I would have married you myself.'

'I am sure that one day you will meet a good woman,' Alice replied. 'You are still a dashing figure, and I am sure we will be able to fit you with a wooden hand when your wound heals.'

'Ah, a one-handed cavalry officer,' Scott sighed.

'You will be up and leading your men in no time,' Alice said, wiping Scott's brow with a wet cloth.

Scott gripped Alice's arm. 'Do you really believe that?' he asked.

Alice nodded. 'Now get some sleep and I pray that the pain will recede with rest,' she said.

Scott lay back and stared at the ceiling of the tent. They both knew that infection could still easily take his life in this Indian climate. Alice pulled down the mosquito net to keep off the clouds of flies gathering to the smell of blood. She said a quiet prayer that her brother-in-law would live.

She hurried back to the wounded men lying on stretchers outside the surgery tent and calmly went about her work of assessing who would be next on her husband's operating table, and comforting those she knew would die.

★

Private Owen Williams sat on a wooden crate in the bivouac on the road to Lucknow, cleaning his rifle. Around him, soldiers smoked pipes, played cards and exchanged gossip about the battle ahead. They ignored Owen, whose morose manner did not encourage company. He stewed in his thoughts about the betrayal of the two men he had once thought were his friends. He was sure they were keeping his share of the loot. Captain Samuel Forbes was an imposter, and both he and Conan Curry were colonials from New South Wales, so neither of them could be trusted. Owen promised the voices inside his head that he would get even with them – one way or another.

'Hey, Taffy,' called one of the soldiers sitting in a small circle a few feet away. 'Want to join us in a hand or two of cards? Winner gets a bottle of gin.'

Owen put down his rifle and accepted the offer. Despite once being their sergeant, the men had accepted him back into their ranks, and a bottle of gin was worth gambling for. Even as the cards were dealt Owen fumed about the betrayal of trust by the fancypants Captain Steele. When Colonel Jenkins returned to the regiment Owen would parade before him and expose the upstart colonial officer for who he really was. Owen did not trust the current acting regimental commander because he seemed to respect Ian Steele as a very competent officer. But Owen knew from their campaign in the Crimea that Colonel Jenkins would listen to him.

*

Colonel Jenkins was pleased to be on leave from the staff college. He found military matters boring and the invitation to Lady Rebecca Montegue's manor was a breath of fresh air. He arrived in his personal coach in the mid-afternoon and knew that he would not be returning before breakfast. India had kept him away from what was most important in life: his future marriage to Rebecca, whose wealth, coupled with her influential political contacts, would help him achieve the highest office in the land.

The occasion was an afternoon tea held in the manicured gardens of the country estate while the last flowers of the English summer still bloomed. Jenkins was greeted by a butler who ushered him into a garden of colourful pavilions erected on the sprawling lawns of Rebecca's grand mansion. Jenkins could see that there were many civilian and military guests. Amongst the civilians he recognised prominent members of parliament, wealthy bankers and captains of industry.

Rebecca radiated beauty and charm when she walked over to greet Jenkins.

'A rather lavish afternoon party,' he said.

'Thank you, Clive,' Rebecca replied. 'I thought this would be a good opportunity to show you off to some very important people.'

'Ah,' Jenkins said, bowing and kissing Rebecca's hand. 'You are the one who should be teaching strategy and tactics.'

'Come,' Rebecca said, and Jenkins followed her towards a small group of high-ranking army and naval officers in their dress uniforms, adorned with the medals of their service. Jenkins was dressed in a civilian suit with top hat.

'Ah, Lady Montegue,' said one of the naval officers when she and Jenkins approached. He gave a small bow of respect, and then focused on Clive Jenkins. 'I have heard that you are currently attending the new staff college, Colonel Jenkins. Not sure if all that book work and theory is really necessary to be a good soldier. We sailors learn about warfare from experience rather than books.'

'Times are changing, Sir Rodney,' Jenkins replied politely. 'New weapons are changing the way we manoeuvre on the battlefield.'

'I am surprised that you made leave from your regiment when it is engaged on a campaign in India, old boy,' a whiskered general commented, and Jenkins identified him as a close friend of General Havelock. 'I would have suspected that to choose a place at staff college under such circumstances would have been a second priority to that of leading your men in the field.'

Jenkins felt uncomfortable. It was almost as if he was being accused of desertion, or worse, cowardice. He glanced at Rebecca and he could see her frowning.

'If you really wish to know why Colonel Jenkins returned to England it was because he missed my company, gentlemen,' Rebecca said, slipping her arm through Jenkins'. 'I must apologise and take the colonel to meet my other guests. I will bid you gentlemen a good afternoon. I am sure you will agree that the French champagne is of excellent quality.'

The small group of military officers raised their glasses as a salute to Rebecca as she led Jenkins away to meet with a couple of members of the House of Lords. All Jenkins received from the two older politicians was praise for his esteemed military service. Jenkins felt much more comfortable in their company, chatting about the demise of morals in this modern world of too many liberal ideas.

The afternoon drew towards evening and the coaches arrived to return the guests to their respective homes in London, leaving Rebecca and Clive Jenkins to their own company.

'It has been a grand day, thank you,' Jenkins said, sipping the last of his champagne.

'I planned the function as soon as I learned that you were returning to England,' Rebecca said. 'You were not born to be a soldier, rather a man destined to lead this country into the future.'

'I could be insulted by your observation,' Jenkins said, 'but I know that a union between us is destined for greatness. I often wonder, though, if you love me or simply see that you can mould me into the man of your dreams.'

'Love is irrelevant,' Rebecca said. 'But I am fond of you, and that is a good basis for a partnership.'

'So, you will marry me after all,' Jenkins said, and felt quite content that he would possess this rare beauty with great ambition.

'When you are no longer playing soldiers, I will,' Rebecca said, turning to walk to her manor as the servants scurried about clearing up after the visitors. 'But I will expect you to do me one great favour before we wed. I want you to destroy Sir Archibald Forbes' son, Charles, who I know is a friend of yours.'

Jenkins was stunned by Rebecca's request. 'Charles!' he exclaimed in shock. 'Why do you wish me to destroy the man?'

'Because I have asked you to,' Rebecca replied. 'If you have any real feelings for me, you will ensure that you use all in your power to destroy Charles Forbes.'

'I do not understand,' Jenkins said, shaking his head in his confusion.

'I want him killed,' Rebecca said without flinching. 'He has done me a great wrong that I do not wish to disclose at the moment, but I trust that in your love for me you will carry out my wishes.'

★

That night Jenkins lay beside Rebecca in the huge double bed, staring at the dark ceiling. He could not sleep. What kind of woman was he marrying? Behind her beauty lay a woman as ruthless as any enemy he had ever encountered on the battlefield. What had Charles Forbes done to her that would warrant his destruction, even his death?

Jenkins was a weak man and he knew it. He was not about to question Rebecca as to her motives. He thought about the conspiracy that he and Charles had entered into to have Samuel killed, and wondered how this orderly society he belonged to could be crawling with vipers – both male and female.

Rebecca stirred beside him, rolling over to face him. In the trickle of moonlight through the panes of the bedroom window he swore he could see a smile of satisfaction on her

284

face. For once Jenkins wished he was back in India facing the dangers of an enemy he understood, but he knew he was a slave to this beautiful woman beside him. After all, he knew she had the potential to make him prime minister.

TWENTY-NINE

Torrential rain fell the night after the battle, and the British survivors huddled in misery in the open, waiting for the sun to rise. Colour Sergeant Leslie moved amongst the cold and wet troops, offering a word of encouragement and a joke where possible. When he came across Private Owen Williams sitting alone, the man was mumbling incoherently and stabbing at the muddy earth with a long bayonet. Colour Sergeant Paddy Leslie had seen this behaviour many times in his long years with the British army. It was something the horror of war did to many soldiers' minds, and he could see that Private Owen Williams had reached that point where the mind no longer controlled the body. The army's cure for such a state was harsh corporal punishment, but Paddy Leslie had never seen that cure any soldier of the malaise induced by combat.

'Taffy, get control of yourself,' Leslie snapped as the rain beat down on them.

For a moment Owen paused to stare at the ground. 'Got to go home, Colour Sergeant,' he said. 'Sarn't Major Curry is out to get me – and so is Captain Forbes.'

Leslie crouched down beside Owen. 'You have to snap out of this, Private Williams, or you will find yourself tied to the triangle for a lashing.'

'I don't care anymore,' Owen said, tears streaming down his face. 'I just want to go home. I don't want to die here.'

Leslie stood, shaking his head. He realised that the soldier was beyond reasoning with and only hoped that when the sun rose he might be thinking more clearly. The word spreading through the regiment was that in the morning they expected to see action near the fortified village of Unao. Leslie knew that he should report Private Williams' condition, but he had a soft spot for the man he had recruited for the war against the Russians in the Crimea. Owen Williams had been a brave and excellent soldier then, but time had clearly taken a toll on his mind. With cholera and heatstroke impacting so highly on the small force, every man who could hold a rifle was needed to fight under General Havelock on his advance towards Lucknow, a mere thirty-six miles away. Colour Sergeant Leslie walked away in the rain, leaving the afflicted soldier to continue stabbing the muddy earth with his bayonet.

*

The sun rose on the following morning to beat down on the heads of the assembled British force. Captain Ian Steele called for the roll to be read and was satisfied to see that all his company was on parade, albeit wet and weary. On either flank of the regiment other British units were assembling, and laid out before them across a swamp were the walled houses outside Unao. A raised road ran through the swamp to the fortified town, and using his telescope Ian could see that the houses had firing loopholes in the walls.

'What is happening today?' Conan asked.

'General Havelock is sending in the Scots along the causeway,' Ian replied, lowering his telescope. Already fire pouring from the defences was ripping into the Scottish ranks and men were falling. Ian could see the terrible price the Highlanders were paying for the assault, but he closed his mind to their casualties as he knew that before the day ended it would be his regiment's turn to face the defences. Havelock's staff had calculated that there were around fifteen thousand mutineers up against their small force of around fifteen hundred.

The enemy artillery opened fire, adding grape and round shot into the advancing Scots soldiers, who were roaring the ancient slogans of the Highlands as they advanced into the wall of lead and iron.

'Poor bastards,' Conan said softly. 'Straight into a frontal assault against an entrenched enemy.'

'Rather them than us,' Ian replied, wiping sweat from his forehead with the back of his hand. The heat was becoming oppressive and Ian wondered how many of his men would succumb to the invisible enemy that dogged them alongside the cholera. 'We are being held in reserve but as the enemy outnumber us I know we will see our share of action. I will brief the junior officers and senior NCOs in five minutes.'

Conan acknowledged the unspoken order to spread the word about the briefing, and afterward the officers and NCOs marched smartly back to their sections to continue with preparations. Only Colour Sergeant Leslie lingered.

'What is it, Colour Sergeant?' Ian asked.

'Sir, it is a matter about Private Williams,' he replied. 'Is there a chance he could be kept back with the regimental HQ when we commence the advance?'

'Why does Private Williams need to be kept out of the advance?' Ian frowned.

'I think he needs a rest from being in the ranks,' Leslie said. 'His mind has been touched and I don't think he will live if he advances as a skirmisher. I have seen this before when a soldier loses his mind.'

Ian thought for a moment, accepting the senior NCO's many years of soldiering. 'I will get the CSM to pass on to Private Williams that he is to be assigned to regimental HQ as a runner for the company.'

'Thank you, sir,' Leslie said, then saluted and returned to his young lieutenant, who would be carrying the colours into battle.

Even as Ian's company went about their duties, the Scots Highlanders were progressing along the causeway towards the fortified town with their two artillery guns supporting them. The town had deep ditches and new earthworks to overcome in the assault. The battle had well and truly begun and in the next few hours they would either win against the seemingly impossible odds, or forever remain in Indian soil if they lost.

Soon enough the remnants of the courageous Scottish brigade were on the first line of the defenders, pushing through with bayonets and entering the town of Unao. The British forces were aided by the fact that the nearby flooded plains prevented the numerically larger Indian cavalry threatening their flanks.

A runner was sent from Havelock's HQ to the regiment, and the order was passed down to the company commanders.

Ian turned to his men.

'Fix bayonets!' A rattle of long knives being attached to the end of rifled muskets sounded, and Ian roared the next order. 'Company will advance. Advance!'

Leading the way, he stepped onto the causeway to follow the unflinching Scots into the town. The company acted as the vanguard for the regiment and soon Ian's men were in the narrow streets, fighting a desperate battle of musket fire and hand-to-hand bayonet combat, as the mutineers quickly deserted their positions. Smoke filled the hot, humid air but Ian noted his men were going about their work well, ever alert to snipers in houses and on rooftops. After many hours clearing Unao they were past the houses and marketplaces and facing their next obstacle: a village called Busserut Gunge which was also heavily fortified.

As night was approaching, Havelock gave the order to bivouac and consolidate the positions they had taken. The small British force had suffered many casualties in the initial assault, and the British general well knew he would take many more on the morrow.

After a rollcall of the butcher's bill, Ian ensured his company had time to take a meal and to check one another for signs of cholera and heatstroke, and for his officers and senior NCOs to be briefed on the next day's fighting. Exhausted as all were, they listened, and very few questions were asked as to their duties. It would be another night of little sleep as men contemplated what lay ahead of them.

When the sun rose, Ian was summoned to a regimental briefing and the orders were issued. They were to participate in a second battle for the village of Busserut Gunge. It, too, had the obstacle of a swamp, and a narrow causeway and bridge leading to it. The mutineers had also reinforced the village with earthworks, protecting their artillery and infantry.

Ian's company was to attack from the left flank.

Weary men looked to their kit and rifled muskets as sergeants and corporals checked the men for their fitness to fight. Cholera continued to stalk the soldiers as surely as the enemy.

Conan joined Ian who was standing alone, deep in his thoughts.

'Reporting that the company is ready to advance, sir,' he said smartly, and Ian lifted his telescope to survey the narrow causeway and village ahead.

'Very good, Sarn't Major,' Ian replied, staring gloomily at their target. Around him the other companies of the regiment deployed into their formations and Owen joined them.

'Order to move out, sir,' Owen said to Ian.

'How are you finding your tasks as the messenger at HQ, Owen?' Conan asked.

'Can't complain,' Owen answered, but his tone was cold, and Conan was hurt by the sullen reply.

'Very good, Private Williams,' Ian said. 'Inform the general staff that we are advancing now.'

Owen saluted, turned and marched back to General Havelock's HQ behind the ranks of infantry.

'He does not appear to be very happy,' Conan remarked.

'I had no pleasure in reducing him to the ranks,' Ian said. 'I am hoping he will redeem himself and get his rank back. But right now we have a fight on our hands. Sarn't Major, fall in with the colour party.'

Conan saluted and fell back with the regimental standard.

For just a moment, Ian hesitated. Behind him he could feel the tension of the men waiting. 'Company will fix bayonets!' he roared. The click of bayonets fitted to the ends of the rifled musket barrels was ominous as it meant the terrible struggle of man on man in a fight to the death. 'Company will advance! Advance!'

Ian stepped off. He did not hold his sword but a rifle instead, despite the orders issued that all officers would lead with swords drawn. In a holster was his six-shot cap and ball Beaumont Adams revolver, and tucked in his belt was Samuel's pistol. His sheathed sword was strapped to his belt.

The company of infantry moved in their orderly ranks towards the causeway, and the Indian rebels commenced firing at them with muskets and artillery.

Ian gave his next order before his voice could be drowned out by the rising noise of battle.

'Company, at the double, charge!'

And so the men following Ian passed through the doorway into a place called death.

★

Colonel Clive Jenkins was in London and pondering the task Rebecca had assigned him. He sat in a deep leather chair in the lounge of his club, sipping a gin and tonic. Around him other exclusive members quietly read *The Times*, following the mutiny in India before turning to the financial section to observe its impact on their stocks and shares.

'Sir, your guest, Mr Charles Forbes, is here,' said one of the club's uniformed employees.

'Fetch him to me,' Jenkins said. 'And bring me another G and T. Also a whisky straight for Mr Forbes.'

When Charles arrived, he sat down in one of the big leather armchairs opposite Jenkins.

'Good to see you, old chap,' Jenkins said. 'If I remember correctly, whisky is your poison, so I have taken the liberty of ordering one for you.'

'A little early for me, but I thank you for your courtesy,' Charles replied. 'Your invitation to meet this early in the morning is rather unusual, Colonel Jenkins.'

'I know you are a busy man, Mr Forbes, but this matter is important,' Jenkins replied. 'How well do you know Lady Rebecca Montegue?'

Charles accepted the tumbler of whisky brought to him on a silver platter by the waiter. He was startled by the question, so directly asked. 'I have only been in the company of Lady Montegue at social occasions – I barely know her – although she has a striking resemblance to a village girl I once knew.'

This revelation caused the hair on the back of Jenkins' neck to rise. He did not know why, but there was something in the statement that made him suspect he'd found the seed for Rebecca's intense dislike of this man.

'You say that the woman you knew has a remarkable resemblance to Lady Montegue,' Jenkins said as casually as he could. 'Where is she now?'

'I was last informed that she had run away from the village near our country manor,' Charles replied with a frown. 'No one has had any news of her whereabouts since; she might be dead for all I know. As a matter of interest, the woman was reputedly pregnant to my brother . . . or should I say, to the man pretending to be my brother, the man you command as Captain Samuel Forbes.'

Jenkins raised his eyebrows at this snippet of gossip. 'What is the name of this woman?'

'Her name was Jane Wilberforce,' Charles said, taking another sip of the whisky.

'You say she was with child to Captain Forbes,' Jenkins said. 'How did you know that?'

Charles paused. 'Your questions seem a little strange, Colonel,' he frowned. 'Why are you so interested?'

Jenkins could see that he had hit a raw nerve with Charles and decided it was best to discontinue his line of questioning.

'Because of Captain Forbes,' Jenkins replied. 'Know your enemy, as they say.'

His response seemed to settle Charles, and their conversation turned to matters financial. Two more drinks and Charles excused himself to attend a luncheon with members of a bank board.

Jenkins watched him leave and ordered another gin and tonic. There were clearly intricate threads that would need to be tied together before he could understand why Lady Rebecca Montegue wanted to see Charles Forbes dead.

THIRTY

Thirst, fear and adrenaline surged through Ian's body as he led the charge on the earthworks. Grapeshot from a cannon blasted past him and two soldiers screamed in agony as the big metal balls ripped through them. A third soldier took the full impact of five balls and was ripped into bloody scraps of flesh and cloth. But Ian kept going; he could see the raised earth just a few yards ahead. His rifle was levelled and the bayonet readied to find a soft target of stomach, throat or chest.

He scrambled to the clinging clay of the sloped front wall and caught a glimpse of one of the mutineers. Before he could lunge with his bayonet the target was gone, and Ian rolled onto his side to unholster his revolver. Rifle in one hand and revolver in the other, he flung himself over the wall onto a startled Indian soldier. Once on his feet, Ian levelled the pistol, firing point blank into the man's face, causing the rebel to fall backwards.

Around him Ian could see the rest of his surviving company tumble down amongst the Indians who had not had time to flee the artillery guns they had manned. Maddened by the terrible wounds the guns had inflicted on their comrades, the British soldiers bayoneted and shot any enemy they encountered, asking no quarter and giving none either.

Ian glanced around and saw that the regimental colours were fluttering from the staff and was pleased to see Colour Sergeant Leslie standing alongside the colour ensign with Conan. The firing tapered off except for an odd shot from his men at the backs of the retreating mutineers.

'We've done it, sir,' Colour Sergeant Leslie said. 'We've put the beggars to flight.'

Ian's ears were ringing as he clambered to the top of the earthworks and looked back down the causeway where he could see the trail of smashed and broken red-coated soldiers. The victory, like so many others on the road to Lucknow, had come at significant cost.

From here Ian could see Private Owen Williams running towards him.

'Sir, General Havelock requires your attendance at his HQ,' Owen said breathlessly. Ian acknowledged the instruction and passed temporary command to one of his senior lieutenants to organise the consolidation of the positions they had taken.

Ian arrived at the headquarters under an open tent where senior officers stood around a table jabbing with their fingers at points on a map. Ian waited patiently, noticing his fellow senior officers of the various units of Havelock's force. Like Ian, they stood back, faces blackened by the gunpowder of battle, their eyes weary and their expressions grim. Eventually Havelock ceased conversing with his brigade staff officers and turned to the assembled officers.

'Gentlemen, my order of the day is that all regiments withdraw from their current positions and fall back on Unao for the night. I have decided that due to our casualties we do not have sufficient force to continue our advance on Lucknow. From Unao we will march to Cawnpore, as I have received a message from the garrison there that they have come under a fresh threat from hostile forces gathering in strength in the countryside. But we can remember that we have fought seven battles and been victorious in each one against greater odds. In the last two days we have captured nineteen cannons, but I have been informed that it is estimated that we have only twelve hundred able-bodied men left. It is my intention to gather reinforcements before we advance. For now, we need to get our sick and wounded to a place where they may be treated. God be with you all, gentlemen.'

Ian listened and agreed with General Havelock's summation of the situation. He was also aware how important it was to advance on the Indian city of Cawnpore once again where a force of British soldiers was holding out in a compound within the walls. Not only were there British and loyal Indian forces facing starvation within the city, but also many civilian men, women and children.

★

Colonel Clive Jenkins wore his dress uniform to the dinner held in honour of the British prime minister at Rebecca's London residence. Rebecca was resplendent in her finest clothes and jewels.

As they waited to welcome the distinguished guests, Jenkins mulled over the conversation he had had with Charles Forbes and broke the silence by saying, 'I met with Mr Forbes this day and he informed me that his brother,

Captain Forbes, knew a village girl, a Miss Jane Wilberforce, whom he supposedly got with child. Did you know this Jane Wilberforce?' He could see Rebecca tense at his question.

'Why do you ask?' Rebecca countered.

'It is just that Charles mentioned how much this village girl resembled you – as if you could pass for sisters – and I feel this may account for your interest in Charles Forbes,' Jenkins replied.

'I did not ask you to meet with Charles Forbes,' Rebecca said stiffly. 'I asked you to ensure he was either disgraced or made to disappear forever.'

'You are asking me to risk everything for this foolish notion and yet you do not do me the service of telling me why,' Jenkins said. 'You have me bewitched, and you know I will do anything for you, but this is asking something that could see my neck stretched.'

'Jane was my twin sister,' Rebecca said quietly. 'We were separated at birth, and it was only in the last few months before her mysterious disappearance that I was told of her existence, although I always had a strange and inexplicable feeling that I was not alone. I found Jane living in the village, and she reluctantly told me that she was Charles Forbes' mistress but that she had found love with Charles' brother, Samuel. Jane's last contact with Samuel was when he was in the Crimea and she wrote that she was expecting his child. After that, my sister simply vanished from the face of the earth. Both Samuel and I strongly suspect that Charles was behind her disappearance, which I can only imagine means that he killed her. If you truly love me you will act as my avenging angel and bring justice for my sister.'

Stunned, Jenkins listened to the hatred for Charles Forbes that was clear in Rebecca's voice. 'Do you have proof that Charles killed your sister?' he asked.

Rebecca turned towards him with a cold stare. 'I do not need to have legal proof. I know he is responsible for my sister's death. Call it intuition.'

Jenkins did not attempt to argue with her zeal. All he knew was that if he did not agree to help her get vengeance then she would sever her ties with him. Jenkins accepted that he must find a way of either ruining Charles Forbes or killing him. Neither would be easy, and there remained the matter of the pact he and Charles had made to have Captain Samuel Forbes eliminated. The latter task of seeing off Samuel Forbes – or whoever he may be – was personal to Jenkins, as the infernal man had witnessed Jenkins' cowardice on the battlefields of the Crimea.

Just then the carriage of the prime minister was announced. As soon as the formal greetings were over, Rebecca manoeuvred Jenkins into the prime minister's company and Jenkins, a hero of the Crimea and recently in India with his regiment, was quizzed on his views on the current campaign to quell the mutiny.

Jenkins was quick to ingratiate himself with the highest level of political power, all the while knowing that it was Rebecca pulling the strings. He knew he needed her, and this reinforced his thoughts of plotting the demise of Charles Forbes. Had Charles not displayed his murderous aspirations when he'd asked Jenkins' help get rid of his so-called brother for his own convenience? Surely such a man had the capacity to kill in his own right? It was a small consolation to Jenkins that he would not be killing an innocent man. But a voice echoed in his thoughts, telling him that he was a coward and that killing Charles Forbes was beyond him.

★

Nana Sahib had mustered forces at the town of Bithoor, sending his cavalry into the outer suburbs of Cawnpore. Ian's company fired on them from the cover of the city's buildings, causing them to retreat under the British riflemen's deadly accuracy. The same story was repeated in other sections of Cawnpore with the result that the enemy commander fell back with his army, but the audacious display against the city captured by the British proved that the mutineers were far from a defeated force.

As usual the heat beat down on the defenders, and Ian found a small scrap of shade beside one of the mudbrick buildings in the city. He flopped down, reaching for his water canteen, and was joined by his company sergeant major.

'No casualties to report amongst our lads in that skirmish, but a few of the mutineers never made it out of the city,' Conan said wearily.

'Good show, Sarn't Major.' Ian sighed as the warm water took away his immediate thirst. His head throbbed, and he forced himself not to allow the listless state he was experiencing to detract from his duties as company commander. Along the low mudbrick wall they had used as a defence he could see his men taking out pipes and lighting them as they chattered amongst themselves, boasting of their marksmanship in the recent melee.

'Oh, the mail arrived and I picked up a letter for you from regimental HQ,' Conan said, reaching inside his jacket to retrieve the precious envelope. 'Somebody back in England must love you.' He grinned, passing the letter to Ian. 'I don't know how any woman could, though.'

'Have you heard from Molly?' Ian asked, holding the precious correspondence and recognising Ella's handwriting.

'I have. She asks after your health. She has written that the two shops are doing a grand trade. It seems she is the bright one in the Williams family. I will leave you to your letter.' Conan rose to walk down the ranks of men sitting with their backs to the wall and enquired gruffly as to their welfare.

Ian carefully opened the envelope, extracting the delicate sheet of paper. He began to read with a serene smile on his face, but halfway through the one-page letter his smile turned to a stricken expression and his hands began to tremble. Ella had written that she was sorry to have to tell him in such an impersonal way that she had met another man who had her father's approval. He was a Russian aristocrat of the Jewish faith by the name of Nikolai Kasatkin who had recently escaped the Russian Tsar via India. Surely Ian remembered him because she believed he had rescued Nikolai during a dangerous mission. He was now a partner in certain enterprises with her father, and the love had grown slowly between them. She wished Ian well and prayed that he would be safe.

For a fleeting moment Ian remembered how he and Nikolai had met during a truce in the Crimean War; he could never have imagined then that the same man would take the heart of the woman he had come to love beyond his own life. He sat staring into the blinding heat rising as a shimmering wave in the street. He tried to convince himself it would never have worked between them when their lives were divided by his soldiering career and their religions. But he had not really believed that this would have been an insurmountable barrier to their love.

Tears trickled down Ian's face, smearing the gunpowder residue and leaving furrows in the black soot stains. He could not remember the last time he had cried. For so long in his life he had been told by his father that tears were the realm of women and not men. Men had to remain stoic in the face of sorrow. But the tears came and Ian wondered if they were all for the loss of Ella – or for something deeper: that of a life of peace beyond war.

Then the order came that General Havelock was to resume his advance towards Lucknow, and the contents of the letter seemed irrelevant as Ian once again faced his possible death.

★

Private Williams could not get the voices out of his head. Captain Forbes and Sergeant Major Curry were plotting to have him killed so that they did not have to share any of the spoils of war. He knew he must do something to protect himself. A stray musket ball would do the trick, and satisfy the nagging of the voices in his head. It was so easy to make a death look like a genuine battle wound. And Owen was one of the best marksmen in the regiment. He would be able to carry out the killings when the time was right.

THIRTY-ONE

After a ferocious struggle, the Indian city of Delhi had been taken by the British forces.

Dr Peter Campbell had immediately sought out one of the better residences that had not been completely vandalised and had it converted to a surgery. The house had accommodation in the upstairs portion for him and his wife and their Indian housemaid who had loyally followed them from Meerut.

Amongst Peter's first patients was Scott, for treatment to the stump at the end of his left wrist. The wound had miraculously avoided infection and, under the clean bandages, was healing. Peter was able to remove the stitches, but the stump still throbbed and the pain was excruciating if Scott bumped it.

'Well, old chap, it is not the end of the world,' Peter attempted to reassure his brother as he examined the wound closely. 'Back in England there are people who design artificial hands.'

'I'm an officer on active service, and I cannot be away from the men of my squadron,' Scott moaned. 'I can't wait till we return to England.'

Alice entered her husband's surgery.

'Did I hear that you need an artificial hand?' she asked with the hint of a smile. She held out something wrapped in a cloth. 'I happen to know a Gurkha soldier who is renowned for his wood carving and he kindly made this for me.' She unwrapped the article from the cloth and passed it to Scott.

'Good God!' Peter exclaimed. 'It looks almost real. Alice, you are a miracle worker.'

Frowning, Scott held the wooden hand with its leather straps in his good hand. 'It does not replace the function of my real hand,' he said with a surly tone.

Alice smiled broadly, suddenly producing a second wooden hand, but this one had the fingers curled with a hollow between them. 'I took the liberty of borrowing your sabre and having the soldier make measurements. I think that you will be able to slide the hilt of your sword into the adapted hand.'

Scott gazed with astonishment at the second wooden hand. 'It just might work,' he said, placing the first hand on the table and taking the sword hand from Alice.

Peter picked up the first hand to examine it. 'I will need to carve out the wrist end and apply padding for the hand to fit the stump,' he concluded.

'Make the sword hand your priority, brother,' Scott said, beaming with renewed pleasure. 'I can use my right hand to hold my pistol and the left my sword. I cannot thank you enough, Alice.' He rose to his feet to kiss her on the forehead. 'There is no time to waste,' he continued. 'I wish to show my fellow officers that I will ride again at the head of the squadron.'

Peter went about preparing the sword hand and carefully fitted it to his brother's wrist, using the leather straps to secure it to his forearm. Scott winced with the pain when the padding came into contact with the bandaged wrist and he broke into a sweat, but he refused to admit to his distress.

'With time the pain will subside,' Peter reassured him, and his brother nodded.

Scott did not dally at his brother's surgery but went immediately to the officers' mess, a large tent with tables covered in white linen and set with his regiment's silverware that travelled with the army on campaign in the baggage train. Silver candle holders flickered light in the dissipating heat of the day as the sun slipped below the horizon. Scott showed off his new hand to the admiration of his fellow officers.

Dinner was served by Indian waiters, and afterwards, when the table was cleared, a few officers of Scott's cavalry regiment retired to smoke cigars and chat with tumblers of a good Madeira port that also travelled with the officers' mess baggage train.

Scott stood outside the mess in the company of fellow cavalry major and close friend, Major Jason Cambridge, who had a reputation for being a reckless adventurer. Cambridge came from a family that had acquired their wealth through the establishment of textile factories in England, relying heavily on cheap Indian cotton. For a moment both men simply stared at the evening sky filling with stars.

'I say, old chap,' Cambridge said, puffing on his thick cigar and watching the blue smoke curl away on the still evening air, 'I have an idea where you might try out that new hand of yours. I have planned a little foray out to a village about twelve miles from here. I have learned it is occupied by a number of sepoys. Fifty of my men and I leave tonight.'

'I have heard nothing about such an operation,' Scott said.

'Ah, but that is the point,' Cambridge said quietly. 'It has not been officially sanctioned by the colonel.'

Scott looked sharply at his friend. 'You mean that you have not received permission to carry out your plan?'

'My men are getting restless just sitting around in the city, and I feel that they need a bit of action to keep them sharp.'

'There has to be a bit more to it than that to warrant this foolish idea of yours,' Scott said.

'Between you and me, old boy, my Indian informant has told me there may be buried treasure in the village, and he will be able to guide us tonight so that we are in place as the sun rises for us to fall on any sepoys occupying the town. I doubt they will be in a mood to stand and fight after the thrashing we gave them here. It is up to you whether you accept my invitation to join us. I would not blame you if you declined the offer, what with that bung hand of yours and all.'

Scott shook his head. 'When do we leave?'

Cambridge flicked the stub of his cigar into the night. 'Right now.'

★

The guards had been quietly informed that a party of cavalry would be leaving the city walls on a mission. That it was not sanctioned was not revealed. Scott sat astride his mount, his good hand holding the reins as the patrol left in single file, following their Indian guide towards the village.

They rode in silence with just one break to eat the cold roast chicken with chapattis they carried as rations, then resumed the silent advance on the unsuspecting village. Hours later, with the sun just breaking the horizon across the vast plain, they saw the thatched-roofed mudbrick houses of the small Indian village.

Scott sat astride his mount and observed the blue smoke curling from early morning cooking fires.

'Look!' Scott said to Cambridge. 'They have two brass cannon at the edge of the village.'

'By Jove, they are not even manned,' Cambridge said, and suddenly three sepoys appeared wandering from the village onto the plain only a short distance away. The three enemy immediately recognised that the mounted force of British and Sikh troops was not friendly and turned to flee back to the huts. Cambridge shouted his order, and already his party of fifty men were dividing into two groups – one tasked to ride in a flanking move around the village, taking up their places to block any withdrawal, whilst the other column charged through the village itself.

Scott knew the deadly effect of brass cannon firing grapeshot at cavalry and took it upon himself to immediately charge the two unmanned artillery pieces as he saw half-a-dozen mutineers scrambling to man the guns. Cambridge ignored the possible deadly threat, leaning over the neck of his horse, sabre in hand, and led the rest of his men onto the main street of the small town.

Foolishly the mutineers had not thrown up earthworks and Cambridge's charge was directed at the panicked sepoys desperately seeking to mount their horses and escape the flashing sabres. The sharp blades came slashing down on the dismounted sepoys, carving away terrible wounds on them.

Scott had been able to retrieve his pistol from the holster and, using his knees, turned his horse towards the men attempting to swing around the two brass cannons. He realised that he was alone in his desperate attempt to foil the Indian gunners but was on the gun position before the enemy could put the cannon into action.

Wild-eyed, they stared up at the British officer, three of them falling as his revolver fired at almost point-blank range. The survivors fled in panic from this mounted bringer of death. Single-handed he had captured the guns, and from the village nearby he could hear the screams of men as they were cut down.

Then it was all over. The cavalrymen herded their prisoners before them back into the village with Cambridge riding ahead, triumphantly waving his bloody sabre over his head. Cambridge had not lost a single man in the attack and they had taken fifty prisoners, two brass cannon and a small herd of Indian horses as their prize.

'Good show, old chap,' Cambridge said when he rode over to Scott, the dead gunners sprawled beside the artillery pieces. 'I see they could have done us some mischief if you had not taken it on yourself to silence them.'

'It had to be done,' Scott said with a growl. 'I am surprised you did not make the capture of the guns a priority in your assault on the village.'

'Can't think of everything, old chap,' Cambridge replied, dismissing the obvious rebuke. 'But now we have our mission to complete. The men are currently occupied going through the cummerbunds of the dead and captured for coins and other trinkets. The Indian guide is going to take you and I to a house where he says a chest has been buried. Are you in, Major Campbell?'

Scott reluctantly left his two captured brass cannons and followed his colleague to a walled house with what must have once been a pretty garden around it. He dismounted and the guide jabbered excitedly at a portion of the garden where the soil had clearly been disturbed. A shovel was found and Cambridge began to dig. His efforts were rewarded when they heard the distinctive clunk of metal striking something hard and Cambridge continued digging until he had cleared away the loose dirt from around a large wooden chest. The three men stood above the exposed chest, thoughts of great riches swirling through their minds.

Cambridge and the Indian guide hoisted the chest from the soil, placing it on the edge of the hole. It had no lock and Cambridge swung open the lid. The three men strained at once to gaze inside at their booty of war.

'Good God!' Cambridge exclaimed. 'All that effort for nothing.'

Scott stared at the pile of papers and stamps the chest held. Not even a single rupee inside. 'Oh well,' Scott sighed in his bitter disappointment. 'The papers may have some intelligence value to the general's staff.'

Cambridge wiped his brow which was streaming with sweat. 'We might have been better off joining the lads and looting the enemy of their coins.'

'We will have to explain our unauthorised raid on the village when we return,' Scott cautioned. 'At least our success might soften their ire.'

'I will order the men to round up the captured horses, prisoners and have the two cannons towed back with us,' Cambridge said. 'Maybe the chest does contain something of military importance.'

Scott left the walled house, riding out to where Cambridge's men were standing guard over the horses that had been taken in the raid. A fine roan mare caught Scott's eye, and he decided she would not be handed over to the army back in Delhi for use as badly needed replacements for the cavalry. He dismounted and walked over to the horse. She appeared to have a good temperament and Scott stroked her nose.

'You may as well take her, old chap,' Cambridge said from astride his mount. 'Otherwise the bloody contractors will keep her.'

Scott took her by the bridle and led her away.

The British cavalry returned to Delhi, pushing their prisoners and the captured horses ahead of them, with the captured cannons towed behind.

Scott rode beside Cambridge, leading the roan mare on a short rope.

'Who is going to explain to the general about our little adventure?' he asked.

'I will,' Cambridge replied. 'I think his annoyance will be lessened when he sees what we achieved.'

'It still does not explain why we carried out an unauthorised mission,' Scott reminded him.

'Military success trumps disobedience in the army,' Cambridge replied, spurring his horse in the direction of the general's HQ. Scott hoped his friend was right. Losing his hand was bad enough; losing his commission to a possible court-martial would be more than he could stand.

Scott broke away from the column and rode with the mare towards his brother's surgery in the city. He arrived just as the sun had set and he could see the light from lanterns within. Scott secured the two horses and made his way upstairs to find Peter and Alice sitting down to dine.

'Where have you been these last twenty-four hours?' Peter asked accusingly, rising from the table. 'Rumour around the city is that you and Major Cambridge decided to desert with fifty of Cambridge's cavalry.'

'Damned rumours. They seem to err on the most salacious side of any mistruth. No, I accompanied Major Cambridge on an impromptu mission to seek out the enemy only a few miles from here, and as a result we had a resounding victory that entailed no injury to ourselves but much to the mutineers. As a matter of fact, I personally captured two of their cannons and we brought back around fifty prisoners. Not bad when one considers they outnumbered us by at least three to one. I hope that you can spare another plate at the table because I am damned hungry.'

'Of course,' Alice said and called for their maid. 'You should not have sallied forth with your wound still healing.'

Scott turned to his sister-in-law. 'Ah, dear Alice, only concern and not accusation from you.' He smiled. 'I have brought back a present for you from our small adventure. So, before we dine I would like to present my gift downstairs.' He could see the look of both surprise and curiosity in her face.

Peter and Alice followed Scott and in the dim light of the darkening sky Scott took the reins of the roan mare and handed them to Alice. 'I thought you might enjoy a mount to get around the city,' he said with a broad smile. 'She is yours, dear Alice.'

Alice stood frozen, stunned by the wonderful gift. She had always been an excellent horsewoman and had a good eye for a well-bred horse. She could see that the mare was of extremely good quality. She reached up to stroke the animal's nose.

'She is magnificent, but such a fine gift is more than I deserve,' Alice said, tears of joy already welling in her eyes. 'I cannot accept such a beautiful present.'

'Both your husband and I would agree that you deserve much more for the grand service you have rendered to the sick and wounded on this campaign. Let us just say she is also a gift from the British army for your sterling efforts.'

Peter stepped forward, extending his hand to his brother. 'Thank you, brother,' he said. 'Alice will accept your gift, as we can both see how much it means to her.'

Scott gripped his brother's hand, experiencing the love in the gesture.

The mare had seemed to take an instant liking to Alice, nuzzling close to her.

'You need to give your horse a name,' Scott said.

'I will call her Molly,' Alice said. 'In honour of a remarkable young lady I once met.'

Cambridge was correct in his assumption that their small victory trumped their disobedience. The matter was quickly forgotten as the general staff pored through the captured documents worth much in enemy intelligence.

THIRTY-TWO

Charles Forbes left his office in London on the Friday morning and took his carriage to the Forbes manor in Kent. Inside the coach Charles leaned back to sip on a brandy flask and smoke a thick Cuban cigar. The coach clattered through the cobblestoned streets until it was out of the city and into the country lanes.

He stopped at a country inn for lunch and an ale or two, and then the journey continued through fields of grain, past copses of trees and the occasional low hill, until in the late afternoon they passed through the village nearest the manor. Charles felt the warmth of knowing that when he arrived home he would make arrangements for one of the maids to come to his bedroom that night.

The coach passed the small hill and its copse of ancient trees. Knowing what was buried in the circle of stones caused Charles a twinge of nervousness.

Suddenly, something smacked into the padding of the leather seat opposite him, and at the same time he swore he heard the report of a gun being fired as the horses reared in their harnesses.

'Go!' Charles screamed to the confused coachman, who instantly obeyed, bringing the horses under control. As the coach clattered away as fast as the horses could manage, Charles cowered in the cabin. It was obvious that someone had shot at him from near the ancient place of the Druids. A wave of terror rolled over Charles. It was as if the ghost of Jane Wilberforce had reached out to kill him.

The coach quickly reached the avenue leading to the Forbes manor and came to a stop at the front entrance.

'Did you see who shot at us?' Charles screamed at the coachman as he tumbled out.

'No, sir,' the coachman replied. 'But I heard the shot. It weren't no musket. I heard muskets when I was in the army and it weren't no musket for sure. Are you hurt?'

'No, but the projectile passed only inches from my head,' Charles replied, his body still shaking with shock and fear. He glanced back at the carriage. 'Coachman, I want you to extract the ball from the leather and bring it to me.'

'Yes, sir, I will do that.'

Charles walked with shaking legs towards the front entrance, where the butler met him. 'You look ill, Master Charles. Did something happen on your journey here?'

Charles did not answer, brushing past the old servant in search of the liquor cabinet in the billiard room. Thoughts of his carnal conquest for the night shrivelled in his mind as he found a decanter of whisky, poured himself a stiff drink, and swallowed the liquid in one gulp in an attempt to steady his trembling hands. Someone had tried to kill him! Who would want to do that – besides the imposter posing as his half-brother?

'Sir, the coachman wishes to see you,' the butler said in a calm voice.

'Send him in.' Charles waved to the servant as he poured another whisky.

The coachman entered the room with his cap in one hand, something clasped in the other. He opened his palm to reveal a strange-looking projectile Charles had never seen before. He was very aware of musket balls from his time hunting on the estate, but this was different. Charles rolled the projectile in his hand, feeling its lethal weight.

'It's a Minié ball,' the coachman offered. 'I seen them just before I got out of the army. The lads have been using the Enfield rifled musket for a couple of years now. They tell me it is deadly accurate as the Minié round engages the rifling in the barrel and spins when it comes out.'

'Yes, yes,' Charles said irritably, experiencing a shudder of fear as he stared at the misshapen, cone-shaped projectile. He sensed that such a round hitting a man's body would inflict terrible damage. 'You say it is only the army that has the Enfield?'

'Yes, sir, as far as I know,' the coachman replied, twisting his cap in his hand.

'You can go,' Charles said curtly, angry at his own fear.

Could it be that Samuel's imposter was back in England? As far as Charles knew he was still in India. Who else would wish him dead? It could not be Samuel because the last report was that he was on a ship bound for the Australian colonies. Besides, the Samuel he knew did not have it in him to carry out such an act.

That night Charles slept alone, trembling at how close he had come to being killed and still mystified as to who would want him dead. He was at a complete loss for an answer and knew that he would once again need the services of Mr Charles Field, private investigator. Charles knew it would not pay to involve the police. He had far too much to hide.

★

It was spring when Samuel Forbes arrived in the southern hemisphere.

The lumbering cargo steamer slipped into an industrial dock in Sydney Harbour amongst the tall masts of graceful clipper ships. It was a balmy morning of fluffy white clouds and blue skies.

Samuel stood beside James at the railing of the ship, taking in this blossoming city. 'We are finally home,' he sighed, despite the acrid stench of a nearby tannery.

'For a short time,' James said. 'It is even risky for us to visit Sir George at Wallaroo farm, you know.'

'I doubt that Charles' reach stretches this far,' Samuel said. 'After I visit my father to pay my respects, we can depart for New York.'

James nodded his head, not entirely reassured. He was aware that fast clipper ships spanned the distance between England and the Australian colonies, and even as they steamed across the Indian Ocean they had watched from time to time those graceful ships pass them by. What if Charles had been so determined to bring down Samuel that he had sent someone from England to find him? After all, the destination of the English registered freighter would have been discovered in Wales by anyone who was interested – and Charles had proved himself interested indeed.

The gangplank was lowered and the customs officers waited at their tables for anyone coming ashore. Samuel and James had little trouble passing through customs as they now produced their real passports, and the name of Forbes was well known to the officials working the docks because of the large amounts of wool Sir George Forbes exported to the English mills.

'Welcome home, Mr Forbes,' said one of the customs officers, signing off on his passport.

'Thank you,' Samuel replied and thought about what 'home' meant. Living in America did not truly feel like home. Samuel was English and he actually felt more at home in this English colony, despite its lack of European culture. But Sydney Town was taking on many commonalties with London, with its grand sandstone buildings rising into the sky. It now had theatres, public libraries and cafes, although it still had none of the genteel sophistication they had left behind in London.

The two travellers passed from the docks into the bustling streets of Sydney where they found stables and hired a horse and buggy to take them to James' vacant cottage at the fringes of the city. He had purchased the cottage on a previous visit to discreetly entertain his small circle of select friends, and this had led to it being a special place for he and Samuel. There they spent the night, and in the morning set out to travel west to the estate of Sir George Forbes.

Back in Sydney, a customs officer met with a lean, tough-looking man with a knife scar marring his face. Their meeting took place in a public house in the notorious Rocks area overlooking the busy harbour.

'They came through yesterday,' the customs officer said in the smoke-filled bar. 'They used their real names and passports.'

The man slipped a note from the wad he carried and passed it to the customs man.

The wait had been worth it, and somewhere far away a client of Mr Charles Field was prepared to pay a lot of money to expose the identity of Samuel Forbes. The man had once been a police constable of dubious reputation. The brutal murder of a young prostitute might have been linked to him had he remained in England, so he had fled to the Australian colonies. Field had discovered his plan to leave before he set foot on the passenger ship and made him promise to remain in contact should Field ever need a favour on the other side of the world.

The man in his early forties now went under the name of Harold Salt, working odd jobs around Sydney for those involved in petty crime. The letter that had arrived on the clipper ship weeks earlier promised a rich reward for carrying out a small task for one of Mr Field's clients. It was an easy job with little risk. Salt even knew from the information in the letter where he was most likely to locate Mr Samuel Forbes. He would in all probability visit his uncle, Sir George Forbes, at the estate of Wallaroo west of Sydney. The job was as good as done.

★

After the securing of Cawnpore once again, Ian attended the briefing by Major General James Outram for the relief of the besieged British garrison in Lucknow. The small garrison had turned a compound into a fortress within the fortress walls of the Indian city and had come under many attacks over the months of the rebellion. Yet against almost overwhelming odds they still held out. The besieged force consisted of British military as well as civilian men, women and children and was on the verge of defeat according to the reports smuggled out.

Although overall command for the relief was granted

to General Outram, General Havelock would accompany the column on the march towards Lucknow. The relieving force was to be divided into two brigades, and Ian's regiment would be at the vanguard of the advance.

Inside his tent Ian prepared orders for his company. The sun was going down but the ever-present heat caused him to sweat beneath his jacket. He paused in his writing to gaze at the vast rain-sodden plains of spindly scrub. How many battles had they fought? They all seemed to blur when he tried to remember. Names meant very little now as they simply continued the endless advance. Ian continually put himself at the forefront of any attack and sheer luck had kept him relatively unscathed, but he knew luck was a fickle thing, and he wondered if he would ever return to England. Since Ella's letter he was not sure he even wanted to return.

'Sir, permission to enter?'

Ian glanced up to see Conan.

'What is it, Sarn't Major?' Ian asked wearily.

'I was able to purloin some medicine for you,' Conan grinned. 'I have noticed lately that you have not been your cheery old self.' He produced a small bottle of rum.

'You know I have never been cheery, Conan, but the rum is the best medicine I can think of right now,' Ian replied with a wan smile.

Conan pulled up an empty ammunition case, sat down and took the top off the bottle, passing it to Ian.

'To us surviving Lucknow,' Ian said, raising the bottle as a toast then swallowing a large mouthful. It felt good and he passed it back to Conan, who silently raised the bottle in response.

'I have a request,' Conan said. 'Private Williams wishes to re-join the company.'

'Do you think he is fit to do so?' Ian asked.

'I think it would do him good to be back with the lads. Company runner does not suit one of our best marksmen,' Conan said.

'You have my approval then,' Ian said.

The two men finished the bottle between them, chatting as friends rather than soldiers, and never imagining that Conan's decision had played into the madness of Private Williams.

★

Even as Conan and Ian sat in the tent sharing the rum, Owen finished cleaning his rifle as the voices continued to nag him. He could not decide whether they were angels or demons come to him. They reminded him over and over that Conan Curry and Ian Steele were evil and had to be killed. Owen told the voices he knew that, and had returned to the company so he would be in a position to shoot them during the next battle. In the confusion of an engagement with the enemy, no one would know from whence came the bullets.

Owen lifted his Enfield to his shoulder and gazed down the sights at the company commander's tent. He could see through the flap the two men sitting together, sharing a bottle and conspiring to kill him. This was not the time, he told the voices.

But the time was coming, he reassured them.

THIRTY-THREE

I an Steele passed his telescope to Conan.

'There it is,' he said as Conan observed the walled city of Lucknow.

The British forces were about to commence their assault. They were six British and one Sikh battalion with three artillery batteries, but only one hundred and sixty-eight volunteer cavalry. From general to private soldier, all knew they were still vastly outnumbered by the mutineers inside the city walls. They were also surrounded by fields of water as a result of the heavy rains, and this severely restricted the use of the small force of British cavalry.

Behind Ian stood his company of riflemen, waiting patiently for the order to advance along a road that would funnel them into long columns. That would make them vulnerable to enemy artillery fire before they even reached a walled park only four miles south of the besieged British force within the walls. However, in their haste to return to the defences of Lucknow the mutineers had failed to destroy bridges, and the order came down to advance. This time Ian's regiment was not at the vanguard of the initial assault, and he was grateful for that fact as he had a terrible dread this battle had a lot in common with the one he had known attacking the Redan in the Crimea.

They reached the walled garden known as Alambagh without any serious resistance, and the captured area provided a good base to leave their baggage train. It was also an opportunity for senior commanders to plan their next move, which did not look promising because of the water-logged fields surrounding the city. The only firm ground led them to a bridge crossing the Charbagh canal.

For the assault, volunteers were called for to organise what was known as a forlorn hope to storm the bridge and open the way into the city. The terrible title echoed those from the Napoleonic wars when volunteers were promised promotion and rewards if they succeeded. In fact, it was a suicide mission and the men who stepped forward knew this.

Ian did not volunteer. Nor did he encourage men from his company. But volunteers stepped forward from other regiments in the desperate hope that they would live to reap the rewards.

The attack went in at company strength, and the volunteer force succeeded in seizing the bridge at a cost of nine out of ten men killed or wounded. Those watching the courageous soldiers storming the bridge stood in silent horror as the enemy cut down the forlorn hope. The bridge was slippery with blood as litter bearers desperately sought out any wounded and the remaining British force advanced under heavy enemy fire.

★

Private Owen Williams heard the voices in his head screaming at him to kill as he advanced with the company across the blood-soaked bridge, his rifle with bayonet fixed. He was just behind Conan and Ian and he knew this would prove the best opportunity as they entered the confusion of fighting. No one would notice a couple of bullets from his Enfield strike down the company commander and the CSM. It was now or never.

★

As usual Ian carried his two pistols, Enfield rifle and sword. The rifle was slung on his back and he held his sword and revolver ready for use in the close confines of the alleys they now found themselves in. The musket fire pouring into their close-packed ranks from rooftops was murderous, and Ian screamed encouragement to his men with orders to clear the windows and rooftops. The accuracy of the Enfield proved itself when the better marksmen in the company were able to stand off, shooting at any puffs of smoke betraying a fired musket. As soon as the musket-eers rose to reload they were killed by the lethal Minié bullets.

Ian hardly felt any fear. He had resigned himself to dying today and only cared that he killed as many of the enemy as he could before he died. He was aware that Conan was always at his elbow with his Enfield; firing, reloading and firing again. Conan did not even have to think about these steps as the weapon was now a part of him.

The air was thick with gun smoke, and the noise of men fighting and dying filled the air. All Ian knew was how thirsty he was but he could not take his focus even for a split second from their advance down the alley, which was bordered by two-storeyed mudbrick houses.

Five Indian mutineers suddenly rose from behind an overturned oxcart when they turned a corner. Ian was in front of his men and directly in the path of any fire. It was impossible for the Indian rebels to miss at twenty paces. Ian froze, waiting for the lead ball that would kill or maim him, but he felt himself crashing into the hard-packed earth instead and realised that someone had tackled him. The volley smashed into two soldiers behind him, and when he rolled over he saw Conan's blackened face. 'Sorry, sir,' Conan said, scrambling to his feet as the enemy musketeers lowered themselves behind their barricade to reload for the next volley.

But they were too slow, and Ian's men scrambled over the upturned cart and drive their bayonets into the small party of defenders. Ian and Conan were just behind their men and pushed past the barricade to advance into another alleyway. Ian was aware that he was leaving a trail of his dead and wounded behind him, as the remainder of the company continued to fight for every house and street. All around them in other streets and alleys the other regiments were doing the same and suffering the same heavy losses incurred in street fighting against a determined enemy that vastly outnumbered them. Time seemed to stand still for Ian, although he was aware that he was still alive, and so too was Conan.

A volley of musket fire erupted from a two-storeyed building to their left, spattering earth and hitting Ian's men. Ian could see that the fire had come from the rooftop and immediately launched himself through a doorway, followed by Conan and Owen trailing behind. Revolver in one hand and sword in the other, Ian glanced around the darkened room to see a sepoy raising his musket, and fired three shots into him. The sepoy fell without discharging his weapon. Then Ian saw the narrow stairway leading to the next level and cautiously began to ascend, every nerve in his body straining to sense what lay ahead. He could see that the next level was as dark as the lower one, but before his eyes could adjust, a shot hit him and flung him face down on the steps. His sword clattered off the stairs, falling below. From the source of the pain Ian was aware that he had been hit just under the armpit.

'Owen, you fool, you've shot Captain Forbes!' Conan's voice yelled from the bottom of the stairs.

Ian felt for the wound and realised with relief that the bullet had ripped through the flesh under his left arm and exited cleanly. Then the pain came and Ian struggled to regain his feet just as a figure with an axe appeared above him. The second shot came from Conan's rifle and the enemy soldier pitched forward, falling heavily into the room below.

Conan scrambled up the steps to Ian's side, helping him to his feet.

'We have to clear the rooftop,' Ian gasped as the pain swamped him.

The two surged forward to the second level of the house where they encountered two more of the enemy. Conan leapt ahead of Ian with his rifle, bayoneting one of the men attempting to rush at them with his own bayonet-tipped musket. The two men met and the sepoy's bayonet caught Conan a glancing slash along his side. Ignoring his wound, Conan's bayonet pierced the Indian in the chest, and Conan twisted his bayonet savagely, ensuring maximum internal damage. The Indian soldier screamed in pain as Conan used all his strength to extract the long pointed blade. Ian had already emptied his revolver into the second enemy, and the two British soldiers panted with the sudden surge of adrenaline. They were both wounded but still alive.

Ian and Conan knew the task was not finished as above them they could see an opening in the ceiling, with a ladder leading to the roof. Private Owen Williams was not to be seen as they prepared to carry out clearing the roof of enemy musketeers.

Conan glanced at Ian. 'Are you all right, sir?' he asked, seeing the dark stain of blood spreading around Ian's wound at the front of the red jacket.

'Let's get this job done,' Ian said through gritted teeth. He still had the use of his left arm, although it hurt to move it. There was not time to reload, and Ian slipped the Enfield off his back where it had been slung. It was loaded and primed to fire.

Suddenly the square of light from the opening was blocked, and Ian realised that one of the Indian mutineers was staring down at them from the rooftop. Without considering the pain, Ian lifted his rifle and fired upwards. He knew it was more luck than accuracy, but the heavy Minié bullet smashed the Indian's face to pulp and he did not have time to scream in his death.

Owen had finally joined them in the room and Conan had turned to say something to him when the grenade fell through the hatch above. It hit the floor, and the round metal ball with the smoke trailing from the hand-lit fuse hung in the air. The three men stared in horror at the explosive device as it lay on the floor between them.

Owen did not hesitate. He threw himself on the object as it exploded, flinging his body in the air as he absorbed the full blast and metal shrapnel fragments.

Ian could hear a scream of 'NO!' and realised that it was coming from his own mouth. His ears were ringing from the concussion caused by the enemy grenade in the confined room.

Conan knelt beside the torn body of the man who would have been his brother-in-law, desperately trying to lift him in his arms.

Another face appeared in the hatch but disappeared quickly.

Enraged, Conan lowered Owen's mutilated and smoking body to the floor and began ascending the ladder without any thought for the danger to himself. Ian was behind him as he poked his head out to survey the rooftop and ducked as a musket ball smashed into the edge of the opening. Without hesitating, Conan pulled himself onto the rooftop.

The rooftop defender did not have time to fire a second shot as Conan launched himself across the short distance, grappling at the soldier fumbling to reload his musket.

Roaring obscenities, Conan grabbed the smaller man by the throat, causing him to drop his musket and fling his hands up to release Conan's grip. But Conan now gripped him in a bear hug, pushing him towards the edge of the roof. He headbutted the Indian soldier, stunning him enough to make him stagger. Conan broke away and shoved the Indian soldier with all his strength towards the edge of the roof, where the man toppled to the hard earth many feet below.

Ian had joined Conan on the rooftop and was sweeping the area for any other defenders, but they could see they had cleared the obstacle to the company's advance below. Both men sat down, hands trembling with the pain of their wounds as the adrenaline surge abated. Below them the fighting continued, but for the moment they sat quietly.

'Owen is gone,' Conan said flatly.

'I will recommend him for a medal,' Ian replied. 'His courageous sacrifice saved our lives.'

'For a fleeting moment back there I could have sworn Owen shot at you deliberately,' Conan said, staring at the pillars of smoke rising from many buildings in the distance. 'There was no threat when he fired, and he was too good a soldier to accidentally shoot you. I heard rumours that he had it in for you and I, but what he did back there just proves that they were false. He died a hero.'

'I will write to Molly and tell her so,' Ian said. 'How bad is your wound?' He indicated the blood on Conan's uniform.

'It hurts a bit but nothing serious from what I can feel,' Conan replied. 'However, I think you should see the surgeon about your wound.'

'In good time,' Ian said. 'I have a duty to show the lads that my luck still stands. We will come back for Owen's body when we take the city.' Ian reached for his water canteen and gulped it dry.

After a moment he reloaded his revolver and rifle then descended from the roof to the room where Owen's mangled body lay. The explosion had ripped him open, and his intestines bulged from his body. Ian paused to salute Owen's body, which was already covered by a swarm of flies.

On the street they re-joined the rearguard of the company and were met by Lieutenant Upton, one of Ian's platoon commanders.

'You are wounded, sir,' Upton said, seeing the blood on Ian's uniform.

'Nothing of consequence, Mr Upton,' Ian replied. 'To your knowledge, what is the status of the company?'

'I think we have lost a third of the men, sir,' Upton replied. 'I have arranged for our wounded to get treatment with the surgeons back at the baggage park. From what the sergeants have told me, we have cleared the enemy from this section of the city and it appears that they have retreated to other defensive positions.'

'Good show, Mr Upton,' Ian said in a tired voice.

'What do we do now, sir?' Upton asked. Ian could still hear the sounds of sporadic fighting from nearby streets and alleys.

'I will send a runner to regimental HQ to wait for further orders,' Ian said. 'In the meantime, make sure those who are able take up defensive positions in the event of a counterattack. Block the alley here with anything you can, and see to the men. Make sure they have shade and water.'

'Yes, sir,' the junior officer replied, hurrying away to carry out Ian's orders, gathering the survivors into a fortified position, using oxcarts and furniture to form barricades.

Ian was not sure of their situation until the runner returned. The orders from their regimental commander, Major Dawkins, were to pull back and re-join the remainder of the regiment a few streets away. Night was falling, and the battle to break the siege of Lucknow had not yet been won.

Ian was able to walk amongst his men who were cheered to see that their respected commander, although wounded, was still alive. This meant a lot to the men of Ian's company. Already the word had gone through the ranks that the commander of their task force, Colonel Neill, had been killed by a musket ball in the narrow streets of the city that day.

THIRTY-FOUR

That evening, Ian reluctantly returned for medical attention to the walled garden being used as the base for the assaults on the city.

The surgeon examined his wound and muttered that another couple of inches and the ball would have shattered Ian's upper arm, which would have resulted in amputation. However, all that was required was that he wash out the wound, stitch it and apply a thick bandage.

Ian thanked him and returned to his company, who were settling in for the night in the outskirts of the city taken by force of arms that day.

'The lads are a bit quiet tonight,' Ian observed to Conan.

'Most lost good friends today,' Conan said as they observed the men sitting in small groups, smoking their pipes or lying on the ground, attempting to sleep in the flickering light cast by small campfires.

'I heard that we were able to break the siege,' Conan continued, packing his pipe and lighting it.

'I also heard that our people being besieged have discovered a fresh stock of supplies so can continue to hold out for a while longer if the rebels counterattack. But it appears they have suffered too many casualties to mount another attack at this stage. Now it appears that we are the besieged. We will be moving out at first light to reinforce the compound and enlarge the defences. The general hopes that our appearance in the city will discourage the mutineers and they will leave.'

But the general was wrong.

★

A world away across the Indian Ocean, Samuel and James arrived at Wallaroo homestead. It was springtime in the southern hemisphere and wildflowers bloomed across the uncultivated open fields around the property.

Sir George Forbes greeted their arrival with joy and tears.

'Welcome home, son,' he said, embracing Samuel on the veranda of the house as servants carried the luggage from the carriage. 'We have been too long apart and have much to speak about.'

Sir George turned to James and shook his hand. 'You must have a lot to tell of your adventures in the Americas.'

Samuel and James glanced at each other with knowing looks. There would be a lot more to tell of than their time in New York.

★

The war went on in Lucknow. The defence of the compound by the original besieged force was expanded, and its control remained under that of Colonel John Inglis, whilst

General Outram took over the larger perimeter. Messages were able to go in and out of the newly established fortifications, but day and night the enemy continued its musket and artillery fire on Outram's freshly dug-in troops.

Tunnelling became a way of life on both sides as the Indian rebels attempted to place explosive mines beneath the British defences. In turn the British defenders sank twenty-one shafts to counter the Indian mine tunnels. It became an underground war, each side attempting to intercept the other's tunnels, but the British were able to keep one step ahead of their Indian foe, whose numbers were calculated at between thirty and sixty thousand troops, opposing their small force of a few thousand.

Ian's depleted company had been left out of the tunnelling duties but manned the outer defences. The continuous skirmishing had taken a toll on Ian, who spent sleepless nights thinking of Ella and listening to the constant artillery barrages and crackle of musket fire. As the company sergeant major, Conan carried out his duties like an immoveable rock and gained the utter respect of the men.

Ian's wound was healing, but it still pained him to use his left arm. News occasionally arrived of battles being fought across northern India, and all were optimistic that the Queen's Indian Empire was slowly being won back, but at a heavy cost. The East India Company was already being called to account in the hallowed halls of Britain's parliament, and it appeared that the Company would lose its monopoly and the British government would step in to rule the vast country with its own appointed civil servants.

For Ian and his men, this news held little interest as they simply fought each day to stay alive against an enemy determined to retake the city. Manning the defensive barriers was both tedious and terrifying as the monotony of sentry duty was often broken by near suicidal frontal attacks on the British forces, who found themselves in a position similar to the small force they had come to relieve in Lucknow. Ian knew from the briefings that they desperately needed a relief force to arrive and break the stalemate. Courage and fortitude alone would not win the day as the rebel forces continued to muster troops outside the city walls.

Occasionally Ian led small parties of his men on night raids to neutralise enemy artillery gun positions. The results were good and the guns were taken out of action, but Ian's men were being worn down by exhaustion and the nervous condition caused by constant fear. Rations were at a stretching point and hunger was starting to become evident in the thinning faces of the British soldiers.

Relief eventually arrived, with Sir Colin Campbell's force of five thousand seven hundred infantry, six hundred cavalry and thirty guns. The tough and dependable Scots soldiers were greeted with cheers by the weary British defenders.

The Scots had eventually broken through the ranks of the rebels outside the city, but the battle was far from over.

Ian was called to meet with General Havelock at his HQ in the compound, a heavily shelled building with fallen masonry lying all about.

He was greeted warmly by the general, who offered him a tumbler of rum.

'I was informed earlier of your wound, Captain Forbes,' he said, 'I commend your sense of duty to your men in remaining by their side.'

'The wound is healing, sir,' Ian said, gratefully feeling the soothing effect of the rum in his stomach. Alcohol was a rare thing as supplies ran short.

'I have asked you here because it has been decided that we must evacuate the women and children from the city.

We all agree that whilst the mutineers remain entrenched, our women and children are in great danger, and Colonel Inglis has been tasked with organising their evacuation. I am assigning your company to escort the civilians out of the city. We want to get them back to Cawnpore, and I know I can rely on you to ensure they arrive safely. There will be other officers with you for this mission, good men who have proven themselves during the siege. The journey is fraught with danger from the enemy forces roaming the countryside, but I am confident your riflemen can deal with that. We have lancers on the road who will also assist you. Here are your written orders.'

The general passed Ian an envelope which contained his authority and the details of the evacuation plan drawn up by Colonel Inglis.

Ian accepted the envelope, saluted the soldier he very much admired, and left the crumbling building. He barely flinched when an explosive shell landed a mere fifty paces away, scattering the courtyard with shrapnel.

Ian then went to brief his company.

'Lads, we are finally getting out of here,' he said simply, and saw the look of happiness in the expressions of the men left in the company. He had only thirty-three soldiers left who were fit to march and fight. Their faces were grimy from days of being covered in spent gunpowder, their uniforms in tatters, but their morale was still high under his leadership.

'Your parade, Sarn't Major,' Ian said, turning to Conan who was standing to attention nearby. Conan called for the salute, and Ian returned it before walking away.

In the early hours of the morning, he gathered his kit for the march and found the letter Ella had sent him informing him of her love for the Russian aristocrat. How long had it been since he had seen her in person? Ten months – a year. Time had lost much of its meaning when some days seemed to stretch forever, and at other times during an action, seconds became hours.

Always he could picture her warm smile and remember the scent of her body from that one night they spent together. The memory of their lovemaking had eased the discomfort of the long nights he'd spent shivering in the torrential rains on the Indian plains or marching under a blazing sun. Thoughts of Ella had crept to him as he retreated into a rare quiet place in his mind, away from the battlefields drenched in blood. But that was all gone now.

Ian sighed. Why did he carry the written reminder of love lost?

'Sir, the lads are ready to march.'

'Thank you, Sarn't Major,' Ian replied, tucking the letter inside his jacket. 'I will join you.'

Conan saluted and Ian let all thoughts of Ella pass from his mind as he followed Conan to join what was left of his battered company.

His men assembled either side of the column of carriages and oxcarts drawn by loyal Indians in lieu of horses and carrying women, children and servants as they prepared to leave the city. In the early dawn light Ian was met by the acting commanding officer of his regiment.

'We will be joining you at Cawnpore,' Dawkins said. 'I wish you Godspeed, Captain Forbes. I know our refugees are in good hands.' The major extended his hand. If only Major Dawkins was able to retain command, Ian thought as he shook hands.

'Thank you, sir,' Ian said. 'I have total faith that my men would lay down their lives to protect the women and children.'

He saluted and Dawkins strode away.

Then the mounted lancers joined the line of refugees departing the city and Ian marched forwards, his Enfield at the ready. He was acutely aware that amongst those he was designated to protect was the young wife of Lucknow's legendary defender, Colonel John Inglis.

They had hardly passed through the outer gate of the city when a sporadic fire opened up on the column from positions off the road.

'Move quickly!' Ian roared to the Indians drawing the vehicles, although they hardly needed urging. Musket balls spattered dirt, slamming into the sides of the oxcarts and carriages. Already Conan had deployed his sharpshooters to locate and fire on the enemy snipers. The enemy fire tapered away as one by one the Enfield bullets reached out to tear into soft flesh.

After the first ambush they were fired at on two more occasions. However, between Ian's men and the mounted lancers they were able to clear the road, and eventually in the late afternoon they reached a house standing in a large garden. Immediately Ian and his men were assailed by the stench of rotting flesh. Glancing around, Ian could see numerous partially buried bodies. He remembered the report he had read before leaving Lucknow of a battle at this place a few days earlier, where around two thousand one hundred rebels had been cut to pieces.

Conan joined Ian. 'Is this where we bivouac tonight?' he asked.

'No, we continue the march as soon as extra troops join us for the rest of the journey,' Ian replied.

At 10 pm the weary column of refugees continued the march to a place called Dil Khoosha Park. In the dark only the creak of oxcarts, the occasional whimpering of children, and the muffled sound of men marching broke the silence of the night. It was important that the train not draw undue attention from the bands of armed rebels roaming the area. Once during the trip, a halt was called, lanterns extinguished and all waited, holding their breaths as the sound of many horses could be heard in the distance. Ian's men gripped their rifles, bayonets fixed, ready for any close fighting in the darkness. But it was their reinforcements arriving, and all were able to breathe again.

Around midnight they came to the camp set up to accommodate them on the route to Cawnpore. Ian had his company settled in for the night with sentries posted and was surprised to see tea, bread and butter distributed to his men. It was a luxury they had not seen in months and Conan was even able to scrounge a couple of bottles of beer.

'Not enough to share with the lads,' he said, holding up the bottles, 'but a reward for senior NCOs and officers of the company – at least the sarn't major and the company commander.'

Ian gestured for Conan to enter his tent and in the dark they removed the tops from the bottles.

Ian raised his bottle. 'To dear friends lost and comrades forever to remain in the earth of India.'

'Hear, hear,' Conan said, and drank down every last drop of the precious amber liquid.

As he did so, he thought of all those people he had loved who had died since he had left the colony of New South Wales. First it had been his brother murdered on the ship that had brought them to London; then Edwin, Molly's brother, killed in the Crimean War, and now Owen, killed in India. He did not want to think of who else might be lost before he could return to England and the woman he loved.

The march for Cawnpore was continued and when they reached the city, Ian turned to look down the straggling column of refugees in the knowledge that they had not lost a single man, woman or child on the march.

THIRTY-FIVE

At Cawnpore Ian and his company paraded with the rest of the regiment. Ian had lost two-thirds of his company to cholera, dysentery and enemy action, but none on the march to Cawnpore. Major Dawkins reviewed what was left of the regiment on a dusty improvised parade ground in a former park.

'Men, you have acquitted yourselves in the finest traditions of the Queen's army. Your courage and loyalty will not be forgotten, and I have good news. Tomorrow, we march out for our barracks in England.' Ian could hear behind him a slight murmur of approval from the troops. 'Silence!' Conan growled, loud enough to dampen any further expression of joy.

'In London we will need to recruit to re-establish our strength for future campaigns,' Major Dawkins continued. He turned to his regimental sergeant major. 'You can dismiss the men to their duties, Sarn't Major,' he said and a general salute was called before the commanding officer left the parade.

Ian raised his sword in salute, and the parade was given the order to fall out. As he turned to march off he reflected on the fact that he would be leaving India without seeing Alice and Peter again. He had heard nothing from them for months and could only pray that they had survived the fighting at Delhi, not to mention the spread of disease and the fury of the sun, and that he would be reunited with them in England.

Conan had already began organising the men of the company to pack, and Ian found his written orders for the march out of Cawnpore at his temporary office. He read that the civilian survivors of the Lucknow siege and his regiment were to be evacuated back to the port of Calcutta and from there they would ship out for England.

In the early hours of the next day the regiment assembled, and Ian's company was given the honour of leading the soldiers from Cawnpore with the regimental colours unfurled.

Conan marched beside Ian at the head of the column as the sun rose over the Indian plains.

'I hope that we never see this accursed place ever again,' he muttered. And Ian could do nothing but agree.

★

In a village tavern nestled in the shadow of the Blue Mountains in the colony of New South Wales, a stranger sat at a sawn-log table with a tankard of ale before him. Across from him sat one of the workers from Wallaroo farm.

'So you reckon that one of the men who arrived recently at the farm is Samuel Forbes?' Harold Salt said, taking a swig from the warm ale. 'How can you be sure?'

'Because I knew Mr Forbes before he left a few years ago,' the farmhand said, enjoying the free ale the stranger had bought him.

'Would you sign a paper swearing to that?' Salt asked.

'What's in it for me?' the farmhand countered.

'A shilling – just to sign a piece of paper,' Salt replied, thrusting a sheet of paper across the table with the shilling coin.

'I can't read or write,' the farmhand said, staring at the paper.

'Just give me your name and then you can put your cross next to it,' Salt said. In anticipation Salt had already written a declaration that Samuel Forbes was currently residing at Wallaroo with Sir George Forbes. All he needed was a witness to the document.

The farmhand gave his name, residential address and occupation, which Salt wrote down, and then made a cross next to it.

'What's this all about?' he asked as Salt neatly folded the paper and slipped it into the pocket of his jacket.

'Nothing for you to worry about,' Salt smiled, swigging down the rest of his ale.

Harold Salt departed the small village on his horse, taking the winding track back down to Sydney Town. He had not taken to the Australian countryside as he was a man who had lived his life in the smoggy confines of London and then Sydney, where he was at home amongst the alleys and mean streets, not the wide-open spaces and dense bushland.

★

Alice's pregnancy was beginning to show, and Peter was worried about her. Alice had suffered one miscarriage already and he knew that she needed a specialist doctor to ensure that this pregnancy ran its full course. He had approached the military hierarchy in Delhi and put forward his case to return to England with his wife. Reluctant as they were to release their best army surgeon, they agreed, and another surgeon would be sent out from England to replace him.

Peter broke the good news to Alice in their quarters and was surprised at her reaction.

'We have a place here,' Alice said. 'You have your surgery, and I know how much good you are doing – not only for the army but for the poor people of Delhi. I can have our baby here.'

'I am not a missionary,' Peter replied, rubbing his forehead in frustration. 'My first concern is for your welfare in these difficult times. I insist that we return to London. As it is, my brother has been recalled by the East India Company to return to London to report on affairs here, so we would travel together.'

Alice sat down on a divan Peter had been able to purchase from a wealthy Indian merchant. 'I suppose there is merit in what you argue,' she sighed. 'I must think of the welfare of our baby.'

Alice could not tell even her beloved husband that she feared her experiences in India had changed her forever. She had witnessed and experienced so much in this exotic and alien country, how would she be able to sit amongst her contemporaries in London's lavish drawing rooms and feel anything in common with her cloistered, pampered friends? But she could see the deep concern in her husband's face and knew that he, too, would miss the adventure of India – despite the fact he had also experienced so much death and destruction. She knew that India and the tiger would forever remain in her dreams – and sometimes in her nightmares.

'We will return to London,' she said finally.

★

Charles Forbes had hardly had a sound night's sleep since the attempt on his life. He was haunted by a recurring nightmare that Jane Wilberforce had risen from the grave, armed with an Enfield rifled musket. Even those he knew from his club remarked on his health. He was losing weight and had the look of a haunted man.

Word had arrived that Samuel's regiment was returning to England from India, and this added to his deep fears, as the man posing as his brother was a recognised war hero and dangerous enemy. Charles Forbes was a shadow of the arrogant and narcissistic man he had been.

It was over a hand of cards at his club that Charles confided to Clive Jenkins the attempt on his life weeks earlier.

'Good God, man, you must report the matter to the police,' Jenkins said.

'I would rather leave the police out it for reasons of my own,' Charles replied.

The news of the attempt on Charles' life disturbed Jenkins because he was not responsible for it. As the two men played cards in the smoke-filled room, Jenkins found his mind reeling with one question. Who else wanted Charles Forbes dead?

★

In the far-flung colony of New South Wales, a horseman was riding towards Sydney to post a signed report to London. Harold Salt reckoned he was about halfway to Sydney and it was time to take a break and boil a billy of tea.

He tied his horse to a tree and went in search of small sticks to make his fire, and when he reached down to pick up some dry twigs beside a rotting log he felt something sharp strike his wrist. He stumbled back and intense pain set in almost immediately. He watched in horror as the big brown snake slithered over the rotting trunk of the fallen tree.

Holding his punctured wrist, he fell on his backside in terror. Harold knew why he hated the colonies of the Australian continent. Everything that crawled and slithered was deadly poisonous. He tried to rise to his feet but fell back, sweating profusely, weakened by panic and poison.

He lay on his back, gripping his wrist as the toxic venom surged through his body. He knew it was senseless to try to ride away. He would surely be dead before his horse had taken more than a few paces. He could hardly believe that he was going to die here, alone, surrounded by the damned eucalypts of this savage continent. He closed his eyes and dreamed of London, awaiting the inevitable.

Five days later, a traveller was drawn by the stench of rotting flesh to a blackened and bloated body. After taking anything of value and pulling a few personal papers from pockets, the traveller buried Harold Salt beside the track. He did not consider the papers to have any value, so he discarded them in the bush and then continued his journey to Sydney.

★

It was Christmas Day and the regiment began boarding their steamer at the busy Calcutta wharves. The atmosphere was euphoric amongst the battle-weary soldiers looking forward to being reunited with friends and family in London.

Ian and Conan stood on the dock supervising the company's embarkation.

'Festive greetings,' Conan said. 'Permission to have a smoke?'

'Why not,' Ian replied. 'It's Christmas Day, Sarn't Major.'

Conan retrieved his battered pipe, plugged it with rough-cut tobacco and lit the bowl's contents, puffing smoke into the humid breeze drifting across the waters.

'When do we sail?' Conan asked, gazing at the last of the red-coated soldiers climbing the gangplank.

'As soon as we have taken aboard a party of civilians, I believe,' Ian answered. 'Then we depart for merry old England, but not in time for plum pudding and roast goose.'

'In my opinion, the best Christmas gift is still being alive and getting out of here,' Conan said. 'But just as good would be sitting with Molly in the kitchen, sharing a port wine in front of the stove while the snow falls outside.'

'I think you might still be in her bed if we were back in London,' Ian grinned.

'What about you, sir? What would you be doing if we were back in England?' Conan asked, and the smile on Ian's face faded.

'No doubt I would be recovering from a heavy night of drinking and remembering the hot Christmas Days we spent back in New South Wales with my ma and da.'

'There is no lady waiting for you when we return?' Conan asked.

'I am afraid not,' Ian sighed. 'No special gifts for Christmas this year.'

'Ah, I see we may have company,' Conan said, gazing at a small convoy of oxcarts arriving, and a carriage drawn by two Indian horses. Ian hardly took any notice, so deep was he in his melancholic thoughts.

'Begorah!' Conan exclaimed, catching Ian's attention. 'Sir, look who it is!'

Ian looked towards the carriage Conan was pointing to, and felt his heart almost stop beating in his chest. He gaped, blinking to make sure that he was seeing correctly.

The obviously pregnant woman was being helped from the carriage by a man Ian knew very well. Without hesitating, he strode up to the carriage.

'Alice, Peter, how the devil are you?' he asked, and saw Alice and Peter turn their heads towards him. Alice immediately burst into tears, and Peter quickly stepped forward, grasping Ian's hand.

'God almighty!' Peter said, gripping Ian's hand as if never to let it go. 'Is it really you, old man?'

Alice pushed aside her husband to embrace Ian, and the tears spilled down her cheeks. 'Sam, I hardly dared believe we would meet again in this life,' she sobbed. Ian noticed a tall and dashing major in Alice and Peter's company.

'My brother, Major Scott Campbell,' Peter said. Ian saluted and Scott returned the salute before extending his hand. His other hand, Ian could see, was a wooden prosthesis.

'Pleased to meet you, old chap,' Scott said with a broad smile. 'My brother has told me so many stories about you that I thought you might be his imaginary friend.'

'Peter never told me about you,' Ian grinned. 'I suppose that is because you are obviously a cavalryman and not infantry.'

Christmas Day 1858, aboard the steamer departing Calcutta, turned out to be one of the happiest Ian could remember. They were even able to feast on a brace of roast duck, followed by tinned plum pudding and precious bottles of beer.

As the steamer plied the calm waters of the ocean late that night, Ian stood alone on the deck, leaning on the railing, smoking his last cigar. He gazed at the moon's bright trail, reflecting on the importance of family and friends in his war-torn life. He knew what lay behind him, but he did not know what lay ahead. All he knew was that he was a commissioned officer in Queen Victoria's army, destined to continue to fight her imperial wars until either he was killed in some backwater of the empire or completed his ten-year contract with the real Samuel Forbes.

★

It was cold. Snow fell gently onto the streets of London. The horse and coach came to a stop outside one of the tenements cloaked in the darkness of night. The appearance of such a grand coach in this part of London, where bank clerks, civil servants and moderately prosperous merchants lived, was a rare sight.

A young woman, swaddled in the warmth of expensive furs, stepped from the coach and went to the front door of the tenement while her coach driver waited atop his seat.

She glanced around before knocking on the door, which was opened by a burly man she knew well.

'Miss Ella, come in,' Egbert said, opening the door to her.

Ella stepped inside the warmth of the modest tenement house, shaking off the cold from outside.

'Can the missus make you a cup of tea?' Egbert asked politely.

'Thank you, Bert,' Ella replied, 'but I must not be long away from home. I have come to see my baby.'

'Just come with me,' Egbert said, and Ella followed him into a small room where his wife sat by a baby's cot. Meg was in her late thirties and still retained some of the beauty of her youth.

'The little fellow is in fine health,' she said, turning to Ella. 'He is a bonny baby.'

Ella stepped forward to gaze down at the face of the baby in the cot and felt as if her heart would burst with the pain she was suffering for her loss. Without asking, Ella reached down to cradle the sleeping baby in her arms, tears welling in her eyes.

'Does your father know you are here?' Egbert asked nervously.

'He does not,' Ella replied, gazing into the face of the child she and Ian had created, and who had been taken from her in the first hour after his birth. Her father had bitterly suggested to her that the baby's father was a man he knew as Ian Steele and, fearing Ikey's reaction and the potential consequences for Ian, Ella had denied it. She couldn't tell if he believed her or not.

Exhausted from the labour, Ella had asked to see her baby. Her memory of the moments after the birth were hazy but someone had taken the child from her and left her alone in the room with her father. Ikey told her that the baby had been weak and sickly and had stopped breathing suddenly. The doctor confirmed her father's story and said that the tiny corpse had already been taken away. Ella instinctively knew that the two men were lying, but she was too weak to do anything about it. She wondered whether her father had smothered the infant, but prayed he would not commit such a crime. She had heard rumours that her father had ordered men killed, but she also knew he had a reputation for protecting women and children.

Within a couple of days Ella had recuperated enough to leave the bed and she played a hunch. Just after the birth of her baby she had noticed Egbert hovering in the background.

Ella had cornered the tough and burly employee and pleaded with him to tell her what had happened to her baby.

Egbert had always cared for Ella; he had witnessed her grow from a child to a beautiful young woman. He felt paternal towards her and could not bear to see her so distressed so he admitted that the baby boy was in the care of him and his wife, Meg. Egbert explained that her father had passed the baby to them as he knew Egbert and Meg did not have a child of their own, and he had promised he would provide financial support for the little family.

Egbert knew from his many years with Ikey that the big man had a soft heart – despite his fearsome exterior. He had agreed to include Ella in the infant's world but had made her swear on pain of his own demise to keep their connection a secret. Ikey might have a soft heart but he did not stand for his orders being disobeyed.

Ella knew she could not oppose her powerful father and was content for the moment to be able to visit her baby. Now she crooned to the baby in her arms, wondering how the future would unfold for them both.

'Have you given him a name?' Ella asked.

'No, not yet,' Meg replied.

'I would like him to be called Josiah,' Ella said. 'Like my baby's father, Josiah was a great warrior.'

'It is a fine name,' Egbert said as Ella gently placed the swaddled baby back in the cot.

Ella stumbled from Egbert's tenement, tears streaking her face. For Christians the following day would mark the birth of their prophet, Jesus. Ella wondered if the man she had loved and lost had survived his war in India. And if he had, how would he react to learning that he was a father? But Ella also knew there was little chance that the man she had loved would ever discover the truth.

EPILOGUE

1859

Spring had come to the fields and farms of England. Fruit trees were flowering and lambs were being born, but in the city of London the stench of industrialisation still lingered in the warm air.

Outside the great synagogue at Aldergate the small crowd did not allow the acrid smell to spoil their enjoyment of the occasion. Weddings always attracted a crowd, and this one was special as the daughter of a well-known and colourful businessman was marrying a handsome Russian count.

Amongst the crowd of onlookers stood Ian Steele wearing civilian clothing. He could not explain to himself why he had chosen to come today, but here he was. A hush fell on the waiting crowd as the new bride and bridegroom exited the synagogue to step into an open coach drawn by a set of fine greys. Ian experienced an emptiness as he gazed at Ella. She was beautiful and radiant, and Nikolai handsome.

Why had he dared hope that he could have been with Ella when everything was against them?

'It was never meant to be between you and my princess, Captain Forbes,' came the voice of Ikey Solomon. Ian had not seen him leave the bridal party.

Ian turned to face the big, bearded man dressed in a very expensive suit and wearing the traditional Jewish skullcap.

'Your daughter is the picture of a beautiful bride,' Ian replied.

'She certainly is,' said Ikey. 'I have always known that my Ella was sweet on you, but we both know it could never have come to anything.'

Ian nodded. 'You are right, I know.'

'I saw you from across the street and wanted to speak with you,' Ikey said. 'You have always been an honourable and honest man with me, so I am asking a favour of you.'

'If it is within my ability to grant it, I will do so,' Ian replied.

'My new son-in-law has accepted my offer to join the family business, and I want you to promise me that no animosity will arise between you and him. If you can grant me that promise, I can assure you I will return the favour if you ever ask.'

'I can promise you that there will be no animosity between us, Mr Solomon,' Ian said, feeling the bone-crushing grip of the big man's hand.

'Thank you, Captain Forbes . . . or should I say, Captain Steele,' Ikey said, releasing his hand. 'I value good men in my life.'

Ian watched as Ikey walked back across the road. It seemed half of England knew who he really was. It was a revelation that made him deeply uncomfortable.

He hailed a hansom cab and directed it to take him to

the barracks in London. There he was obliged to meet with Colonel Jenkins, who had resumed his command of the regiment. He was riding on the tributes showered on the regiment for its courageous service in India. The fact that he had not been with his men under fire but instead lounging at staff college in England seemed to be overlooked by the press, who hailed his service to the public anyway.

Already the rumour was spreading through the officers' mess and the barracks rooms that the regiment was to be shipped to China or Africa to confront the enemies of the empire. Another war in another country. As the hansom cab clopped through the streets of London, Ian reflected that his life was destined to be lived or lost in the far-flung parts of the British Empire, leading his riflemen. Love and marriage were but an idle dream for a man such as he, certainly until his agreement with Samuel came to a conclusion or was exposed.

He consoled himself with the fact that he had accrued a small fortune from his military enterprises. He could disappear back to the Australian colonies and establish himself as a rich and successful man.

Yet his beloved company of infantrymen was as close to a family as he had ever had, each and every man like a brother to him. Leaving them behind was something he could not imagine. It seemed he was destined forever to be travelling from one battlefield to another until his time for travel in this world was ended once and for all.

AUTHOR NOTES

Captain Ian Steele's regiment is purely fictional, but the events portrayed in *The Queen's Tiger* are real. I have been fortunate that many of the historical sources have been preserved in books, now reproduced on the internet, as the original manuscripts are almost non-existent.

As such I was able to refer to *Memoirs of Major General Henry Havelock K.C.B* by John Clark Marshman, originally published in London in 1867 by Longmans, Green & Co, for the material concerning the obscure Anglo-Persian war. The reproduction originated from the University of California Libraries network. It was interesting to discover within the pages of that biography that the Persian referred to themselves as belonging to the land of Iran.

The Indian Mutiny is better known, but to Indian historians today it is viewed as the first revolutionary war of independence from the British colonists. It is also my amateur opinion that what started as a military mutiny soon turned into an Indian rebellion for independence. Its failure to do so appears to be the lack of overall agreement between Hindus and Moslems for a united country. That would be an issue echoing down the years leading to the partition of India and Pakistan in the twentieth century.

For background to the sepoy mutiny I referred to the memoirs of Colonel A.R.D MacKenzie CB, from his biography published in Allabadad in 1891 by Pioneer Press, titled *Mutiny Memoirs: Being Personal Reminiscences of the Great Sepoy Revolt of 1857.* This was found through the University of Pittsburgh. Colonel MacKenzie was an eyewitness to the events that unfolded at Meerut, and the character of Lieutenant Craigie is a real person.

The events at the siege of Lucknow are taken in part from the diary of a truly remarkable woman, Lady Julia Inglis, wife of the military commander, who held out against overwhelming odds until relieved as portrayed in *The Queen's Tiger.* I recommend going on the net and searching for *A Celebration of Women Writers* to read her full account of the Lucknow siege and her vital role in assisting her husband.

The private investigator in this novel, Charles Field, is a portrayal of the real Charles Frederick Field, who was once a noted detective inspector with the Metropolitan Police and friend of Charles Dickens, and who became a noted private investigator after leaving the police force. I doubt that Inspector Field would have approved of the character of Charles Forbes in his real life.

It is worth mentioning that the Enfield rifled musket, and its projectile, the Minié bullet, would feature heavily in the American Civil War and change the course of history for both the British Empire and the Union of the United States.

Something that stood out in my research was the competency of two British generals, Havelock and Outram. Both men are largely overlooked by military historians, who continue to concentrate on Wellington. The event of my fictional characters rescuing General Outram is based on an actual incident – although the original account did not explain why he did so, so I have filled the gap to explain the general's gratitude to Captain Steele.

Needless to say, there are no shortages of campaigns for Captain Steele and his company of riflemen to march to in the many virtually forgotten battlefields trod by the British army in the nineteenth century.

And no, the next in this series will *not* have the title *The Queen's Corgi*!

ACKNOWLEDGEMENTS

As always, my thanks go to my publisher, Cate Paterson, who has been there from the first book. Completing this project would not have been possible without the work of Julia Stiles, Libby Turner, Brianne Collins, Rebecca Hamilton, LeeAnne Walker, Tracey Cheetham, Lucy Inglis and Milly Ivanovic.

I would also like to acknowledge the following people who have contributed to my writing year: From the USA, John Kounas, in Australia, Kevin Jones OAM and family, Dr Louis Trichard and Christine, Peter and Kaye Lowe, John and June Riggall, Kristie Hildebrand, John Carroll, Rod Henshaw, Geoff Simmons, Mick and Andrea Prowse, John Wong and family, Rod and Brett Hardy, Jan Dean, Betty Irons OAM, Chuck and Jan Digney, Bob Mansfield and all members of the Gulmarrad Rural Fire Service Brigade.

I will extend that thank you to all volunteer emergency service volunteers in the Clarence Valley – and beyond.

To my family of cousins; the Paynes and Duffys. To my brother, Tom Watt and family, as well as my sister Lindy Barclay and husband, Jock, and family, Ty McKee, Kaz and family.

Best wishes go to a few of my author mates, Dave Sabben MG, Simon Higgins, Tony Park and Greg Barron.